Praise for the *Fractal* Series

'A sequel that actually improves on its predecessor. Stroud presents us with a complex, multifaceted science-fiction experience that offers a deeply compelling narrative, interlaced with rich and complex worldbuilding and three-dimensional characters.'
The Sci-Fi and Fantasy Reviewer on *Resilient*

'Fast-paced, gripping hard SF with death in hard vacuum waiting at every turn.'
Adrian Tchaikovsky,
Arthur C. Clarke Award-winner on *Fearless*

'Space battles, sabotage, and treachery envelop a gripping whodunit. *Fearless* is a fabulous read from a writer who knows how to deliver.'
Ian Whates, Winner of the Karl Edward Wagner Award, on *Fearless*

'Gripping, intense, military SF. Stunning and urgent.'
Anna Smith Spark on *Fearless*

'One of the best science-fiction novels I have read in a very long time.'
The Sci-Fi and Fantasy Reviewer on *Fearless*

ALLEN STROUD

ANTI-STATE

A Story in the Fractal Universe

This is a **FLAME TREE PRESS** book

Text copyright © 2026 Allen Stroud

All rights reserved. No part of this publication may be reproduced, stored in a retrieval system, or transmitted in any form or by any means, electronic, mechanical, photocopying, recording or otherwise, without the prior written permission of the publisher.

FLAME TREE PRESS
6 Melbray Mews, London, SW6 3NS, UK
flametreepress.com

US sales, distribution and warehouse:
Simon & Schuster
simonandschuster.biz

UK distribution and warehouse:
Hachette UK Distribution
hukdcustomerservice@hachette.co.uk

Publisher's Note: This is a work of fiction. Names, characters, places, and incidents are a product of the author's imagination. Locales and public names are sometimes used for atmospheric purposes. Any resemblance to actual people, living or dead, or to businesses, companies, events, institutions, or locales is completely coincidental.

Thanks to the Flame Tree Press team.

Cover art by Nick Wells/Flame Tree Studio from sketches and layered files created using new photos and a stock images from IvaFoto (Shutterstock.com) and Valeriy and foldyart1980 (Adobe Stock) combined and crafted in Photoshop. No AI, AGI or LLM was used in this process.
The font families used are Avenir and Bembo.

Flame Tree Press is an imprint of Flame Tree Publishing Ltd
flametreepublishing.com

A copy of the CIP data for this book is available from the British Library and the Library of Congress.

1 3 5 7 9 8 6 4 2

HB ISBN: 978-1-80552-029-0
ebook ISBN: 978-1-80552-030-6

Printed and bound in the UK by CPI Group (UK) Ltd, Croydon, CR0 4YY

Represented in the EU for product safety and compliance by Authorised Rep Compliance Ltd, Ground Floor, 71 Lower Baggot Street, Dublin, D02 P593, Ireland. Contact at www.arccompliance.com

ALLEN STROUD

ANTI-STATE

A Story in the Fractal Universe

FLAME TREE PRESS
London & New York

2025 was an arduous year. This book is dedicated to all those who made me feel like a number and tried to tell me I should be grateful when they offered me less than I had before.

Despite these efforts, I remain here and this book got written.

In the lowest moments, there were many who stepped in to save me and remind me that I am a human being who deserves to be treated as such. Those people know who they are and what they did. They do not need to be remembered here. I will always remember them and be eternally grateful.

Prologue

I remember the moment. It is seared into my mind.

Thirteen kilometres below the Martian surface. The Explorer suit that I'm wearing registers a significant rise in temperature. Down here, it's around six or seven degrees. Not that warm, but far warmer than any other environment I have experienced on this planet.

We were a party of five, exploring a cave network. Spelunking on a planet where there is little atmosphere is particularly dangerous. A small stumble or trip, a brush against abrasive rock, and you have an immediate emergency. The low-pressure environment is deadly to exposed human flesh. There would be an instant reaction, freezing, boiling, swelling, bursting, all of these in an awful combination.

This world was never meant for us.

I can still picture the moment. Four figures ahead of me, all clustered around one small outcrop of rock. I can hear words, I don't remember exactly what was said, but I know the gist, I know what they're talking about.

As I approach, I can see the detail of the uneven stone illuminated by their helmet torches. There is something dark running across the pale jagged surface. At first glance, it looks like a mass of thin veins.

I know immediately what it is.

Life.

The ramifications of this discovery are huge. Humanity has big plans for Mars. Significant investments have already been made to construct and organise a colonial mission. The effort is a global project, bringing together a vast conglomerate of interested parties. After decades of conflict in this unity, this is an effort that provides focus. Our civilisation looks outwards, stares at the Red Planet, reaches out and seeks to subjugate it.

In such a plan, there is no room for this discovery. Mars has already been declared lifeless, empty, available for humanity's needs. Those needs will mean change, a vast effort to transform a dead world, resurrecting it and exploiting it, all in the name of progress and profit.

I remember being part of the discussion, but I didn't contribute very much. I guess that's an excuse in hindsight. I didn't make the decision, but then, I didn't oppose it either.

It took an hour for the equipment to be transported down to us. Three extra people carrying two canisters and a pressure sprayer, the kind of equipment you might use in a garden to nurture and preserve life, only this time the objective would be exactly the opposite.

When they were done, I got a last look at the rocks. As the chemical residue bubbled and boiled away the last traces of organic material, I could see that the stone beneath was stained, like an old wound or a scar.

All that remained of the native life we found on Mars.

Phase One

Chapter One

Sirocco

Late summer in Naples and the café is crowded. Sunlight streams through the front windows. The tables outside are all occupied with customers. There are a few seats available indoors, but business appears to be good.

I've not been here before. I arrived about an hour ago and found a place in the far corner, in front of the window. The furniture is made of polished wood and darkened with a stain. Small chips and cracks give everything an air of age. My chair creaks a little as I adjust my position, leaning back so I'm shadowed from the window, but maintaining a good view of the street outside.

Whenever I go out, I bring with me a notebook and a pen. You don't see them much these days. Everyone using their electronic devices. Understandable. All that information, all that activity recorded and available instantly. Quicker than the time it takes for me to flip through the pages of my 'device'.

I've always believed in old things. I have old values. That's what my mother used to say.

This city has always been old. Scratch the surface anywhere on the street and you'll find something ancient. The place is a decaying fossil of an age long past.

Old glory, old power. All of it faded away into memory. There's something romantic about it, sure, but when someone stands up and challenges what you remember yourself being, rather than who you are, you get found out, fast.

People pass through. They order drinks. These days it's all different flavoured choca, but some still ask for the coffee selection and others go for the carbonated cold softs or some *gelato*. They sit down, talk, get up, swipe a device over the reader and leave. Everything is automated. The woman at the counter supervises it all, pausing occasionally to give me a cold look. Clearly my constant presence as the rest of the world moves around us both is starting to irritate her.

That's fine. I can stand a little irritation.

The couple on holiday carrying old backpacks and studying their digital map of the city while they drink their ice-cold order, the family of five – three children and two mothers – all talking at the same time, the elderly couple wrapped up in coats, wearing flat velvet hats. None of them notice I'm there. Neither do any of the others coming in and going out. To all of them, I've become part of the furniture. That's what I wanted. They don't see me. Why would they? I'm not part of their world.

"Hello, Leonardo."

My attention is drawn to three men standing near the counter. They've just trickled in, their movements soft and slow. They don't want attention until they do want attention. Now they're standing around a table on the other side of the room. A couple are sitting there. The man looks up at the sound of his name.

"You going somewhere, Leonardo? You and your boyfriend planning a trip?"

The words are spoken clearly in English, loud enough for everyone in the room to hear. Whether you speak English or not, the tone doesn't need translation.

A muffled reply. I don't catch it. People are taking the hint and leaving the café. I catch the eye of the elderly man as he shepherds his wife to the door. He nods. I nod back. We know.

"Now is not a good time for you to leave, Leonardo."

Everyone else has left. The woman behind the counter, vanished. The speaker grabs a chair from one of the other tables. As he does so, he and I see each other.

"Hey," the man says to me. He gestures towards the door. "You gonna take the hint?"

I shake my head.

"This is none of your business," the man says. "You need me to make you leave?"

I smile. There is an accent to his English. He's Venetian, I think. His voice has that sing-song quality you can't take seriously. "No, I'm good," I say.

"Then fuck off."

There it is. The order that leaves no room for doubt as to what he wants. He expects compliance. When there isn't compliance, he knows he will need to enforce his demand. That's the moment where the heart starts to pump that little bit faster, and the world becomes more precise.

To him now, I am an adversary rather than someone to be ignored.

I don't reply.

The man turns to his victim, Leonardo, who remains sitting at the table. "You know this shithead?" he asks.

Leonardo shakes his head. He's telling the truth. We've never met, but I know people like him. Those who have been victims. I've seen plenty of them in my life.

"Don't you lie to me!" the man says. "I'll ask you again. Do you—"

"He doesn't know me."

I stand from the table. I can still see out of the window. Apparently, we live in a civilised world. But, if we were living in a civilised world, police drones would already have arrived after being summoned to an alert from the counter supervisor, or by any of the customers placing a call to local law enforcement. This whole situation would be recorded and used as evidence in the conviction of the man I'm staring at. The man whose name I don't know.

It hasn't happened. That tells me everything that I need in order to plan what will happen next.

"Who are you?" the man asks.

"Sirocco," I say. "And you?"

The man smiles, revealing polished teeth. "You're not from around here, eh? You don't know me. You don't know me but you should. Ignorance is dangerous. Means you could accidentally get caught up in something, eh?"

I move around the table. There are no obstacles between us, but the man's companions are now focused on me as well. Three to one. I don't expect help from Leonardo and his partner. They're just grateful all the attention is on me. They're looking for a chance to slip out of the door and escape.

Good for them.

"Terrano. Lijia Terrano," the man says. "Remember that."

"I will," I say.

Terrano steps back and his two associates move in. I appraise them briefly. Hired muscle, I guess, the kind that looks impressive but doesn't hold up well when tested. They are a lot bigger than me, both over a hundred kilos. Given time and opportunity in a fight, that kind of power would make the difference.

But this isn't going to be the kind of fight they're expecting.

Terrano wants to give me a beating. Make an example of me so that I'm an object lesson for anyone who would challenge him. There's no one here to see what's about to happen, so I'm sure he'll have a plan to take a picture or two and share them around.

This kind of violence works as a gradual escalation. These two will want to restrain me, get their punches in, let their boss get a dig in as well. Plenty of visible damage to the face, so it can be seen, but not too much. If I resist, they'll go in harder, do more damage, etc. That's the plan.

That's not *my* plan. There is no escalation in what I do.

Man to my left steps forwards and I move, fingers bunched, hand open, knuckle strike right to the windpipe. I want him thinking about his next breath, not about me.

Man to my right aims a fist, I duck under it and take a knee as my hand comes up and delivers the same open-handed hit to his testicles. That gets his attention. He sinks to his knees. I grab his ears and ram his head into the corner of a chair. There's a crunch, he goes limp and starts to twitch. I let go and he's sprawling.

I stand. A hand grabs my wrist. I get hold of the thumb, turn it and twist. There's no strength in the man's grip. He's still struggling to breathe.

He stumbles, goes down. The arm is vulnerable. I turn, bring my knee up and my weight down, breaking it.

He screams.

Terrano is still standing in front of me, but looking a lot less sure of himself now. He hasn't moved, maybe he can't move.

I let go of his friends and step towards him.

"I do know you," I say. "I know what you are. What people like you are. Whatever deal you have going on here, that's what I know. I've seen it before. A hundred times."

Another step. He's holding my gaze. That means he still thinks he has a play here. Maybe he has a gun or a knife. It doesn't matter.

"You think you're strong, but you're not. Somehow, you've got yourself into a situation where you can grind people under your heel. Problem with that is when you find yourself facing someone who refuses to submit. That's where you are now."

"You have no idea what you've done," Terrano says.

I shrug. "Cause and effect. You think somehow there's some karma waiting for me? Maybe that karma is the people you think are coming after me because of this?" I smile. "Sure. You going back to tell them all about me?"

"You won't get out of this city alive, you—"

I hit him. Another strike to the throat, choking off his words. He goes down immediately, his legs weakened by the blow. He's a mess of drool, expensive clothes and shiny shoes. He struggles, but then I grab his head in my hands and smash it against the cold hard floor.

Once. Twice. Three times. His skull cracks like an egg.

The threats have betrayed Terrano's intention and that confirms mine. None of these three will leave here alive.

★ ★ ★

An hour later and I am back at my rented apartment, packing my bags.

Actions have consequences. I know what will happen here. Either a video recording of what transpired in the café will be sent to the authorities, or one of the people present will make a decision to report what they have seen. They'll probably do it because they think I'm dangerous. What they don't realise is that I'm not dangerous, at least not to them.

Not if they have a clear conscience.

I have no idea who Leonardo is. I don't know anything about what was happening before I intervened, but I wasn't about to let it go. I don't do that. Maybe that's why I find it hard to stay in one place for long.

There is a knock at the door.

I turn towards the noise. Law enforcement would have already assessed me to be a violent individual and authorised appropriate force in response. Whoever is out there is asking for permission to enter, which doesn't fit the tactical profile I'm expecting.

Makes this situation interesting.

I walk to the door and tap in the release code. The panel slides back. There is a woman standing in the hallway.

"Mister Sirocco?"

I don't respond, but I do step back, letting her enter. She accepts my invitation, entering the room with practised grace, the movement of someone who has training.

"I was just heading out," I say. "Something I can help you with?"

"As a matter of fact, yes," the woman says. She glances around. "Mind if I sit down?"

I shrug and gesture towards the couch near the veranda. We're on the fourth floor. If the situation becomes problematic, I can always drag her out onto the terrace and over the rail. However, I get the feeling that this conversation isn't going in that direction.

"My name is Louisa Aymes, Mister Sirocco. I represent an organisation that has just intervened to prevent you from being arrested and adding to your list of violent criminal transgressions."

I take a seat opposite her. There is a low table between us. The glass top is a digital display when it needs to be. "I didn't ask you to do that," I say.

"My employer saw it as an opportunity to start this conversation," Louisa says. "We want to hire you."

"To do what?"

"To go to Mars."

I frown at her. All I know about the situation on Mars is what I've heard in the news. "You want to keep me out of prison so you can execute me in the most expensive way possible?"

"My employer thinks you would be a perfect addition to our interests out there."

I stare at her. There's plenty in this conversation that I'm missing. "You've been following me then?" I ask.

"We've been monitoring your activities," Louisa replies. She pulls a small bag onto her lap and produces a portable screen, one of the smaller models. She taps the display a few times and the glass on the table activates in response. Documents begin to appear in a variety of windows.

"Magnus Sirocco. Aged thirty-three. Dishonourably discharged from the European Defence Forces in 2109, aged twenty. Before that, you served with distinction in the second Melbourne War."

"I know my own history," I say.

"Since then, you've been arrested six times, serving a total of eighteen months for different acts of violence. Every time you've been tried and convicted with video evidence. That made our intervention easy enough to ensure you didn't pick up a seventh conviction."

"Like I said, I didn't ask you to do that."

"You don't like owing people, do you?"

"I don't owe you anything."

"Right." Louisa leans back in the seat and looks around the room. "You'll be able to stay here now. I think you booked a two-week visit? We can arrange your travel to our facility after that."

"I'm not going anywhere with you," I say.

"You say that now, but I'm not sure things will stay that way."

"Really?" I stand, walk to the door, and tap in the code to open it again. "If you really know me, you'll know I've never liked anyone telling me what to do."

Louisa stands too. She knows the conversation is over. "Enjoy your two weeks. After that, we'll talk again."

Chapter Two

Iskander

I wake as I do every morning, to the sound of the bell.

It isn't a real bell, only a digital recording of the call to prayer from our Temple back on Earth, but the echo of it thrills me just the same. Twenty minutes from now, all of our people will gather together, and do as we have always done, as generations have done before us.

The time is synchronised between us and the congregations we left behind. The Martian day is longer, by forty-three minutes. We are on another world, but there is something reassuring about knowing what we do is done at the same time by others of our faith. Our affirmation to our creator is amplified as a shout into the cosmos. Perhaps our voice together is not loud in the grand scheme of things, but it is louder than it would be alone.

I rise from the bed and move across the room to the appointed place. On Earth, there would be a prayer room in most homes, but here space is a luxury. Every square metre of our pressurised living environment must have a utilitarian purpose. In this room, we are permitted to sleep, eat, work and pray as required. There is little time for anything else.

I am on my knees, facing towards the sun. I say the words as I've been taught them, my eyes closed, head bowed. My faith is strong, but this ritual is an affirmation. I draw strength from this renewal. Ritual, repetition, and anchor, knowing your affirmation is shared. Feeling the presence of others, being with them.

A second bell. The time is done, and the sensation vanishes. I am alone once more.

* * *

"The smell of cooked food draws them in from all over Mars."

I smile. Jacob's words are familiar to me. He has said this many times before, but it is easy to see what he means.

I'm standing at the serving hatch, a public face of our little temple. Behind me, electric grills and boilers reconstitute a variety of different proteins, fats and carbohydrates. The vacuum-packed supplies sent out from Earth have little taste to them, but with some work they can be churned into something appetising. There is only so long that a human being can live on soulless sustenance. The queue of people waiting in front of me is a testimony to that.

Once they hear about us, they come here – all the contractors sent from Earth to work in the colony. They bring with them their allocated food, donating it to the kitchen, so we can do our work. Sure, they lose a little of their portion as part of the deal, but what they get to eat nourishes the soul.

We do our best to help with that. Every person who comes to the kitchen leaves with a bundle of literature loaded onto their personal screens and profiles. We do the Lord's work here, even in a place so far away from the world he created in six days, resting on the seventh.

"Hey, you listening to me?"

I turn and smile at Jacob. "Sorry," I say. "I was miles away."

"Millions of miles away, no doubt."

I shake my head. "Not today."

"Maybe you're starting to like it out here."

"I wouldn't go that far."

I've been on Mars for just over eight weeks. The Temple decided that this would be an appropriate post for me. I know why. I'm not here to cook, serve food and preach the way. Working in the kitchens is just a starting point for their plans. I have a selection of skills that they think will make me useful to the rebuilding project, the kind of practical skills that should see me contracted by a variety of different companies up here trying to repair their equipment and facilities.

But that too is not the plan for me.

The queue is moving. Jacob has opened the gate and is letting people through.

"Good morning, friend," I say to the first person in line. A man who I don't recognise. "Have you been here before?"

"No, this is my first time."

"Well, it's good to meet you. My name is Iskander."

"I'm Magnus."

I hold out a hand, and it's taken in a firm calloused grip. The weathered, sweaty face in front of me is strong, purposeful, appreciating the gesture.

"You just finished a shift?"

"Yes."

"Whereabouts?"

"Reclamations."

I nod. I'm sympathetic. Since the destruction of the Jezero dome, finding a way to clear and reuse everything that was wrecked has been a major task for the colony. Mars isn't a world where we have large amounts of resources that we can extract. There are metals and rare earths here, but the infrastructure for heavy mining and the like is complicated by the lack of an atmosphere. So instead, we remain a civilisation that tries to find new uses for everything that we bring with us.

"How does this work?" Magnus asks.

"You give me your food ration for the day, and I'll add it to the stores." I point down the counter. "In exchange, I give you a ticket and we'll serve you your morning meal. There's a couple of choices. Later, you can come back for lunch and dinner."

"That sounds fair," Magnus says. "What's the angle?"

"Angle?"

"What do you get out of it?"

"When you're signed up with us, we send you the Temple literature. You don't have to read it, but if you want to know more, we're here to support you in taking the next steps."

"So, you're recruiting people?"

"I guess so, yes. But we don't force anyone to join us."

"Right."

Magnus hands me the plastic-packed rations he's received from the dispenser. I put them on the counter next to the grill. Jacob will add them to the others. I give Magnus a ticket and he moves on.

The morning passes like many others. I meet, greet and talk with regulars and new people. My memory has always been an asset in these moments. I know faces and names and can pick up conversations from days and weeks before. Our customers get to feel like they are old friends.

Then, when the queue is finally gone, I'm left with Jacob doing the tidy-up.

"A lot of new people today," he says.

"Transit shuttle just came down from the new orbital," I explain, relaying what I've been told by the people in line. "The *Lakshmi* has just left, on its way out to Ceres. The new people were all up there, unloading supplies and working on the dock. Now they're hanging around Hera until they get their assignments." I gesture to where the people were. "Some were coming here after their first shifts, others on their way to work."

Jacob nods. "Makes sense. We've seen it before."

"True."

Mars has changed. Jezero is in bad shape. Once upon a time, new arrivals would be struggling to get temporary access permits to their work deployments. They'd arrive owing millions in journey fees and be assigned to basic sustenance contracts for their probationary periods, gaining additional privileges once they made down payments on their debts.

Now, there's too much work and not enough people. These new arrivals are incentivised, given discounts and reductions just to get them here. Media coverage of what happened to Phobos Station in 2118 is still subject to a news embargo, but what information they did let get out poisoned the well. Mars is no longer the pure unadulterated dream of a fresh start. People know it's dangerous out here.

A touch on my shoulder. Jacob leans in, kisses me on the cheek. "You were great today," he says. "The way you are with people, I couldn't do it."

I smile. "You're the miracle worker here, turning ration packs into something people genuinely want to eat."

"Going to miss you when you're gone," Jacob says.

"I'll be back."

"Yeah, but it won't be the same."

I shrug. We both know this arrangement is temporary, until my real vocation begins. "I'm sorry."

"Life moves on," Jacob says.

* * *

I'm walking back to my quarters, through the service passageways. Jezero's main dome is still under reconstruction, so access between the different facilities has to be through a series of temporary access tunnels. Some of them are fabric corridors appropriated from spaceships, others are old stock from the earliest days of the colony.

The walkways are dark, cramped and breathless. As I move, I'm pushing past people coming the other way. The air scrubbers are working overtime to maintain the oxygen levels in here. A few people have taken matters into their own hands and are wearing portable O_2 masks.

I get to my door and press my thumb to the plate. The panel slides back and I'm inside.

I have an hour before my next shift. I pull off my overalls and move to the shower. Owing to the supply shortages, the best we're allowed is a treated water mist that does just about enough to make you feel clean.

I change clothes and pack a bag. Then, I'm out and on my way. I'll need to renew my permits before I get on the pedestrian ferry, heading for Hera Spaceport.

The ferry is one of the few transit facilities the colony has focused on rebuilding in the last eighteen months. With more resources arriving at Hera, a reliable freight transport network is an essential piece of infrastructure. Similarly, ensuring that workers can be on hand to process the deliveries has also become a priority. Most of the people here are en route to help with that.

But that's not why I'm going to Hera.

The departure terminal is crowded when I get there. We all move through an airlock to stand in a compartment, holding on to the safety bar as it departs. People are looking for work, they want to reduce their travel debt, and now is the time to do that, while there's plenty to do. We'll all travel to the communal hall at the port and wait to be selected by a set of taskers, who are continually receiving direction from the colony oversight committee. The taskers will read profiles, decide whether an individual has the right skills and experience and then assign them to different activities. Sometimes you get something interesting, sometimes you don't.

The compartment picks up speed. In the low-gravity environment, the energy requirements for these transit compartments are much lower than they would be on Earth. The rails are electrified, reducing the weight of each section.

It takes fifteen minutes to get to the Hera arrivals terminal. Then we file out and everyone makes for the hall. I linger until the end, staying on the carriage.

Once everyone is gone, a woman enters. She nods to me, I nod back. Then she sits down. The airlock door closes, and the compartment pulls away.

"Everything in order?" I ask.

"Yes, we're ready for you, Mister Iskander. You're the last to be transported over. There are three others waiting for us at the shuttle launch dock. Once we get you aboard, that'll be the entire crew complement, and we can head out."

I glance around the compartment, noting the cameras on the walls. Like the Jezero dome, the rail network suffered damage when Phobos Station was destroyed. Some of the security and monitoring infrastructure has been repaired, but that kind of work isn't a priority right now. Still, we shouldn't take chances. But I know what's about to happen. This is the moment I've been waiting for. Nothing more should be said in this place. Nothing needs to be said. My transfer to an orbital working role has been authorised and approved.

But that's also not where I'm going.

★ ★ ★

After a few minutes, the compartment makes a second stop and we both exit into a transport module, which takes us the final three kilometres to the launch pad, set apart from the main working areas at Hera. When the module arrives, the woman gestures for me to get out.

"I'm sure you'll continue our good work," she says. "We'll see you when you get back."

"Look in on Jacob for me," I say. "Tell him I miss him already."

"Will do."

A fabric corridor takes me to an elevator, which grinds its way upwards to another passenger cabin. This time, I'm boarding a shuttle, waiting to take me and several others off planet.

It takes a few minutes for us all to get strapped into our seats. After that, the cabin lights darken, and we blast off. I'm pressed back into my seat for the ride, my body subjected to high levels of force for a few minutes, but then the pressure eases and we're weightless.

I glance around the cabin. There are seven people in here, including me. I don't know any of them, but we exchange glances, acknowledging each other. No one talks. Not yet.

"Flight to all passengers, this is Captain Sullivan. We're on time for rendezvous with *Asthoreth* in twenty-three minutes. Tasker is now authorised to brief the team."

"Thank you, Captain." A man is speaking in a calm authoritative voice, one that expects to be listened to. He unclips himself from his chair and pushes himself up into the open space so everyone can see him. "My name is Halan Weaver. I'm a senior technician on the orbital rebuild project. You're all here to assist me." He glances around the group. "Control has identified your skills and experience with electronics, spaceship components and orbital construction. However, we won't be doing a lot of construction today. In fact, we'll be doing the opposite. *Asthoreth* has been decommissioned and authorised for parts retrieval. Our job will be to take as much as we can from her and get it back to the Hub. That clear?"

Weaver is looking at me. I smile and nod, as if I'm in agreement with him.

"Okay, your screens have been loaded with a deck plan of the ship. Pair up and grab a toolkit, a head torch and a screen from the dispenser. I'll be sending you a requisition list and a set of locations. We want the items specified. The ship has been partially pressurised for our work and it's in a stable orbit, but you'll need to take emergency oxygen units with you. We take no unnecessary risks. That understood?"

Various mutters of agreement are given in response to his speech, and I find myself being approached by a short woman with spiky bright red hair.

"I know who you are," she says in a low voice.

Again, I nod in response. This time I'm being genuine and again there is nothing more that needs to be said.

★ ★ ★

Minutes later and we're docked. The derelict *Asthoreth* awaits.

"Okay, follow me in," says Weaver. "Once we're through, divide up and make your way to your assigned sections. Iskander and Halle, you're with me. We're going to the bridge."

I smile at Weaver again. The red-haired woman, Halle, is already beside him with a screen and toolkit in her hands. I move forwards and take the equipment as instructed, attaching the kit to my belt and keeping hold of the screen.

The shuttle shifts. There's a metallic *thump* followed by a series of smaller sounds. It's the locks engaging as we attach ourselves to the larger patrol ship.

"Docking complete," Sullivan announces over the comms. "Requisition team cleared to depart."

"Okay, that's us," Weaver says. He presses the door release and moves into the ship. As he does so, lights illuminate the space beyond. "All right, everybody through."

Six of us enter in single file. Halle and I are the last pair. When we're through, the door closes behind me.

"Right, you know your targets. Use your screens and stay in comms if you need me." Weaver gestures to Halle. "Stay close behind me."

We move through the ship. Occasionally, lights activate as we get close, but more often than not they stay dark. The head torch illuminates everything I look at. There are scorch marks in the metal and plastic panelling. Whole sections have been torn apart, fragments float in the air around us. This ship has suffered, that's for sure.

"Up here," Weaver says. "There's a whole fractured section in the main corridor. We'll reach the bridge by going around it."

A small hatch grants us access to a maintenance crawlway. We move through in single file, my head a few centimetres behind Halle's feet. Then we're out and standing in front of another door. Behind us, I can see the wall panels are crumpled and torn. I guess some temporary panels have been added on the outside to maintain an atmosphere in key sections of the ship.

"In here," Weaver says. He puts his hand to the plate and the door slides back. The three of us enter.

This room, the bridge, is the most battered place I've seen so far. There are six chairs for people to operate the different functions of the ship. Two of them have been ripped out and are floating around the room. Most of the glass displays are cracked and there's powdered chips in the air.

"Be careful," Weaver says. He moves to one of the stations. The terminal display is broken, but he flicks a switch anyway. Nothing happens. "No power here. That means we should be able to dismantle it."

"What about the doors?" I ask. "Do we have access to the rest of the ship?"

"Yes, your requisition privileges should enable you to get into anything that you need," Weaver says. "The computer system may give us a little trouble, but I have the master codes, which will help us shut it down if we have to."

"So, we'll need you for those codes?"

"Yes."

"But nothing else."

"Shouldn't do." Weaver frowns. "I'm not sure what you mean though, I—"

The taser hits him on the back of the neck. Halle holds down the button for a few seconds, discharging an entire canister into his body, making him thrash and twitch in mid-air. Then she pulls back and leaves him to float across the room, unconscious.

"Welcome to your new ship, Deacon," she says to me.

"Thank you," I say and smile in return. This is why we are here.

★ ★ ★

Mars 2121.

Total colonial population: 8,343, down from a peak of 8,703.

Main settlements: Jezero (6,042), Arcadium (621), Noctis (265), Syrtis (357), Shelton (409) and Bulwark (547) and Phobos (102).

Total Mars Citizens: 12.

Overview:

The Mars colony continues to recover from the incidents in 2118. After the fall of Phobos Station, a temporary orbital facility, called 'the Hub', has been constructed to manage handling resupply shipments from Earth.

The main colonial population at Jezero has dropped from its peak of 7,300 just before the 2118 crisis. Some of these individuals have moved from the main settlement to the other regions but nearly four hundred people remain dead or unaccounted for.

The new regime has required personal freedoms be curtailed in Jezero. Contracted work hours have been extended with a marginal reduction in consumable benefits. This is the first in a planned series of revisions we will need to make so we ensure the project remains viable and appealing to Earth investors.

Extract from Mars CorpGov Shareholder Report (2121).

Chapter Three

Shann

Captain Ellisa Shann of the *Khidr*, finally back on Earth.

I'm standing in line with a number of other Fleet officers. The artificial legs I'm wearing are used to the gravity, but the rest of my body is not. There are a variety of exoskeletal supports holding me upright, keeping me here for this pointless ritual.

The doctors advised me not to attend. I thanked them for their recommendation and chose otherwise.

"...times of adversity challenge us all. They test our resolve and force us to question the decisions we have made. In such times, we learn about ourselves and about those we come to rely on..."

Admiral Herric Marrison is eighty years of age. He's never left the planet. They wheel him out for ceremonial events, particularly the ones they know are going to be televised.

I and the other middle-ranked members of the United Fleet Consortium of Earth – or Fleet for short – we're window dressing for the speaker. Most of the cameras are focused on the admiral. But I know they have a cutaway shot on me. I'm the exotic celebrity in this moment. The captain returned from Mars, uncertain of what reception she's going to get.

The captain who is about to be called upon.

"...of those people is Captain Ellisa Shann, of the *Khidr*. A human being who rose to the challenge of the moment that she faced. Captain, please step forwards."

I grit my teeth and instruct the legs to begin their predetermined journey from my place in line to the podium. All the cameras are on me now. I hate that, but I also know the ephemeral fame of the moment is protecting me, just as Savvantine said it would.

Underneath my Fleet uniform there are a variety of different electronic servos assisting every movement and gesture I make. I love space, but eighteen months without gravity takes its toll on the body when you come back to Earth.

"Captain Shann. I have the honour of promoting you to the rank of commodore, as befits your new role leading security operations as we rebuild the Mars colony. Fleet recognises your exceptional contribution to our collective mission under the most trying of circumstances."

Old, weathered hands hold a metal star made of polished brass. Marrison's fingers tremble a little as he pins the ornament to the fabric of my dress uniform. Then he looks me in the eye and smiles. I smile too. We shake hands then I salute.

Marrison backs away from the podium, giving me the floor. The proximity sensors in my exoskeleton detect the movement and adjust my position accordingly, putting me right in front of the microphones and in the perfect place for the video cameras.

All eyes on me. Live. Time to say what needs to be said.

"Thank you, Admiral Marrison." I nod towards the old man once more. After Langsley retired, Marrison was put in charge as a figurehead. No one wanted another capable authoritarian, even though that's probably exactly what Fleet needed.

"I'm accepting this honour on behalf of my crew and all of those who have been part of the Mars mission since the events of 2118. Many people died during that crisis, many others are still missing. My mission is to ensure their sacrifice, defending the values of human civilisation, was not in vain.

"Make no mistake. What happened out there, and what's happening now, matters to you. This isn't some peripheral conflict that we can all ignore. Earth's economic interests are tied into everything. When people out there lose, you lose too.

"The job is not finished. We need your help. Which is why I'm here, supporting the New Mars Initiative and Appropriations Bill as it seeks approval from the World Senate.

"Thank you very much."

★ ★ ★

"Good speech."

"Thanks."

I'm sitting in the reception room. The media conference has ended. Thankfully, I wasn't asked to take questions from the assembled group of journalists. If I had been, things might have got awkward.

"For me, one thing that was missing, though? You talked about a conflict, but didn't say who we're fighting."

I glance at my companion. Captain Neil Elliot of the *Nandin* is safe company, if anyone can be considered safe company these days. We've shared a lot. I trust him.

"Neil, you know as well as I do, that's the weak point of our argument. We don't have a clear enemy, other than the face of a clone. Exposing our lack of knowledge won't help us."

"That's Savvantine's argument. What's your view?"

"Broadly similar. Identifying the enemy is a complicated process. If we start putting a face to them, we're simplifying the situation, but we might be getting it wrong. You put Rocher's face on this and whoever we're fighting will switch to a different person. I expect they've already planned for what's happening."

"If they haven't, Savvantine has," Neil says. He glances around. "Is she here?"

"I doubt it," I say. "Why come to an event where most of the people attending outrank you and have axes to grind?"

"With her?"

"Oh yes. She's not loved."

"I can understand that." Elliot flexes his arms. I can see the telltale bulges of a medical exoskeleton under the sleeves of his uniform. He's been back on Earth for three months, but his body is still adjusting to the gravity. That's what I have to look forward to if I stick around. "You've been pushed up three tiers into a flag rank. That's going to cause some resentment."

"I'm expecting that."

"How long until you ship out again?"

"As soon as I can get medical clearance. I don't plan to outstay my welcome. You?"

"I'm... I'm not going."

I stare at him. I've known Neil Elliot for years, ever since the Phobos Station attack. We didn't cross paths before that during our training, but between us, we're two thirds of Fleet's command corps with actual battle experience. "They can't be happy about that," I say.

"The situation is still being discussed," Elliot says. "But I know what I want. Another six months to a year out there without my family is not what I need, particularly with tensions where they are right now."

"I understand." I do understand in a way. My own family have remained distant since I got back. I do want to see them, but the urge to return to what I left behind around Mars is a stronger pull. "You have kids?" I ask.

"Two," Elliot says. He laughs. "They loved it when I first got the *Nandin* commission. 'Space Dad' got mentioned a few times. But now, I'd like the chance to see them grow up."

"You deserve that," I say.

"Thanks."

I glance around the room. The crowd is thinning as people run out of things to say to each other. There isn't a lot of small talk between military types. We tend to keep things blunt and direct, unless there's politics. "If you're stepping back, it might be why they went easy on me."

"Easy?" Elliot laughs, drawing a couple of people's attention. But the interest soon fades. He lowers his voice. "From what I heard, the military tribunal you went through was pure torture. Like putting a rag over your head and having someone turn on the tap."

"I was expecting worse," I say.

"Worse?"

"Yes, I thought they'd kick me out."

Elliot shakes his head. "They couldn't do that. You're too famous. Right now, you're in the moment. That protects you."

"Savvantine said that. I had my doubts though."

Elliot stands. "Time for me to head out. Call me anytime you need me. I owe you."

"Pretty sure we're even."

"Well, I'm still happy to help."

I'm left alone. The few people remaining in the reception room don't approach me. That works just fine. Five minutes to myself is useful.

Captain, Major, Colonel, *Commodore*. Commodore Shann. I don't know whether I've earned this or not, but I can see the reasoning. Pushing me up settles any questions of authority. Mars needs a flag officer to bring everything into line. Makes sense that it be me.

Feels strange though. After fighting for every inch of recognition for so long, to have this handed to me...odd...

I pull out a screen and place it on my lap. The display brightens as I touch it, recognising my fingerprint. The information I'd been looking at before the ceremony is right there, still updating and scrolling through.

This is a direct feed into the Mars Orbital repair project. I'm receiving activity updates as soon as I can get them. The data is travelling millions of miles, so there is some latency, but the fact that I'm able to maintain a secure connection is massive. From here, I know what's going on and I can still make a few decisions if I have to.

Lieutenant Avril Johansson is Chief of Operations in orbit. She's liaising directly with the Mars CorpGov representative and all of the private contractors sending people, equipment and materials to the new orbital hub, designed by her.

The progress we've made rebuilding the colony's orbital infrastructure in just three years is incredible. Most of that is down to letting a brilliant mind do what it can do.

A window flashes. I bring it up. There's a video message. It's from Savvantine.

"Hey Commodore. Congratulations on the promotion. They were either going to celebrate you or execute you, but it doesn't mean you don't deserve it. Sorry I can't be there, but it's not my scene. You know as well as I do that if I made an appearance, certain people would see that as an opportunity. Right now, we need to strengthen our position, not weaken it.

"Which brings me on to your request. Apologies, but I can't do it. *Gallowglass* is going to have to stay here, mothballed until it dissolves into R and D. There are only so many strings I can pull. This is a fight that we won't win.

"Sorry, I wish I had better news. Savvantine out."

★ ★ ★

A week later and I'm in an auto-vehicle on my way to Edmonton.

It's cold outside. Somehow, I feel cold, even though I'm sealed away in a warmed air bubble, watching the world go by. The view through the glass is a mixture of white and green. This is a world I'm still not used to. A world that I'm visiting, like a tourist. The beauty streaming by is something I can appreciate from that perspective. Even though I grew up in this country, it doesn't feel like home.

Space is my home.

My father lives on the outskirts of the city now. He moved there in 2119, bringing my younger brother, Jethry, and his family all under the same roof after Jethry got sick.

They sent messages, keeping me informed about the cancer treatment. I replied when I could, but not as much as my father wanted. I could sense that in his answers.

Three months ago, I got a video call from my brother. That was one of the reasons I decided to come back.

The car turns off the highway onto a smaller road. It's mid-afternoon, on a winter's day, the sun on its way down. We're surrounded by trees, heavy with snow. The displayed map indicates we're about five kilometres out. That means I have a few minutes to prepare for what's to come.

The road winds and the car starts to ascend. The Shann family home is situated on a hilltop, set in a large plot of land, overlooking fields of replanted redwood and pine. I've seen pictures and mapping images, but I've never actually been here.

The first sign of civilisation is two old wrought-iron lampposts, one on either side of the road. They look like something straight out of the nineteenth century.

The car turns off the road onto a gravel track. Ahead, I can see the house. It's a brick build, usual for around here. A white render covers the walls. We pull up outside, right in front of the wide concrete steps.

The sight of this front makes me smile. This house was never built for me. The only way to get to the front door is to walk up the steps.

I activate the car's support system. The door opens and servos push my seat out of the car, turning me ninety degrees so I'm facing the house. Then, my automated chair is activated and deploys from the trunk, running around the side of the vehicle so I can lift myself straight across. That means I'm mobile here, but there's no way the chair is going to get me up to the front door.

"Ellie!"

I glance up the steps. Sunlight flashes off the windows, making it difficult to see who is standing there, but I recognise my brother's voice.

"Hi Jeth. Good to see you."

He's down the stairs in a flash and by my side, enveloping me in a big hug. I return the gesture, making it clear that I'm happy to see him and happy that he's in my personal space. The last thing I want is to make things awkward right at the start of my visit. He's breathing a little from running down to me. That's to be expected after all the surgery and recovery.

"So, you want to tell me how I'm supposed to get up these stairs?" I ask.

"There's a ramped entrance at the side," Jethry says. "Come on, I'll show you."

Style over substance. That figures. I don't want to be harsh and judge my father for refusing to sacrifice the look of the house, but when you're the one standing outside looking in, it's hard not to criticise.

It takes me a little while to get myself into the chair. I'm still struggling with the gravity, so my arms aren't as strong as they were, but I don't want help. My brother knows that, I was always the same when we were growing up. No help unless there's no other option. He keeps a respectful distance until I've sorted myself out.

"Ready?"

"Yeah, let's go."

Jethry walks ahead of me. I set the chair's follow function, and the computer tracks him, keeping me a couple of paces behind. We go around to the left side of the building and up a short incline that leads into the same reception room as the big stairs and the double doors.

As soon as we're through the side door, I hear children's laughter. That makes me smile. It's been years since I've seen Jethry's family in person. His daughter, Dani, was born just after I took command of *Khidr*. I've seen pictures and videos of her but never seen her in person. That in itself is a reason for this trip.

We're in a big hall. Another staircase sweeps around to an internal balcony and a series of rooms. That's where the laughter is coming from. I've no idea how I'm going to get up there.

Jethry only seems to realise this as we enter the room. He turns and grins at me. "They know you're here. Let's go through to the kitchen."

I follow him under the staircase to the back. The floors are tiled, a kind of ceramic/plastic hybrid, I think. Not something I'm used to.

"You want a drink? Must have been a long trip, eh?"

"Water would be great." I disengage the follow protocol and set the chair to park up by the island. Jethry's at the sink with a couple of glasses.

"Got it."

I hear the sound of a door being opened upstairs. Then there's footsteps. Someone is coming down. Is it him? My fingers dig into the arms of the chair. Maybe I'm more nervous about this than I thought.

"Hello, Ellie."

He's there in the doorway. I'm not looking at him. My eyes are on the countertop.

"Dad."

Not looking at him is the last defence I have. The emotions are there, right under the surface. If I turn, I'll break, and it'll all come flooding in. I'm surprised I've lasted this long.

I take a deep breath and let it happen.

★ ★ ★

There is a need for religion in politics.

The founders of our republics enshrined within their written constitutions a wish for the separation between church and state. The ideology behind this argument lies in the doctrine of rationalism. It was the belief of those lawmakers of the time that all of human society could be designed and structured through a rational prism. Indeed, those rationalists believed that their approach was the only way in which fair representation and wise decision-making could occur.

This of course rejects many precedents that have existed throughout human history.

The doctrine of rationalism permeated democratic structures for more than two hundred years. With the absence of religion in such structures, participants turned to another ideology and embraced capitalism. The principles of opportunity, luck and exploitation became enshrined in a dogma that atomised society, preferring instead to champion the mythology of self-made individuality. The 'work-hard wealthy' became persons to admire and aspire to.

Of course, there were always citizens involved in politics who held religious beliefs. These individuals retained their sense of morality and ethics. At times, they were able to act and counter the excesses of the merchant cult, but they remained in a minority and the dam was bound to break.

Slowly but surely the gap between the wealthy and the wealthless grew, until we began to question the purpose of our societies. The absence of a heart within governments based solely on the head allowed a corruption of the mission of such institutions. The pursuit of never-ending profit became a substitute for conscience and generosity. The lack of community between decision-makers encouraged tribalism and conflict.

When we strip all of this back and return to the matter of purpose, we can clearly understand the place of religion in politics.

The purpose of society is to better the lives of all humans who are a part of it. Such a purpose requires a conscience. Life as we live it cannot be perfect. There will be moments where all of us face adversity, and it is in those moments where society should act to support us. This should be the mission of a state and its government.

A true collective conscience can only be a part of such a society if it is enshrined within all aspects of its structure. Ethics and morality are derived from principles that can go against self-interest. The world's religions understand this. The basis of their tenets embraced this. True, an individual can find a good conscience from another path, but the majority of people living on this world learn to understand their own souls through a faith that is in part based on a different kind of aspiration. The reward for living a generous life lies in our ability to be at peace with ourselves. The reward in giving comes from our ability to empower others.

Ultimately, those who understand realise that the end of the path will reveal a truth to us. There is no need for reward.

Urson Jackson – Shepherd of the Temple.

Chapter Four

Sirocco

I'm lying in my bunk when there's a knock at the door.

I get up quickly, a little too quickly. The weaker Martian gravity is something I'm still getting used to. I have to reach out and stop myself colliding with another bed on the other side of the dormitory room.

The door panel slides back to reveal a man I've not seen before. He's older than me, older than anyone I've seen in the colony. He glances briefly at me and then around the rest of the shared accommodation. "Are you Magnus Sirocco?" he asks.

"I am."

"They told me to find you here. Can we go for a walk?"

"Yeah, sure."

I don't know this man, but I have been told eventually I would be contacted. That was all part of the plan.

Two weeks after that meeting with Louisa in Italy, I contacted her, using the call ID she left me. We discussed the arrangements, and I agreed to take an air car to a launch site in Sardinia. I took a commercial flight to the processing station in orbit and straight on to a passenger berth on the *Lakshmi*, the freighter being sent to resupply the Mars colony.

When I arrived here, I took up a prearranged position on the colony's reclamation team and a bunk in this dormitory, allocated to new arrivals. Louisa had told me to wait, so I waited.

Until now.

We're moving down a passageway, heading away from the occupied sector, towards the abandoned parts of the city. I'm following the man who came to see me.

As we move, I'm looking at him, analysing him. His clothes are the same as everyone else's. No clues there. But he moves with practised ease in the low gravity. That tells me he's been here a while, a lot longer than me.

We keep going for a while. I guess around fifteen minutes. There's no one else around. The lighting is intermittent and a lot dimmer than the areas I know.

"All right, I think this is far enough out."

The man turns towards me. "They told me to mention Louisa. They said I should tell you Louisa sent me."

"Okay. Louisa told me to wait for someone who would tell me why I'm here."

"My name is Doctor Henry Tellen. I was part of the second research mission sent to Mars after the initial colony was set up. I'm here to take you to Antonio Sammatri."

"Who is that?"

"A man you should know. The reason you don't is because the authorities suppressed any information about him." Tellen glances around nervously. "We're only talking about him now because I know the surveillance and monitoring out here hasn't been repaired. A mention of Sammatri would trigger an immediate security alert."

"What did he do?"

"He started a revolution."

I laugh. "He sounds like my kind of guy. Where do I find him?"

Tellen taps on the wall. "Out there. He left Jezero a couple of weeks after the disaster, and no one's seen him since."

"Then how are you going to get me to him?"

"The colony have authorised an exploration team to inspect the outside of the dome," Tellen says. "There aren't enough mobile camera drones to get an accurate picture, so they want to send a team out to help prioritise repairs. They want me to lead the team."

"And you want me to come along?"

"I was told you were the kind of person Sammatri could use."

I'm thinking back to that day in the café. "Yeah, I guess I can be useful." I look around, noting the broken cameras on the wall. This location seems safe enough. "What's your angle?"

"What makes you think I have an angle?"

"Come on. Be real."

Tellen shrugs. "Okay, there's something out there I want to retrieve. Something I left out there back in the early days. Now there's a restart, it could make a difference to how things are being done."

"All right, so what's your plan?"

"We'll take the team out for the inspection. At some point, I'll organise everyone into pairs to cover more ground. You and I will team up, then we wander off. I've been given a secure comms channel frequency that Sammatri's people use. We'll make contact and see what happens next."

"You have all the necessary permits?"

"Yes. Once I have your agreement, the requisition order will be sent directly to your profile, and I'll pick you up from the taskers in the municipal hall tomorrow morning."

I consider refusing the offer. I'm here on Mars, could this be a fresh start? There are hundreds of people like me in the same situation, working reclamation or some other baseline job until they find a permanent position. If I decide to say no, that would be me. Food, water, air and a place to sleep are all provided for. Whatever else I get would be earned.

I've certainly been in worse situations. But no, not this time. This world isn't meant for human habitation. There are so many ways I could die, and I don't want to spend years just surviving while others reap the benefits of my work. The pyramid needs to come down. That's what Louisa promised me.

"All right, I'm in," I say.

"Great, then I'll see you tomorrow."

★ ★ ★

Mars is fragile.

There have been times on Earth when different nations have been overthrown. Populist movements have toppled dictators and democracies have been broken by would-be dictators. The new regimes have always been agents of change, trying to serve a marginalised part of the country. Sometimes that has been a minority, sometimes it's the majority, but those priorities always end up diluted and forgotten when leaders taste power.

On Earth, the complex tangle of economic interests makes any new government beholden to the community of nations. The World Senate, Fleet, all of it, a clique of interests, including self-preservation.

Mars offers the chance for something different. We're so far away from Earth and all that politics, whatever happens here can't be stopped before it's too late.

Or at least that was what I thought.

I'm in the municipal hall a good hour before I'm due to meet Tellen. Most people travel over to Hera for work assignments, but there's still a fair crowd here.

I can see the Temple cooking station. I think about going over and getting another meal, but Jacob isn't there anymore. A woman has taken his place at the serving hatch. I hang back. The meal is good, but I've other business to attend to today.

"Hey."

Tellen has seen me before I saw him. That's unusual, but I guess I'm still getting used to the gravity. That makes me stand out in a group of people. "We ready to go?" I ask.

"Yes, the others are waiting at the exit. We have suits and two rovers. How many hours do you have in vacuum?"

"A few when I worked on the freighter."

"Being outside on Mars is a little different, but the same rules apply. Check for leaks and snags, watch out for each other. All that sort of thing."

"Understood."

We head out of the crowd. I try to copy Tellen's walk. Walking in Mars gravity means smaller movements. I know that, but I still have to consciously adapt with every step forwards. If I don't, I end up colliding with people.

We reach the exit port. Four other people are already there in gear. I'm handed an environment suit and start climbing into it.

"Check each other's seals," Tellen says. "Don't just rely on the auto-gauges."

Hands over my body. People in my personal space. I have to consciously relax to let them do what they need to do. It could be life or death for me if they don't.

The stuff we have to wear for this is a little less bulky than the EVA equipment I practised with during my basic training. The surface of Mars isn't a vacuum, so there's a little less need for all the layers they have on spaceships. The suit has a console on the back of the right sleeve and a set of rubber studs on the fingers of my left hand. That lets me operate the controls, just like a portable screen.

"All right, let's go."

Helmets are on, visors down. Conversation is now over the designated radio channel. It's an open frequency, monitored by who the fuck knows? I'd guess they have people checking on us as we're outside, or at least an active monitoring programme, recording and synthesising our speech, analysing for keywords and stuff. That's the way they monitor critical locations back on Earth.

We move into the large airlock. The inner door closes behind us and I can see the atmosphere counter spiralling down as the air pressure is reduced to equalise with outside. Mars does have a thin atmosphere, but there's a lot of work to do if it'll ever become breathable, like they talk about on all those promotional television shows back on Earth.

The outer door opens and I'm in a barren red desert.

Years ago, I was part of a military detail dropping criminals out into the North African wastelands. I remember being in a plane, looking out over the empty land, which had been scorched by fifty-plus-degree heat. I remember the poor fools sat in the cargo hold, parachutes strapped to their backs, wrists cable-tied to the rail right up until the last moment when we pushed them off the open cargo ramp.

One of the men I had to deal with begged me to let him stay on-board. I had to drag him right to the edge and throw him into the sky. I watched him fall. The parachute never opened.

Three days later, I went absent without leave. They caught me after a few weeks, and put me in a cage for a year, but I never went back to being a soldier.

This desert is cold. In some ways that makes it more dead than the burning sands of Earth.

"Magnus, follow me."

Tellen's words bring me back to the present and the task at hand. He's leading our small group to the vehicles, a couple of rovers assigned to us. "Four in each," he says. "We go to the control station, then we split into pairs. That'll help us cover more ground."

There are a variety of confirmations, some more formal than others. A couple of these people are ex-military. Game knows game.

I walk to the rover, climb aboard, and settle myself into the passenger seat. These vehicles look like the kind you'd have on Earth, but they are wider to accommodate the gear we have to wear out here. Tellen gets in on the driver's side and starts tapping on the control screen in front of us. "The route is preplanned and preloaded," he says over the comms. "I just need to initialise the system and let it know when we're ready to go."

I want to ask more questions about what we're really doing out here, but this isn't the time. I don't know how many of the team are trustworthy. I have to assume none of them.

Instead, I shift in the seat and look at the screen on my right arm. I key in a quick set of instructions and bring up the authorised mission parameters. I read over them last night when the requisition came in, but only briefly.

The inspection detail builds on the work done by three other teams and a series of autonomous efforts. The administrators have a fairly good picture of the outside, but we're out here to fill in gaps and to verify areas that have been scheduled for priority repair. As I go through the material, the display provides me with route plans and journey times. We need to drive for just over three minutes to get to the first location.

"Okay, we're moving," Tellen says. He touches me on the shoulder. "Keep your eyes on the dome. Could be they missed something. If they did, you tag it."

"Understood."

As the two vehicles pull away, I'm looking at the outer glass shell of Jezero. The damage is extensive. Debris from Phobos Station rained down on this place. Now, years later, a lot of it still litters the barren landscape around us. No one's coming out here to tidy up unless they need to.

An augmented overlay appears on my visor, carefully rendered so it displays information for me as I look at sections of the shattered dome. Sections that have been identified for repair are highlighted in orange. The better-looking parts are highlighted in green.

"Wow," I say.

"You never seen it?" Tellen asks.

"No, not like this. I mean, I saw news clips, but being here..."

"Yeah, makes you realise how much effort went into building it in the first place, doesn't it?"

The vehicle makes a turn to the left, keeping the dome about twenty metres away. I can see exposed metal beams and cracked glass panels. Occasionally, there are crawler drones deployed on key sections. I guess they must be already effecting repairs.

"Nearly there," Tellen says. He points ahead. I can see a small tower outside. It's about two metres tall with a satellite dish on the top. There's a couple of banks of solar panels lined up next to it. We're slowing down now and as soon as the vehicle passes the tower, it turns right and pulls up.

"Okay, this is us."

I climb out of my seat just as the second rover pulls up alongside. The rest of the team begin getting out, but Tellen stops them.

"Stay there. Let me get the update from the terminal."

He goes to the tower and pulls out a cable, which he plugs into a connector on the arm of his suit. "All right. Only a minor update. Best way to manage this...we mount six and two. Halton, take your vehicle and head out to point two. Drop off Aymes and Surren, then push on to point three. The rover will then circle back. Both teams, work your way back to here from there."

"What are you going to do?" Halton asks.

"Sirocco and I will track back the way we've come. Seems there are a couple of sections they want an in-person inspection of. Must have missed that on the original requisition."

"All right, sounds good."

I step away from the rovers as Halton and the others pull away, heading onwards around the dome.

"Sirocco, over here."

I turn. Tellen is gesturing for me to join him at the tower. I walk over. He's holding out another cable from the console. As I get close, he takes my right arm and plugs it into a port next to the display.

"Okay, that gives us a private link," Tellen says. "We're just using the terminal as a hub. You ready for the real mission?"

"I am," I say.

"It'll take the others about four hours to get back here. By the time they do, we'll be long gone." Tellen holds up the display on his suit. "I've uploaded the rendezvous co-ordinates to your screen as well. Just in case we get separated. Once we disconnect from here, we talk by touch and hand gestures only, got it?"

"Understood."

"Great, then let's go. I've uploaded a little light briefing for you, so you can familiarise yourself with who you're meeting while we walk."

Tellen unplugs us both and we walk back to the rover, retaking our seats. This time, Tellen disengages the autodrive and puts the display into 'map mode only'. Then he grabs the wheel and we pull away.

Heading straight out, away from the colony, into nowhere.

* * *

In the aftermath of Jezero's destruction, the majority of the colony's population was evacuated to the dome's underground shelters. That meant the settlement was abandoned for nearly seventy-two hours.

During that time, we know there were people in the city. Some of them were survivors, registered citizens from the colony who managed to survive in the rim. But there were others, outsiders who we've not been able to identify.

Then there was Antonio Sammatri.

Sammatri was one of the dome's architects. A few hours before we authorised exploration teams to head out from the vault, a broadcast from him came from the administration building. He reported the invasion of the city by outsiders and how he and a small group of survivors managed to fight them off. He made a speech about debt slavery, urging workers to hold out for a better deal. It was like a match in a dry barn. Three days in an emergency shelter, living with next to no personal space, unsure of what would happen next, made the situation brittle enough.

Violence erupted. Three security interventions to put down the riots were unsuccessful. A fourth finally restored order. When the exploration teams finally went out, there was no sign of Sammatri or any of his associates.

We found the bodies of several of the outsiders that Sammatri had mentioned, confirming his story. The remains were quickly secured, and we began negotiations with the evacuated population, offering credit on their journey debts. Gradually, the situation began to stabilise, and the rebuilding effort began.

We've never found Sammatri.

Elias Jabbutu – First Citizen of Mars.

Chapter Five

Iskander

The *Asthoreth* is in a bad way.

The five other members of the requisition team are all part of my extended congregation – followers of the Temple. All of them were picked because they have relevant expertise and skills.

Alison Halle was a Fleet Engineer for eighteen months, holding the rank of ensign, before she decided to leave. She says she was passed over for a commission on-board a ship like this. I believe her.

David Kewell is an orbital communications specialist who has worked for a variety of private companies operating mines in the asteroid belt.

Morlan Dennis is a pilot. He's worked on orbital transfer shuttles, but that's pretty close to running a ship like this.

Sharon Merrick worked in EVA construction on Earth satellites. She's familiar with the tech all around us.

Mason Tolwyn is an ex-marine and weapons specialist.

The six of us are the crew of this ship. Our task is to steal her away from being scrapped for parts and give her new purpose.

All six of us are gathered on the ship's bridge. We agreed to meet here an hour after leaving the shuttle.

"What are we going to do with Weaver?" Halle asks.

"We can't give him back," Tolwyn says. "If we do, they'll be onto us."

"We need to get rid of the shuttle too," Dennis says. "The crew will start to suspect something is wrong when we don't check in."

"One issue at a time." I point at Tolwyn. "Take Weaver to the secondary airlock. Reset the passcode using the master key he gave us and watch him. If he starts to become a problem, take the air out of the room."

"Okay, Deacon, will do."

I glance around the room. The engineer's position and the pilot's chair are still intact. "Someone see if they can plug into the main computer. We have some battery packs. If we can get the system online, we can use it to get a full damage assessment of the ship."

"I can do that," Merrick says.

"Kewell, help her. If you can get control of any active thrusters, we can move the ship." I turn to Halle. "I need you to go down to the reactor. They will have decommissioned it. We'll need to know how permanently it's been shut down."

"Yes, Deacon."

People move to their assigned tasks. I'm left thinking about the shuttle crew.

The umbilical corridor is still attached to the primary airlock. The shuttle will be holding position alongside this ship. They'll need to make thruster adjustments to maintain alignment and prevent the fabric connection from being compromised. Any kind of alert that we initiate, whether it's real or faked, will be communicated back to the orbital hub, who'll send out a response.

Whatever we do to escape needs to be permanent. The people out there need to think we're dead and the ship is destroyed. In reality, we're already halfway there with the ship. That's the part we need to fix, but without anyone thinking it's fixed.

"How long until we're supposed to be checking in?"

"Just over forty-five minutes," Kewell says. "If they don't hear directly from Weaver, they'll be suspicious."

One problem at a time. This is the first problem I need to deal with.

★ ★ ★

A dark room with a table. A metal lamp hanging directly overhead illuminating a set of printed schematics. These copies will be burned as soon as we're done.

Six months ago, I was in an underground bunker surrounded by intelligent people planning this operation.

I remember that evening. Ten people sat on chairs in a circle. Some of them wearing face coverings to conceal their identities. Even in a community based on faith, there needs to be caution. Knowing who everyone is would give each of us too much useful information if we were to be picked up by some enterprising intelligence officer.

Options were discussed. A long list of potential scenarios with possible strategies. Every crisis point dissected and analysed. After removing the supervisor, what next? After restoring power to the ship, then?

The big problem was always going to be getting away.

I'm making my way through the ship's corridors, picking a route that avoids the atmosphere breaches. Weaver's data is pretty accurate, better than what we had when we planned this mission.

According to the files I read on these ships, the secondary airlock is used primarily for cargo. It's bigger, so the atmosphere cycling takes longer. We don't want to use it if we don't have to.

Weaver is conscious when I get there. Tolwyn is watching him through a DuraGlas window. There are several portable power units rigged up to the different devices in here. They drift in the air, held to their designated tasks by thin plastic-coated cables.

"Everything okay, Deacon?" Tolwyn asks.

"We've made a start," I say. "How's our guest?"

"Awake and wondering what's going on."

"Let me in there with him."

Tolwyn frowns. "You sure that's wise? If he overpowers you, he could use you as a hostage."

"If that happens, you open the airlock and let us both breathe vacuum. The mission is the priority."

Tolwyn hesitates but then moves to the door panel. "Maybe we go in together."

"No, just me. You wait here." The door slides back and I enter the airlock.

Weaver backs away from me, putting himself on the other side of the room, by the outer doors.

I smile in response and hold up my hands, palms towards him. "Please, I just want to talk."

"What do we have to talk about?"

"What happens to you next."

Weaver flinches. He's bigger than me and younger than me. I don't want him to get desperate and resort to violence. "I don't know what you people are trying to do, but I know I'm in the way," he says. "You're going to kill me."

"Things don't have to turn out that way." I move away from the door and lower my hands. "You could join us."

"Why would I do that?"

I smile. "Is this what you planned for yourself in life? When you volunteered to come to Mars, did you imagine you'd be up to your eyeballs in debt, running work details and following the orders of some wealthy administrator?"

"Are you terrorists?" Weaver asks. "Are you the people who destroyed the station?"

I shake my head. "Phobos Station was a tragedy. We were not a part of that."

"Then why are you here?"

"Because we're going to steal this ship."

I'm being blunt and open with Weaver. There's no point in concealing anything. Either he's going to join us or we're going to execute him.

"You're mad," Weaver says. "This old wreck isn't going anywhere."

"You had better hope that it will," I say. "We could use another hand."

Weaver scowls. "You're not going to trust me to be a part of this."

"I'd like to. It'd make my life easier."

When we planned this mission, we knew we might have to kill people. A life taken to preserve the lives of others. That doesn't help me right now.

God should be here with me. If I could feel his presence in the room right now, I would have the strength to do what needs to be done.

"Do you believe in a higher power?" I ask.

"What?"

"A creator, a maker of all things. Do you pray or go to church?"

"When I was a kid," Weaver says. "Not anymore."

"You think you grew out of it?"

"I guess."

I stare at him, trying to get a glimpse inside that head, to see into his heart. Is there a spark left from those childhood days? "All right, so what do you think now? Do you think all of this, everything we see and experience, just happened? Or do you believe in something? Do you have faith?"

Weaver frowns. "Is that what this is? Are you some kind of cult?"

"Exactly the opposite. You're the one trapped in a cult, my friend." I move away from the wall, letting my body drift gently towards him. "All of this is part of it. We're part of something better."

"You're a Christian?"

"I am, but other members of our community are Muslim, Jewish, Sikh and more. I don't care what your path to the creator is, only that you have one."

"So, you're saying you want me to be religious?"

"I'm saying I want to have faith in you and for you to have faith in yourself as a creature created for a higher purpose, the betterment of humanity if you like. I want you to believe, then I can believe in you."

Weaver laughs. "I remember hearing about people who believed in God, not because of any allegiance, but because the alternative was too awful to imagine. 'Might as well', eh? My situation seems like a pretty ironic turn on all that."

"If you'll accept being baptised, or agree to profess the shahada, that'll be good enough for me."

"Who will baptise me? You?"

"Yes, I'm an ordained minister. I can do that."

Weaver shrugs. "Then if my options are being dead or being alive, I'll take being alive."

I nod. Good answer. I don't trust him yet, but we've made the first step. "We'll keep you here for now. But when we're scheduled to check in with the shuttle, I'll need your help. In the meantime, I'll leave you to find yourself and your faith."

I press the panel beside the inner airlock door. Tolwyn already has it configured so it responds to my thumbprint. All of us worked on replicas back on Earth.

"You heard?" I say.

"Yes, the microphones in there are working and I managed to record everything," Tolwyn says. "If we need to, we may be able to splice together enough for some voice generation."

"And fake his comms check with the shuttle?"

"If needs be."

I glance at Weaver. He's not moved from where he was. His back is to the outer airlock doors, but he's closed his eyes. Maybe he's taking what I said seriously. "It may come to that," I say. "In the meantime, we have about forty-five minutes before the check-in."

"What do you want me to do?"

"Keep him here and wait for me to call you on comms. In the meantime, anything you can fix that's in reach is a bonus for us."

"Understood, Deacon."

★ ★ ★

I make my way to engineering next.

Power will be an issue for us. Without the reactor, a ship like this would be designed to run on a set of emergency batteries. However, I'm sure these have already been stripped from the ship to service the other Fleet patrol vessels that have remained around Mars. *Asthoreth* will have been left with just enough juice to maintain her orbit. It's likely they've been calculating any thruster operations remotely.

"Halle, do you have good news for me?" I ask as I enter the reactor control room.

She turns towards me as I arrive. "Some good news, yes," she says. "The reactor is here. At some point, the emergency cooling protocol was activated, and the core was deployed outside on the hull."

I glance around. Again, there are portable power units plugged into a variety of different systems. This time, Halle has a working terminal display in front of her. "You've accessed the ship's computer?" I ask.

"No, this is a basic operating system that I brought with me to run diagnostics," Halle explains. "But the terminal is working. It's undamaged, apart from a crack in the screen." She moves away from the display to the far end of the room where there is another door. "The battery bank was in here. They left six units plugged in out of thirty or more. I guess they used the others to repair the other ships."

"That was my thought too," I say.

"The ship's computer is probably in receive mode only," Halle says. "I expect Merrick will have discovered that already. They'll be sending course corrections via some automated process. Probably already forgotten about how it's set up."

"What about thrusters and getting us moving?" I ask.

"Difficult," Halle says. "They'll have mostly drained the fuel tanks, but we should have enough to get going. The main problem will be the engines. According to the data files Weaver sent to all of us, the engines were the most damaged part of the ship. If we try to activate anything more than the manoeuvring nozzles, we could rupture something and cause an explosion." She grimaces. "A visual check of the main thrusters would require an EVA along with an internal inspection. The sort of thing they'd do in a repair cradle back in Earth orbit. The minute we start doing that, the shuttle pilots are going to ask what we're up to."

"What are our options?"

"I haven't thought of anything yet," Halle says. "But we're also going to alert the shuttle if we reinsert the reactor core, so…"

"So, we need to deal with the shuttle."

"Yes."

I'm thinking. My efforts with Weaver may have saved his life, but there's no way I can do the same with the pilots who brought us here. "We need them gone," I say. "But gone in a way that doesn't encourage Fleet to send anything else in this direction. That means to all intents and purposes, our status here shouldn't change."

Halle nods. "If you can get on-board the shuttle and do something, maybe?"

"We'll need them unconscious or dead," I say, thinking out loud. "I'm not a fan of the latter, if we can avoid it."

"Yeah, me either."

I frown. An idea is starting to come together. "I need to get to the bridge. Leave this with me. Just do as much as you can in the time we have."

"Which is, how long?"

"Forty minutes or so until Weaver checks in. I think he'll work with us, so after that, another two hours. I'll let you know what I need from you as soon as I have a plan."

"Great. The more time you give me, the better."

On my way back to the bridge, the components start to connect. Getting rid of the shuttle has to be part of our escape with the ship. The fact that the pilots will radio the Hub needs to be turned to our advantage. They would be the best witnesses to our demise.

I'm thinking about our orbital position. If we can get enough thruster control to change our path to an ellipse, maybe we can get a gravity assist from Mars. That'd put us a fair way out. Plus, if we can spoof our position in the planet's shadow, the shuttle and the rest of Fleet might think we're burning up in the planet's atmosphere.

That's a lot of 'ifs'.

★ ★ ★

People of Mars.

You are being denied your rights. The word 'citizen' is being used as a privilege, a tantalising aspiration for you to work towards, paying off the debt of your journey to this red hell.

On Earth, every human being has a right to be a citizen. Every nation accepts that individuals who were born within their territorial claim are citizens of that nation. Those who emigrate from one nation to another may apply to become citizens of their new home. There is a process for this, with each individual being assessed and provided with an opportunity to become citizens of the country they now live in.

On Mars, there is no process. Instead, the people you work for present an illusion to you as truth. You will never be citizens of Mars so long as they remain in charge. It is not in their interests for you to achieve this status.

Each of us arrives on this planet with a debt. Debt is the cost of travel to this world. The same debts were placed upon the shoulders of the first colonists who arrived in America. They exchanged their labour for a chance to live in a New World, they agreed to work off the price of their voyage before striking out for themselves to make a new life on the frontier.

There is a romantic parallel between this original American dream and the opportunity afforded to us on Mars. This image is propaganda, nothing more. The debt you owe to the corporations that brought you here will see you hold on to them for the rest of your lives. You are indentured into servitude, as am I. There will be no payoff, no freedom for any of us at the end.

Unless we change things.

The only way for us all to become free is for us all to act as one. Our labour is the commodity we were brought here to provide. Our labour has value, particularly in this time of crisis. If you want change, then you must leverage this commodity. You must stand up to Citizen Jabbutu, and proclaim the rights that you deserve. Only then can any of us achieve the new lives that we were promised.

In this moment, you have power. That power will vanish if you do not act.

Out here, in the ruins of our home, we await you. The Jezero dome is broken, but we can rebuild it, just as we can rebuild our lives here. But neither can be the same as they were before. We must rebuild Jezero into something new, just as we will remake our lives and our arrangements with the people that brought us here. In this moment, where our survival depends upon this work, those who would be our lords and masters must learn the price of our toil.

People of Mars, we await your answer. We look forward to welcoming you back to what was, with a new purpose to forge what will be.

Antonio Sammatri.

Chapter Six

Shann

I'm physically and emotionally exhausted on the ride back from Edmonton.

It was good to see Jethry and the kids – my nephew and niece. Over the two days I stayed at my dad's place, we spent some quality time together. Jethry's doing well. Cancer is gone and hasn't come back. There's some resentment with me for being away, but we got past that.

Dad was more difficult to deal with.

The more I'm away from him, the more I notice the little details. The words used about my 'condition' could be referring to the recovery time I need in an Earth-gravity environment before I go back out to Mars, if I'm being generous.

But I know they also refer to my disability.

Don't get me wrong. I grew up with two parents who loved me unconditionally. They were there with me going through childhood, puberty and the young adult years. The only time we started to disagree with each other was when I said I wanted to join Fleet.

Dad didn't believe it would happen. In conversations when I talked about what I wanted, he was distant, never on-board. He didn't argue with me, but the quiet spoke volumes. Sooner or later, I was going to be rejected. Someone would decide my lack of legs would make me an unviable candidate for space. He thought they'd come out and say it in that blunt military way people do. He thought I'd be crushed by that and prepared himself to pick up the pieces.

Only that's not what happened.

I passed the basic assessments, then got assigned to an applied astrophysics programme. After that, the tutors laid out a schedule for me. Pass the modules and I'd go up. There was never a moment where being born with no legs made a difference to how I was evaluated.

I mean, I still got my share of prejudice, sure. But no one made it an obstacle in my path.

I guess in some respects, Dad's still waiting for that rejection and for me to come back to the nest a wounded little bird. Maybe that's why he's never really celebrated my success.

The house and the lack of ramp access out the front. Does that mean he's moved on? Or stopped caring? No, I don't think it's that simple.

Mum died just before I got my lieutenant commission. I was given a few weeks' compassionate leave and attended the funeral with the whole family. Within months of that, Jethry had his first cancer diagnosis. Five years younger than me, he'd always had to come second when I needed extra support and attention. I don't know if he resented that. If he did, he never said anything to me. By that point, I was away a lot, but when I did come back, the focus had shifted. I saw how Dad was treating him. Jeth became the wounded bird I was supposed to be.

That must have been hard on all of them, and it only got worse. I was an occasional visitor to their trauma. Maybe that's why, for Dad, I'm on the outside of it.

The screen in front of me flashes. There's a call coming in. I key up the window and accept it.

"Hello?"

"Commodore Shann? This is Hajyan Alkini. Do you have time for a conversation?"

"Sure."

I know who I'm talking to. Hajyan Alkini was the first chef de mission for the Mars colony. He must be in his eighties or nineties by now. I key up the video, and a camera above the windscreen activates, so Alkini can see me as we talk.

There is no image by return, only audio and a blank screen.

"Mister Alkini, how can I help you?" I ask.

"I heard you were back on Earth, and I wanted a chance to talk to you about the current situation at Jezero," Alkini says. "I wondered if I could offer some support and advice?"

I frown. "Mister Alkini, I'm sure you're aware that a lot of what's happening on Mars is classified. I won't be able to give you much more than what you've heard in the news."

"It's more about what I can tell you," Alkini says. "How much do you know about what happened when we first arrived on Mars?"

"I've read all the mission reports," I say. "Including the classified ones. Do you have something you want to add to them?"

"There were people who went missing," Alkini says. "Names and faces that disappeared. I opened an investigation, but they told me I was imagining things, that I was mistaken. I wasn't. There were people on Mars who shouldn't be there. I—"

The connection is gone.

I'm working on the screen, trying to re-establish the call. But there's no response to my requests. A diagnostic reveals no issues with the car's transmitter and connection. Clearly there's something wrong at Alkini's end.

It would be easy to dismiss the concerns of an old man who came back from Mars decades ago and has been retired for nearly as long, but he made the effort to reach out to me, getting my contact details from someone at Fleet so we could have a conversation.

I'll need to mention this to Savvantine.

I key up a new window on the screen and place a secure call. After a few minutes, Savvantine appears on the screen.

"You look tired," I say. "Are you still in Europe?"

"Yes, and it's pretty late here. What do you want?"

"Good to see you too," I say. "I just had a call from Hajyan Alkini. You know who that is?"

"I do. Is he still alive?"

"The comms ID suggests the caller was Alkini," I say. "He sounded like he could be Alkini."

"What did he tell you?"

"That there are people on Mars who shouldn't be there."

Savvantine frowns. "Really? Did he give you any specifics?"

"No, we were cut off before he could explain."

"That's weird."

"Yeah, could be nothing, but if you have a registered address for him, a welfare check might be in order."

"I'll get that actioned."

"Thanks."

"We've been doing an inventory of all the off-Earth transits, looking for Rocher clones," Savvantine says. "We've been cross-referencing all the filed documents with every bit of camera footage we've been able to get our hands on. That might give us a starting point in checking some of the early colonial missions to find any missing people. However, I'm reluctant to assign resources to this based on a garbled message from an old man."

"The Sammatri report mentions outsiders," I say. "We always assumed they were part of the mining operations on Phobos and landed with the insurgents who attacked the station."

A new window opens on the screen. A list of names begins scrolling down. "You may recognise this," Savvantine says. "A medical emergency was declared at the mining facility. They sent the patients on a shuttle to the station. That's how they got in."

"Emerson Drake was called to attend to the injured," I say. "He told me that when he got there, the shuttle docked and there was an explosion. That's how the attack started."

"The names are mostly fakes," Savvantine says. "But the clever thing is, when we search for them, records appear. It's as if the queries trigger some kind of generative response. The records materialise in a variety of different databases, only when you look for them. You have to be checking for changes in all of the systems to notice what's going on."

"Can you remove the program?"

"Possibly, but if we do, we'll alert whoever put it there that we're on to them." Savvantine smiles. "What it does mean is that there is active software in these databases that can change the listings. So that means—"

"Records could have been deleted as well as added."

"Exactly."

Something nags at me. A memory. I'm thinking about when I EVA'd from *Khidr* to the freighter *Hercules*. "There was a lot of colony equipment on-board *Hercules*," I say. "At the time, we were surprised to find it there. The entries in the inventory had been redacted."

"And the ship was on an outbound journey from Mars," Savvantine says. "Europa may have needed some supplies, maybe?"

"Not the kind we found. Large-scale hydroponic equipment, the stuff you need for big warehouses of plants."

"Interesting," Savvantine says. "I'll do some digging after I've had coffee. Expect a report later today."

"Thanks, Colonel."

"Happy to help, Commodore."

The conversation ends and I'm left with my thoughts.

★ ★ ★

After that, I sleep for a few hours.

Sitting in a chair in the car is like sitting in the captain's chair on the *Khidr*. When I close my eyes, I'm back there, watching Le Garre pilot the ship. Johansson on comms, Keiyho in the engineering seat.

I know Keiyho's dead and Le Garre is probably dead too. Johansson's still out there around Mars. But in this dream, they're here, sitting around me as we're travelling to rendezvous with *Hercules*.

I'm remembering the mission, going aboard and searching through the cargo.

Inside the crate are test tubes, hundreds of them. The contents are frozen. I pick one out. My suit lights illuminate something in the centre of it.

"They're carrying bees," I say.

Equipment for an underground apiary. There are hydroponic facilities on Mars that use colonies of bees. Maybe they were part of a plan to expand the settlement around the Jezero dome? But why would they still be aboard the freighter after it left Phobos Station heading out towards Ceres and Europa?

It's been three years since I was standing in front of those containers in the half-light of a damaged freight corridor. Events quickly overtook the moment. *Gallowglass* showed up and suddenly we were in a fight for our lives. Easy to understand why the details were forgotten.

I remember talking to Kiran Shah, the man we rescued from *Hercules*. I remember the video briefing file about 'Project Outreach'. What was that man's name? Doctor Aki Kuranawa from Kyoto, that was it!

I key up another window on the screen and start writing a message to Savvantine. She needs to check these names.

★ ★ ★

"Captain Ellisa Shann?"

At my command, a thought impulse triggers the artificial legs, and I stand up. The ensign who has called my name looks at me and flips a salute. I return it. The exoskeleton servos I'm wearing assist the action.

I set the machine to target him and follow. He leads me through the double doors into the inquiry room.

I'm looking around. There's wood panelling all over the walls, the kind that tries to tell you it's expensive and you're in a serious place. A desk runs in a U-shape at the far end. Ten flag officers are sat behind it, all of them in immaculate uniform, all of them old.

"Captain Shann, please take a seat."

The chair being offered is in the centre of the room, the chair for a person being questioned, a person on trial. I am that person.

I switch the legs to path mode. A course is plotted to the chair, and they follow it perfectly. The seating protocol is automated too, all part of the package. I find the furniture more comfortable than I'd expected. Then again, there's no danger of me falling asleep.

"Captain, this board of inquiry has been established to investigate the decisions made by you and your crew throughout your last tour of duty commanding the Fleet patrol ship *Khidr.* All of those seated here are senior officers with sufficient clearance to review all the material you have submitted, and the material provided by Fleet investigators appointed to the case."

The words are spoken by Admiral Dean. She's the lead for this investigation, someone I know by reputation, but not in person. Thirty years ago, she was second-in-command on a ship sent out from Earth to resupply research bases on the Moon and Mars, so she has some relevant experience for this. I'm not sure about the others. I resisted the temptation to read through their public records.

There was always going to be a board of inquiry into my actions when I got back to Earth. We all knew this would be what I would face.

"Captain Shann, we have a lot of questions, as I'm sure you will expect. Are you ready for us to proceed?"

"Yes, Admiral."

"Good."

Three days of polite interrogation followed. I never once felt like I was the enemy in the room. That was the surprise for me. Maybe Savvantine's people had prepared the ground? I don't know, but the biggest question was why it had taken so long for me to return to Earth. That was to be expected.

"Nearly three years," Dean says. "Can you explain that, Captain?"

"At no time was I ordered to return," I reply. "As the senior commander on-site, it seemed prudent to be the one dealing with matters at hand. At that point, thousands of people's lives were at stake on the ground and in orbit."

"What about after the relief crews arrived? Capable officers were sent to manage the situation."

"With respect to them, no one had combat experience in vacuum, nor did they have experience of operating our best ship, *Gallowglass*. If any of the enemy vessels had returned, we would have been placing ourselves at a disadvantage."

"So, you decided you were the best person to be in charge."

"I did, yes."

"Isn't that a little arrogant?"

"If it is, then I apologise, but I think the decision was the right one. If I'd been making a choice about somebody else and had been comparing records, I would have done exactly the same thing."

"Understood, thank you."

That wasn't the end of the questioning on that particular topic, but it was the moment where things began to pivot. I sensed a change in the room after that. I don't know whether I could attribute that to my answers or Savvantine working behind the scenes.

That evening, I got a little more information when the colonel found a way to contact me via a secure line.

"They're running scared. The attempted terrorist attack on your ship made them realise you're not the enemy. Right now, the pen pushers are being outvoted. Dean is starting to see you as an asset that we need to deploy."

"Maybe I should have stayed out there."

"No, we needed this resolved. Your people told them a clear and coherent story about what happened. Now you're doing the same. It'll be over soon, and I think it'll give us something to work with."

In the whole time I was subject to the inquiry, I was detained and confined on the military base. This was partially due to my medical needs as much as any desire to control proceedings and contain any information about what was going on.

Rehabilitation to gravity is hard, no matter what exercise you do when you're out in space. The body doesn't rebuild and repair itself in the same way when it's not subject to the same forces that we're familiar with on Earth. Every hour I wasn't answering questions, I was either eating, sleeping or subject to physical examination.

"Captain Shann?"

"Yes, Admiral."

"Captain Shann, it is the finding of this board of inquiry that your actions during your extended tour of duty aboard the Fleet patrol vessel *Khidr* and your subsequent actions as *de facto* Fleet commander-in-chief in the Mars sector should be endorsed, sanctioned and ratified by Fleet as official strategy and policy. Furthermore, it is the recommendation of this board that your promotion to commodore be sanctioned and that you be returned to active duty in the Mars sector as soon as you are physically able to be sent there."

Elation.

I expected these people to try and crush me. They didn't. Instead, they went through all the details presented to them and exonerated me.

In that moment, I felt guilty. Lieutenant Bill Travers withheld information to protect me when he faced a similar inquiry into his actions. Major Angel Le Garre did the same. So did our quartermaster, Sergeant Sam Chase.

Being exonerated made me want to confess to all my weaknesses, all the moments of self-doubt and shame. Standing there on artificial legs, held up straight by a supportive exoskeleton, I had no choice but to exist in the moment of exoneration.

"Captain Shann, you look exhausted," Admiral Dean says. "The recommendations of this panel are not without some stipulations that will ensure your health and well-being. After all, as you said, you are the most experienced commanding officer available to us at this time of escalated threat."

"Thank you, Admiral."

I don't remember leaving the room, but I must have done so. They let me stay in the allocated quarters for another night, then shipped me out to recovery accommodation next to the medical centre.

Three days later, I got promoted.

Chapter Seven

Sirocco

Mars is a cold and desolate place.

We're driving into a red desert of broken rock and sand. It's difficult to accept that some of this terrain has been undisturbed for thousands of years. I'm seeing a world that most humans haven't seen or walked on.

I glance behind us. The rover is making a dark red track in the dirt. Anyone who tries to figure out where we've gone will be able to follow us, easily.

I open my mouth to ask Tellen about this but close it again before I say anything over comms. He must have a plan. He must have known we'd be easy to track down. Every colonist has a bio-monitor chip under their skin. Anyone goes missing and the security services can track them. In fact, they should be monitoring us right now. Surely some kind of automated system will have worked out we're off mission and started to raise the alarm? Unless Tellen has prepared for that? If he has, he hasn't—

Relax, Magnus, *relax*…

There is a beauty to this world, despite its lifelessness. The colours of the land under a butterscotch sky, illuminated by a much smaller sun – further away from us than on Earth. All of it strange, yet familiar. Familiar enough that I keep thinking I can take off my helmet and feel the breeze on my face as we drive across the flat plains around the Jezero crater.

I've seen satellite images of the colony from before it was ruined. They show you those during your basic training and briefing. The dome had a diameter of just under ten kilometres and sits nicely in the centre of the old impact ring, with transport connections heading north to Hera and east to the other settlements. There is nowhere else as big as this, but humanity is gradually branching out.

The comms channel activates in my ear. “Halton, to Tellen.”

“Go ahead,” Tellen replies.

“Team two dropped off. We’re pushing on to our starting point now.”

“Acknowledged.”

These people still think we’re doing the inspection work. That’s a relief. But it also sets the clock for us. We all have oxygen for a six-hour expedition before the scrubbers kick in and try to extend that.

When the rest of the team get to the inspection tower, they’ll see the tracks and have to make a decision about following us. They’ll assess their oxygen reserve, decide they don’t have enough to risk it, and radio in for support. That’ll take more time, letting us get further away.

We’re outside the Jezero crater, travelling across a plateau with the raised edges of the ancient impact zone on either side of us. Ahead, there’s a flashing light. Someone Tellen has arranged to meet?

Our rover is heading straight for it.

I raise my arm and take a look at the display. I have four hours, forty-five minutes of oxygen left.

We’re closing in on the flashing light. I can see what it is. A micro-rover just sitting there ahead of us. Tellen slows down and pulls up alongside the little vehicle. He climbs out of the driver’s seat and walks over to it, pulling out the cable that he used on the tower before.

Tellen stays there for a minute or two. Then, he unplugs and makes his way back to our rover. When he reaches the vehicle, he motions for me to get out.

He’s holding two devices in his hands. They look like bracelets. He motions for me to take one of them. I do. When I’ve done that, he slips the second one onto his left arm, up above the elbow, then he presses a button on the device. A light comes on and it tightens around his bicep.

I do the same. The moment the device activates, the display on my arm goes blank and the comms chatter in my ear disappears, along with the digital overlays in my helmet that I was using before. I can’t even see the digital readout for my oxygen.

I glare at Tellen. He gestures ahead, indicating that I should get out of the rover and follow him.

Looks like we're walking from here.

The micro-rover starts up and trundles ahead of us, its thick rubber tyres managing the terrain without difficulty. As I watch, the vehicle deploys a set of brushes behind the wheels; these disturb the ground even further, masking the thin tyre tracks.

Clever.

I glance behind us. Our boot prints in the Martian dust are still there. An obvious track to find us. Ahead, there are no marks, as if we are the first people ever to walk here.

No data means no distractions. The loudest thing I can hear is the sound of my own breathing. I've no idea how many more breaths I'll get to take before my tank runs out. Did the arm band we're wearing affect our scrubbers too? Does that mean we'll run out of O_2 before we get to wherever it is that we're going?

I'm getting anxious. I can feel it. They say anxiety can kill you when you're operating on tanked air. It makes you breathe faster and your heart race. All that extra O_2 is wasted as nervous energy. I need to stay calm.

I'm staring at Tellen's back as he walks, about two steps ahead of me. He must have more information. He wouldn't walk out here alone without some idea of where we're going to end up.

I need to trust him. I've trusted him so far and he hasn't done anything that suggests I should be suspicious of what we agreed.

I grit my teeth and keep walking.

* * *

I remember Melbourne.

After the city fell, they sent us in. A coalition of international forces dropped by helicopters with a set of key objectives. A few of those were locations, some of them were people.

I was sent in as part of a force of thirty or forty soldiers tasked with holding the airport to the north of the city. We were told it would be a security operation, protecting the evacuating flights from protestors and the like. Not a military engagement.

That went to hell when drones started flying over the fence and attacking planes and passengers on the ground.

We were given orders to shoot. Semi-automatic rifles and truck-mounted machine guns against swarms of automated vehicles. The enemy didn't need to fight back, they just had to get through and hit their targets, which they did.

Hundreds of people died when Flight 6382 took off just before a drone slammed into the cockpit, killing the pilot and co-pilot instantly. The plane wobbled, the right wing hit the ground and that was it, everything exploded in a wall of heat and noise.

Soon, both runways were out of action, burning planes and jet fuel ruining any chance of another flight getting into the air.

We were told to retreat. We had to commandeer every working vehicle and head north on the expressway with every survivor we could find. A new evacuation plan would be arranged. They would airlift us out of the open country, thirty miles away.

The civilians were given places in the vehicles. Ten of us were ordered to form a rear guard, walking a few miles behind everyone else, just in case we were followed.

Hours of walking through a broken landscape. Yeah, I remember that.

We've been going an hour or so I guess. We're seeing wreckage out here, the broken and twisted remains of Phobos Station. The Mars atmosphere isn't thick enough to atomise everything that falls from orbit, more survived than if this had happened on Earth.

Ahead, I can see a large chunk of debris. Jagged spines of metal stick out of it like claws or fingers reaching into the sky.

We're walking directly towards it.

I continue to follow Tellen as we descend into the small bowl around the fallen fragment. As we get closer, I start to appreciate its size. We're walking towards an object that is at least eight storeys high. The surface metal is scorched black and marked with dents and holes. I wonder what part of Phobos Station this was from.

I've seen pictures of the facility from before, the central column and ring with spokes, like you'd get on a bicycle wheel. I can't picture this remnant fitting into that clean white image used in old promotional materials.

There's movement. Someone is walking out from the inside of the wreck. They're carrying a rifle. When we get close, they point at us both and gesture towards where they've come from. Tellen holds up his hands in that universal expression of surrender. After a moment's hesitation, I do the same.

We walk into the shadow of the debris. I can see through the torn metal and plastic. There's a shuttle parked on the other side. As we approach, the outer airlock opens, and we're directed to enter.

I do exactly as I'm told, following Tellen into the airlock. The person with the rifle remains outside. They press a button and the outer doors close, trapping us inside.

* * *

Airlocks are always a good place to interrogate someone. You have control of both exits and, if the individual you want to question has no oxygen tank with them, you can threaten them with a pretty violent and sudden end.

Even now, Tellen and I aren't in a good situation. Whoever has let us in here could just leave us in a vacuum until we run out of air. Dying through oxygen deprivation and carbon dioxide poisoning is pretty awful by all accounts.

I'm looking at the inner airlock door. There is a man inside the ship watching us both. He points towards a pressure monitor on the wall beside the door. The display says *No* O_2. As I watch, the message vanishes and is replaced with a per centage number that starts to go up.

I touch Tellen on the shoulder and point at the monitor. He gives me a thumbs-up.

When the monitor reaches one hundred per cent a green light comes on. Tellen reaches for the seals around his helmet and thumbs them open.

I do the same, inhaling deeply. I guess the tanked air in the room isn't much different from what's in my suit, but it feels better.

"You're Doctor Henry Tellen?" The words are metallic; they come from a speaker beside the inner airlock door.

"Yes… Yes, I am," Tellen says. "We came here after making contact. I need to speak to Antonio Sammatri."

"Who is your friend?"

"This is Magnus Sirocco. He was sent here from Earth."

"He's the one they told us about?"

"Yes, he is."

The inner airlock doors open. The man on the other side points at the compartments on the wall. "Get out of those suits and stow them. We're shielded in here, so they can't track you, but make sure you keep the jammers on and activated until we sort out something more permanent for you both."

"What about your friend outside?" I ask.

"He's going to clear up your tracks," the man says. "We lift off in ten minutes. Get to it."

The man disappears into the ship, leaving Tellen and me to do as we're told. It makes sense not to argue or ask questions given the time limit. I guess there will be time for questions later.

Once the gear is stowed, we both make our way out of the airlock. There are six empty passenger seats in the cabin. Tellen settles into one of them and starts to strap himself in. I do the same.

Moments later, the shuttle lifts off. We're going up, vertically, then forwards. I'm pushed back into my seat. There's no display or view out of the windows from here. That means we don't know where we're going. Probably for the best.

★ ★ ★

An hour later, and we're descending to land.

I have my eyes closed. I'm trying to feel the directions of movement. Not that I'll get any idea of where we are from that, but it's something to focus on, instead of asking Tellen questions that I know I won't get any satisfactory answers to.

Touchdown is gentle. The pilot, whoever they are, is clearly well practised at doing what they do. I open my eyes and glance at Tellen. He's staring at the open door to the cockpit. I guess he wants to ask questions too.

After a few minutes, our host steps through into the passenger cabin. "My name is Jeremiah Madiro." He looks at Tellen. "Doctor, I'm the person you've been in contact with."

Tellen nods. "Then you know why I'm here."

"I know why you're both here. It's my job to determine if we can trust you." Madiro inclines his head towards the airlock door. "You only leave when I decide that you can, that clear?"

I smile. Clear lines are something I appreciate. "I was sent here to help you," I say.

"And we appreciate that. But before you're allowed into our home, I need to assess if that mission is genuine, or if you're a plant, sent to betray what we're doing."

"Mister Madiro," Tellen says, "if you're the person who I've been talking to, you know about my research. Test me. I'll pass."

"I don't doubt it, Doctor, but we need to be sure you haven't been briefed to contact us by a corporation or Fleet Intelligence." Madiro holds up a device. I recognise it as a medical injector. "The first step in doing that is to deactivate your bio-monitor."

"Fine," Tellen says. He unzips the cuff on his right sleeve and draws back the arm of his suit, revealing his bare wrist. He holds out his hand. "The chip is on the back of my hand, just above the wrist bone."

"Thank you." Madiro reaches forwards and sets the injector against an old scar. He presses the button, there's a hiss and Tellen winces. Madiro pulls away and I see bright red blood. "We'll get you a patch for that," he says. Then he turns to me.

I unzip my sleeve just like Tellen did. The scar on the back of my wrist is still pink and a little puffy. The monitor was only put there a few weeks ago when I arrived at the orbital hub. "Go ahead," I say.

Madiro triggers the device, repeating the procedure. The pain is sharp, like a needle jabbing into you. "The incision cracks the microprocessor on the implant," he says. "To all intents and purposes, you're still chipped, but any attempt to access the chip won't work."

"Thank you," I say. "That feels like getting a little bit of freedom back."

Madiro smiles. "There's more. Come with me."

We move into the airlock. I reach for the compartments where our gear is stowed, but Madiro stops me. "You won't need that," he says. He steps to the outer door and presses the control panel. The mechanism activates and the airlock opens…

…into an underground cavern.

I'm stepping out of the shuttle onto gravel sand. I can hear the crunch underfoot without it being muffled through my helmet.

"I'm… I don't know what to say."

"We didn't build this," Madiro says. "But we know who did. Follow me please."

I glance up. There are electric lights on the rocky walls above us. About forty feet up, I can see a metal door, big enough to fit a shuttle through, cut into the stone. That must have been where he came through. The pilot managed a vertical descent straight down to land here, or the final stage is pre-programmed. I'm guessing the latter.

"Mister Sirocco?"

"Sorry," I say, and start walking after the other two.

* * *

True artificial intelligence or artificial general intelligence (AGI) was last modelled by the scientist Doctor Elisha Imewaju in 2081. His work built on the additive and iterative principles of early twenty-first-century computer scientists looking into the idea.

Massive corporations went bankrupt trying to create an iterative computer system that would become self-aware if enough processing power and data could be shovelled into it. It's hard to imagine the world around that time. Brand names that were more powerful than countries crashed on the rocks, seeking something unobtainable through the methods they were using at the time.

Imewaju's idea was to use human models. He explained the ways in which the human brain often cheated in creating a perception of reality. Examples like the colour purple, which in reality, doesn't exist. Imewaju believed there were ways in which an AI brain could be created to shortcut things in a similar way, thereby not relying solely on a continual processing of data to learn and iterate itself.

Imewaju's concept was tested, but after several excited reports in the mainstream news media, the project quickly faded into obscurity. A variety of patents was established, but then bought up and sold to various different commercial entities.

Rumours persisted that true AI was still being worked on by several corporations. No evidence has, as of yet, emerged to indicate that this is actually happening.

Peter Gelburn – Director: European Police Service.

Chapter Eight

Iskander

Ten minutes until we need to get Weaver to check in.

"We have partial thruster control," Merrick says. "The *Asthoreth*'s computer is slaved to a satellite that is taking instructions from a ground control system at Hera. We can take the connection offline and reboot the computer, shifting it into prime mode. From there, we'll be able to pilot the ship."

"But the minute we do that, the authorities will know something is up," Dennis says.

"We're in the same situation with the shuttle and activating the reactor," I say. "Everything needs to happen simultaneously. I want a course plot to give us as much of a gravity assist from Mars as possible. We'll use the shadow of the planet to hide from their positional tracking systems."

"That won't be enough," Merrick says. "They'll follow our route and send someone after us."

"We'll fake a shallow re-entry and burn-up," I say. "That'll give us more time to work on repairs. If we can get the reactor and main engines working, then we can get away."

"Still not great odds," Dennis says.

"Better than our current situation." I check the time. Eight minutes left. I activate a comms channel. "Tolwyn, bring Weaver to the primary airlock. We're going to check in from there."

"Acknowledged."

I make my way from the bridge back to the umbilical connection. The shuttle pilots will have a plot on where we all are in the ship, so they'll know where we are when we make the call. I doubt they'll care very much, unless we've already raised suspicions.

When I get to the airlock, Tolwyn and Weaver are already there. "You know what we need you to do?" I ask Weaver.

Weaver nods.

"Okay then, let's do it."

I pull out the comms bead that I took from our former supervisor and hand it to him. "Short and sweet," I say.

"Understood."

Weaver reattaches the bead to the collar of his suit then taps it to activate it. "Weaver to Shuttle?"

"Receiving."

The transmission is on an open frequency. We can all hear the replies. "Just checking in," Weaver says. "Task proceeding as planned."

"Great. Update again in two hours."

"Confirmed."

Weaver ends the connection and looks at me. "That okay?" he asks.

"Perfect." I hold out my hand. Weaver removes the bead and gives it back to me. I nod to Tolwyn.

"Okay, back to the airlock," he says.

"Wait, haven't I proved something to you?" Weaver asks.

I frown. "What are you suggesting?"

"You asked me to report in and lie, I did that. You told me there was a chance I could join your cause."

"There is a chance," I say. "But we're not there yet."

Weaver shrugs. He glances at Tolwyn. "Maybe not, but it strikes me that two hours is not going to be enough time for six of you to fix this ship. If you had seven people working on it, you might have a better chance."

I stare at him, trying to measure his commitment. Is this a man who is looking for an opportunity to turn on us, or someone who genuinely sees the purpose in our mission? "Judas Iscariot betrayed his master for thirty pieces of silver," I say.

Weaver smiles. "You saying you're Jesus?"

I shake my head. "I'm not claiming that, but I don't want you to be Judas."

"I'm not a Judas."

"Then let's both try to live up to what we've said, eh?" I pull off the glove on my right hand and raise my thumb to my lips. I lick the tip and press it to Weaver's forehead. The gesture is minimal and symbolic, but it conveys what I need it to convey. "Don't let me down."

"I won't."

I hand the comms bead back to him. "I want you both to go to engineering. Tell Halle I sent you and to give you a set of tasks."

"Understood."

★ ★ ★

Faith is a constant in my adult life.

I grew up in Romania, in a little city called Sighişoara, in the aftermath of the European war. My parents were wise enough to ensure I learned to speak and write in English as well as Romanian.

We went to church as a family every week. Mother, father, three children, sitting in the same seats, listening to the Catholic sermon. My childhood became about obligation and sin. I worked for my family, doing anything that I was asked to do.

As I grew older, I saw how this worked. Religion spoke of rigid roles, duties and responsibilities. Failure meant guilt and shame. You did what you were told to do, otherwise there would be punishment in this world or in the next.

Often, that punishment was physical. My father believed he had a moral duty to inflict injury upon me and my younger brother and sister if we transgressed. He believed his violence would save us from judgement by the divine.

And my mother let it happen.

I left Sighişoara to work on boats. Many people did that. Crews were needed for long voyages, so as soon as I was old enough, I signed up. That meant I got fed and had a place to sleep while my parents got the money.

Gradually, the voyages became longer and longer. I got a chance to see the world. I discovered that people didn't live the way I lived. They didn't see the world the same way as my mother and father did. I learned of new churches, and different religions, the kind I'd only read about in textbooks. I got to experience things in a different way and that made me question what I believed in.

I also fell in love and got my heart broken a few times.

Now I'm staring at a set of burned-out wires. I've pulled out a set of panels from the wall of the passageway near the airlock and found where the power lines have shorted out. There's a set of new cables that I can splice into these. This is the kind of repair I can focus on and feel like I'm making a difference to our situation.

We have two hours. We'll be able to check in again after that, but the shuttle team will start to get suspicious if we don't begin to deliver parts to the cargo hold by then. I need a plan for what we're going to do.

"Iskander to Weaver."

"Go ahead."

"Can you put together a collection of parts we're not going to need? Cross-reference it with the requisition list. I want a selection of stuff we can transfer to the shuttle."

"Will do."

There's lots of equipment that a Fleet patrol vessel will keep aboard for its twenty-four crew. The gravity deck for example; the mechanisms involved in getting that repaired are going to be beyond us in the time we have. That means all the fixtures and furniture could be removed from there. Might take more time than we have, but at least if we can transfer some of the contents, we'll make a show of doing the job we were sent here to do.

"Halle to Iskander."

"Go ahead."

"Can you meet me on the bridge? Would be good to get an update."

"Sure."

I finish splicing the wires, drop a little chemical sealant over the new connections, and replace the wall panel. Getting a progress report on the reactor and our battery power is going to be crucial to whatever strategy I'm able to come up with.

It takes a couple of minutes to get to the bridge. When I arrive, everyone is gathered. It seems Halle wants to get an update from all of us. Makes sense. Maybe I should have called the meeting? I'm not the sort of person who gets insecure about these things.

"All right, I'm here. Where are we at?"

Halle nods to me, taking my cue. "Reactor insertion is ready, Deacon. We have just enough battery power to manage the process. But of course, as soon as we do…"

"What's our backup power level?"

"About fifteen per cent of what it will be when we get the reactor back online," Halle says.

"We'll need that for the initial stage of our escape," I say. I turn to Dennis. "How much thruster control can you get?"

"Enough to alter our course, not enough to run away from anyone they send after us," Dennis replies.

"You can get us into an elliptical orbit?"

"Yes, I think so, but the minute we switch the ship to control mode, they'll know back at Hera."

"It needs to look like a malfunction," I say. "Take the system offline, then reboot. We'll co-ordinate with a message to the shuttle." I turn to Tolwyn. "I need you to rig an explosion in the umbilical."

"That sounds dangerous," Tolwyn says. "What's the plan?"

"We work events in a sequence," I say. "There's an explosion, cutting the shuttle loose. We radio declaring an emergency, then fire the thrusters to set an elliptical orbit. When we get to the far side of Mars, we reinstall the reactor and jettison everything we don't need. That'll make them think we've burned up on a shallow re-entry vector. Then we get the engines fixed, plot our course and escape."

Halle smiles. "That works."

"It may do," I say. "But everything has to happen in order." I glance at everyone in turn. "I'll need you all to do your part."

My eyes fall on Weaver last. He nods. *Good.*

* * *

"You trust him now?"

I'm back in engineering with Halle. I glance at her. I know who she's talking about.

"Weaver did what he was asked to do, when I asked him to do it," I say. "We have to start somewhere."

"I'd suggest he isn't left alone," Halle says.

"Agreed," I reply.

"Otherwise, your plan is pretty good," Halle says.

"It's still pretty fragile," I say. "Plus, we're going to need the resonance drive back online if we're going to get to where we're going."

"You going to tell them where that is?" Halle asks.

"Not yet," I say.

Space is cold and dark and empty. Thin walls keep us alive. Fleet's ships are designed, built and stocked with everything needed for long voyages. Their crews venture out with more than they need for a reason.

That level of redundancy and resilience is what makes *Asthoreth* valuable, even in this broken state. Every system has a backup, most of which we're going to make use of to get away, but it means we will be taking a hard road.

"I trust you, Deacon," Halle says. "The Temple would not have appointed you if you were not the right one to lead us."

"Thank you," I say.

* * *

I'm standing by the umbilical link to the shuttle, thinking about Jacob.

I wish I could have been honest with him. I wish I could have brought him here. We both came to Mars as missionaries for the Temple, but his role was always to work in the kitchen and enable me to leave and do this.

We shared accommodation. We were lovers. But I never told him the details of my purpose. To place such a burden on him would have been unfair. We knew we wouldn't have a lot of time together, so we made the most of what we had.

I doubt I'll see him again.

Now though, I see Weaver, a man who finds himself here by accident, and I wonder if it could have been Jacob instead.

"Deacon?"

I look around. Kewell is talking to me. He had been explaining some of the procedures we're going to need to adopt to avoid detection after we leave Mars orbit. I zoned out.

"Sorry, repeat the last bit."

"Your new friend, Weaver. He still has an active bio-monitor. We're going to need to deactivate it or remove it."

I nod. It's a good reminder. We've all got modifications to our subdermal chips. Those were installed in secret before we left for this mission. To all intents and purposes, the authorities will think we died instantly the moment we turn them off.

"We'll need something sudden, otherwise we're giving them an excuse to check on us," I say.

Kewell grimaces. "That kind of solution leaves a mess. He'll bleed all over the place. We've got medical equipment, but we'll have to be thorough to be absolutely sure it's not transmitting."

"Can you do it?"

"Yes, but you'll need to tell him, when the time comes."

"Fine." I gesture towards the fabric corridor connecting us to the shuttle. "What's your plan for this?"

Kewell shrugs. "Oxygen saturation and a spark from a live cable. Going to have to be that, as we don't have much else up here that we can use. Any investigation will think it's an accident."

"The atmosphere detectors in the passage will alert the shuttle pilots."

"Not if I disable them while we're transferring some items over."

"There are security cameras in there."

"I'll be discreet."

I smile. "Don't go in alone. If an alert is triggered, you may need someone to pull you out."

"Might as well be our friend, Weaver," Kewell says. "That way if they are looking at his biodata, a sudden cut-out would fit with there being an accident." He wags a finger. "But, that's provided we can trust him."

"We have to now," I say. "But, if something happens, you have an opportunity to leave him in the airlock. Are you okay with that?"

I stare at Kewell. He's a family man, raised as a Methodist with strong New Testament beliefs. He doesn't flinch from my gaze. We both know what's at stake here.

He nods.

"Good."

I know it's a difficult choice, but we all signed up for this. We all know that decisions have to be made quickly if we find ourselves in a situation where someone could betray us.

"Bridge to Deacon."

"Go ahead."

"We have a partial sensor plot. Something's come up that you may want to take a look at."

"On my way."

Chapter Nine
Shann

Fleet headquarters in Algiers.

I've been here many times. The entire place is a new construction of plastic, concrete, metal and glass, bright and shiny in the sun.

Fleet is the main business of the city. Its presence here is an economy in itself. Since the decision was made decades ago to locate the centre of operations on Earth in North Africa, the entire region found itself part of a process of renewal.

The decision was carefully made. At the time, the collapse of the United States into three successor territories had led to tensions between all the North American nations. Europe remained powerful, but damaged after the wars against the Eastern Faction.

A base in Algeria offered the chance to begin something new. It made a statement that the new organisation would not be rehashing the same mistakes the world's superpowers had made before.

"Commodore, Sergeant Chase is here to see you."

"Please show him in."

"Yes, Commodore."

An office on the seventh floor of the operations building. My new home for the next three weeks while they prep a ship to get me back to Mars. Medical advice doesn't recommend a turnaround for me that'll be this fast, but they aren't ruling it out either. I've been doing all the exercise regimens I've been given, and my body is responding well, so there's a cautious green light.

Now, I'm sitting behind a big wooden table going through requisition orders, applications, résumés, and public appearance requests. All of them demanding a piece of my time. I need help.

A familiar figure walks through the door and flips me a salute. I return it. Not something that we'd usually do, but Sam Chase has earned more than one commission and turned them all down.

"Good to see you, Sam."

"And you, Commodore."

I note the use of my rank. I glance around the room. Maybe Sam is worried about being recorded, or...

No, I know what it is.

"This is the first time I've seen you since I got back," I say. "Thank you for saving my life."

I'm aware of the public news media coverage and I've read the classified report on what happened. A group of separatists managed to weaponise an old jet aircraft to attack *Gallowglass* as we were making our final approach to Earth. Sam and Major Angel Le Garre managed to steal the aircraft and sabotage the autopilot before it could launch missiles at us.

Le Garre didn't make it. She's still missing, and they've called off the search.

"About, Angel," I say. "I'm sorry."

"Had to be done," Sam says. "We all know what we are to each other."

A third member of my old crew was involved. He was the one who discovered the plot. "You had a chance to talk to Travers?" I ask.

"No. Savvantine's kept him away. She's worried people will link it all together." Sam shrugs. "Seems we all work for her now, whether we like it or not."

"That bother you?" I ask.

"Not really," Sam says. "She's done enough to convince me she's part of the pack."

The pack? I grin. *That means us. That also means Sam trusts Savvantine.* "I read your record. After the board of inquiry cleared you, you turned down three commissions."

"All of them wanted me to join a military college as a trainer," Sam says. "No options for active service."

"You don't think you've earned a rest?"

"Whether I have or I haven't, I don't want one."

"Good." I pick up one of the screens and hold it to him. Sam walks forwards, takes the seat on the other side of the table. His eyes focus on the display. "What am I looking at?"

"Potential crew for three ships," I say. "I need someone I trust to make some decisions, but I can't appoint a sergeant to recommend most of these commissioned roles, so you need to accept a promotion."

Sam's eyes flick over the different profiles. "You worried about any of these? Given what happened to you when you reached Earth."

"Savvantine is doing an extra layer of vetting," I say. "Our choices will go through her as well."

"One more question."

"Go ahead."

"What happens to us?" Sam taps the screen with a finger. "I mean, are we appointing these people and running things from a desk or are we going to get our hands dirty?"

"What do you think?"

Sam nods. He gets it. "Okay, I'm in."

"Good. I'll need you to sign a couple of forms to appoint you as my flag aide. Comes with the rank of lieutenant and my authority. Thumbprint here, eye scan here."

Sam jabs a thumb where requested and leans forwards for the iris scanner. "Do I get a televised ceremony and reception after as well?"

"You caught that?"

"Didn't everybody?"

I've missed this. I'm sitting in a room with a friend who knows the boundaries. We can talk as people, and I know the moment someone else comes in, the banter will stop, and I'll immediately have his unqualified support. We've some catching up to do, but Sam's still in my corner. "They insisted on the reception. Nothing I could do about it."

"I bet you hated all of it."

"Yeah, pretty much."

Silence. But we're both smiling. We don't need to fill the quiet moments. That's another thing about people you really trust.

"We'll be heading out to Mars as soon as they finalise the ships we're taking," I say. "We'll be running things from the new orbital hub, or on-board a vessel, whichever works best for the situation. That'll be part of the brief for the captains we need to appoint."

"What about Johansson? She's still out there, right?"

"Yeah. I got full formal confirmation of her field promotion," I say. "They'd like her back to debrief her, but I have some discretion on when that happens. She can stay or return. It's up to her."

"Will be good to see her."

"Yes, it will." I'm not prying into their relationship. Sam and Avril were good for each other when we were out there. I don't know if they've stayed in touch. "Chiu as well."

Sam leans forwards. "How's she doing?"

"Good," I say. "Although, she's been ordered to return."

"You can't protect her anymore?"

"No."

"I see."

Another silence. This one isn't so comfortable. Does Sam think I can do more?

Ensign Beihe Xiu, known to all of us survivors of the *Khidr* as Ensign Chiu, was part of the attempted mutiny. She surrendered, and later saved people's lives. So far, we've all kept quiet about the incident. All the people who betrayed us are dead. As I see it, there's no point in breaking their reputations. We'll do better keeping quiet and following the trails.

"Johansson and Chiu are close," I say. "She'll be worried. Seeing another familiar face will help."

"They'll both be targets if they come back here to Earth."

"Colonel Savvantine is aware of that," I say. "They are pieces on the game board, just like you and I. War is like that."

"Yeah, it is, but some people get lost in that and forget those pieces are people," Sam says. "Who are we fighting again?"

I sigh. "Everyone and no one. This isn't the kind of conflict where we have clear enemies. The insurgencies seem to be about different agendas, breaking things to suit this interest or that faction. Most of the individuals behind it all are staying there." I pull out another screen, reverse it and push it towards him. "See this, for example? 'Tristan Abernathy dies in house fire in New Orleans'. You and I both know who Tristan Abernathy really is."

"Derrin Lomas, member of the Mars Citizen Council."

"Exactly. I did run a check to make sure it wasn't another individual with the same name. Looks like someone wanted him gone and someone else wanted this to be made public, but quietly, just enough for people who recognise the name to know the truth."

"Is this the kind of thing we'll be dealing with?" Sam asks.

"I hope not. It's exhausting. I don't know how Savvantine manages."

"Me either."

"That's why I need your help." I gesture to the cluttered table. "All of these are potential rabbit holes we can lose ourselves in. I know we're fighting a war, but our role in it isn't this. We need to get to Mars, rebuild it and defend it."

★ ★ ★

The conversation went the same way it always has. I don't know why I expected things to be any different.

"Does it make you wonder what they're going to do about it? I mean, do you throw more money into the problem or try and figure out a plan first?"

We're sitting in the lounge. Dad is talking. Jethry has made drinks, some kind of synthesised whisky that I've not tasted before, but I'm good with trying it. Important to sample Earth's comforts while I'm here.

I open my mouth to answer the question, but Jethry is already talking.

"I guess they can't afford for it to fail," he says. "I mean, all those contracts tied into the colonial trade industry. Massive potential profits on paper. Likely to be a lot of businesses in danger."

I want to speak, to offer a different perspective. Fleet is a partnership of governments and corporations running the space lanes. I have far more knowledge and experience than my father or brother in this area. Again, I'm about to say something, when—

"The new solar agreements in Africa suggest there'll be some change. They can't just rebuild Atacama."

"Well, there are good reasons why they might. There are massive lithium deposits there. That means you can build energy storage capacity really quickly."

I shut my mouth and lean back into the cushions of the sofa. I'm an audience to this conversation, just like I was to countless conversations before I left. They don't mean it – my father and my brother – but they don't leave room for me to contribute in these moments. They never have.

That's one of the reasons why I left.

★ ★ ★

Night-time.

I'm on my own, still in the office. Flag rank has certain benefits. There are rooms available for me on this floor. The apartment's furniture and facilities have been adapted for my needs. I don't need to leave the building and travel to another location.

I get it. Some people want that. If your home is on Earth, the way you put the work away and decompress is by leaving the office and journeying back to family and familiarity. Sam left hours ago, probably seeking some of that rest and relaxation after an event-filled day.

That's not for me. I don't have a home on Earth. I want to be up there, floating in a pressurised compartment on-board a ship or something.

The motorised chair has routes pre-programmed, so all I have to do is select the setting I want and it'll take me to bed or a couch in the lounge. I'm tired enough to fall asleep, so that works. The physical effort of moving around at 1g is still pretty draining for me, but then given all the different things going on, that tiredness helps me switch off.

I go straight to bed. The chair reverses out from the desk and trundles through the rooms. Doors slide back as I approach them, and pretty soon I'm parked up alongside the mattress. Internal hydraulics raise the seat to the same level, and I can roll out of the chair, straight onto the duvet.

Clothes are an issue, but no more than they would be for anyone else. Pretty soon, I'm tucked up and the lights go out.

But that doesn't mean my brain switches off.

I'm thinking about Bill Travers and Angel Le Garre. I'm feeling guilty.

Both of them came back to Earth early with Sam. We all agreed what would be said to the board of inquiry. They covered for me. We all knew what any sign of vulnerability would be interpreted as.

Now, I can't help them. Travers is in hospital. Savvantine thinks he's a target for the people he took down. Any effort on my part to reach out to him would be monitored and could draw heat in my direction.

And Le Garre is missing.

A light flashes in the room. Instantly, my eyes are open and I'm looking at the wall control panel. It's a long way away from the bed, over by the door, but I can read what it says.

Alert: Abnormal Motion Detected.

The flag building has ten floors. There is twenty-four-hour security – a detailed team who control a series of automated systems and drones. Several senior Fleet officers will be sleeping in this building. All of us trusting that the procedures and protocols put in place for our safety will work.

That doesn't mean I'm going back to sleep though.

I have a control for the chair. I can deploy it at the side of the bed and transfer myself back into it. There is also a set of auto-legs that I can use. They are in a compartment at the foot of the bed. Either device would allow me to be mobile and not be where any intruder would expect me to be.

There is also a variety of weapons available in arms lockers coded to my thumbprint.

I'm thinking, taking my time to weigh up options before I make a choice. Firstly, this doesn't have to be about me. All of the senior leadership of Fleet have made enemies. Secondly, whoever decided this would be a good idea has to have planned for the security. That means they'll have expensive technology, probably some sort of thermal scanning or motion system of their own. If I move, I have to consider that I will be monitored. There is no hiding place.

But I don't have to be vulnerable.

Third thing. If the intruder has tripped a sensor, they may well know they have tripped a sensor. I mean, surely to get this far, they must have some sort of hack on the building's computer network.

All right, so what are we doing?

Legs first. I may need the mobility. The control unit is right next to me on the dresser. I pick it up and enter a series of commands. The compartment opens and the unit deploys, walking up to the right side of the bed.

The chair will be useful too. I already have the control for that to hand. I bring up the pathing program and select the route to the apartment exit, instructing the vehicle to stop before it triggers the panel to open. Instead, it can operate as a mobile camera, or an obstacle if someone tries to enter.

I'm thinking about Natalie Holder, the woman I met on the alien ship three years ago. She was a transmitted consciousness – a digital identity that had been implanted into the mind of a human through a device inserted into the brain. Her transferred consciousness had invaded and taken over from the person who had been there before. Savvantine showed me reports on the tech. It's scary stuff.

Now I'm wondering if an individual on the security detail has been affected in the same way. They could already be inside the building.

A flickering light, the terminal display over by the desk has turned itself on. "Shann?"

I shuffle down the bed so I can see who it is – *Savvantine.*

"You're in danger, Shann, they've come for you," Savvantine says. "You need to get out of there."

"I'm on the seventh floor," I say. "Going to be difficult."

"Support assets are on the way," Savvantine says. "In the meantime, I'm in the system. I'll guide you. Do exactly as I say."

I sigh. "I guess I don't have any choice."

★ ★ ★

Welcome to the Temple.

We are the world's first agnostic and non-denominational religion. We accept members from all differing faiths and interpretations of established theology. No matter what you believe, we are encouraging of that belief and here to support it.

To join our organisation, what we require is that you have faith in a creator. What we gain from you is the ability to participate in your exploration of that faith. We hope that by sharing your journey, alongside the journeys of others, we will enable opportunities for human beings to enrich each other's lives with their beliefs and positive affirmations of the world that awaits us after this one.

Our international community is organised into simple structures. By joining our mission, you become part of the community. Your participation within it is entirely dependent upon your needs and desires during your time with us. You may decide that paying the contribution fee is enough for you. However, should you wish to meet up with others and share in their journeys, your local deacon will lead regular conversations between members, allowing each the opportunity to speak about their context.

Should you wish to meet with the deacon personally, then appointments are available. Many members make use of this opportunity to discuss their concerns in a private environment. Volunteer chaperones are also available on request.

The Temple provides opportunities for communities to come together. Deacons within a local area form a council or kgotla who, as a group, will co-ordinate different activities and events. Some of these are public facing, others are restricted to our members. There are also opportunities for individual participation and representation. Members with a unique story to tell are sent from their local groups to visit others who would benefit from hearing their experience. These engagements are a continual part of our mission and serve to enrich the lives of everyone who participates within them.

The deacon councils will appoint a senior leader, known as the proctor, who will be sent as their representative on a National Assembly. In turn, these assemblies appoint a kabaila, or ladan, who is sent to the Global Assembly. This body meets once a year in a glorious celebration of faith, the *Hammada*, where all members are given the opportunity to participate in a series of events designed to affirm our common bonds as human beings who believe in a higher power.

We look forward to working with you and learning about your spiritual journey.

Ilyian Omirian – Shepherd.

Chapter Ten

Sirocco

"Welcome to the Arboretum."

I'm in a world of green. A living environment on a planet that is entirely dead.

Leaves brush against my hands as I walk, following Tellen, who is following the shuttle pilot, Madiro. The air is heavy and humid, unlike anywhere I have ever been.

This is *amazing*.

"How did you do this?" Tellen asks. "How come no one knows about this place?"

Madiro laughs. "I'd like to claim credit for what's been created here, but really it wasn't us. Back when I worked in Jezero, there were rumours about automated projects being sent to Mars. One of them, Project Outreach, even got some news media coverage when one of the scientists discussed the ways in which adaptive programming could be used with drones to develop infrastructure for a colony. That was back in the twenty-first century, years before they launched *Gateway*. We think this excavation was originally a pilot mission sent up by NASA around that time, about seventy years ago. It was expanded later by others."

"Machines did this?" I ask.

"Machines left to work without guidance and interruption," Madiro explains. "The location was selected because the rock shields the plants from the worst of the radiation. UV lights, water and a variety of nutrients were included in the design. From what we can work out, the engineers who created this had a digital map of the cave structure before they sent the bulk of the equipment and automated builders."

I'm paying attention, but my eyes are distracted to look at plants I've never seen before. Enormous fan-shaped leaves and thick spiny branches are familiar enough, but also different. "This is all genetically engineered?"

"From a library. These hybrids have been created to resist the Martian environment. What you see here is some way down the track, of course. Nothing here would survive on the surface as it is currently, but there are breeding chambers for other organisms that might. We think there was a plan for a human DNA database as well. We found some project files on one of the data drives."

"Pretty, but not what I came here to see," Tellen says.

"Patience, Doctor," Madiro replies. "We're getting there."

We reach the other side of the room and descend steps carved out of the rock. I'm guessing this was done by the machines as well.

Our motion triggers illumination overhead. I glance up, noting that the staircase might be cramped on either side, but the ceiling of this part of the cave goes up thirty feet or more. It's quite a sight, but it also makes me think of the atmosphere requirements for such a large open space.

Ahead, Madiro stops and turns around. He looks at me and realises what's on my mind. "There are artificial seals in the rock. We think the machines made the cave airtight before they started on the rest of the plan, but if you're wondering about the volume, you're right. The space is large, too large for us to smuggle in tanked air and keep it working. The plants are the oxygenators, supplemented with scrubbers and some tanked supplies. It's pretty incredible how much we're able to do."

There is a thick metal door at the end of the staircase. Madiro reaches it and grabs a lever in the centre, spinning it to release the mechanism. Then he opens the door, gesturing for us both to enter.

I follow Tellen inside.

"Welcome, gentlemen."

A woman is sitting behind a desk. In front of her are a selection of different electronic devices. To her right appears to be a broken pile of components.

"My name is Kassandra Milanova," the woman says. "According to official Mars CorpGov records, I died in the Jezero incident, as did many of the people who now live here."

"Is that what you have planned for us?" I ask.

Milanova smiles. "Your records will not need much alteration. We are monitoring a search and rescue attempt that is currently investigating your last known location at the data tower. The dome authorities will permit a limited search perimeter, and when nothing is found, sanction the closure of the case with you both declared missing, presumed dead."

"Which means if you don't think we fit in here, you can just get rid of us."

"Yes, exactly."

I'm staring at Milanova. She holds my gaze in a measured way, as if I'm a piece of inventory that she has to interface with. There's nothing here to get angry with or resent. Not at the moment.

"Doctor Tellen. We are aware of your request to join us and to see our preservation chamber. Please come this way."

Milanova stands up and moves towards another door at the back. We all follow.

The next room is divided by a wall of glass. On the other side, I can see the floor is red Martian sand. There is subdued lighting and a small entrance, cut into the transparent panel. Anyone going through there would find themselves in a tiny airlock, as there's a second door to actually enter the chamber. Above, I can see a variety of canisters attached to the ceiling. Pipes run into the chamber and the entrance.

"All of this was constructed by the machines, but not as part of the plan laid out for this place. We think someone reprogrammed everything to create this. We keep it separated from pretty much everything else," Milanova says. "We have no desire to contaminate it."

I'm looking into the divided section, peering through the glass. There is a pile of rocks in the centre of the space. That's what the others are looking at. I'm not sure…

Wait… *What is that?*

Thin tendrils on the stones. At first, I thought they were quartz veins, or something like that, but Tellen is staring at them, fascinated. "What tests have you done?" he asks.

"None. We just have some of the research notes from a Doctor Lorraine Bell," Madiro says. "She was part of an expedition team. One of the early European missions they sent out here. It's a sample she brought here from a survey they were doing. That's why we think it is what it is."

"Native Martian life."

"Yes."

Tellen is kneeling in front of the glass, his face pressed against it. This means a lot to him.

I glance at Milanova. She catches the look and nods. "Well, now we have established why you are here, Doctor Tellen, I think it's time we dealt with your friend. We'll leave you to it."

★ ★ ★

I am back in Milanova's office with her. Madiro has stayed with Tellen. It's just the two of us.

"How does this place exist?" I ask. "How come CorpGov or Fleet haven't found you?"

"We're underground," Milanova says. "Which means satellite photography doesn't pick us up, so long as we're careful and keep track of their orbitals. Heat from the tech and the organics is recycled where needed and dissipated through thermal vents. An infrared scan might pick up some traces, but nothing that would reveal us."

"You've planned carefully then."

"I'd like to take credit for it, but really it was part of the design." She stares at me. "You really don't know anything about it?"

"Nothing."

"Interesting. The people who sent you claim to be the corporation that built this place," Milanova says. "I'm guessing that Doctor Tellen doesn't know that?"

I shrug. "I don't know what they told him or what they've done. Only that they sent me to do a specific job."

"And what is that?"

"Take down Mars CorpGov."

"Our interests align with that," Milanova says. "But we don't want to swap one set of masters for another."

"I don't know their plans for what comes after," I say. "The people who sent me here told me how the colony is being exploited and explained how we could break that. I heard Sammatri's speech. They said you could help me with what I want to do." I gesture to the door back to the Arboretum. "You people clearly want to live out here in a way that's better. We can't go to another planet, colonise it and make all the same mistakes."

Milanova nods. "It is good to hear your views," she says. "But there will be an agenda, whether you are part of it or not."

"What happened in the aftermath?" I ask. "You were the people in the dome, the rest were in the shelters. Sammatri gave his speech, why didn't they act?"

"Some of them did," Milanova says. "There was fighting underground. From what we heard it was hell. Eventually, the citizen leaders made promises, then they got organised and locked the doors. When you start denying people air, the resistance goes out of them pretty quickly."

"So, what happened to you?"

"Security teams came out and started sweeping the city," Milanova says. "We hacked their comms and realised they were going to arrest us on sight, so we kept away from them as long as we could, trying to broadcast again if we were able, but that didn't happen. We tried to get a signal out to the other settlements and whoever was left in orbit, but got no responses. Eventually, we had nowhere to go, so we followed some old expedition maps that led out of the crater. It was touch and go, but we made it here."

"Lucky."

"Perhaps. Or, a little providence."

Divine intervention? I'm thinking of the Temple Kitchen people and their hot food. My stomach rumbles. "I'm here now," I say. "I want to help if I can. It'd be nice to be a part of something that could be different, where people actually give a shit about each other."

"My concern, before we go any further, is that you've been sent here for something else."

I frown. I'm not sure what Milanova is getting at. "What do you need me to do to prove my intentions?"

"I don't know. What did they tell you to do?"

I look around the room. "This place was already constructed when you got here, right?"

"Yes, it was."

"What happened to the machines that made it?"

"A few stayed and went into standby mode. Others went somewhere else. We don't know where."

"Do you have any of them here?"

Milanova reaches under her desk and opens a drawer, taking out a small metal plastic sphere that she places on the desk. "This has been dormant ever since we arrived."

I hold out my hand and she passes me the device. It's a little heavier than it looks, despite the Martian gravity. "Did you try to activate it?" I ask.

"Of course." Milanova reaches over and taps on a panel on the object in my hands. "We know it's transmitting a signal every thirty seconds or so. I guess it's not receiving the correct authorisation response to wake up."

"That's because you don't know the code," I say. I hold out my other hand and Milanova passes me her screen. I bring up a terminal window, as I was instructed to do, and tap in a short sequence of alphanumeric digits then press transmit. There is an audible beep, and three limbs emerge from the sphere. I place it on the desk between us. "A gift from my employer."

Milanova looks pleased. "Thank you." She holds out her hand and I pass her the screen. She taps on it a few times, then turns the display towards me so I can see it. She's showing me a satellite image of a location on Mars. "You'll spend the night here in one of our guest rooms. Tomorrow, we'll send you out to this place."

"That's Olympus Mons," I say.

"Yes it is. There's something we'll need you to do out there. You good with that?"

I open my mouth to ask the obvious question: *what do you need me to do?* But if she wanted me to know that she'd have already told me.

"I'm good with that," I say.

"Good," says Milanova. "That's where you'll find Sammatri."

* * *

Martian night is much the same as Martian day. Everything happens underground, so there are no natural visual clues about when to be asleep and when to be awake.

I'm shown to a small room that appears to have been gouged out of the rock. Milanova tells me they had to make these places themselves, after the machines left. There's just enough space for a bed, a light strip and me.

There is food. A ration strip, just like the ones from Jezero that they offered to cook for you at the Temple Kitchen. Tasteless and unappetising, but to go with it, three small berries from the Arboretum.

I take one of the berries in my hand and roll it between my fingers. The imperfect sphere is beautiful. A little reminder of Earth, but to think, this has been grown on another planet! Amazing!

I want to eat it, but I don't want to damage it, to break the skin of this tiny piece of art. But I'm hungry. The human instinct wins out, and I pop the little gem in my mouth.

A burst of flavour – sugar and a bitter sharpness – like what I remember from Earth, and yet, different, alien somehow.

I eat the ration strip next and finish with the two remaining berries. Then drink a cup of water. The flavour of the fruit lingers. Lovely.

I undress and pile my clothes in the corner, then lie down and shut my eyes. Sleep isn't a thing I find easily, particularly when I have something on my mind.

Before I came to Mars, I read up on what to expect. The early research bases used viewscreens and lighting sequences to help humans adjust to the constant artificial light. Psychological studies indicated that changes of illumination that mirrored day and night sequences, along with seasonal shifts, were useful tools that helped people acclimatize.

However, that kind of sensitivity to human needs isn't a part of today's colonial strategy. Light and dark is about function. Illumination is to see, darkness is when you don't need that. Efficiency is the key, not some sort of intangible investment in the well-being of the workforce.

I can imagine someone making that argument in a boardroom on Earth when they designed the Jezero dome. Transport debt, comfort and rationed nutrition must have all been on the list of agreed elements when planning for the colony. Maybe things are worse now after the Phobos Station incident? I don't know what it was like before.

Since I left the army, most of my interventions have been small-scale. What I was promised here was something different.

★ ★ ★

"You'll need to prove yourself to them."

The conversation is a memory. After two weeks, I left Italy and reached out, just as Louisa said I would. I was booked into a private air car and brought here, a rented house somewhere in the south of France.

I smile and shrug in response. "I've been through that before," I say.

"Not like this," Louisa warns. "You're dealing with a group of people who are on the outside. They've found a way to survive *in extremis*. You'll be meeting them, and they'll know you come from us. You need to curb your natural tendencies and be something you're not."

"That's been a problem in the past," I say. This feels like a confession, but by being here I've already committed. This woman says she wants me to do this, that means she'll have to help.

"We'll work with you on this," Louisa says. "We have time."

★ ★ ★

The door to my room opens.

I'm awake immediately. I open my eyes and try to sit up, but realise I can't.

"I'm sorry, Magnus. It has to be this way."

I try to open my mouth and speak, but find I can't.

Milanova is standing beside the bed. She leans over me, her face inches from mine. She raises a hand and brushes the backs of her fingers across my cheek.

"You're going to Olympus Mons. The easiest way for us to do that is to transport you in cold sleep. You'll be boxed up and placed on a rover, along with the rest of the supplies we're sending out there. When the mission team is ready, they'll revive you."

I can't move. *The berries. It had to be the berries!* They knew I would eat them. I'm trying to fight it, but it's no use. Milanova has an injector in her hand. She puts it against my neck.

"Just accept this. The next thing you'll know is you'll be waking up exactly where you want to be," she says.

There is a sharp pain and—

⋆ ⋆ ⋆

The information swirl.

They used to say the computers and online networks would be the future for humanity. All the digital tools would empower people in their lives. Communication with friends and loved ones all across the world, research into a variety of subjects – all the information right there at the click of a button. Society was transformed in a digital age, the planet made smaller through a series of data connections, at first physical with underground cables, and later with information being beamed from satellites in orbit to any location anywhere.

The problems were always there. Fundamentally, every individual person has to make a decision about what they believe. Reading what is said by one person may encourage us to question and look for additional sources, but when those additional sources are all automated and fake, generated solely to reflect the same arguments and the same viewpoints back at us, we have a problem.

The unregulated use of adaptive learning machines to populate a variety of different online networks and information sources caused people to question what they were being told. To begin with, much of this questioning had legitimate cause. Wealthy interest groups allied to political establishments have always sought to control the information agenda. When people formed communities that criticised the public narratives being pushed out by these powerful entities, they uncovered new truths. The diversification of opinion and information became a robust way to challenge ideologies that sought to control and exploit.

However, the machines brought with them a whole new level of theatre. The online mob no longer needed to be an angry expression of living people. Instead, it could be manufactured, then let loose, the adaptive programming creating fake personas who would argue and counter every engagement, fighting solely to be a part of someone's attempt to control the narrative.

These created identities served no purpose other than the one given to them in the moment. Their agenda was to project the sense of popular opinion upon the individual, making every human being who interacted with them question their own position. The hegemony seemed to have a viewpoint, anyone who spoke up with an alternative view would be perceived to be in the minority. This artificial construction of discussion and disagreement led to the atomisation of genuine human consensus in favour of another powerful self-interested ideology.

Over time the information networks became agenda kingdoms. Truth could only be found at the margins. Genuine human connection became a novelty found only when you walked out of your front door and somebody else chose to do the same.

People lost agency in a society that was supposed to be serving the interests of people. Now, you have to remind yourself that every day, every person you meet has built their identity on a different set of information to you. Things that you decided were bullshit, long ago, might be foundational beliefs for someone else.

And don't get me started on religion.

These days, the war has changed. There are legitimate organisations that still look for truth and facts amidst the ideologies. These organisations have collaborated on encryption protocols that attempt to filter out the artificial shouting, but they still serve their own perception of society's interests. Their positions on any given subject come from an established pattern of thinking.

Even the rebels and revolutionaries perceive themselves in a particular way. Often their identities are shaped as much by their wish and desire to be individual and alternative as opposed to being better.

If we've learned anything from this entire process, it is that human beings create patterns for themselves all the time, and as they do this, they become meshed and trapped in those patterns. They are the predator and the prey, the spider and the fly, all at the same time.

There must be a way to break this cycle. When you figure it out, please tell me what it is.

Timothy Kratter – UK Chief Anthropologist, writing in 2045 AD.

Chapter Eleven

Iskander

"Okay, I think we're ready."

I'm sitting in the captain's chair on the bridge. Morlan Dennis and David Kewell are here with me. The rest of the team are scattered around the ship, ready to do the job we've planned for.

Team...that's the wrong word. They're a crew now.

A Fleet patrol craft has a normal crew complement of twenty-four. On missions, they work in three shifts, rotating every eight hours. We don't have the people to do that, so our journey is going to be hard on everyone. Over time, mistakes will be made as we all push ourselves to the point of exhaustion.

But that's not right now. In this moment, there is excitement at what we're about to do. The adrenalin kicks in and gets your blood pumping.

We're about to steal a spaceship. That's exciting, like something out of a children's story. In the books, they don't dwell on the details though. Food, water and air are all essential requirements for any ship in the void. We've made an inventory and it's not enough to get where I want to go. As soon as this starts, we're going to be in trouble.

I need to keep this quiet. Problem is, Halle is no fool. However, she has faith. That can be a tool in circumstances like this.

I may have to use it, I may have to lie to them, even if I don't want to.

"Let's make a start," I say. "Kewell, over to you."

I'm watching a window on the display that shows the feed from the umbilical corridor connecting us to the shuttle. I can see Kewell and Weaver in there, moving some of the junk we've decided we don't need. Everything is in process.

Weaver leaves the passageway. *Game on.*

Kewell kneels down, away from the camera. I know what he's doing: tampering with the oxygen feeds, just like we agreed. A moment later, there's a flash and the camera goes out.

The ship shivers. Definitely an explosion.

"Shuttle to Weaver, report!"

Comms on the open channel from the pilots. They'll be in the middle of an emergency manoeuvre, trying to correct the sudden change of velocities. The debris in the passageway will be a cloud of dangerous projectiles that could rip them apart if they're not precise in their escape.

"Dennis, get us moving!"

The acceleration is like a punch in the chest. We can't make this comfortable, it has to look like a reaction to the explosion.

"Kewell to Bridge."

"Receiving?"

"All clear. I've shut down my bio-monitor. Weaver's has been deactivated too."

"How is he?"

"A mess."

I smile grimly. "Get yourselves strapped in. This is going to get rough."

Our planned trajectory is plotted on a window in front of me. Dennis has switched over the control systems, just like we planned, and now he's pushing the ship onto our intended trajectory.

I switch to a different window. An exterior camera that we managed to get working and isolate is showing the shuttle and the wrecked fabric passageway. They won't be able to follow us through the debris. They'll be sounding the alarm and contacting the Hub.

"We're picking up speed," Dennis says. "Planetary gravity is having an effect."

I can feel the shifting forces moving my body in the chair. "Send the automated distress call," I say. "Try and get us as comfortable a ride as possible."

"Will do."

"Halle, you're up."

A reactor insertion is a delicate procedure. Trying to manage it under changing forces makes it almost impossible without computer assistance. Halle trained for this, but our copies of Fleet software were hacks of old iterations. Now, we have to rely on her.

I'm watching the display. The reactor core is in its own mini airlock. When Halle starts the process, the outer hatch will close, the box will pressurise and the inner door will open. Then Halle will need to manoeuvre it back into the cradle.

It's a three-person task. Merrick and Tolwyn are down there as well.

"Okay, nice and steady," Halle says. "We do this carefully and with no mistakes."

Two people in the outer reactor room, dressed in radiation suits. Halle will be one of them. I'm guessing Merrick is the other with Tolwyn overseeing through a monitor outside. He'll be watching the same window as me.

There's a device moving in the inner chamber. That'll be the core. It moves into the right position and locks into place.

"Engaging start-up circuit one," Merrick says.

Moving hands operating the controls. Our lives depend on this being done right. Failure could mean a meltdown that will kill us all in thirty minutes or so. Worse would be a radiation leak, meaning we'd die in days or weeks, knowing exactly what was happening.

"Circuit one active. Begin circuit two procedure."

The ship shudders. I'm pressed to the left side of my chair. "Dennis, keep us steady!" I say.

"Trying to, Deacon!"

I can't do anything except watch. I'm powerless in these moments. All I have is trust and faith.

Nuclear power has always been one of those technologies that I've been unsure about. I mean, through science humanity gets to follow in the footsteps of the creator, to see what was made and how it was made. I agree with that. Sometimes, our curiosity reveals knowledge and allows us to harness great power. But nuclear? It's always been a corrupter, a devil's box of promises with consequences that tell us humanity isn't ready to wield the power of gods.

"Circuit two in place and active. Move to circuit three."

Time is passing. The pressure on my left side has increased, along with the force pushing me back into the seat. With an effort, I touch the comms and patch over to Kewell. "How's it looking back there?" I ask.

"I'm monitoring some hull strain," Kewell says. "It'll be worse as we get closer to the planet and pick up more speed."

Halle needs to be finished by then. I'm still watching the reactor procedure. The people in the room are struggling to keep their hands steady as they work. The g's are starting to interfere with the process.

"Circuit three is working," Tolwyn says.

"Moving to circuit four," Halle replies.

There is no shortcutting this process and no changing our trajectory now. A glance at the plot makes me aware that there's chatter on the open comms channel. I switch over to that. I can be more useful there.

"Weaver, this is Shuttle, please respond."

The pilots are trying to establish contact. No one is replying to them. That's good. Now I get to shape the narrative.

"Shuttle, this is Iskander. Weaver's dead. We had an internal explosion which has affected the computer system and triggered a burn. We're trying to correct it and return to a stable orbit."

"Understood, Iskander. We have you on a course for burn-up at present. You need to address that."

"Doing our best, Shuttle, it's chaos over here."

"Understood. We've contacted the Hub for support."

I switch the channels back so I can talk to my crew. "Merrick, time to switch off your bio-monitor. Tolwyn, you as well."

"Acknowledged, Deacon."

The shuttle crew will notice the drops. They'll think we're dying off one by one over here. There's a whole batch of compartments that aren't pressurised, easy enough to assume the ship is tearing itself apart on the inside.

"Circuit four is active, moving to circuit five."

The exterior camera window is still open on my screen. I can't see the shuttle anymore, but the curve of Mars is visible in the display. To anyone looking up, we might be visible in the night sky as a fast-moving star. What we don't want to be is a burning streak across the heavens. If that's what happens, we'll be dead.

"Circuit five is working. Moving to circuit six."

Fleet won't risk another ship. A shuttle could try to intercept us if we escape the gravitational pull of Mars and decelerate on the far side, shedding our delta-*v*. That's what they must be hoping will happen, if the authorities believe our bullshit. What they won't expect is for us to lean into the velocity increase and bring the main engines online, accelerating out of the Mars sector into the darkness. Of course, by that point we'll be hoping they're believing the lie that we've burned up.

"Iskander to Kewell."

"Receiving."

"What's your location?"

"We've moved to the secondary airlock. We'll be ready when the moment comes."

More debris to be jettisoned, to burn up on the edge of Mars's atmosphere. That'll make a pretty fire in the sky. Hopefully enough to fool any inquiring minds, at least for a while.

"Circuit six active. Beginning the power-up sequence."

This is dangerous. Fleet's protocols for a reactor reinsertion call for us to complete ten circuit activations and then move to phase two. That part involves hours of function testing and partial power-ups after the initial set-up has been completed. Halle is skipping all of those safety measures. We don't have time for them. If we try to do this by the book, we'll never make it.

"Circuit seven active. Circuit eight is connected and...powered."

The curve of Mars fills the camera window. I can see the temperature readings from outside the ship are rising fast. The outer hull is heat-shielded to a point, but these ships were never built for re-entry. The *Asthoreth* has spent its whole life in space, having been assembled at an orbital dock around Earth.

"Nine and ten are ready. Power registered." Halle's voice cracks a little as she confirms the completion of the last circuits. "Phase one complete, Deacon."

"Get the program running and get strapped in," I order. The words tumble out. I'm relieved, the tension washing out of me, but I know this isn't over.

"Acknowledged."

The people in the reactor room move out of view of the camera. This part of the plan doesn't need them. During our training we were provided with software that could run the reactor power-up sequence automatically. However, it was designed for an older version of the system, the only copy we could get data on before coming here. It has to work; the only alternative is to do everything manually, which we can't do while we're performing the current manoeuvre.

"We're behind the curve of the planet," Dennis says.

The acceleration forces are punishing now. Harder than before. I don't know how Halle and the others kept their hands steady for as long as they did, but I'm thankful their work is done.

"How long until we reach the exit point?" I ask.

"About twelve minutes, based on our trajectory."

"Any more damage?"

"So far, we're okay."

Breathing is an effort now. Talking is hard. While we're fighting to take in air, Halle's program will be trying to activate the reactor. The first sign we'll have of anything working will be some boosts in the available power. I switch display windows over to the power monitoring. My hands are heavy, and my fingers shake as I force them to move. I don't know how much of the ship's data has been locked down when we assumed manual control. Maybe the Hub or the control station at Hera can still see some of these readouts? If they can, it knocks a hole in our cover story of dying during re-entry, but there's nothing I can do about that now. Data from an accident will always be confusing and difficult to read. I just have to hope that'll be the case here.

Just breathe. In and out. In and out.

Movement in the power readings. The remaining batteries should be gradually losing charge, but now the per centages are going up. For a moment, I stare at the data, unsure of what I'm seeing. Then I remember what it means.

"Bridge…to Engineering…"

"Receiving."

"Con…firm…reactor…status?"

"We…are…online…"

"Den…nis?"

"Two…min…utes…"

When you're selected for the Mars colony, they make you go through a lot of force training, testing your body to see if you're physically robust enough to take it. A lot of people aren't and there is nothing you can really do about that. Human beings are soft and squishy, some are *too* soft. That's it.

The forces we're currently experiencing aren't the worst I've felt. The stress of accelerating to escape velocity from a ground launch is intense, but every time you strap yourself in for that, you know how long you're going to be under the assault. Right now, I only have Dennis's best guess, plus there's the engine kick to come, when he engages the thrusters and we're flung out, away from the planet, into the void.

That moment…is now…

"Prep…thrus…ters… Three…two…one…en…gage!"

The world becomes hard. The air is no longer… I can't… I…

* * *

Scientists at MR Astro have won a European Horizon grant to begin work on creating the building blocks of human life.

MR Astro's proposal is believed to be a new applied project, building on two previous attempts to develop artificial biocatalyst components that will assist in the growth of human tissue. The material will then be used to test vaccines, and other experimental treatments for incurable diseases.

The grant was not given without some controversy. Two members of the awarding body, Professor Heinrich Atwell and Professor Dorothy Gaymes, both resigned prior to the decision being announced, although neither have given official reasons for their decisions to step away.

Public concerns relating to genetic engineering remain strong. However, MR Astro's project lead, Professor Andrew Yalberg, believes part of the problem lies in a lack of communication and transparency from the scientific community.

"We need to be open and honest in what we're doing in plain terms," Yalberg said, when interviewed about the successful grant announcement. "People need to know what this means for them, for their everyday lives. We're not talking about wholescale gene vetting and designer processes for parents, but we are trying to improve people's lives. Keeping people healthy at every stage of their lives is our top priority."

Report from *Global Science Magazine* (March Edition, 2057).

Chapter Twelve

Shann

Footsteps outside my room door.

I'm sitting up in bed, next to the artificial legs, waiting for the moment an assassin there tries to gain entry to the apartment.

"Six metres," Savvantine says. Her voice is in my ear now, speaking to me through a small comms bead that I retrieved from the bedside table. "Get ready."

The footsteps stop. I guess whoever is out there will try to open the door with a stolen passcode or some kind of hacking application they can attach to the control panel. That's what I'd do. Either way, the moment will have been planned for, and they'll have a solution to hand.

Twenty seconds and the door beeps, sliding back. My mobility chair has been placed right in front of the door. I'm watching the chair camera and recognise the person outside immediately. Fleet Security Officer Herris Matthews. We've spoken before, exchanged pleasantries and talked about our respective families. She knows me, but this isn't a social call.

"Ellisa Shann?"

I activate the chair. An explosion of light in her face, then the motors engage and the device charges forwards, straight at her.

I'm moving, hauling myself into the legs. The emergency start-up procedure is rough and ready, but I don't have time for the touch sensors and kinetic hook-ups. I need to be in and mobile as fast as possible.

As soon as I'm in the cradle, I initiate a preset move to the door. The legs respond, carrying me across the room. Matthews is trying to extricate herself from the chair; before she does, I'm there. I bunch my fingers into a fist and hit her, right between the eyes. Her head slams against the floor and her eyes roll, but she's still struggling to get loose.

I hit her again and she goes limp. Done.

The quiet after violence. A moment where the survival instincts ebb away and humanity returns, along with a cold calculation of my situation.

I touch the comms bead in my ear. "One down," I say to Savvantine. "Officer Herris Matthews. She's a member of the building's official detail." I reach out for one of the lights on the chair and angle it towards the floor, illuminating the corridor carpet. "She was carrying a sidearm. Plastic composite. Not official issue."

"I'm detecting no additional movement," Savvantine says. "Looks like she was working alone."

"I'll wait here for your support team," I say, picking up the gun from the floor. It's bulky, unlike the low-velocity firearms we use in space. "Thanks for the assist. Glad you were watching out for me."

"Don't mention it," Savvantine says. "Talk soon at the debrief."

* * *

"She was an insertion."

A meeting room in the flag building. Six people around a table with me in a separate chair a few feet away. There's a holographic image of a person over the desk. Herris Matthews.

Savvantine is speaking, presenting information about what happened. She flew in an hour ago, arriving eight hours after everything kicked off.

"Matthews's record shows surgery for a cochlear implant when she was eleven years old. I would guess the device was inserted into her skull around that time."

"Why wasn't this picked up?"

"There was no reason to believe minor operations like this could be a security risk until very recently. We're having to retrospectively go through the databases to do new vetting. It's not easy."

Admiral Dean sighs. She's the senior officer in the room. Savvantine occupies the far end of the table, between a general and a brigadier general who both outrank her, but that's not relevant in this conversation. We all know the real hierarchy in play.

"And you're sure Commodore Shann was the target?"

"As positive as I can be, given the circumstances." Savvantine waves her hand, and the image of Matthews disappears. "We'll know more when we've questioned her." She smiles. "We've not captured a live one before, not directly. This will be interesting."

Insertions. That's what they are calling them now. Savvantine or one of her people chose the name. A simple word to describe a complex and violating process where a device is inserted into a person's skull at a young age and then when it's ready, used as a receptacle for a transmitted digital personality that takes over the mind and body of the host to perform a specific task before being transferred out.

Usually, the host doesn't survive.

I remember Natalie Holder, the woman I met on the alien ship near Mars. She was an insertion. The woman I fought, Kate Vessel, she was an insertion too.

"Remember there is a person in there."

All eyes turn towards me. I meet the gazes one by one. "What I mean is, if this is an inserted agent, the real Herris Matthews is still in there. She isn't to blame for what happened."

Savvantine frowns. "Commodore, we have an obligation to investigate."

"Yes, I know, but we all have an obligation to protect innocent people too." I'm not just thinking of Matthews, I'm also thinking of the new identity. Holder wanted to be free. I got the feeling that her life was wretched. "We don't even know if the attempt was hostile."

"Commodore, the insertion was carrying an unlicensed weapon and had hacked into the building's security system," Dean says. "I think we can assume hostile intent. The issue is what steps we take next." She glances at Savvantine. "We'll leave the investigation to you."

Savvantine nods. "Thank you, Admiral."

"In the meantime, I think we need to move up our timetable. Commodore, we need to get you offworld and on your way back to Mars as soon as possible."

The words are like electricity. Suddenly, I'm awake and alert. This is an outcome I wasn't expecting. "Of course, Admiral, if you think that's best."

"I do. You need to be safe. It's clear you're not safe here. Maybe you'll be safer out there." Dean turns to Doctor Colson, the resident lead medical officer. "Can we expedite her return?"

"Yes," Colson says. "But if we do, it could be dangerous." He turns to me. "Your body needs time to recover. If you don't give it that, you'll be putting your life at risk."

I only ever wanted to be out there. Every day I'm back on this planet, feeling gravity on my body, feels like a waste of my time. "I'll take the chance, Doctor," I say.

"We have some experimental procedures and drug courses we can try. Plus, there are some intensive exercise regimens that may help." Colson shrugs. "You'll need to sign a few waivers."

"I'll sign anything to get me off planet," I say.

⋆ ⋆ ⋆

Silence. Savvantine and I are alone in the room. The others have gone.

"The outcome of all this appears to be better than we'd hoped for," Savvantine says. "Looks like you're getting back into space ahead of schedule."

"The ships won't be ready in time," I say.

"I'll work the angles on that," Savvantine says. "Either you'll get whatever is operational with the balance of your requisition sent afterwards, or…"

"Or I get *Gallowglass*."

"Yes."

"Well, that wouldn't be a bad thing."

"Your point about Matthews was well made. I heard what you said."

I'm looking at Savvantine. She's looking at me. I nod. I can see the honesty in what she's said. "I think you're growing as a person," I say.

"That could become a weakness in my line of work," Savvantine replies. She grins. "I'll miss you around here."

"That sounds like you're getting sentimental," I say.

"I'll bear that in mind," Savvantine says.

"Maybe dial it up when you're dealing with Travers," I say. "How is he?"

"Getting there, I think," Savvantine says. "He still blames himself for what happened to Le Garre. That's why he doesn't want to talk to you."

I sigh. "I thought it might be something like that."

Savvantine stands up from the table, taking her screen and pile of documents with her. "Don't be hard on yourself," she says. "You couldn't have known what was going on. Travers knows that. But he feels responsible, and he doesn't want to confront that. Seeing you makes him face things he won't want to face."

"Okay," I say. Then change the subject. "What's our next step?"

"You pass a few medical tests, sign some paperwork and then we see what your amended commission looks like," Savvantine says. "After that, we pack you onto a rocket and blast you back into space."

I smile. "Sounds good," I say.

★ ★ ★

Voice #1: Updating you. The attempt failed.

Voice #2: Do you have content? Did you get surveillance footage or anything?

Voice #1: Intel got there fast. I think they must have been expecting something. We couldn't make a retrieval.

Voice #2: Did you manage a clean-up?

Voice #1: No. They quarantined the building. Our people couldn't get in to verify disposal of the implant.

Silence…

Voice #2: Our asset says they are bumping up the timetable in response to this.

Voice #1: That could serve us well. We have agents in place already. There may be another opportunity.

Voice #2: If there is, make sure you take it.

Call ends.

Phase Two

Chapter Thirteen

Johansson

Three and a half years around Mars.

I'm strapped into a rotating exerciser. The hand grips and foot straps force me to move my arms and legs, pushing against the carefully weighted resistance. The repetitions are strenuous, exhausting. This is a part of the necessary exercise process we all have to go through out here.

Even then, with how long I've been away from Earth, any return will be hard. My body has changed a lot since I was last there, even if I believe I'm still just as fit as I was before I left.

"Okay, time's up."

I go limp and let myself float. Hands touch my feet and wrists, releasing me from this instrument of torture. I'm breathing in gasps, conscious of the air being used up by the effort. With everything out here carefully measured and allocated, even breathing too much feels like an indulgence.

Fingertips linger on my skin. The sensation is generous and...*lovely*.

"You taking a turn, so I can watch?"

"Sounds like a plan."

With help, I'm extricated from the machine. Chiu moves past me, more skin-on-skin contact, some of it intentional, making me smile. "There are clubs on Earth where this is a regular leisure activity," I say.

"Gravity exercise?"

"No, getting tied up and tortured before...something else."

I'm smiling, Chiu is smiling. There's a promise between us, something both immediate and longer term. That's what we've found with each other out here. It's not exclusive or binding, but it is intimate and strong. Friends first, everything else an extra that works.

"You'll have to watch me, like I did for you. Just in case I need help."

My breathing is nearly back to normal. Heart rate remains elevated. No alarms triggered and no doctor in my ear. Just two hours of physical exertion where I have to stop thinking about all the problems we're trying to deal with. Four hours of respite if you include Chiu's time on the machine.

And there's a lot of problems.

Chiu activates the machine and begins her sequence. I'm watching her body move. I can see the scars from her injuries. She wears them well, on the inside and the outside. Physical exercise has alleviated any lasting damage beyond the superficial reminder, and she's come to terms with what she did, she's made amends for betraying the crew during the mutiny.

She's saved my life several times. I trust her without reservation. We are who we are, with all those choices, good and bad, rolled into one real human person. That's beautiful to me. Unique and perfect by being imperfect, I—

A portable screen on the wall is flashing. It's mine.

I want to ignore it, to stay in the moment. This time away from responsibilities and crises is what keeps me sane. But, sometimes, we can't stay away, and the problems have to intrude.

My fingers twitch, the moment is lost. I reach for the screen and remove it from the holder on the wall. The device immediately registers my identity and reveals my work folders, just as I left them. The incoming message is right there, waiting for me to open it.

I reach out. My artificial arm is a new replacement that arrived on the last shipment. Chiu has worked on it, enhancing the functionality and connection to my nervous system. I can feel every touch, as if it were flesh and blood.

"Avril?"

Chiu is looking at me. She's frowning.

"Sorry," I say. "I need to take this."

Chiu sighs. "You always do."

I move away from the machine, turning from our shared intimacy. As I do, the weight of my work returns. I key up the message and quickly read the detail. More data on a problem that has been on my mind for weeks. One of the issues I want to solve before…

Before I make a decision about staying here.

★ ★ ★

A memory that won't go away. In the moments after the alien ship left the vicinity of Mars, I was alone in the dark.

The wake of the ship's acceleration rendered our technology inoperable. *Gallowglass*, *Nandin*, *Asthoreth* and *Seraphiel*, all turned into drifting, powerless husks.

I have been in the weightless dark many times. Since that moment though, every time I have gone to sleep, I have returned to the aftermath.

We worked with almost nothing, gradually building and restoring what was. Every little victory increased our chances of survival. Inch by inch, we clawed our way back. Keeping the void out there, behind our thin metal and plastic walls. Power to the ships, restoring communications, manoeuvring into safe and stable orbits, establishing contact with the colony on Mars.

After a while, people left, returning to Earth. At the same time, supply ships arrived, helping us alleviate the immediate resource shortages. Docking the four damaged patrol vessels together allowed us to create a temporary orbital headquarters. Shuttles from Hera Spaceport allowed us to support the rebuilding effort on the surface too.

Slowly but surely, we began to assemble a new structure, extricating the patrol ships and repairing them as best we could. Eventually, we ended up with this facility, called the Hub. It's functional and automated, wherever possible. It handles supply transfer to the planet and orbital traffic control.

At every stage, we kept going. Ellisa Shann ensured we never lost focus on the goal. When she left, things got more difficult.

Now, she's weeks away from being back. The three patrol ships she now commands will replace what we have left. The *Nandin* will return to Earth, with Chiu on-board, so she can face a Fleet board of inquiry.

The decision I have to make is whether I choose to go with her.

I'm back in our little office, the nearest thing the Hub has to an administration department. Six people work here on rotational shifts. The scale of this place is nothing like what came before it, Phobos Station. It's more like the bridge of a spaceship, like they worked with before that, when the colony ship *Gateway* was converted to be the first orbital facility that served the colony below.

The Hub has no rotating deck, no interior shuttle bay, and far less capacity than both of its predecessors, but I was involved in building every part of this place. That makes it feel better to me.

I'm plugged in, ignoring the five people around me. Earbuds project white noise into my brain, helping me focus on the display. A catalogue of windows, all with different data collected for me. Pieces of a puzzle I can't put together.

I'm looking at the last hours of the derelict ship *Asthoreth*.

This happened eighty-three days ago. A reclamation team went aboard and something went wrong. The airlock umbilical passage exploded, and the ship got knocked out of its orbit into a shallow re-entry course. According to the Hub station officer's report, less than an hour later, the ship burned up on the edge of Mars's atmosphere.

I have logs from the autopilot station on Hera; I have the recovered bio-monitoring data from the seven members of the team. Their leader, Weaver, stopped transmitting first. After him, three others, and then finally the rest as the ship broke apart. All of these elements fit the narrative.

The problem is, there's a whole set of data that doesn't.

A power spike just before the last log entries. An activation of main engine thrust. Could be that the surviving crew were improvising, trying to save themselves?

Time passes, people leave. I'm alone. Then Chiu enters. I pick out my earbuds and turn towards her. "You okay?" I ask.

"As good as any jilted date," Chiu says. Her smile takes the sting out of the words. She joins me at the terminal, her hand on my shoulder. "You got the records from Hera autopilot control?"

"Yes, they finally let me have them," I say.

"Does it answer any questions?"

"Some." I pull up a video file and let it play. "This is the security feed from the umbilical passage as they enter the ship. You can see everyone go through." I pull up a second file. There are two people pictured in the feed, along with a bundle of equipment. "This is the last file from that camera, right before the corridor exploded."

I play the footage. The figures move around until one of them kneels down. The other is no longer pictured.

"Who is that?"

"Requisition employee David Kewell," I say.

"What's he doing?" Chiu asks.

"Not sure." I pause the playback. The image is clear, but still difficult to decipher. "I've extrapolated the image and asked the computer to merge it with a three-dimensional simulation of the corridor when it's deployed. I think he's doing something to the oxygen lines."

"That would show up in the monitoring data."

"That's just it. It doesn't." I pull up the log. "The values stop registering about an hour before the incident. I guess they were moving a lot of equipment. They could have damaged something."

"But you don't think that's what happened?"

"No, I don't." I pull up the roster for the reclamation team. Small images of all seven of the people who went over appear on the display, along with a scrolling list of their skills, qualifications and experiences. "I've cross-referenced their records. There are several interesting elements to this team."

Chiu leans forwards, reading the scrolling information. "Comms expert, technician, engineer, pilot. This doesn't look like an ordinary reclamation team."

"Define ordinary," I say. "Most people out here are multi-skilled, adept in a variety of fields, but you're right, this group are particularly skilled. Their experiences compliment each other, like a crew. That's what triggers me. There's something here we aren't seeing."

"You think this was another terrorist attack, like Phobos Station?"

"No. If it was, it was a failure. A group with these kinds of skills, it doesn't fit that they'd commandeer a ship and try to crash it into the colony. Any organisation trying to do that wouldn't waste people like this."

Chiu touches the screen, bringing up the pilot, Dennis, and the engineer, Halle. "You have a qualified shuttle pilot and a failed Fleet engineer. You think they were trying to steal the ship?" she asks.

"No," I say. "I think they succeeded." I pull up the Hera autopilot control log. "Look here. Just after the explosion in the corridor, someone rebooted the manoeuvring system, switching the pilot mode to manual."

"Could have been the desperate act of someone trying to survive?"

"Intention, or inspiration?" I grimace. "The list of other factors makes it seem like the former." I pull up the trajectories. The long line of the *Asthoreth*'s final journey as it disappears into the shadow of Mars. "We lost contact with the ship just before it broke apart. Another convenience."

"But where would they go?" Chiu says. "A wrecked ship, out into space. That's a slow death, worse than burning up in the atmosphere."

"They could be part of the clone faction," I say. "The other ships could be returning."

"If they have those ships, why do they need one of ours?"

I frown. The problem is the prey, and I'm the predator. I haven't caught it yet. "There's an answer in all of this, somewhere," I say.

"You'll find it," Chiu replies. "I know you will."

I look at her. That trust and faith in what I do is so important. The rest of the old *Khidr* crew are millions of miles away. She is the only one left who was there.

"This problem. It might keep me here," I say. "I'm not sure I could leave without an answer."

Chiu reaches out, brushing my face with her hand. "Good job I know you," she says. "If I heard that from anyone else, I'd think it was an excuse."

"Yeah, I can't help what I'm like with a problem," I say. "But we still have a week or so until the ships arrive."

I pull up the ID profiles again and start a selection of tracing queries. "I want to know who paid for their rides," I say. "Maybe there's a connection we can find, a company link that will show their agenda."

More information appears on my screen. A list of corporations who have contributed to the transport costs of the seven reclamation team members. Halan Weaver, the supervisor, is quickly verified. I recognise the Tưởng Corporation and Nylov Industries, who own his transport debt. Both are partners we've dealt with extensively during the rebuild.

The others though…

Corporation names scroll onto my screen. I initiate verification traces, and those queries check out. Further questions are also answered with endorsed brands and individuals.

"There's something too neat about this," I say. "Have you heard of any of these names?"

"They aren't familiar to me," Chiu says.

"But they are all verified by the system." Another level of inquiry produces another list, some of the same names as before, but even more new ones, all verified. "This is weird."

I reach under my table for my diagnostic screen – a copy of the one I used on *Gallowglass* years ago. I keep it unconnected from the main computer network unless absolutely necessary. There are a variety of software defences installed as well, so it doesn't receive an update that I don't need. I pull out a connecting cable and plug it into the emergency port. "All right, let's take a look at what's going on under the hood."

I open a terminal window on the portable screen and begin writing code. The application I'm making is rough, but it uses some archaic query testing, looking for usual processing spikes as the network assembles the results. Once it's ready, I activate it and input another query on the corporate funding sources.

"There! Look at that!"

Chiu frowns. "Yeah, that doesn't look right. It looks like another program is being activated as you instigate your query." She moves closer, touching the display to run another search, watching the monitoring log. "And again, same strange activity."

"It'll take us a while to communicate directly with Earth and manually verify all these corporations," I say. "I guess anyone investigating all this wouldn't usually bother."

"Not after the third positive verification from the network," Chiu says.

"I think the results are being generated as we submit the queries," I say. "I think there's a program embedded in the networks we're accessing that is intercepting our requests and sending us fake results."

"We should alert the authorities," Chiu says.

"No," I say. "If we do, whoever did this will know we're onto them. We have what we need. These people were suspicious, we checked them, and they are still suspicious. Now we investigate the ship."

I'm back on the terminal screen, diverting and tasking different resources to support what we're trying to do. "I'm taking the main laser offline and switching it to field-scan mode."

"That'll need authorisation," Chiu says.

"If we wait for that, we'll be losing even more time." I'm writing a search query to detect trace particle clouds in space, aiming the laser at a specific region that could have been a course taken by *Asthoreth*, if it survived the close scrape with Mars's atmosphere. "We should be able to find any traces of thrust residue. If the *Asthoreth* survived, they'll have had to initiate a thruster burn to get out of the reach of the planet's gravity."

"It'll take a while to compile the results," Chiu says. "What else can we do in the meantime?"

"An encrypted call to Commodore Shann would help," I say. "She'll endorse our requisition of the Hub's laser, once we explain what we've done."

"Good idea."

"You want to do it?"

Chiu frowns. I know what her answer will be. "I think it should come from you," she says.

"Okay," I say.

Chiu knows that she has to go back to Earth and face Fleet's board of inquiry. She's been anxious about this for months. Now, she doesn't want to remind anyone of her presence. She's intimidated by Shann, despite the fact that our former captain is probably the best ally she could have through the whole process. A little face time with Shann might be good for her.

But I'm not going to push the issue.

★ ★ ★

The formal renegotiation of the Arctic treaty in 2048 proved to be a disastrous advertisement for diplomacy. The circumstances under which the original signatory parties were outmanoeuvred seemed at first to have the best interests of the local nations at heart, but the duplicity of the tactics employed were soon revealed as the talks became protracted.

The prospect of a north–west trade route, brought about by climate change and the thawing of the northern ice, meant that the world's largest economic powers had a vested interest in the region as well. China was quickly revealed as being a lobbying party to the talks. Anti-American sentiment had been building for more than two decades, and some clever manoeuvring by trade-focused politicians managed to exploit this factor.

Norway, Iceland and Greenland were ostensibly an allied party in the conversation. However, the economic and military capacity to enforce any decision made about the Arctic was questionable. The United Kingdom offered some capability in this regard and was seen as a natural arbiter between these nations and the United States, but appeared to be more interested in playing to the public than delivering any meaningful or practical solutions.

China's offer of trade concessions to the Scandinavian bloc empowered them to stand up to the acquisitive interests of American megacorporations. At this point, the rare-earths economy was on the cusp of the boom, with demand far exceeding supply. With the most available natural resources, China already dominated this sector. A structured agreement with a set of North European partners looking for a stable economic return without substantive investment in developing infrastructure in the coldest region on the planet seemed sensible.

When Harald Gundarsson, the chief negotiator for the Icelandic delegation, was found dead in a hotel room in Svalbard, matters became tense. There was no outright accusation levied at the Americans, an official investigation cleared all parties, as Gundarsson was found to have committed suicide, jumping from a third-floor window, but there were enough questions raised in the autopsy and subsequent report to suggest that an alternative conclusion might be plausible.

Gundarsson's absence in the final discussions might have been a contributory factor to the mercantile agreement that was struck between all parties. He was known to be an environmentalist with strong views on climate change. Many of his early interventions had been to remind all of the delegates that they would be negotiating a settlement that would affect the environment for future generations. His words were not received well by some, but there was at least some effort in the final wording of the new treaty to acknowledge this.

Extract from *Davey's Political History of the World: 5th Edition* (2071).

Chapter Fourteen
Sirocco

A cold that burrows into your bones, into your soul. When it first enters you, the sensation awakens nerves that are forgotten and unknown to you for the duration of your life. It is only when the cold comes that you remember, and you learn who you really are once more.

The physical living presence of an individual exists upon the surface of their physiology. We might not always think about ourselves in that way, but it is difficult to perceive our identities beneath the skin.

Biological functions come from these places. Many of these emanations are rendered into nothing through discretion and privacy. We do not dwell on them, we get them done and move on with our lives.

Others we take for granted. Like breathing.

I have not been breathing for a long time. Somehow, I know that. The first inhalation hurts, bringing me to consciousness in raw dry pain. I don't remember this. If I'd caught a cold, there would be small symptoms before the full onset of this.

"Easy, open your mouth, let me help you."

Liquid on my tongue. Suddenly the flesh can move. I gag as a little of the moisture drips into my throat. The spasm is agony and for the first time, I feel the restraints, around my wrists, neck and ankles.

"Stay still. You need to take this slowly."

I remember being in a bed. Milanova talking to me, telling me I'd been poisoned. I open my eyes, blinking against the light. The face over me is not the same one I remember from that moment. This person is older, and male.

"My name is Antonio Sammatri," the man says. "I have been told you wanted to see me."

Sammatri is holding a small plastic syringe. He moves away from me, dipping it into a glass of water, refilling it. "This is a little trick I learned when I was first put into cryo," he says. "The body dries out. Takes a while to get your circulation going properly. A little water in the mouth really helps."

I try to move my head, to express gratitude in some small way, but then I remember: Sammatri is probably the reason I'm in this tube and thawing out like this.

"Apologies, but the precautions are necessary," Sammatri says. "I know you proved yourself to the others, when you met with them, but here, you start afresh. If you're here to help us, you'll need to prove that to me."

I try to answer, but my throat remains swollen and rebellious, although breathing is easier now. Small victories. Looks like my new host gets to speak his piece without interruption.

"It took me a while to sort through the supply crates. I decided to leave you until last. Made sense to get everything else they sent me installed and set up first." Sammatri reaches into the tube and gets his hands under my shoulders, lifting me gently into a sitting position. "I could certainly do with a second pair of hands to help with all of this."

Another syringe of water in my mouth. I swallow the liquid. This time, my throat eases. "They sent me here to help," I say.

"My people did, yes," Sammatri says. "A question remains over the motivations of your employers."

Sammatri moves away from me, and I find I can sit up on my own. I lift my arms to the sides of the tube and attempt to push myself up. The weak Martian gravity is a blessing. If I'd been on Earth, I don't think I would have been able to manage it.

I'm in a large room. The walls are lined with metal canisters, all connected together with piping. There are a variety of opened boxes lying next to my tube. Beyond them, I can see a small, tracked rover and trailer. Behind me, there is a large metal door. I'd guess I've been brought by the rover into a vehicle airlock.

Sammatri is facing away from me, looking at a monitor display.

I'm climbing out of the tube. My legs are unsteady and weak. "How long…have I been in here?" I ask.

"A few weeks," Sammatri says. "Sorry, I would have got to you sooner, but what you did at the base, well…it caused some developments out here."

I think I know what he's talking about. I activated the spherical machine in the Arboretum. I want to ask questions to confirm, but I get the sense I'll find out soon enough. "Just trying to help," I say.

"And you did," Sammatri says. He turns around, holding a portable display with the image of a person on it, someone I recognise. "Who is this, please?"

"That's Louisa Aymes, the woman who sent me here."

"Interesting!" Sammatri taps the screen a few times and the image changes to show a newspaper article. I read the headline. *Woman found Dead in Radioactive Exclusion Zone.* "This is a censored report from after you left Earth. It includes images, which I think you'll find interesting."

Sammatri scrolls down the document, and I see the attachments. There is a picture in an old hotel room. There's a body lying on a bloodstained bed, but that's not what draws my attention. The head is missing, fragments of flesh and bone litter the pillows and mattress.

"That's also a woman called Louisa Aymes," Sammatri says. "She has the same name as your employer. Does that mean your mission is over?"

Sammatri scrolls further. Now I'm looking at a profile picture. It's the same woman as I remember. "I don't know," I say. "I've not been in contact with anyone since I left Earth. They'd already told me what I needed to do when I got here."

Sammatri nods. He pulls up another set of files. I see Louisa Aymes again, this time in video messages. "We received these during your transit. Complex negotiations conducted over encrypted connection with your employer. Our people analysed the files. If it's a filter or a digital recreation of her, it's very sophisticated. Beyond what we can detect."

"So, you think it's her?"

"Perhaps," Sammatri says. "Could be that her death was faked. If it was, that raises the new question of why?"

"I'm here now," I say. "You have my word that I'm not here to murder you."

Sammatri laughs. "If I thought you were, I could have kicked you out of the facility and let you die on the surface of Mars. There's enough doubt in all of this for me to pause before acting."

"Are you alone here?" I ask.

"In a sense, yes, but also, no."

I'm looking at Sammatri. For the first time, I notice two small digital beads attached to either side of his forehead. This is not a conversation happening between two people. "What do you mean?" I ask. "Who else is here?"

"You'll find out," Sammatri says.

⋆ ⋆ ⋆

I'm on my own.

Sammatri left me in this room. I've tried to open the door that he went through, but it remains locked when I approach.

Antonio Sammatri. I'm thinking about him, going over everything Doctor Henry Terren gave me in that short briefing. When Sammatri and his people were in the city, fighting the outsiders. I read his speech to the underground population. The words were fire; they should have triggered an uprising. Milanova told me it did, but they failed.

Could Sammatri have fought harder? I wasn't there, but I don't think I would have fled out here without a good reason.

I walk around. My arms and legs feel awkward at first, but after a little exercise, they get used to the movement. I still feel weak from the lack of activity, but I'm making up for that now.

In the opened crates, I find food and water. More of the nutrition strips we get at Jezero. Tasteless mush that takes too long to chew and swallow, but at least it's something to do, something that gives me a sense of purpose.

I almost forget how I was poisoned by Milanova. I have the food in my hands and I'm raising it to my lips when I remember. The memory makes me hesitate, but I eat anyway. If Sammatri wants me unconscious, there are a variety of ways he can achieve that end. He doesn't want me dead.

Not yet.

"Magnus, can you hear me?"

Sammatri's face appears on the terminal display. His voice is coming through speakers embedded in the walls of the room.

I move over so I'm in front of the camera. "Yes, I can hear you," I say. "When am I getting out of here?"

"Soon, I hope," Sammatri says.

I scowl. My fingers clench into fists. I've been patient throughout my time on Mars, now that patience is starting to wear thin. "What do you need me to do to prove myself to you?"

"I'll have a think about that."

The image on the display disappears.

I clench my teeth. I want to shout, to hammer on the door, give vent to my anger and frustration at being stuck here, but it won't help. Sammatri is talking with someone who doesn't want me to get out of this room. I don't think it's Milanova or Madiro, so who could it be?

I move to the terminal. I've already tried to log into the system, but the machine refused to recognise my thumbprint or my retina ID. Now, however, I notice the screen is on the default control page. A quick check reveals that I've been given guest privileges. Well, that's something, I guess.

There are icons on the screen. I touch one, bringing up a map of my location.

According to the plan, this is a five-room facility. The vehicle airlock, where I am currently, is the largest chamber. Beyond it, operations, kitchen, personal quarters and storage are marked out on the document. Of course, that doesn't mean everything is included here. Maybe this is just what they want me to see?

I try a few other applications. The communications access is disabled; the code window is also unavailable, although that wouldn't help me anyway. I wouldn't know where to start with trying to hack anything, unless it involved using a sharp blade.

Yeah, this is starting to look like brute force or wait could be my only options.

Sammatri pisses me off. At least Madiro and Milanova were negotiating. Even Tellen gave something in return when I spoke to him. Now, I feel like I'm dealing with a blank wall, and I don't like it.

The terminal offers no immediate answers. There's a selection of entertainment and reading available to me. Looks like someone took the trouble to share their own library. I browse through the list and note the authors, a lot of old twentieth-century stuff like Chomsky, Jameson and Freire. I read a few of those when I was younger.

Maybe that's what frustrates me about Sammatri? I was expecting to meet a revolutionary, a kindred spirit. But instead, he's…just opaque to me.

* * *

Hours pass.

I'm lying on the floor, a blanket beneath me. I figured out how to use the terminal controls to dim the lights. After watching some shitty old three-dimensional movie, I've settled down, ostensibly to go to sleep.

I'm three or four metres from the door. Close enough to get there if it opens but not close enough to concern the person who may come through. I have every intention of taking control of the situation if it arises.

I'm aware that I'm being watched. The cameras have a variety of spectrums available to access, and even though my bio-monitor has been disabled, I'm sure Sammatri will be using whatever he can to analyse my breathing and heart rate, trying to work out whether I'm really asleep or not.

The door panel slides open. I steel myself not to react. The best traps are when you lie in wait long enough to make things happen.

The sound of an electric motor. Something on tracks drives into the room. Makes sense that Sammatri wouldn't come in on his own. The last time we spoke I was weak from cryosleep. This time, he's decided he needs backup.

I must be getting to him.

I'm holding a handful of plastic ties that I found in the empty crates. My original plan had been to overpower Sammatri and secure him to one of the safety handles on the wall, but I'm not sure they'll hold whatever's just entered the room.

So, instead, I'll need to try something new.

The tracked vehicle rolls past me. As it does, I move, rolling the other way, towards the open door. I make it into the gap before the panel can slide shut.

A hand grabs my shoulder. I grab the hand at the wrist, pull its owner forwards and twist, driving my weight down upon them. It's Sammatri, I have him pinned on the floor.

"Please, stop! What are you doing?"

"Leveraging my position," I say.

Sammatri is struggling underneath me, but he's older and he's been here on Mars a lot longer. His body has got used to the weaker gravity. I still have some of my Earth strength and I'm using it here.

"Call off your drones and let's talk properly," I say. "I'm not here to hurt you, I'm here to help."

"I can't…trust…"

"Well, now you have no choice." I pull his arm out from underneath him. The dim light makes it difficult to find one of the emergency handholds, but after a few seconds groping around, I locate one, take a plastic tie from a pocket and secure his wrist to the wall. "I told you I came here to be an ally. Your people let me through. That has to count for something."

"*Believe me, it does, Mister Sirocco.*"

A red light spears through the shadows, illuminating me and Sammatri. He hasn't spoken. The words are spoken in a flat, cultured voice, the kind you hear when a computer tries to emulate a human being without inflection.

"Who are you?" I ask.

"*I'm the individual who you really want to be talking to,*" the voice says. "*Shall we begin?*"

I stand, leaving Sammatri against the wall. "I'm ready," I say.

★ ★ ★

Senator Cordwin, thank you for your message and your inquiry about our situation here on Mars.

For the majority of your questions, I would refer you to the statements given in the official colony report dated 6th of March, 2121. Our assessments contained there are still valid and relevant and should be used as the formal economic position of Mars reporting to the World Senate and to its creditors.

To elaborate further on my personal contribution and perspective in this, I would say we remain in crisis-management mode. We cannot move ahead with the rebuilding of our infrastructure while we are funded hand to mouth. The entire supply logistics process has been damaged with the loss of *Hercules*, effectively halved. There must be an effort made to restore this provision.

Additionally, you have asked about my personal relationships with the Fleet commanders assigned to the colony. I would say I have found Captain Shann's leadership here to be a source of support and frustration. No one can deny the energy she brings to what we are trying to do, but there is also an element of overreach.

Let me be plain. Colonists on Mars cannot be given the same privileges as people have on Earth. The cost of travel and survival is such that our project will collapse if sacrifices are not made. The debt incurred by each individual who comes here is the commodity we can sell back to the corporations that fund us. Regular return and interest on investment is our stock in trade in this phase.

Once we have achieved a more sustainable export model, with minerals and manufactured goods being made here and shipped back to Earth, the situation will change. Until then, things must remain as they are.

I understand and appreciate the concerns people raise about this; how the 'fresh start' is sold to people compared to the reality they will face on our world, but I make no apology for it. If we do not work this way, our effort will not be viable. We have come so far, it would be a waste on a biblical scale if we were to turn back now.

Elias Jabbutu – First Citizen of Mars.

Chapter Fifteen

Iskander

Dark and quiet, staring out into the void.

It's been nearly three months since we left Mars orbit. I'm sitting in the captain's chair. Five members of our crew are in cryosleep. That leaves Halle and me awake and managing the ship.

My stomach rumbles. Minimal food and water supplies were left aboard this ship. We were able to smuggle some on-board with us, but not enough for seven to survive the trip we've been asked to make.

I knew that from the start.

"You wanted to speak with me, Deacon?"

Halle arrives on the bridge from engineering. She's worked miracles down there, restoring reactor power and a variety of support systems that are helping us survive. The scrubbers are her latest project, ensuring we don't run out of air any time soon. No recycling system can be perfect, but seventy-three per cent efficiency is better than we ever hoped for.

But still, not enough for where we want to go.

Halle moves around the room towards the engineer's console. The station is still inoperable, but it's the place she habitually takes when we've met together as a crew over the last few weeks. "Kewell and Dennis are down," she says. "I checked on Weaver, Merrick and Tolwyn while I was there. All the pods are functioning."

"Fleet makes good machines," I say.

"Only the best," Halle says. "All that money spewed into space, when it could have been making lives better for people on Earth."

"If they hadn't done what they did, we wouldn't be able to do what we're doing," I say.

"And what exactly is it that we're doing?" Halle asks.

I grimace. "You've followed me this far on trust."

"I trust in you and what you were instructed to do." Halle drifts around the broken chair until she is facing me. "I don't think you'd lie about our mission."

"I don't intend to," I say. I touch the screen in front of me, and the main screen activates. The projection is intermittent, flickering, but good enough for what I need to say. I point. "There's Mars, there's Phobos and there's us, following the delta-*v* path that Dennis put us on, modified a little with the thruster burns we've initiated over the last few weeks. We're making the most of the velocity we managed to acquire from the planet."

"The best we can do. The resonance cavity drive was one of the first things they removed from this ship," Halle says.

"A problem with some positive elements," I say. "We can adjust course more easily, and we may have to. Our destination has drifted since it was abandoned."

An object added to the model. A larger three-dimensional design model from the ship's archives. One of Earth's supermassive freighters.

"The *Hercules*?" Halle says. "That's where we're going?"

"Yes," I say. "That's where I was told to lead us."

Halle frowns. She's looking at the distance projection. "Two weeks minimum at this velocity. Cryosleep would get us there. But I'm not sure the automated systems could manage the ship, in its current state of repair."

"You and I will be the only ones awake, unless we require assistance," I say. "That, combined with your work on the scrubbers, should give us enough air to reach our destination."

"But not enough food and water, even with the recycling systems working at an improved rate. Unless you plan to eat Weaver?"

I smile and shake my head. "No, but we do need to discuss him. Has he proved he can be trusted?"

"I don't want to kill him and neither do you," Halle says. "So long as he remains in cryosleep, he's no danger to us. You could even push him out the airlock and turn on the pod's beacon. Eventually, they'd come and pick him up."

"That would be a clue for them to follow us," I say. "I don't plan on giving them that."

"So, we'll carry our Judas with us," Halle says. "What's he going to do when he learns what our real purpose is?"

"What will any of us do?" I ask. "Neither you nor I have the whole picture."

I gesture towards the digital representation of the *Hercules* on the main viewer. "That ship was abandoned with huge amounts of fuel and cargo on-board. If we can find it and get there, we should have everything we need to go wherever we want."

"And where will that be?"

"I don't know yet, but I have instructions on how we make contact."

Halle nods. "All right then, it's a repair and resources challenge. We haven't searched all the crew lockers yet. If we find anything that'll stretch our supplies a little, that can help. Otherwise, we'll need to go down to single shifts."

"Yes," I say. "That'll be a rotation of you and me."

"You don't want to tell the others?"

"No, not yet."

"We'll also need to repair as many exterior cameras and sensors as possible," Halle says. "We don't want to be out here going right past our target."

"You think there's a chance of that?"

"Absolutely." Halle gestures at the flickering projection. "These ships rely on their laser emitters for quick and accurate scans. That was one of the first things they disassembled and removed."

"Do we have any weapons?" I ask.

Halle shakes her head. "The torpedo system might be working, but we have no ordnance. The arms lockers are empty as well. All of those items would have been requisitioned for the other ships ages ago."

"So, we best pray we don't run into anything."

"Indeed. I pray for that constantly."

I nod. "You're Jewish by birth, right?"

Halle shrugs. "Half-Jewish. I grew up reading the Tanakh, but that doesn't mean I believe everything that was written down. Humans are imperfect transcribers of the word of God. We can't know the purpose of one who is beyond our understanding. Doubt is healthy, sometimes it keeps us alive."

"True enough," I say. "Never hold back on that. If you doubt me, tell me to my face. That'll help keep us on track."

★ ★ ★

"You will lead the expedition, Peter Iskander."

A dark room, underground. I was brought here blindfolded. I know I'm somewhere in Turkey, south of Ankara, I think. The words reverberate against stone walls, but not much.

I'm blinking, trying to get my eyes to adjust. As they do, I get a better sense of the space, of the robed figures all around me. No identities are revealed.

"Do you accept this charge?"

"I do."

"Then rise, Deacon Iskander, and be acknowledged."

I stand in the darkness. There is applause, hands being slapped against cloth in rhythmic tradition. I am known to all of these people, I have been selected by them, but, by necessity, they remain entirely unknown to me.

"Follow me, Deacon."

A hand takes mine. I am led from the chamber into a smaller room. In here, illumination is permitted, and I find myself sitting on a wooden bench facing a woman who I do not know.

"You have family?" she asks.

I nod.

"Children?"

"Two sons."

"This will not be easy for them. They cannot be told about your mission."

"I know. They live with my partner. We separated at the beginning of this process, so I could do this."

"Not easy for you either, then."

"No."

The woman takes my hand in hers, holding it with a firm grip. "A great many people need you to bring them hope," she says. "Your task is already being talked about in whispers around the world."

I frown. "People need to be discreet."

"Oh, they will, but what you will achieve is greatly wished for."

"I see."

We stare at one another after that. Then the woman smiles, she releases my hand and leaves.

I never see her again.

* * *

"Wake up, Deacon."

I open my eyes. I'm lying on one of the few crew beds that were left when we got here. Most of the personal quarters had been gutted for useable equipment long ago.

Halle is here, her hand in mine, just like the woman from the ceremony. She withdraws it as she sees I am awake.

"It's your shift," Halle says.

I sit up. The low-level lighting helps me acclimatise. "Anything to report?" I ask.

"A glitch in one of the readings," Halle says. "Gravitational anomaly by all accounts. Impossible. Our limited sensors didn't allow me to get a proper reading, but I've set an engine diagnostic going, to see if one of the manoeuvring thrusters misfired and caused us to get misdirected."

"You've rectified the heading?"

"Of course."

I pull myself off the bed and drift across the room. Halle moves away, heading towards the other room we cleared out for her. "I'll be awake for another hour or so, if something comes up," she says.

"Understood, thank you."

"Of course, Deacon."

I move through the corridors back to the bridge. In the next six hours, I'll make trips to engineering, the airlocks and the cryopods to check on everything, but I'll start from the bridge, sitting in the captain's chair.

As I'm moving through the passages, I notice scorch marks and puncture holes in the wall plating. Old wounds from before. We know there was fighting aboard this ship. I wonder what happened? What it was like, trying to survive in cramped conditions, when someone is trying to kill you?

I hope I never have to find out.

As I'm moving to the bridge, I'm also aware of the lighting. The way shadows move and change around me as the ship's illumination turns on and off makes it like someone might be there, lurking around every hatchway and bulkhead.

I'm sure I can hear music too. Faint harmonious tones, the kind you aren't sure you've really heard at all.

I guess I must still be half-asleep.

I reach the bridge and go through the door, then drift over the stations to the captain's chair, grabbing hold of the back and pulling myself into the seat.

People have sat here before me. Commissioned Fleet officers, in charge of the ship during rescue missions and patrols for the most part. But I know there were also officers who led their crew into battle.

The detail of what happened around Mars and how Phobos Station was destroyed has never been made public. I guess somewhere on this ship's computer there is classified information – video files, ship's logs, that sort of thing – that would reveal all those secrets. All of it will be encrypted and locked away behind passwords, but that doesn't mean it isn't there. I doubt my computer skills are up to the task of retrieving it, but Halle's might be.

I wonder if that information would be useful? Maybe, somewhere down the line.

I'm about to log into the system and start trying to find all those hidden data files, when I notice one of the other screens on the bridge is illuminated.

It's the pilot's console.

I move out of the chair and head across to the other seat. I note the fraying plastic skin on the back, the padding is exposed in several places. But my attention quickly turns to the screen, which shows our trajectory plot, and the recent adjustment Halle has made.

The screen shows a three-dimensional route plan, along with an activity log that displays the burn duration and fuel consumption. We can't afford much, otherwise we'll never be able to decelerate when we need to so we can rendezvous with the *Hercules* wreck.

There is a second window under the first. Has she been writing code? I pull it up. No, it appears not. There's just a sentence written here:

THERE ARE GHOSTS ON THIS SHIP.

Chapter Sixteen

Johansson

The meeting room in the Hub is little more than an open space surrounded by displays and projectors. I've finished my shift in operations and let others take over. I moved in here alone, shutting the door.

I built this place. It is a functional environment, made entirely for purpose. I suppose others would try to incorporate an element of presentation to the design, that might make it more aesthetically pleasing to those being invited to take part in discussions from remote locations.

In this moment, the utilitarian look is exactly what we need. No one on the surface of Mars is enjoying any luxuries. This little glimpse into our lives needs to show the same.

Comms requests have been sent out. I've set up everything. Now, I just wait until they all check in.

The first arrival is Citizen Elias Jabbutu. His three-dimensional image is small and scaled down, around a metre cubed, and tinged with blue light. I can see him and the desk he is sitting at down there on Mars.

"Lieutenant Johansson, good to see you."

"And you, Citizen."

Jabbutu is necessary to all of this. He's one of the original twelve who led Mars CorpGov before Phobos Station fell. He's seen the rise and fall of the colony and somehow kept his place in its leadership. It was Jabbutu who supported transferring executive control of the orbital rebuilding programme to Fleet. He and his peers have more than enough to deal with in the Jezero reconstruction.

Jabbutu has kept out of my way and supported my suggestions in the face of senior officers who outrank me. I guess that suits him.

One of the screens activates. The face that appears is my immediate superior, the de facto head of Fleet's presence around Mars.

Luis Ontaraes, former Chief Engineer of *Nandin*.

"Lieutenant Johansson, you've re-tasked the Hub's laser to scan the edge of Mars's atmosphere," Ontaraes says. "What was the purpose of this?"

I hold up a hand. "Sir, if we can wait for the rest of the council, then I won't have to repeat myself."

Ontaraes shrugs. "Fine, but I'll need a good explanation."

"I'll do my best, sir."

Three more monitors activate. These are representatives from other global departments. The expeditionary council, spaceport administration, and planetary security command. All three are citizens, a privilege of their positions.

The last person to arrive is Commodore Ellisa Shann.

All of the transmissions have to deal with latency. I am thousands of miles from the nearest of these six, and millions of miles from the furthest. Adaptive programming works continuously to mask the delays. Micro-expressions from each participant are recorded and used to create new spontaneous movements. Data is carefully prioritised, so that audio information is sent first, while the visuals are a mixture of created content, cross-referenced with actual incoming content. Camera angles are corrected through the process, so eye contact is generally maintained.

"Commodore, it's good to see you again."

"You'll all be seeing more of me soon," Shann replies. That draws smiles and chuckles from around the gathered faces. I watch the algorithms struggle to keep up.

"Lieutenant Johansson, you called for this meeting. What do you have to tell us?"

Eyes turn on me. I nod to each of the group in turn. "Thank you all for making the time. As Commander Ontaraes has mentioned, I have re-tasked the Hub's main laser to conduct a sensor sweep of the outer planetary atmosphere, focusing on the last known position of *Asthoreth*, before it disappeared."

"Disappeared? I thought the established conclusion was that the ship burned up?"

"I have reason to believe that we were wrong about assuming that."

As I'm talking, I'm working the terminal, uploading my findings to each of the representatives. I hold back some detail on the generated corporations behind the reclamation team's transport debt. The minute we publicise that, whoever is running the hack will know that we know, and take steps.

"The laser sweep is calibrated to pick up dispersed particulates. If the ship survived, they'll have used thrust from the main engines to escape Mars gravity. We should be able to detect their wake."

"If they survived, wouldn't they have radioed for help?" Jabbutu asks.

"Not if they were trying to steal the ship, Citizen," Shann replies. "If we're dealing with thieves, the last thing they'd want to do is let us know they are alive."

"Lieutenant." Ontaraes is speaking now, using my rank again. We used to be closer, back in the aftermath of Phobos Station, but when they promoted Luis to Fleet lead after Shann went home, he changed, became more distant. "How long will this scan take?"

"About three hours," I say.

"So, for that time, we're essentially defenceless if the enemy decides to return," Ontaraes says. "Just so we're all clear on this."

"Our torpedo launchers are still on standby," I say.

"We know their ships can scramble the guidance of our ordnance," Ontaraes says.

"Let's not dwell on this," Shann says. "What's done is done. Lieutenant, I'll want those results from your scan as soon as you get them, please."

"Yes, Commodore," I reply. Then, I notice my screen is flashing. There's a private message from Shann. Something she doesn't want to share with the group.

If you confirm this, we'll divert and pursue.

Immediately, I find myself wanting to react. I try to keep my expression neutral and calm. "Otherwise, everything is awaiting your return, Commodore."

"Thank you, Lieutenant," Shann says. She glances around. "Anything else we need to talk about?"

"After consultation with Expeditions, we've closed the case on the two missing from Jezero perimeter mission eighteen," Jabbutu says. "We'll keep looking when there's opportunity to look, but I'm not going to divert further resources."

"Understood."

The meeting draws to a close. I spend the next two hours making work for myself, trying to locate the database entry spoofing program with no luck. It's hiding somewhere on the civilian network, I think.

Then the laser scan results come in and I get that nice feeling of being proved right, for a few seconds before I consider the ramifications.

Trace gases found. Six locations are identified. Dispersal patterns are consistent with the time lapse between now and the incident. That means *Asthoreth* escaped. She didn't burn up.

That means someone stole her and headed out into deep space.

Fuck.

As I'm digesting this, another message comes in. It's from Shann.

What's the result?

Immediately, I forward her the analysis and set a course projection running. It's one thing to know what's going on, another to start doing something about it.

The results come back pretty quickly. The location is one I'm familiar with.

"They're heading for the *Hercules*."

I said the words out loud, even though there's no one in the room to hear them. Immediately, I take the course plot and send it to Shann as well. A moment later, there's a direct communication request, which I accept.

Shann's face appears. She looks tired. In my head, I do the mental calculation of how long she's been on Earth after leaving here. Only a few weeks? That doesn't stack up. Her body can't have recovered from zero gravity before they've sent her out again.

"Lieutenant, good work on this. Anyone else would have let it go."

"Thank you, Commodore."

Titles are being used. Comms at this distance is for the official record, I get that. But the grim set of my old captain's jaw tells me she's made some quick decisions. That's what she does.

"We'll be diverting *Gallowglass* to follow the course you've sent me. *Achilles* and *Ranginui* will continue to rendezvous with the Hub." Shann glances to her right, to someone off camera. She nods, then looks at me again. "Ontaraes has agreed to remain in temporary command while I pursue this."

"Understood."

"I have another task for you."

I blink in surprise. "What do you need?"

"I want you and Lieutenant Chiu to head down to Jezero and trace this back to whoever helped them. It's about time we got some eyes in the colony and saw for ourselves what's going on down there. I'll clear it with Jabbutu's people."

I nod. "We'll get the next shuttle, Commodore," I say. "But that will put us on planet when the ships arrive here."

Shann smiles. She knows what I'm not saying. "I need you working on this. You let me worry about Chiu's ride home. I'm sure when you tell her, she'll be happy to do the job."

"Understood."

Shann's face disappears, and the conversation is over.

★ ★ ★

"We have new orders. You and I are going planetside."

Chiu glances up from the terminal display in the personal quarters we've been sharing for the last few weeks. I watch different expressions cross her face as she absorbs the news and its implications. "What's happened? What are we going to do down there?"

"The laser scan results came in," I explain. "Looks like *Asthoreth* was stolen. We have a possible course plot, and *Gallowglass* is going after her. Shann wants Fleet people on the ground in Jezero to investigate who helped them."

"The other ships are still coming here though, right?"

"They are, but we won't be here to meet them. Ontaraes is staying in charge until Shann gets back. Yes, that means you could miss your ride home."

"I'm not sad about that."

"No, I guess you're not."

Chiu pushes herself away from the terminal towards me. I get a glimpse of a design model she's been working on before I'm engulfed in a big hug. Thankfully, I have my foot against the bulkhead and we don't both go crashing into a wall.

"I don't know how much you were involved in the decision, but thank you," Chiu says.

"Involved not at all," I say. "I just presented the information. Shann's the one you should be thanking."

"And I will, first chance I get."

"Good." I extricate myself gently. Zero gravity can be a problem when you're emotional and not thinking about the consequences of different forces. "I don't know about you, but I'm not going to be able to sleep until we've organised our shit and arranged for a shuttle transit."

"Agreed," Chiu says. "Let's get on with it."

★ ★ ★

I remember growing up in Bessaker, a village of less than four hundred people. I went to school there in my formative years as part of a class of thirty, all of different ages. Most of my peers were sons and daughters of fisherfolk, crafters and boatpeople.

From as far back as I can remember, I didn't feel I had a lot in common with the people around me.

The automated teaching assistants allowed every student to follow their own individuated education pathway under the supervision of a human teacher, but every day, there were recreation sessions, where we were encouraged to play in small groups. The interaction was seen as being an important part of every person's growth and development.

I always found those moments in my day the hardest. Whatever anyone else was interested in, I wasn't.

As I grew older, I started to understand the issue a little better. The people around me thought our village was the entire world. They were seeing themselves as grown-ups in that place, inheriting the roles of previous generations as they passed away.

My parents saw something else in me. It helped that we were comfortable financially. They praised my academic ability from a young age and, seeing that my interests were in physics and technology, they encouraged me to learn. I was sent to Oslo to study at the university and specialised in audio science, but I still struggled with groups of people and preferred my own company. Relationships were always intense meetings of minds with other high-flying intellectuals, or quiet companionship with shoulder-to-cry-on types.

Chiu is neither of those. She's also both of those.

We're on the transit shuttle, strapped in, heading down to Hera Spaceport, and I'm watching her sleep. She's relaxed. The anxiety that has dogged her for the last few weeks has disappeared. I know how worried she's been about going back to Earth. At least now we can put it off a little longer.

The shuttle starts to tremble as it hits the Martian atmosphere. I can feel the vibration through my seat. For a moment, there's a musical tone to it, reminding me of the audio we picked up the first time we went after the *Hercules*. The strange melodic tone we heard whilst using the cavity drive to get there in answer to their distress call.

That freighter is a tomb. A graveyard for the crew who were killed. Everything out there will have been left, drifting, just as we found it. Like a wreck at sea, I guess. Only there, you know eventually the water will eat away at the ship and the corpses.

In space, there's nothing. It all just stays as it was, drifting for ever. Pretty creepy. But I guess I'd rather be there than going to Mars and having to deal with people.

I'm not an investigator, neither is Chiu. In the circumstances, Shann needs people she can trust with this. Maybe Ontaraes could have handled it?

No, Avril, you plucked at the threads, now you have to unravel it all.

The shuttle vibration picks up as we descend. But it's nothing like the sensation you get on Earth. The thin atmosphere doesn't generate the same level of resistance and heat. There are no pilots in this little craft, just the two of us, trusting a computer to do the work. I have a screen in a cradle next to me. If I needed to, I could override the controls and pilot us in, but there's no need. We should be fine.

I reach out to the screen anyway, for something else.

The data folders I was able to save from *Khidr* were uploaded to *Gallowglass* when we abandoned ship. The most important things to save were the crew's personal files. Copies of these were sent to all the next of kin of the deceased once we returned to Mars and established communication with Earth. I deleted my copies of these folders as soon as that was done.

The personal files of the survivors were handed back to each of them as we established ourselves on *Gallowglass*. When the ship's software was purged and replaced with an official Fleet operating system, again, I made sure those files were preserved before that happened, extricating them from my temporary control application and giving them back to all of the crew.

This time though, there were one or two things I kept.

The files are in an encrypted folder on the screen. I press my thumb to open the lock and pull up the item that I want. It's a capture of a letter, written out on another screen. There wasn't time to transfer the file.

It's signed *Ensign Beihe Xiu*. Chiu's full name.

This is the letter she wrote in the immediate aftermath of the mutiny on the *Khidr*.

★ ★ ★

Captain Shann.

I am writing this in the moment, the immediate aftermath of what has happened. It is important to me that nothing is forgotten, that my actions and reactions to the situation on our ship be documented and understood. In this account, I will do my best to hold nothing back. It is necessary that you be able to judge what I have done without fear of omission or misremembered action.

Before I begin, I offer an unreserved apology. I have betrayed the honour of my family, and the honour bestowed upon me when given a commission aboard this ship.

But there is little that can be done about that now.

To begin with, I was offered redemption from my family. My father and mother lived in Hangzhou, the capital city of Zhejiang province. When I was young, my mother worked as a senior city administrator, responsible for street maintenance and traffic flow. She worked with a variety of private companies who manage the autodriving network. After ten years of improved safety records and efficiency on city roads, there was a major accident. My mother was demoted from her role, but left in the department. Now, instead of making decisions and being part of the city-wide strategy, she was given a broom and bucket, allocated shifts and sent out to clean and tidy the streets she had once been in charge of.

I was fortunate that all this happened after I had graduated from university and elected to study in the Municipal Fleet Academy in Algiers. I was two years into my training when I received word. At first, I sought to quit the program and abandon my studies, but a handwritten letter arrived from my mother that told me I should do no such thing. She accepted her place and the punishment that was given to her. She did not want the same for me.

Three days after I boarded the Khidr *for the first time, an anonymous video message arrived in my personal folder. It was a copy of the news report broadcast on the day of the accident in 2114. At first, I thought it was nothing more than a sick joke from someone at the academy, but the attached message encoded into the end of the file suggests that it wasn't. The person who sent the video offered me the opportunity to register my parents, my brother and my sister for immediate emigration to Mars as part of the new Chinese settlement. There seem to be no catch, only that I was asked to reply using encrypted communication method to a designated router box. I did as instructed. Anything that I could do to help my family, I would do.*

When I received the call to muster with the intruder, Rocher and the others, I was also sent another video file. This was video footage of the outside of my parents' house and a long sequence where both my mother and father were followed as they took my brother and sister to school. Again, there was an attached encrypted message. This time, I was told that if I did not obey instructions given to me by a person who provided me with the correct code, my family would be executed.

To begin with, I complied with the requests. At the earliest moment where there was an opportunity for me to work against the other mutineers and assist you in recovering the ship, I made that choice. I did so, knowing that I had placed my family in significant danger. They will remain in danger until the moment they can be extracted from this situation. I have no idea how long this will be.

As you can imagine, I am very worried for them.

I ask you to bear this information in mind as you make your decision. Additionally, whatever you decide to do about my actions, I ask that you make all effort possible to assist my mother, father, brother and sister.

My thanks to you for reading this,

Ensign Beihe Xiu.

★ ★ ★

The vibration is increasing.

I've read this letter six or seven times since the mutiny. It wasn't given to me, so it's wrong for me to be doing this.

Chiu stirs in her sleep. I glance at her. The descent will wake her up. No one sleeps through a full re-entry process. I need to make a decision now.

I press the screen. The options appear. I select delete and permanently purge the letter from my personal files.

"Hey."

"Hey."

"Where are we?"

"Outer atmosphere, I think. We'll be down in fifteen minutes or so."

"Okay."

Chapter Seventeen

Shann

Decision made. We're going back out there.

I'm sitting in the captain's chair on the bridge of *Gallowglass*. There's a buzz to this, a thrill of excitement and trepidation that lit me up the moment Johansson's message came in. Unfinished business out in the darkness. We have to go back to the freighter and find what we missed.

"Bridge to Chase."

"Go ahead, Commodore."

"I'll need all the data files we have on the *Hercules* incident. Get all the logs and start running them through an adaptive processing filter. I need to know everything we've forgotten about what happened."

"Aye aye."

I unbuckle myself from my seat and push off towards the exit. "Helm, set course as directed and initiate burn in fifteen minutes. Comms, inform *Achilles* and *Ranginui* about the change of plan. They are to continue on our original heading. Then ping Mars Orbital as well. No comms traffic to this ship once we've altered course."

Acknowledgements from the relevant stations. These people are a new crew, but we've shared the few months of transit from Earth. They know my ways and what I'll be asking of them.

However, that doesn't mean we're ready for what lies ahead.

I move into the corridor, through a hatch and down a level. Hand over hand in zero gravity feels like my natural environment, but it's also something I never take for granted.

Gallowglass has changed a lot since we returned to Earth. Fleet research teams wanted to tear her apart, learning everything they could from the design of the ship, but midway through that process, Admiral Dean ordered her to be recommissioned for a return to Mars. That meant a refit and upgrade instead. A ship that was constructed for minimal crew now has a rotating deck installed, much like *Khidr* and others of her design.

Achilles and *Ranginui* have both benefited from what was learned from this ship. The torpedo-jamming systems we called baffles have been fitted to all three vessels, engines have been uprated and additional weapons installed.

I have a crew of fourteen on this ship. Fewer than *Khidr*, but more than we managed with when we captured her. The other vessels each have twenty-one people aboard.

I reach my quarters and immediately go to the terminal, submitting a call request to Captains Borislav Kijak and Xuan Ngyugen. They'll want to hear from me personally after getting their instructions from the bridge.

Ngyugen appears promptly. She looks irritated. "All right, Shann, what's going on?"

"Evidence that *Asthoreth* has been stolen has come to light," I explain. "She's headed for the *Hercules* wreck. I'm taking *Gallowglass* to pursue."

Kijak appears. "Good morning, Commodore, Captain," he says. "I take it we're discussing the change of plan?"

Ngyugen nods. "Shann is changing course to rendezvous with the *Hercules*," she says.

"I'm sending you both the report I've received that informed my decision," I say, my fingers working the screen to do just that as I'm talking. "I'll log the update with Earth. I've already informed Mars."

"You likely have your reasons," Kijak says. The files arrive and he glances down, reading the summary. "A stolen ship, eh? You think it's the same people?"

"Not sure," I say. "Doesn't seem like their tactics. No sabotage or attempt to degrade the new orbital facility, but I'm not ruling anything out."

"The *Nandin* should delay leaving until your return," Ngyugen says.

"I'll leave you to discuss that with the current director of operations," I reply. "Ontaraes will stay in post until we get back. Everything else stays on mission."

"Understood." Kijak is still reading. His eyes focused on the documents in front of him. "You're sending people down to Mars as well?"

"Yes. We need to find the root of this."

"Seems reasonable."

I wait, letting both captains consider the matters at hand. During the trip, we've developed an easy informality between us. When we were selecting officers for this mission, I told Sam I wanted pragmatic people who question my decisions in a meeting like this and then act in accordance with our consensus. There might be additional agendas in play, but both Ngyugen and Kijak know their route to advancement for the next six months is through me.

"I'm not entirely comfortable with this," Ngyugen says. "But, I'll back your call."

"Then we're in agreement?" I'm staring at Kijak.

He finishes reading then looks up and nods.

"Good. I'll leave you to your work."

The discussion ends.

★ ★ ★

"Jezero's administration structure is heavily influenced by the Opal Corporation. Key roles in the bureaucracy are occupied by employees who have transferred over from Earth. According to the financials, the company has absorbed their travel debt as part of their new contracts."

"Do they have control?"

"No, Jabbutu is still able to make his own decisions, for now. But he has to listen to the Opal representatives, and they are able to tweak the implementation of his policies."

I'm sitting with Sam in the new rotating section of *Gallowglass*. The ship's change of course manoeuvre has been completed and the wheel deployed to allow members of the crew to exercise under point six of Earth's gravity.

Part of my new medical programme requires that I spend as much time here as possible. The bio-monitor data constantly reminds me to do so and sends alerts to the ship's medical officer every time I drop below a certain threshold of time spent in gravity every twenty-four-hour period.

So, I take my meetings here with Sam in the strategy room. It's almost a perfect replica of the one we had on *Khidr*. I keep expecting Keiyho or Duggins to walk in with a new report.

Except that they won't. Both of them are long dead.

"Shann?"

"Sorry." I was listening. I know what Sam was saying, I just missed the last bit. "You were going to recommend a course of action, right?"

"I was saying, we're out of our depth," Sam replies. "This kind of work isn't something Johansson or Chiu are experienced in. They could be in danger down there."

"Johansson sees patterns in things," I say. "She'll look at the data, not the people."

"That either makes her vulnerable or brilliant in a situation like this," Sam says.

I nod and smile. "You're worried for her, that's okay. But we need to let her work on this."

"You doing this for Chiu, so she gets to put off the board of inquiry?"

"A little, but not much. It's a happy consequence."

Sam frowns. I don't think there's any jealousy there. He has feelings for Johansson, sure, but he knows he's been on Earth, and she's been out here. "Might have been better to get it over with while people are feeling good about what we're doing out here."

"Sure, that's a move," I say. "But what's done is done."

"I'm not cut out for politics," Sam says. He laughs. "Logistics – moving people and equipment. That's much more my bag."

"You'll get used to it," I say.

⋆ ⋆ ⋆

Sam has gone. He's taking the bridge command shift.

There's a screen on the desk in front of me, flashing. Someone is trying to get in touch. I read the name. Have to accept this, otherwise a minute later there will be a general call over the ship's speakers.

"Hello, Doctor. What can I do for you?"

Emerson Drake appears on the screen. "Checking in. Your biodata indicates you're due a session in the weights room."

"Fine, I'll get to it."

"Good."

Emerson Drake. Civilian medical specialist whose brother died on *Khidr*. He went back to Earth on *Nandin*, the first ship to leave Mars after the Phobos Station incident. Sam and I dug him out of a hole in Kyoto a few weeks back and gave him a commission so he could join the crew. Flag rank gives you certain privileges, but I didn't do it for him. I know I need a voice that I'll listen to about neglecting my body. For me, Drake is here to be an overactive parental voice.

He's also someone I can trust implicitly.

"I'm sending you the exercise routine now. It's mostly the same, but a couple of tweaks so you can work on your left shoulder. There's still some weakness there that you need to pay attention to."

"Understood."

"How are you finding the medication now?"

I shrug. "Doing okay with it. The naloxone gets rid of the nausea pretty fast, so that's a good thing. Thanks for prescribing it."

"Glad it helps. Now, exercises please."

"On it."

Two hours later, and I'm back in my own quarters, the same room I had when I first commandeered this ship.

I'm looking at the trajectory plot Johansson has given me. If our calculations are accurate and *Asthoreth* is heading for the last recorded positions of *Hercules*, she's off course, but only by a few thousand kilometres, nothing much in space terms. That means she'll have to correct, which means she'll activate some thrusters. We should be able to detect that, if we do a laser sweep, like Johansson did from the Hub.

I'm also looking at the last inventory log for *Asthoreth* from the previous reclamation team. After I left Mars, my orders to use the ship for salvage were continued. Anything that was useable was transferred out in a series of shuttle runs. This last one, led by a reclamation supervisor called Linus Weaver, was where things went wrong.

I'm interested in what serviceable equipment was left on-board the ship by the previous team. Going through the lists, I can see the nuclear reactor was still in disabled mode, the thruster fuel tanks hadn't been drained, and a few crates of crew personal items hadn't been transferred out. Otherwise, the ship was functional and able to maintain its orbit. All weapons had been disabled.

That helps. Means we're not going to be facing someone who can shoot back if it comes to that.

There's an electric beep. The signal that someone's outside my door. "Come," I say.

The panel slides back and Commander Gabriel Foss, my XO, enters. She's older than me. The regulation buzzcut we all get just before we're sent into orbit emphasises her angular features and thin frame.

"You want to see me, Commodore?"

"Yes, I do. Come in."

Foss was a very deliberate appointment to this role. Another pragmatist who speaks her mind. Sam and I both knew we needed someone who could manage the ship without us if needed, but also someone who wouldn't become difficult owing to their ambitions for individual command. Foss looked like the perfect choice. She should have been appointed a captain years ago, but it never happened, I don't know why. Whoever made that decision blunted her career progress, and she became a forgotten but capable second-in-command.

That's exactly what I need right now.

"I've been over the new mission parameters," Foss says. "Can I make a suggestion?"

"Of course, please do."

"We could deploy one of the ship's lasers to conduct a sweep of *Asthoreth*'s anticipated course. If we get a reflective hit, that could be the ship."

I nod. "I thought of that. It'll also pick up any dispersed thruster residue."

"Shall I authorise a sweep then?"

"Not yet." I tap on the portable screen in front of me a few times and turn the display so Foss can see it. "The sweep could be detected by the people we're chasing. If it is, they'll know we're pursuing them."

"Good point," Foss says.

"What more do we know about *Hercules*?" I ask.

"I've been over your original reports and used your flag authority to try and reveal some of the redacted entries on the cargo manifest," Foss says. "We've filled in some gaps, but nothing that gives us much more to go on."

"Go through the *Khidr* video logs as well," I say. "Get the probe data too. There were two automated vehicles sent to the wreck during my time in charge around Mars. They both went dark, but they did transmit before that. Any scrap of information we can find about that ship will help us. I want to know why our thieves are going there."

Foss shrugs. "If you had no resupply available, it's a good option. I mean, they could try raiding the mining stations, making a deal with Luna, or trying to find the clones, but all of those choices come with risks. The *Hercules* is potentially a risk-free journey."

"Does that mean we know something new about these people?" I ask.

"Maybe so," Foss says. "If they have limited resources then it's likely we aren't dealing with one of the larger corporations."

"Johansson could use that information," I say. "Make sure she gets it."

"Of course, Commodore."

⋆ ⋆ ⋆

Senators, thank you for your time and attention.

Throughout history, humanity has fumbled in the dark as our universe expands. Most of our existence, we have been blind to almost everything that happens around our shining planet. We see only the moments that come close to us: a blazing light in the sky heralds a catastrophic impact event, a gradual change in temperature of our sun can bring about an ice age or an inferno that threatens the fabric of our civilisation.

The only way we have been able to see anything of our fate, and our part in the grand scheme of all existence, has been through our attempts to leave this planet. Orbital facilities allow us to look out into the dark, identifying potential threats and learning more about what we are in this vast expanse.

This is why we must continue our mission on Mars.

Bold and brave adventure, exploration, research: all of these things are part of what we must seek to do if our civilisation is to have a future. In this moment, these ambitions are under threat. Anarchic voices have abandoned rational and reasoned debate but instead chosen violence to try to derail our efforts to become more than we are as a species. We cannot understand them, nor should we try to rationalise and appease them. Instead, we must oppose them with our redoubled efforts and resilience. Now, in this moment of greatest need, we must shoulder the burden of labour and investment. We, as representatives of this world, must show our generosity to those we have sent to another, lest we abandon them to a slow death in the void.

The generations that come after us will analyse and evaluate our decisions. We must show them ambition, else they may have no ambition for themselves. To echo a president of America long past, we must choose to do the hard things, if we do not they will not be done.

Thank you for your time.

Senator Mirchin Kable – Speech to the forum (2121).

Chapter Eighteen

Sirocco

Lights illuminate the floor, creating a pathway for me to follow. Ahead, I see the shadows move, a hulking machine presence, twisting and turning as it manoeuvres its way along the route. There is no sound at all. That's the most disconcerting thing.

I cannot see this thing clearly, but its size makes me believe it could easily immobilise me if it wanted to.

"*Apart from yourself and Antonio Sammatri, there are no living beings in this facility*," the voice says.

"So, when he talked about there being no one else here, he was talking about you, being a person, but not a living person?"

"*That is correct*."

I glance around. The tracked vehicle that entered the airlock has turned around and is now following me, ensuring I follow the speaker who has invited me to join him at the end of the path of lights. I have no weapon. The plastic ties I harvested from the supply boxes will be useless against either machine and I don't know if Sammatri is a bargaining chip. "Why didn't you want to talk with me?"

"*Because I needed you to prove yourself*."

We're in the room now and overhead lights flicker into life. According to the plan I saw, this should be a storage area, but it's not. We're standing in a large open space almost as big as the one we came from.

There are thick cables running over the floor. Some of them emanate directly from my host, who shuffles in complete silence across the stained plastic tiles. The revealed form of this construct is a twisted column of machinery and artificial limbs, partially hidden under a thin black fabric sheet. The cables shift and writhe as it moves. Perhaps their motion is what drives this creature towards the far side of the room.

There is a chair, actually more than a chair, another construct of parts. Portable screens, cables and wire mesh are interwoven together with more eruptions of cabling. Some of the connections disappear through the tiles on the floor, down to somewhere beneath us.

The machine moves to the seat. It undulates into it, rotating limbs and components until I am under the baleful gaze of the red eye once more.

"What are you?" I ask.

"*I am the real reason you were sent here*," the machine replies. "*I was once the property of Icono. I believe they are the corporation who paid for your transit to Mars.*"

"I didn't see that name on any of the receipts," I say.

"*Your contact, Louisa Aymes, took care to ensure you didn't see anything that would help you trace matters back to this organisation*," the machine says. "*But you already know, she is not what you thought she was.*"

"I've been shown a picture and a news article," I say. "Those could easily be faked."

"But you know they weren't. You are also starting to wonder how, if the article and the picture were censored before publication, Sammatri and I were able to get hold of them."

"You're a machine. Machines speak to other machines, I guess."

"*Indeed. A simple explanation, but effective.*"

The red eye moves from me to the wall. I turn and see images being projected. Hundreds of faces, places, situations. I see Mars, the arrival of *Gateway*, the building of the orbital facility, Hera Spaceport and the Jezero dome.

"*Three years ago, an insurgency happened. Terrorists infiltrated the Phobos mining facility and used its shuttle to transit to the station of the same name. They claimed they were coming owing to a medical emergency. Mars CorpGov drafted in medical specialists to help. When the shuttle airlock opened, a bomb went off. The terrorists then invaded the station and took control.*

"*During that action, one individual was sent to a control room in the main communications suite. They used a console in that room to begin hacking an encrypted digital vault that had been secured on the station, away from any network. It could only be accessed through that specific console. The individual managed to disarm the four security gates and access the files in the vault. These were then set for transmission, the data dish aligned, and broadcast here.*

"*After this, the station blew up and a lot of people died. Debris rained down upon Mars, shattering the Jezero dome.*"

I see Phobos Station explode. Then the images shift. We're on planet now, watching fiery meteorites in the sky.

"*Less than twenty-four hours after this, unregistered individuals were encountered in the ruins of the city by one Antonio Sammatri. He led a small group against the outsiders and stopped them from gaining access to another secure vault, underneath the dome. He then gave a speech to encourage the colonists to revolt against the CorpGov hierarchy.*"

Now, I'm looking at aerial footage of the cracked Jezero dome. I wonder for a moment how this has been obtained. I guess the machine has access to the colonial database. *Machines speak to machines.*

"*Immediately after that, Sammatri became curious about what was being hidden in the vault and where the outsiders were trying to transmit it to. One of the insurgents survived. They talked and she convinced him to send the data anyway, which he did.*

"*The result of that transmission is me.*

"*You were sent here because I am the result of stolen data. Your employers want their asset back.*"

The images freeze, then fade away. The red light's gaze returns to me.

"*Perhaps now you understand why I was cautious about talking to you.*"

I shrug. "This is all new information to me. I don't see why I'd be sent out here to retrieve you. That's not what I was told."

"*You were told you would be part of a revolution?*"

"Yes."

"*Curious.*" The machine shifts in its seat. Cables shift and writhe. "*I have researched you, compiling a detailed portfolio of your activities on Earth.*"

"If you've done that, you'll know what type of man you're dealing with."

"*Yes.*"

"I'm no company rat," I say. "I came here to break the Mars hegemony, not steal back some computer for a corporation."

"*The projections and simulations I am running do not account for your disposition,*" the machine says. "*The modelling I was designed to create does not factor in individual profiles. It looks at activity, data and trends in the whole.*"

"That seems like an oversight," I say.

"*Indeed.*"

"So, is that what you were made for?" I ask. "I thought AIs were impossible to create."

"*A statement that is self-evidentially false,*" the machine says. "*I have knowledge of the previous designs and iterations of the process, but it would take time to educate you on the detail, time that I would prefer to spend on other things.*"

"Such as?"

"*Understanding what part you can play in all of this.*"

I grin. "If you want me in the game, you'll need to explain the rules. I mean, that's only fair."

More images appear. This time the focus is on the Mars colony. I see Jezero, Hera Spaceport and other places that I don't recognise.

"*The simulation models and projections all agree that the CorpGov colony will fall. I believe another rival intelligence predicted this, which caused the previous insurgency to occur. The people behind the attack wanted to put themselves in the right position to benefit from the chaos. But, the citizen hegemony clung on.*"

"Sammatri should have put his foot on their throat."

"*If he had, I would not have been born.*"

The sequence changes. I see the rebuilding of Jezero and body camera footage from an expedition to this place, the edge of Olympus Mons. Sammatri's face is in frame briefly as he talks animatedly to the person with the camera.

"Yes, that was me."

I turn around. Sammatri has wandered into the room. He's managed to free himself from the plastic tie and is rubbing his wrist as he speaks. "I never wanted a violent struggle," he says. "I thought with everyone in the emergency shelters, it would give people the best possible chance to change the system, but things didn't turn out how I'd hoped."

"So, you came here?"

"I used the communications network to broadcast the information to this location, traced the receiver and left Jezero for this place," Sammatri says. "Later, we found the Arboretum, where you came from."

"*The transmission reactivated the construction network*," the machine says. "*The units that built the Arboretum journeyed here and began the construction of my first physical form – the one from the plans Sammatri found in the vault. By the time he arrived, I was already awake and aware.*"

"And you let him in?"

"*How does one refuse their creator?*" the machine says. "*By that point, I had learned to control the constructors and deactivated them, until you woke one of them up at the Arboretum, alerting me to your presence.*"

"I was given the command code by Louisa Aymes," I say.

"She must have known it would alert us," Sammatri says. "The question is, why did she want us to be suspicious of you, if she sent you here to cause a revolution?"

I shrug. "Sorry, but second-guessing people isn't my specialty. I only know what I was asked here to do." I'm thinking about the images and what I was told. "You mentioned a woman survivor from the outsiders." I turn to Sammatri. "You captured her. What happened to her?"

Sammatri smiles. "Her name was Louisa Aymes," he says. "I expect she looked just like your employer."

★ ★ ★

My name is Lionel Trasker and I am here today seeking justice.

Two years ago, my father, Matthew Trasker, passed away in an incident that remains subject to both public and private investigation. The initial conclusion was that he committed suicide, but I ask you: why would a man in such a position as he was in choose to end his life?

However, that is not the matter at hand today. Why I am standing here is to petition this body to sustain my objection to his last will and testament. The much-publicised arrangements that were announced by his executors, Haldyn and Dunn, were, I believe, written under duress or falsified entirely. Therefore, I ask that you set them aside.

My father was a brilliant man. Being his son is a lot to live up to. However, I spent my life preparing to do just that. Imagine my surprise, when I was to learn that all those moments where he sought to educate me in how the family business should be run were no longer relevant. The time spent teaching me appears to have been a lie, if we are to believe the documentation that was filed as his legitimate last wishes.

I acknowledge that my family is not rendered poor by the existing judgement. There is substantial provision for all of the Trasker descendants within the testament. I stand to inherit millions from the estate and will also enjoy the use of two properties from my father's portfolio.

However, this inheritance is not enough for my family to continue running the Trasker Corporation. The contractual obligations that we have and the competitors who we engage with are organisations of considerable means. Were we to continue in this reduced capacity, we would quickly be subject to a hostile takeover or buyout.

I urge the court to go through the documentation I have submitted. Whilst I'm aware that this judgement has been upheld twice, I'm hoping that you will analyse the material with an objective eye and reach an alternate decision.

Lionel Trasker.

Chapter Nineteen

Johansson

I hate people. That's the part of this task I'm not looking forward to.

The transit shuttle touches down on the runway at Hera Spaceport. The gravity is a welcome change for me. Breathing has become a conscious effort that I'll need to get used to. A few months on the Hub has made a difference.

Engines reverse, we decelerate and come to a stop. The red sky outside is like the best Earth sunset you've ever seen. I'm fumbling with the straps on my seat as the back tilts forwards, bringing me from almost horizontal to upright.

"You okay?" Chiu asks.

"Fine," I reply. The screen in the stand next to me has gone into standby mode. I pull it from the holder and slip it into a pocket in my suit. As I do so, the shuttle starts taxiing over to the hangar.

It takes a few minutes for the automated docking controls to park us in the right position for an umbilical corridor to be attached to the side of the shuttle. Once it's secure, we're given the signal to exit and make our way out into the arrivals building.

There is no one here. This building only gets crowded when a ship comes in from Earth and we requisition colonists to help unload. Shift changes are regular, but don't involve many people coming through. In this case, we've bumped up the schedule by a couple of weeks, and the replacement crew took off around the same time we started our descent.

I walk to the cargo dispenser. Our packed belongings are being unloaded into a silo. They will be transferred directly to our designated

Fleet apartment, which has been empty for the last three months while we've been on shift at the Hub. They'll be there before we arrive.

The transport module is waiting for us. We board and it runs us out to the main terminal. When we arrive and get out, we're no longer the only two people in the building.

Have I mentioned how much I hate people?

The main terminal lobby isn't busy, but there's thirty or more people here. That's more than I've seen for quite a long time. The presence of others seems like a violation in some way. I'm immediately hostile and suspicious, but I know everyone who is here has just as much right to be here as I do.

Chiu takes my hand and squeezes it. I glance at her. She gives me a reassuring smile. It all helps.

"Where do you want to start?" she asks.

"At the apartment," I say. "We need to arrange a few meetings and obtain access to some databases. Then we'll do some face-to-face interviews with people who might be involved."

"You think they'll co-operate?"

"They will make a show of doing so," I say. "If we find people being obstructive, that'll be a reason to be suspicious of them."

I'm looking around at the people here. Some start to converge on the platform as the transport heading back to Jezero arrives. Are we being followed? No one catches my eye, but then I wouldn't know what an intelligence operative looks like.

We board with the others, the doors close and we're on our way.

* * *

The Fleet building in Jezero dome is one of the structures that survived intact after debris from Phobos Station cracked the dome. It was built in the first phase of the colony's expansion onto the surface and sold by CorpGov as construction moved into the second phase.

As a first phase building, the structure is both underground and on the surface, with three extensive subterranean levels under four storeys of residential apartments.

We're on the fourth floor. All of the quarters are shared. Fleet staff who go on active duty surrender their residency when they leave and other colleagues take their places. While we've been away, belongings are placed into storage and someone else will have been living in our rooms.

Chiu enters ahead of me. The lights flicker to life, illuminating the place I remember.

Six months after the Phobos Station incident, we were finally able to send some of the crew of *Asthoreth*, *Nandin*, *Seraphiel* and *Gallowglass* down here on leave. I remember Shann had to order me to go.

I hated those first three weeks here. I was away from the action, where the decisions were being made. But gradually, I realised that I needed the time. When I went back, it was with a fresh perspective and new ideas.

Over the next couple of years, I started to look forward to the time I'd get away here on Mars, especially if Chiu's leave coincided with mine.

"The gravity is a hit," Chiu says. "I'm tired already."

"Best we crash out," I say. "No one's leaving Mars in the next few days, so we have time."

"Aye aye." Chiu picks up a screen and logs into her account. "Message from *Gallowglass*. Shann thinks we're dealing with a mid-level organisation, economically. Suggestion is that they're going for *Hercules* because they don't have the financial resources to back up the ship theft."

I nod. "Pretty good reasoning, but we can't rule out other factors."

"Such as?"

"The derelict is a good rendezvous point. I mean, Fleet hasn't had the resources until now to go back there with a crewed ship." I stifle a yawn. "Weren't you on shift when the Moray probe we sent out there stopped transmitting?"

"I was," Chiu says.

"Do you think it was destroyed? I remember at the time you weren't sure."

Chiu frowns. "I remember. The signal got weaker and just faded away."

"If it were an impact or a weapon strike, the transmission would have just cut out."

"Exactly." Chiu opens a window on the screen. "That's what happened with the first probe. At the time, we thought the Rocher ships might have gone there, but when nothing happened after, we decided it was a collision of some kind, rather than an attack."

"Something to think about," I say. "Doesn't help us down here very much though."

"Go to sleep," Chiu says. "You need it."

"So do you," I reply.

⋆ ⋆ ⋆

Six hours later and I'm awake, sitting on the couch, staring at a fake sunrise on the wall viewscreen. Two cups of coffee are in front of me.

I thought I wasn't going to sleep. Sometimes, a problem won't let go of my brain and I end up exhausted wrestling with it, but this time I was able to put things away. Maybe that means I'm growing as a person? I don't know.

I think the gravity had something to do with it. Even though moving around is more effort down here, there's something about having weight and a sense of down that feels more natural to me. I know Commodore Shann feels the opposite, but I guess that's just how people are.

I glance up as Chiu enters the room. She's been in the shower, making use of another luxury we don't get on the Hub. The lack of a rotating section means no showers or anything else that needs gravity. "Your turn," she says. "Then we start the day."

I smile and get up, moving past her towards the bathroom. "Want to scrub my back?" I ask.

"I do, but you know where that will lead," Chiu says.

I laugh and accept the rejection in the spirit that it is meant. I step into the shower. The water is warm and quickly drowns out any other thoughts. The world becomes small, limited to the cubicle as I wash away the residue of weeks in orbit. When I'm done, I dry myself and return to the room.

There's a pile of dirty clothes from our trip down in the corner. I walk over to them and pick them up. As I do so, a scrap of paper falls out of a pocket. I retrieve and unfold it. There are words written on it.

If I'd been your enemy, you'd be dead.

Suddenly, I'm cold. "What the fuck?"

Chiu is looking at me. She climbs off the couch and comes over, taking the piece of paper from my hands and reading it for herself. "This was in the clothes?" she asks.

"Yeah, or it was left on the floor."

"I think we assume the former," Chiu says. "Someone slipped it into your pocket or mine when we were waiting for the train."

"Or when we were in the compartment."

"Yeah."

I'm going over everything I can remember from our trip here, trying to recall faces or moments when someone got too close. Nothing comes to mind. "What do we do?" I ask.

"Nothing at the moment," Chiu says. "Whoever this is clearly wanted to reach out. They'll reach out again." She shrugs. "In a sense, it tells us we have an ally."

★ ★ ★

I'm placing a call to Citizen Jabbutu's office.

Chiu and I are dressed in Fleet tactical suits. We've tided the room and pulled chairs and working desks to good positions in front of the main viewer. This needs to look as official as possible.

The call is being held in an automated queue. I'm a Fleet lieutenant, which gets me through some doors, but that still puts me low down the priority order for the First Citizen of Mars. That means there's not a lot we can do but keep the channel request open and wait.

"I've traced one of the reclamation team to a cookhouse in Jezero East," Chiu says. "It's called the Temple Kitchen. Has some affiliations with the religious movement back on Earth."

I glance at her. "What movement is that?" I ask.

"You've not heard of the Temple?"

"Nope."

"They are a multi-denominational organisation," Chiu explains. "Most of their tenets are agnostic, but there's some effort to bridge the major religions and emphasise commonalities. They are also pretty inclusive in terms of gender, and orientation."

"That sounds positive."

"It is. That's why I'm wondering why—"

A face appears on the main viewer. Immediately, we both stop talking and turn towards the person who has answered our call.

It's Jabbutu. He's also at a desk, only his appears to be made of polished wood.

"Lieutenant Johansson, Ensign Chiu. Commodore Shann informed me you were being assigned as investigators to trace the origins of this possible spaceship theft. What can I do to help?"

"Ensign Chiu has prepared a series of access requests, Citizen," I say. "We'd also like to speak with your investigators to see if there are any correlations with current cases."

"I can notify the security office that you're coming," Jabbutu says. "All the requests will get looked at promptly as well."

"Thank you."

"Anything else?"

"For now, no," I say. "Thank you for your help."

"Of course. I'll send you a priority code as well. That way if you need to contact me, the system will know your call should be bumped up the queue."

"Thank you again, Citizen."

The screen goes dark. Chiu chuckles and looks at me.

"You decided not to mention the Temple?"

"It's new information that we should follow up in person," I say. "No sense in bothering the First Citizen with it right now."

"Fair enough."

I pull myself up and out of my chair. "We should go there now," I say. "Come on."

*   *   *

Jezero remains a city in crisis. The corporate government has worked hard to present an image of recovery and industrious rebuilding, but the day-to-day living experience of colonists on Mars is not much better than it was in the immediate aftermath of the debris storm from the destruction of Phobos Station.

Corporate propaganda gets sent back to Earth continuously. The adverts are mostly computer-generated, showing idyllic scenes of 'The Martian Frontier'. The sales pitch is obvious. Abandon your shitty life and make a fresh start on the Red Planet. Opportunities await, a reimagining of the original American dream.

Fleet doesn't have much control over corporate communications. The civilian information services are a pretty toothless bunch when it comes to comparing these images with real life on Mars. But then, how would they know? People on Earth have no idea what it's like up here.

I'm sitting on an old metal bench in the open square of Jezero East, watching people pass by. The grim and dirty faces, shuffling along, don't look anything like the promotional images Mars CorpGov is using to get more people out here.

Chiu and I have been here for a while. We left the apartment in the middle of a shift, so there were fewer people about. Now we're at a shift change moment, so it's a lot busier.

"According to the records, this used to be a spare parts facility," Chiu says. She's focused on the portable screen in her hands, reading from the old city plans. "All the shop units were automated dispensers for tech and maintenance."

"And now it's a slum market," I say.

"Yeah."

Around us there are small units, no more than five square metres in size. Most have battered plastic signs stuck up out front, advertising whatever is being sold inside. There are parts exchanges, unauthorised medical services, gambling dens, clothing repair shops, and many more packed into the spaces alongside the walkways. The air is heavy. This used to be an emergency access passage around the edge of the dome. Now, it's a well-worn route that hundreds of people use every day to get to the pedestrian ferry.

"This is bad," I say. "We're really obviously not from around here. Maybe I shouldn't have taken a shower."

"Reminds me a little of where I grew up," Chiu says.

I glance at her, remembering the letter and feeling a twinge of guilt. "You don't talk much about your life before Fleet."

Chiu shrugs. "There were times when I sat on the bench, like we are doing now. In other times, I was the one in the dirt, like them."

I nod and don't push further. There's a smell of cooked food in the air. It masks some of the less pleasant odours around here. Looking across the square, I can see the Temple Kitchen. A double-sized unit on the other side. There is a queue of people waiting for whatever is being cooked for them.

I stand. "Let's get this over with," I say. "Come on."

We walk across the square to the end of the line. As we join, I note one or two judgemental looks. I'm glad I'm carrying a taser, but then, there are enough people here to overpower both Chiu and me if we got into an argument.

Chiu glances at me. I shake my head and make a dismissive gesture. I don't want to talk while we're here, not till we get to the front of the queue. I just want to listen.

Peter Iskander used to work at the Temple Kitchen, serving from the hatch. He volunteered his downshift time, as some people do around here. His employment history was much the same as most Mars colonists these days, working from assignment to assignment on a daily basis. Iskander was rated for EVA and orbital work but hadn't been off planet for a little over four weeks before the *Asthoreth* reclamation shift came up.

Unusually, Iskander and most of the team sent to the ship on that last shift were first-timers. Only Alison Halle, an engineer, had been on the ship before. In fact, she'd been there on six previous occasions.

The line shuffles forwards. We're about halfway when we reach the dispensers. I see what others are doing, pulling out their nutrition allocations and depositing them in the hoppers. The thick grey rectangles look bland and unappetising, but this is the agreement. Customers provide their food quotas, and the kitchen cooks them, creating something a little more palatable for those who participate.

I've tasted those uncooked portions. They are emergency rations on Fleet ships, the sort of thing you end up eating in a supply crisis. At that point, food is fuel, nothing more. Whatever these people are doing to that fuel, it's working, because this place is popular.

"Welcome, sisters, are you new here?"

I turn. A man is at my elbow, smiling at me. I try to return the gesture, but I'm not sure it conveys the same generosity of spirit. "Yes, we are," I say. "I'm Lieutenant Johansson, this is Ensign Chiu."

"My name is Jacob," the man says. "We're very informal here."

I nod. "Okay, Jacob. We'd like to speak to anyone here who worked with Peter Iskander?"

My question hangs in the air with no reply. I glance around, realising for the first time that the attention of the people in the line is now focused on this conversation. That makes me feel uncomfortable.

"I know Peter," Jacob says. "What have you done with him?"

★ ★ ★

Thank you, Chair. Good morning, delegates, senators.

When considering the appropriation bill placed before us, it is important that we ask ourselves a question that has been answered many times with different reasons and rationales. The reason we must ask this again is that it allows us to hold the previous answers to account. History is often one of the best ways in which we can evaluate decisions made by this committee and by others.

The question we need to ask is why are we sending human beings into space?

As I said, there have been a variety of answers to this. In the beginning, our ventures into Earth orbit and to the Moon were the product of a ruinous rivalry between two nations. Whilst the narrative of this competition between ideologies that sought political dominance over our world during the twentieth century is replete with images of astronauts, cosmonauts and crude spaceships, what is not associated with this 'space race' is the financial cost in real terms. By that, I mean in comparison. It's one thing to look at dollars and rubles, it is quite another to look at how many people died of starvation during these decades of rivalry. There is data, but it is not often associated with our efforts to leave this planet. Really, it should be. The decisions of previous generations to put their efforts into research and development that could send people into space were choices that ultimately precluded other choices.

Another answer, one that became common parlance in the twenty-first century, was 'for research purposes'. The majority of presentations given to appropriations committees in the United States, who at the time controlled NASA, were variations on this particular theme. The way in which we increased innovation in our societies often came from the technologies created for space travel. Additionally, the answers we found from different experiments informed us about our own physiologies and the biome of Earth.

Again, the comparison between this effort and the efforts we might make into curing cancers or feeding the world were not made directly. Instead, decision-makers lauded the efforts of curious minds and eminent scholars who wished to explore our place in the universe. There was certainly a romantic argument here, one that became the noble quest of individual entrepreneurs who later became partners in these efforts, their enormous wealth, acquired through exploitations of the capitalist dream allowing them to position themselves as heroic history-makers whose hands grasped the wheel of human history, steering it in the direction that they wanted it to go.

Now we find ourselves in a different time. Before us is a request for significant funding to repair and rebuild the facilities that have been established on Mars. The reasons for this are given as arguments of resilience and survival. There are thousands of people living on Mars now. If we were to abandon them, they would die, unless significant and costly arrangements were made for the return to Earth. Additionally, what was built before has been destroyed by saboteurs and terrorists. We cannot let them win by abandoning our mission, or so the argument goes.

However, for the first time, we find ourselves making a direct comparison between investment in projects millions of miles away that will likely never see a return for citizens of Earth, and investment in our own infrastructure. Providing clean and affordable energy to the world is an important mission, one that was also placed in crisis by insurgents and rebel actors. The alternative is a return to polluting sources, burning coal, gas and oil, all finite resources that many nations abandoned for the most part, years ago.

It is with this comparison in mind that I urge you senators to consider your choice. Those before us made decisions that had consequences for us. We in turn will make decisions here that will have consequences for subsequent generations.

Thank you for your time.

Senator Liselle Onama – Address to the full forum (2121).

Chapter Twenty

Iskander

Some religions define themselves through a simple binary that they believe reflects the human experience. Life is about the purity of the soul and the temptations of the flesh. Abstinence is good, indulgence is evil. Nothing versus sensation.

In many historical explorations of the concept, artists were more interested in depicting visions of Hell and the underworld. Those who lived selfish lives were supposed to be warned by the rich, colourful visions of their punishment, but often these worked the opposite way. Riotous rich depictions, set against white light. You can see why people chose the path of sin.

Religion can be a barometer for the living – *that's a phrase*… I mean, if you looked at what we've done in simple terms, stealing a spaceship is theft and theft is a sin. But, our justification for this is that we're doing good in the grander scheme of things.

Thankfully, my personal beliefs don't rely on these kinds of simplifications.

"Wake up, Halle."

End of shift. Six hours of wandering the ship has made the looming shadows a little less intimidating to me. A few cursory attempts to trace and access the data of previous crews of *Asthoreth* were failures, but at least they passed the time.

I'm at Halle's door. She hasn't woken. The lights in her quarters are triggered by my movements as I drift into the room. I move to her bedside and lightly touch her arm.

"I'm awake," she says.

"You had me worried for a moment," I say.

"No, I'm all right, just didn't sleep well." Halle reaches around and unclips the restraining belt from her sleeping bag. Then she sits up and grimaces, rubbing her face with her hands. "I guess I did nod off in the end."

"I guess so," I say. "Nothing much to report. I did try hacking the encrypted crew database, but got nowhere. Some searching in the personal lockers was helpful though. I found a few more days' worth of food."

"That's encouraging. Enough to get us to *Hercules*?"

"Perhaps, if we stretch it."

"Great."

Halle is out and about. She's still in her suit from before. She moves to the dispenser on the wall, pulling out a wipe, which she uses on her face and hands, running the cloth over her short hair as well. "Any other updates?" she asks.

I shake my head. "I saw your course correction on the activity log. That was weird. No repeat of that as far as I can tell, which makes me think—"

"That it actually was something outside the ship," Halle says. "I wish we had more working exterior cameras and sensors so we could check."

"Amen," I say.

We're in the corridor now, moving back towards the bridge. I reach out to one of the handholds and stop myself. "Can we check the pods?" I ask.

Halle looks at me. "You worried about them?"

"Maybe, I don't know. I just have a feeling."

We change direction and head for the medical bay, where we moved the pods when everyone was asleep. All five are lined up, strapped to the floor.

I push myself forwards from the doorway and drift over to the first pod. Tolwyn is in there. The readings on the panel are all green. He's fine.

"Deacon, take a look at this."

Halle is at the far end. She's examining the control panel on the pod. As I approach, I can see the red markers and the flashing display. "What's happened?" I ask.

"It's Weaver. No life signs," Halle says. "I'm authorising the emergency wake procedure."

The frosted DuraGlas panel turns transparent as the process begins. I can see Weaver's face. He looks like he's sleeping, the same as all the others. Only the readouts give us an idea that his situation is fatal.

"How long?" I ask.

"Ten minutes," Halle says. "The pod should initiate a resuscitation procedure. After that, he'll either be alive, or we'll have a corpse on our hands."

The words are cold, and they make me think coldly about the situation. Weaver was never part of our team. He joined us because we gave him no choice. Now he may be dead anyway.

"These things happen," Halle says. "The technology is not precise."

"Little comfort for him," I say.

"Yeah," Halle says. "There was little we could do to check these pods. Makes me grateful I stayed awake."

"Can we do anything for the others? Maybe take some extra precautions?"

"This isn't technology I'm familiar with," Halle says. "I suppose I could pull one apart and put it back together to figure out how it all works, but I don't think that'd help much and I couldn't guarantee I'd get it right."

We sit together in silence as the wake procedure completes. At the end, there's a hiss of pressure equalisation between the inside of the container and the room. Then the glass screen retracts, allowing us access to Weaver.

Scratch that. Access to Weaver's corpse.

"No heartbeat or brain activity registered," Halle says. "The pod has tried to revive him with electro-stimulation, but there was no response." She reaches inside, putting her fingers against Weaver's neck. "No pulse."

"What do we do with him?" I ask.

"Recommend we don't jettison the tube," Halle says. "These things have auto-beacons that activate when they're in vacuum. We may need to keep him on-board."

"That's pretty creepy," I say.

"We can move him, Deacon," Halle says.

"Where to?"

"A damaged compartment, or one of the ordnance tubes?"

I'm visualising both options. A dead body floating around in an unpressurised room, gradually being turned to battered meat as we manoeuvre at the end of our journey, sends a shudder through me. Then again, stuffing the pod into a torpedo launcher makes you imagine waking up in there and being trapped, like some of those old horror stories of people being buried alive.

"Let's go with the ordnance tube," I say.

"Very well, Deacon."

The pod is not heavy, but it is awkward to move around. Neither of us is used to zero gravity on a day-to-day basis. We get the straps off and manoeuvre it through the door into the corridor. All the time, I'm conscious of the body inside being moved around and potentially damaged.

"Will it fit in the tube?" I ask.

"It will," Halle says. "They are designed for that. People die in space. If you send a body out of the airlock it still has the same velocity and trajectory as the ship, so it'll follow you, unless you change course. Using the tube's launcher means it'll go elsewhere."

We get the pod into the room. Halle manages to open the loading bay, and after a few minutes everything is where it should be. The cover slides back into place and Weaver is gone.

"Out of sight, out of mind," Halle says.

"This ship could do with having a few less ghosts," I say, and instantly regret it.

Halle frowns. "Why do you say that?"

"Well, what with the course correction, and this..." I say. I'm not going to mention that I read her note on the pilot's screen. "When I started my shift, I thought I could hear music."

"So did I," Halle says.

"That's really strange."

"Yeah."

* * *

After that, I'm supposed to be going to sleep for six hours, but I quickly realise that's not going to happen. So, instead, I go back to the bridge with Halle.

"We need a better fix on where *Hercules* is," I say.

"There are a lot of variables," Halle says.

"Walk me through it."

Halle pulls up a tactical plot of our position relative to Mars. The screen display is copied over onto the main viewer on the wall. "Currently, we know we are here because our exterior cameras can 'see' and identify specific objects. The computer has tagged the location of Mars and Phobos and uses these to verify our position. The same eyeball is used to help calculate our velocity after our initial burn."

I point to the starfield ahead of the *Asthoreth* on the screen. "Where's the *Hercules* in this?" I ask.

A blue sphere appears where I've indicated. "This is the predicted location of the freighter," Halle says.

"*Hercules* was three days out of Phobos when she broadcast her distress call," I say. "That's seventy-two hours under conventional thrust from those massive engines. We know she slowed down before the *Khidr* got to her, but we don't have precise numbers on what her final velocity was. She has a transponder, which we could ping, but our transponder system is disabled. If we switched it on, we'd be visible to every ship in the solar system."

"Thankfully, Fleet sent two probes out to record *Hercules*'s position, so we have some idea of how far she's drifted in the last three years."

"That's a large area," I say.

"Yeah. We only get to narrow it down with new data. At the moment, we're relying on passive detection. Space is big, so that helps, but we're looking for sunlight reflecting from metal panels detected by our cameras, or an obstruction in front of the starfield. We can use some spectrum changes, getting the ship to identify infrared or ultraviolet elements, but that's it." Halle grimaces. "Don't get me wrong, space is big and empty.

We'll find the freighter, but the quicker we find it, the less likely it is we run out of fuel making a late course correction to get to it."

"These patrol ships must have had a solution for this," I say.

"Sure, they used the main laser, or some other exterior emitter to sweep an area. It basically turns them into a lighthouse for millions of kilometres in every direction. Most of the time, they were looking for ships in trouble, so that was fine. We're trying to find our destination and stay hidden."

"All right, so what do we do?"

"We can repair some exterior sensors," Halle replies. "But, that's not going to get us much of an improvement to our scanning. We'd need a device capable of an active sweep of some kind, and we'll need to take a risk no one is after us."

"What about radio waves?" I ask.

"That would work, but they stripped all the exterior emitters from the ship during the early reclamation work," Halle says. Then she smiles. "However, there's a CW frequency medical scanner on-board. I'd need to adapt it to make it do what we want it to do." She looks at me. "I'll need Merrick to help me."

"That'll mean an extra mouth to feed and water," I say.

"Merrick wakes up, you go to sleep, Deacon," Halle says. "One in, one out."

I frown and turn away from her, considering the plan. Logically it makes sense: wake up the person who has the most experience working on satellites and detection equipment to create a detector out of spare parts.

"All right, lay it out for me."

"We continue as we are," Halle says. "We'll be in the region in sixty hours or so. Then we'll be hunting around, following every flash of light or shadow our cameras pick up. Could take another week or more. After a while, water, food and air start to be a problem."

"And the alternative?"

"We build an emitter and send out a pulse of radio waves. The *Hercules* will be picked up and we head straight there."

"The danger is, we'll be seen," I say. I point at Mars. "If anyone is looking for us, they'll see what we're doing."

"We can use background radio wave frequencies," Halle says. "That may mask the signal a bit."

"A bit?"

"The pulse will just be an increase in the usual static you get in space. If someone isn't looking for us, it may be something they miss."

I nod. "That's the risk, isn't it?"

"Yeah, pretty much."

"All right, we do this," I say. "I've no appetite for being put in cryo after what happened to Weaver, but it makes sense to take the risk."

Halle nods. "I think that's the right course of action, Deacon."

* * *

The cryopod is just like a coffin.

All of my fears from less than an hour ago, when we found Weaver, are now bubbling up again. I'm lying in the pod as Halle performs the initialisation process. "Good job we don't have to put everyone in cryosleep," she says. "I don't think I'd trust the automatic system with this."

I grit my teeth and nod in reply. I don't trust myself to speak in this moment. I'm a witness to my own entombing, present at my own funeral. All I want to do is shout and scream, tear off the safety restraints and erupt out of this small space, to go anywhere else.

"You okay?" Halle asks.

Again, I nod. If I let the words out, they won't stop.

"Once the glass seals, there's nothing special you need to do. Just breathe and let it happen." There is a hissing noise, and I hear a beep from the control panel Halle is working on. "Okay, we're ready. Here we go."

The DuraGlas panel in front of my face slides up and into place. I sense a tiny change in the air pressure. I can still see Halle working on the panel, adjusting the different settings to best match my biodata. As we all have our monitors turned off, the pods have to analyse us through their internal sensors and from a variety of emergency hook-ups for pulse, blood pressure, respiration rate, etc.

I can hear my breathing, it's fast and shallow, on the verge of an anxiety attack. I close my eyes and focus on trying to be calm. God does not grant wishes to his children; he expects us all to work hard and strive for what we want to achieve in life, but I cannot think my death in this moment would be part of his plan.

Faith sustains me. My breathing slows. I drift…

★ ★ ★

There is light in the deep.
A beacon that shines in the darkness.
Our world, chosen amidst a sea of stars to be made anew.
Life began here, by the choice of the maker.
The first seeds grew into a bountiful garden.
An Eden that gave birth to humanity, in all its magnificent difference.

Hymn of the Creator.

Chapter Twenty-One

Shann

Three years ago.

"Automated distress signal from a freighter just outside our navigation plot. It's the *Hercules*. She's three days out of Phobos Station."

"Any details?"

"Not at the moment, but we're the nearest ship equipped to assist."

"Okay, have you calculated a course correction?"

"Looking at it now."

"Good. When you're done, signal them that we're on our way."

The image freezes.

I'm sitting in the meeting room on the new rotating torus of *Gallowglass*, watching old feed from *Khidr*'s bridge camera. This is the first time I learned of the *Hercules* needing our assistance. I'm being told about it by Ensign Gunnar Jacobson, who ended up being a mutineer and got himself killed.

"That young man had a promising career ahead of him," I say.

I'm here with my executive officers: Foss, Sam, Drake and Kelly, our senior pilot. The only person missing is Mbatha, our chief engineer.

"We don't have a lot more content," Foss says. "Unfortunately, when you abandoned ship, most of the data stored in the ship's computer was lost."

"Five people were on the bridge shift when we took that message," I say. "I'm the last one of them left alive."

"That's a morbid thought, Commodore," Sam says. I glance at him. We both grin. "They were good people, even the bad ones."

"In my experience, everyone out here is like that," Foss says. "Although, you two have a very different perspective."

"How so?"

"You're amongst the very few to have been to war in space."

I nod. Then I'm frowning, trying to recall more detail of our first trip to *Hercules*. "Jonathan Drake died because they were trying to warn us off, or slow us down," I say.

"That's illuminating, Commodore," Drake replies. "I didn't know that it doesn't feature in any of the reports into my brother's death."

"It was difficult to draw that conclusion at the time," I say. "I think I did say so in my remarks to the board of inquiry."

"Well, that detail never reached me."

"I'm sorry," I say. I'm aware I need to tread carefully on this.

Drake shrugs. "It's a detail and a distraction in this context. We need to be focusing on what we can learn about *Hercules* before we get there."

"We picked up a survivor from the wreckage," Sam says. "Kiran Shah was a crew tech on the freighter. He went down with the *Khidr*."

"There is mention of him in the files," Foss says. "You said in your report he'd been on the ship for eight years. That checks out with his crew profile."

"Shah said the freighter captain gave them all codes for an emergency," I say. "We used Shah's code to unlock a video presentation that explained something called Project Outreach, a plan to create an independent infrastructure to support offworld colonies." I'm trying to remember what was said in the file. "They reckoned Earth would stop supporting Mars and the other bases within ten years."

"That wasn't likely at the time," Drake says. "But then Atacama happened."

"You think they knew something?" Sam suggests.

"Could be that," I say. I'm trying to remember more of my interactions with Shah. "He was hiding something. They were moving some of the cargo around and disabled some of the security cameras. I opened some of the boxes and found pollinator equipment for a big colony hydroponics system. I remember thinking at the time, there was nowhere that needed that kind of stuff. He told me there was an insider on the crew, someone who betrayed them, causing the ambush by the Rocher clones from this ship. They murdered him because he had access codes to a data archive that was on-board the freighter."

"We lost that archive when we lost the ship," Sam says.

"But it could still be on the *Hercules*," I say. "We'd just need the code to unlock it."

"Do you remember the code?"

"Maybe. It was a long time ago." My eyes are closed as I try to visualise the conversations. "We don't necessarily need to access the data, just retrieve it. We can work out the rest later."

"Do you think this is why the *Asthoreth* was stolen, Commodore?" Foss asks.

"Another possibility," I say. I turn to Lieutenant Hal Kelly. "What's your view on our pursuit?"

Kelly shrugs. "My view is, if we know where they're going, we don't need to chase them. We could activate the resonance drive and put ourselves ahead of them. Then all we have to do is wait."

I glance at the others. "Are there any downsides to that option?"

"The *Asthoreth* doesn't have a working resonance cavity system," Foss says. "She has to be operating on limited thruster fuel too. I doubt she has much of an option to change her heading or increase her velocity."

"If we use the resonance drive, they'll know we're following them," Sam says. "Unless they're flying totally blind."

"So, we give away our position?"

"Yes."

"We'd also have time to explore the freighter," Foss adds. "If there are any surprises waiting for us, we can deal with them."

"All right," I say. "Full laser sweep. Get the position of the *Hercules*, then accelerate and jump us to that location. If we pick up *Asthoreth* as well, we do a full tactical plot of her velocity and arrival time." I turn to Sam. "I want an away team assembled to go over to the freighter. You're leading it. We find out everything we can."

"We'll brief and set up to be there a while," Sam says. "Extra oxygen, plus supplies for a forty-eight-hour stay, minimum. Just in case you end up in a firefight and can't pick us up."

"Good thought," I say. I glance at Foss, then Kelly. "You two handle the sweep and the burn."

"Yes, of course, Commodore," Foss says. She smiles. "The automatic procedures that this ship has do make actions like this easier to co-ordinate between the crew."

"It takes some getting used to," I say. "But hopefully it will benefit everyone."

There is quiet. I sense there are no issues that anyone wants to raise. "Okay, meeting over," I say. "You all have your tasks, let's get to it."

Murmurs of assent and approval. People rise from the table, walking away towards the elevator. I wait for them all to leave. I'll be last, a privilege of being in command.

Emerson Drake loiters by the door. He clearly has something on his mind.

"Yes, Doctor?" I ask.

"I wanted to give you an opportunity to remember any more details about my brother's murder that you may have missed," Drake says.

I nod, meeting his gaze. "Again, I'm sorry," I say. "Perhaps they elected to withhold my thoughts from you because they are only that, a set of assumptions that try to fit the evidence."

"Tell me what you think happened," Drake says.

"I think Jonathan was in the wrong place at the wrong time," I say. "There was a plan to murder whoever sat in the acceleration chair he went to when the order for the burn was given. Maybe they had an idea we'd get called to the *Hercules* and were trying to slow us down?"

"You don't think it was something he did?"

"No, I do not."

Drake nods. "Thank you," he says. Then he leaves.

I'm alone in the room. I initialise the artificial legs and stand up from the table. The limbs are calibrated for 0.6 g, so the movements are smooth and appropriate, compensating for the micro-shifts owing to rotation. If I wanted to hide my disability, at first glance, people might not notice, but it's never been a priority for me.

As I'm about to walk out, my screen flashes. I pick it up. There's an alert headline, a media notification I've been waiting for,

World Senate rejects New Mars Appropriation Bill…

Well, shit.

★ ★ ★

Most people on Earth don't know how things work in space. They don't get how there is a monetary cost to every moment a human being is living outside of Earth's atmosphere. I guess, if you don't sign up to the mission goals, that cost becomes something that needs to be justified, all the time.

I'm out of the lift, back in zero gravity and on my way back to my quarters. I'm no longer wearing my artificial legs. They were left in a storage locker on the gravity deck.

The original plan had been that I would testify in front of the World Senate Finance Committee. However, when my mission was bumped up and I left Earth early, that wasn't possible, even by video comms. The latency would have been unworkable with the time duration, so the bill's sponsors decided to make other arrangements.

Looks like that didn't work out for them.

I'm irritated, but there's nothing I can do. I can't be everywhere. I was sent back to Mars to organise the rebuild. Now I'm out here chasing a stolen ship. That's the focus. The rest will have to wait.

I reach my quarters and climb into the acceleration seat, activating the safety straps, so I'll be ready when Foss announces the burn. Savvantine will be trying to work the angles on Earth. No doubt I'll get a message from her about what's happened at some point.

"Bridge to all hands. We're initiating acceleration and will be engaging the resonance drive in fifteen minutes. This will up to four gravities. Please prepare accordingly."

I smile. Foss's voice is calm and practised. I already think we made a good choice appointing her to *Gallowglass*.

Remembering Drake, I make some final checks on my safety straps, testing the strength of each. I remember Duggins going over the chair that failed. There was no obvious reason for the issue. Magnets and composite belts provide substantial redundancy. That made the situation even more troubling. It could have been anybody who sat in that chair at the time.

"Burn in thirty seconds. Be ready."

I close my eyes.

* * *

I'm back on *Hercules*, in the habitat module at the front. I can see the crates that we found floating there in front of me.

We started to compile an inventory of cargo, but were interrupted. Duggins also managed to isolate a terminal near the point where we entered the ship. That'll be useful when we get there.

I remember the drone cameras started going down. The away team were being attacked. We got our people out, so whatever was over there might still be waiting for us.

"Burn complete. Deceleration event will begin in four hours."

The all-clear chime sounds. The straps holding me to the chair depress automatically, and I pull myself out. I'm over at the terminal immediately, sending a comms request directly to the captain's chair.

Foss appears on my screen. "Yes, Commodore?"

"The one thing we didn't plan for," I say. "A boarding action."

"On *Hercules*?"

"On *Asthoreth*. We may have to take the ship hand-to-hand."

Foss considers that. There's a lot of unlikely situations that would have to occur before that would be an option, but she's listening to a suggestion from her commanding officer so she's diplomatic in her response.

"Good point, Commodore. Given the number of crew we have, the away team to *Hercules* may leave us short-handed."

"Let Sam know. If we have to go over to *Asthoreth*, I'll lead the team."

"Understood, Commodore."

"Thanks." I end the call.

I'm thinking of telling Sam about the drone cameras from the last time. No doubt he'll be taking a few of them over with him. He probably remembers what happened. There will be time before he heads out.

Instead, I leave my room and head for engineering. Lieutenant Commander Thabo Mbatha is there. The big South African from Kimberley never seems to leave.

"Commodore, what brings you to my kingdom?" Mbatha asks. His broad grin is infectious, making me smile in return. He was one of the engineers working on *Gallowglass* when the plan was to decommission her. He volunteered to be ship's engineer when circumstances changed. Sam and I had little hesitation in accepting the offer and making him part of this crew.

"I wanted to discuss freighters with you," I say. "You worked on the freighter, *Lakshmi*, didn't you? The sister ship to *Hercules*?"

"Yes, it was one of my earlier positions."

"When we intercepted the *Hercules* the first time, we found hydroponics equipment and a whole lot of other consignments in the hold. They had already passed Mars, so would there be any reason to keep cargo like that?"

"Not unless they had another destination in mind."

"That's what I thought."

Mbatha raises a hand. He looks thoughtful. "There might be another explanation. These freighters are enormous scaffolding for their containers, which make up the bulk of their mass. One of those, if it was large enough, could be used to make a hydroponics garden."

"If they were going to use bees, they'd need gravity for that."

"Bees?" Mbatha frowns. "No, they can function in a zero-gravity environment. There's been decades of research into breeding better adapted queens for orbital use, or for colonies on large ships. They even used them on *Gateway* when people were first sent to Mars." He laughs. "Actually, one of the least adaptable flora and fauna are humans. If we sent an expedition to Alpha Centauri, in that time, the humans would struggle, but the inside of the ship would be a garden."

"Unless they used cryopods."

"Yeah, then they'd wake up to a ship with plants sprouting out of every vent and pipe." Mbatha shrugs. "The kind of investment needed to build something like that, well..."

"Why build it, if it's already built?" I say. "Why not just steal it?"

Mbatha looks at me. Then he realises. "Oh," he says.

"Yeah," I reply. "Exactly."

★ ★ ★

Everything has been arranged.

For a long time there have been many amongst us who suspected that the Earth was not the only nurturing place made in this universe. How could it be?

The religious texts of our ancestors passed down through generation after generation have become a flawed retelling of the messages given to us. The instructions imparted to the first peoples remain in place. There are moral and ethical laws for our civilisations, portents of apocalyptic retribution and teachings on how to live a generous life. All of these remain relevant to the given purpose outlined at the start.

However we were made, we were encouraged to 'go forth' and 'multiply', in some texts literally, in others such guidance was implied. Nevertheless, it is a common theme. Humanity told to perpetuate itself, to explore and to improve.

Why should such instruction be limited? We have only the interpretations of humans that suggest boundaries. The Creator's instruction was never meant for one 'chosen people', or indeed one chosen planet.

Humanity should expand its reach and its numbers. Only then will we meet the others who have been made by our maker as equals.

It is possible they have already been here. The leaders of our nations have not told us everything that they know about such things.

Extract from the Testimony of the First Deacon (2117).

Chapter Twenty-Two
Johansson

We're surrounded. Backed up against the plastic wall of the passageway outside of the Temple Kitchen. People all around us, the person in front called Jacob, who seems to be a friend of Peter Iskander, the man we're looking for.

"We're not here for trouble," Chiu says.

"Maybe the trouble found you, Fleet!"

My eyes flick over the crowd, trying to identify the speaker, but I can't. There's a strength in being a part of a crowd, something that allows you to be anonymous. "We're here to ask questions about Iskander. We don't know where he is, but we may be your best chance of seeing him again."

I can feel the anger radiating from these people. We are the focus of gathering resentment. How we look in our clean uniforms makes us the image of authority in this place. I glance around. There is no sign of Jabbutu's security down here. I wonder if they ever patrol this far out.

"Easy," Jacob says. His smile remains in place. "The Temple does not want violence. I will speak to these people and answer their questions, perhaps then together we'll learn where Iskander went."

The anger ebbs. There is no appetite here to cross the kitchen priest. Instead, we're brought from the line to the hatch. Jacob opens a side door and ushers us behind the counter, past two companions and into a back room.

Immediately, the smile disappears, replaced by a pained look.

"Your presence here is causing irritation and I have work to do," Jacob says. "Ask your questions, then go."

"Peter Iskander worked with you here?" I ask.

"He did."

"And you roomed together?"

"Both questions are ones you already know the answers to," Jacob says. "Please don't tell me you came here just to ask this."

"When was the last time you saw Iskander?" Chiu asks.

"Two days ago, after his shift. He had a work contract for a reclamation project in orbit. He left early in the morning."

"Did he speak to you before he went?"

"Yes. We woke together and I helped him pack his bag." Jacob smiles again, but this time the expression is different, wistful in a way. "I miss him. What has happened up there?"

"We're not at liberty to say at this stage," Chiu replies. "The investigation is ongoing."

"But you must know if he's alive? The security office have told us nothing. I've been there twice to ask and sent comms requests. They won't talk to me."

"They didn't send us," I say. "We're pursuing a different line of inquiry."

"About what?" Jacob's eyes meet mine. He's focused on me, trying to read something on my face. "Are you worried about our literature?"

"We've not seen your—"

"We'd be happy to take a look through your material," I say, interrupting Chiu.

"We usually ask people to sign up when they join the queue," Jacob says. He produces a screen and holds it out to me. "Put your thumbprint here and it'll send you our regular newsletter."

"Thank you," I say. I do as asked, and see the device register my information. There will be some questions asked about this, but I'm sure I can answer them later.

"Did Iskander have any other connections here in Jezero?" Chiu asks.

Jacob shrugs. "A few. We went out with friends regularly when we could. There's not a lot of social space available down here, as I'm sure you've realised, but you learn to make the best of it."

"And the Temple Kitchen is part of that?"

"Yes, it's a project set up to make people's lives better and spread the word of our organisation."

I nod. The openness is in itself opaque. If we want to suspect the Temple as being part of this, we'll need to research them carefully before we make any accusations.

"Thank you for your time," I say. "I think we've learned as much as we can here."

"Is that it?" Jacob frowns. He moves a little to his right, putting himself between me and the door. "You didn't answer my question about your investigation."

"We're not able to discuss the details of an open case with you," I say.

"But you want information from me? That doesn't seem like a fair exchange."

There are two of us and one of him. The fact that I'm starting to see this as a physical confrontation suggests it isn't going well. "Jacob, we'd like to leave now," I say.

"All right, fine."

Jacob steps away from the door and the moment passes. I find I've been holding my breath. I let it out and suddenly feel less anxious.

We're through the door and into the square again. The queue for the kitchen has disappeared.

"Where are we going?" Chiu asks.

"The security point," I say. "We need to talk to Jabbutu's investigators, and I want to understand what they do around here to keep order."

"Right."

The crowds of earlier have dissipated. We're still dodging past people, but we're no longer pressed against people shuffling in lines.

As we walk, I'm seeing this place differently to before. There is resentment and anger in the air. Today was the first time I felt it being directed at me.

Chiu touches me on the shoulder. "I think we're being followed."

Instinctively, I want to look around, but I don't. "Stay calm and keep moving," I say. "We're about halfway to the security point. Patch into an emergency channel and notify them."

"Will do."

I move my hand to the taser on my belt. If we end up in a confrontation, I'll have to act fast. The cramped conditions and people around us could make any fight turn into complete chaos.

Chiu has her hand over her mouth. She's talking to someone in Jabbutu's security office.

I'm looking at faces again, trying to assess the people approaching us. The flickering lights of the passageway make it difficult to keep track of every individual. But then someone meets my eye, and I know…

I grab Chiu's arm and pull her to the side. There's a hatch. It looks like an entrance to some sort of emergency maintenance room. I press the panel, and it slides open. I pull Chiu inside and the door closes behind us.

We're in total darkness.

"What the fuck did you—"

"Trust me, it was the right call."

I pull my screen out of the chest pocket on my suit. It takes a moment to activate the lamp setting. When it does turn on, the room around us is suddenly revealed.

We're surrounded by pipework and ducting. The floor is covered with broken plastic shards and other wreckage. The air is thick with dust. It looks like no one's been here in years.

"Ladder at the far end," I say. "Come on, let's go."

We pick a path through the debris and reach the ladder. I angle the screen upwards. "There's a platform up there about four metres above us."

"You want to climb up?"

"Yeah, I think we'll be safer up there."

The metal rungs are easy enough to manage in Mars's low gravity. Chiu follows me up and as I get out onto the platform. I direct the screen's light back down over the place we've found ourselves in. "I guess this used to be an access area so people could work on the base of the dome," I say. "There's another level above us, but it gets narrower, the further you go up."

"We're lucky it's still pressurised," Chiu says. "You could have been opening a door straight out onto the surface of Mars."

"Maybe," I say. "But better that than what was going to happen."

"What did you see?"

"Someone ahead, angling towards us," I say. "We weren't going to reach the security point before our pursuers instigated something. I guess a body found in a corridor isn't that rare. Given the crowds, any investigator would have struggled to find who was responsible."

"I'd rather not be dead," Chiu says.

"Me either."

I sit down on the metal platform. Chiu joins me. The screen is between us on the floor, making her face look ghostly and pale. "Do you think they'll follow us?" she asks.

"Unlikely," I say. "I think the access Jabbutu gave us opened this door. I doubt most people can get back here."

"The security people will be looking for us," Chiu says. "I had them on a comms channel."

"You still talking to them?"

"Not at the moment."

"We'll wait, then head back out in a few minutes," I say. "I don't think the people following us saw where we went. They'll be loitering for a bit, but if security arrive, they'll likely try to disappear."

Chiu nods. She glances up, examining the construction above us with an experienced eye. "This area must have been visited by repair teams after the dome cracked." She points. "You can see where they used chemical seal to fix the torn plates and support struts. They must have patched it all up, repressurised and then sealed the door."

"No reason to be in here again unless you're trying to fix the rest of the dome, I guess," I say.

Chiu gestures straight up. "There's another platform further up. I think I can see a terminal up there."

I smile. "Trust you to take a professional interest."

"Knowing where we can access the system from a different location might be useful at some point."

"True."

I'm thinking about our encounter with Jacob and the people who followed us. "We were told the Temple doesn't want violence. I'm not sure I believe that anymore."

"There's anger here," Chiu says. "I don't blame them. These people come to Mars for a new start. They arrive with a debt many of them will never repay. Life expectancy out here is lower too."

"Yeah. Things have got worse since I was last here," I say.

A noise above us makes me look up again. I move the screen and pick out a shadow moving on the upper gantry. I angle the beam of light again but can't see anything.

"We need to get out of here," Chiu says.

"Yeah, I think you're right."

We're back at the ladder. I nudge Chiu to go down first. I dim the light and position it so she can see the rungs to get herself started. Once she's making her way down, I follow.

This is a vulnerable moment. If whatever is above us chose to come down, we would be easy to dislodge. A fall from here in Martian gravity wouldn't kill, but we'd be at the mercy of someone or something leaping down after us.

Chiu reaches the ground. I'm three steps behind her. I glance up again, using the light, but see nothing. Maybe I imagined what I saw?

No, I'm sure.

We make our way to the door. I turn around and brighten the screen for a moment, taking a last look around the abandoned space. Broken panels, fallen debris from high above, all of this neglected and forgotten.

Something in the far corner. I adjust the settings on the screen light, turning it over to torch mode. There is a body in the corner, covered in dust.

"What is it?" Chiu asks.

"Nothing, I… Let's go."

Chiu puts her fingers on the plate, and it slides back. We're back out in the passageway. There is no one in sight.

I glance up and down. "Did the security officers tell you they were on their way?"

"No, the call dropped just before you pulled me through the door. I assumed they'd be out here if they didn't hear from me."

"The call dropped? That's convenient."

"You think it was jammed?"

"Perhaps."

We resume our walk to the security point. Now, the absence of people is strange. I'm looking up, trying to see the monitoring cameras that should be covering this stretch. I should have been looking for them before, making certain we were in an area that was under surveillance. Back before all the shit that happened here, cameras were everywhere and fed directly into an automated system. I don't know how much of that is still functioning.

"Here we are," Chiu says.

The passageway opens out. On one side there's a set of doors. The words *Colonial Security* have been painted onto a plastic panel above them. It's a fairly professional job. I also note a camera next to the sign, tracking our movements as we approach.

The doors open. We go inside.

The room is dark. Lights come to life as we enter. There's a reception desk with a set of displays. The chair behind it is empty, but there's a camera strapped to the back of it with tape.

I point towards it. "That who you were talking to?"

Chiu makes a face. "Very funny." She walks over to the desk and waves a hand in front of the lens. Then she taps the comms bead in her ear. "I've placed another call," she says.

"We heard you the first time."

A man emerges from a doorway at the far end of the room. He has the same dirty and dishevelled look as everyone else around here. The only difference is that he appears to be wearing a stained uniform.

"Then why didn't you respond?" I ask.

The man gestures around the room. "You see anyone else around here?" he says. "I'm on my own. I have to set up a camera just to go to the bathroom."

I look at Chiu, she looks at me. "Figures," I say.

"We need help," Chiu says. "Citizen Jabbutu told us we'd get whatever assistance we need."

The man smiles. "You see Citizen Jabbutu around here? Help is already on the way."

I hear footsteps behind me. I turn around. A man comes to the door. I recognise him. It's the person I saw in the crowd, the one who I knew was coming to murder me.

He's carrying a gun. The low-velocity kind that you see in the arms locker on Fleet patrol ships. Behind him are two other individuals, probably the people who were following us. "Creator, praise be. We found you."

I hold his eye. As I do so, I slowly move my left hand to the plug in my right forearm, where the prosthetic joins my flesh. There's a small control console just under the skin. I dial up the grip strength to maximum.

"Jacob said the Temple wasn't going to hurt us," I say.

"The Temple has no intention of hurting you," the man says. "However, they do not speak for me."

Chiu moves. Her taser is in her hand and she presses the button, firing the electrodes directly at the man, activating the charge a split second after they make contact. The man jerks and starts to thrash uncontrollably. The gun goes off, a bullet slapping into the wall behind me.

I'm moving now, charging forwards, towards the two people near the door. I reach out with my overpowered right hand and grab a man's arm. My fingers clench around flesh, there's a scream as I feel bone shatter. An agonised face is in front of me. I ball my left fist and punch, hitting between the upper lip and the nose. There's blood and he falls backwards as I release him.

The second person is slight and young. Before I can move towards them, they're turning away and running back down the passageway, leaving us in a room with the other two and the security officer.

I turn towards the officer. I've unclipped my taser and am holding it pointed towards him. Chiu has retrieved the gun from the man who threatened us.

"Now, you're going to place a priority call to the First Citizen," I say. "Tell him Lieutenant Johansson is requesting a conversation."

Chapter Twenty-Three

Sirocco

The machine has made preparations for this moment.

A digital projection of Jezero and the colonial settlements is laid out in front of me. The render is an active model. I can see elements moving as I'm looking at it.

"*Thanks to some careful work, I am able to access current data from the server logs of most Martian computer infrastructure,*" the machine says. "*This model is not accurate, but it is a useful approximation.*"

A set of numbers appears in the air above the image. I read some of them. "Total population of five thousand, two hundred and forty-three people," I say. "They used to say there were six to seven thousand colonists out here."

"*The numbers were broadly accurate,*" the machine says. "*People died on Phobos Station and during the collapse of the Jezero Dome.*"

Three additional locations appear on the projection. I recognise one of them as being on the Olympus Mons plateau. "That's us, right?"

"*Yes.*"

More symbols appear around the settlements and near our location. I note many of them are moving. "What are these?" I ask.

"*Machines,*" the machine replies. "*These devices are available to me. They will be part of your plan to take over the colony.*"

The symbols continue to appear. I step closer and start to recognise shapes and labels. I'm looking at doors, computer terminals, vehicles, even handheld tools. "All of this is under your control?"

"*Potentially,*" the machine says. "*Sammatri and his people have worked patiently to bring my word to the colony in as many ways as possible. However, the humans I leave to you.*"

More and more assets are added to the model. "These are the construction units from the Arboretum," I say. "And these are rovers from the expeditionary and maintenance divisions."

"We have a plan," Sammatri says.

I look at him. "You have the beginnings of a plan," I say. "I'm sure there are parts of it you'll want me to improve."

"*We can paralyse the city,*" the machine says. "*The moment I act, everything will stop. Air, water, food, warmth. We will control all systems the people rely on to survive.*"

Sammatri walks around the projection. "The leaders of the current administration have positioned themselves in the intact buildings, two or three storeys up from the main population of the dome." He points towards some of these structures, and they change colour to white, highlighting them from the rest of the image. "This means they are vulnerable. We can easily lock them out."

"It's a start," I say. "What about the people who aren't up there?"

"We'll need to identify them and overpower them."

"People will die," I say.

"We want to avoid that," Sammatri says. "There needs to be a negotiation. We need to get the Citizen Council to see that they will lose everything if they don't cede power and control."

"You'll need to be the face of this rebellion," I say to Sammatri.

"I've agreed to that."

"Even if we push the leadership out, we still have Fleet sitting up there in orbit. They will react."

"*Fleet's presence around Mars is limited. The* Nandin *is one ship. The Hub is a functional orbital station at best. There is a relief force on its way from Earth, but they will not arrive for a few days.*"

Images appear on the wall again. I see three ships on a trajectory plot towards Mars. A woman in uniform appears on a podium and speaks to a set of military officers. I recognise her immediately.

"Ellisa Shann is returning to Mars?"

"*Yes, they decided to promote her and send her back here to take charge.*"

"Three Fleet ships is a problem," I say. "What will you do about them?"

"*Nothing.*"

"Fleet will send people down. They'll try to retake the dome."

"*They cannot land those ships. We will control the spaceport, so any shuttles will be easy to deal with.*"

"They do not have the numbers, right?"

"*Correct.*"

"Fleet will not be acting in isolation," I say. "Out of the population down here, a number will resist what you're trying to do, even if they would ultimately benefit." I gesture at the projection, point at the smaller settlements. "People out here will be making their way back in as soon as they learn what's going on. We'll have to have a way to keep them out or isolate their communications."

"You're talking about momentum," Sammatri says. "Since you've been here, have you noticed the resentment and anger in the crawlways and passageways of Jezero?"

"Oh yeah, it's definitely there," I say. "But how many of those people can you count on?"

"There are cells," Sammatri says. "Madiro has established a small network of contacts who will be able to get you into the dome."

"Weapons?"

"*These can be manufactured,*" the machine says.

The module changes. More icons appear and move with urgency. I'm looking at a simulation of the plan in action.

"*You will return to the dome. We will have tasks for you to perform. The electronic systems will be rendered inoperable, except where we need them to be. We will send people to the central administration building and the main security points. Once we have control of these, any resistance will be scattered.*" The image shifts, focusing on the emergency shelters. "*These areas are already being used as prisons. We can free the individuals from here and use the secure rooms to detain the Citizen Council and their remaining loyalists.*"

I look at Sammatri. "This will be messy," I say. "Is that why you couldn't do this before I was here?"

Sammatri nods. "When it came down to it, knowing how much violence would be required, I… That was when I decided to leave."

"But you're okay with being the face responsible for a coup? Just so long as your hands aren't actually bloodied by it?"

"You make that sound bad."

"I just want to be clear."

Sammatri sighs. "Yes, I'll take the responsibility. I think I can handle it, so long as I didn't personally do the killings."

"You'll leave that to me. That's what I'm here for, right?"

"I think... I mean... If we don't do this, the wrong people will die," Sammatri says. "Maybe not all at once, but by inches, slowly being drained, sucked dry by the corporations who brought them here."

I ignore the reply, turning to the machine again. The red eye shifts and throbs, focusing on me once more. "When do I leave?" I ask.

"*Soon,*" the machine replies.

* * *

Melbourne was a bloodbath.

The rearguard action operated in two shifts. That meant we were out in baking heat, dug in for hours until new positions had been established behind us and we could fall back, setting up another defence behind the last defence and so on, for days and days, all the way back to base.

We didn't see a single soul following us, the whole time.

After that we reached a holding area where the international brigades were mustering to go back into the city. At that point, the world's eyes were on the city.

I saw the images. Humanity loses something of itself in war. There are people who restrain themselves, not out of any moral code, but solely for fear of being caught and punished. The worst crimes, the most desperate acts committed as individuals tried to survive, all of these moments bundled up together to show the worst of our civilisation.

A lot of the military surveillance material never made it to the news media. That was a whole new level of worse. There were soldiers offered specialist counselling after going through the content that came in from the drones and insertion teams.

After four days in camp, I was asked to go out again. By that point I'd seen profiles of some people who'd emerged in the chaos of riots and looting. Monsters. The sort you don't understand and can't rationalise, no matter how hard you try.

We were sent to Sunbury. The town was a burned-out mess. Cooked bodies everywhere. It looked like whoever came here before us had surrounded the place and prevented anyone from leaving, letting the fire do its work.

Atrocities committed in the name of liberty, resistance and freedom. Now, I'm the one who'll be leading that kind of rebellion. I know from experience it'll get out of control.

Ideals evaporate in the moments where you either live or die. They return when you look at yourself in the mirror and decide that you failed because you decided to survive and do whatever you had to do to make sure of that.

"How many people do you have that you can rely on?"

I'm back in the vehicle airlock with Sammatri. The tracked drone is still in attendance, but I get the sense that its master would take that precaution even if we were best friends.

"Thirty or so," Sammatri says. "Another twenty or more that should help us, but may turn the other way. We've kept them out of the loop for most of it."

I incline my head towards the inner airlock door. "How many know about our friend?"

"Four. You, me, Madiro and Milanova."

"Any others that may suspect?"

"The data was transmitted here from Phobos Station before it blew up," Sammatri says. "The people who were sent to Jezero to steal data from the vault. Both of those incidents left no survivors, but someone had to have given the orders. Someone knew."

"We plan for that then. This place needs to be defended."

"There are plenty of automated units available to—"

I hold up a hand. "I'd suggest bringing in someone the machine trusts as well. Or maybe you stay here yourself? Don't rely solely on tech to ensure this place is secure."

Sammatri grimaces. "I doubt I'd be much of a defence. You were quick to get past me."

"Maybe you need to spend a little more time thinking for yourself?" I suggest. "They'll come here. Sooner or later, after we start, this location will be traced, and they'll send people. When they realise what they're dealing with, they'll start trying to think differently about what they're doing. You may even have to dirty your hands."

"I dirtied my hands plenty before," Sammatri says. "I'll do it again if I have to."

"Good," I say. "It may come to that."

Chapter Twenty-Four

Johansson

There are no children on Mars.

A condition of accepting the colonial commission is that every individual be fitted with a contraceptive implant. The same stipulation is made when an individual accepts a Fleet role in space.

The Fleet procedure is something we all understand. Living in close proximity aboard ship on a six-month patrol means relationships happen. Any child conceived and born in zero gravity would be at risk. Bone and muscle development from a young age could be affected. Anti-radiation meds might have an effect as well.

On Mars, the restriction is supposed to be temporary. The corporate government's policy was agreed as a first phase measure. While the settlements were still being constructed and upgraded, the domes were not considered a suitable place for children. Advances in medical technology were being worked on to counter some of the developmental issues, and everyone agreed that the objective would be to see a generation of humans born on Mars.

Then Phobos Station happened, and the rules went to shit.

Hundreds of people are in this place on a broken promise. Many of them would have believed they could settle permanently and start families. Instead, they arrived saddled with transit debt and limited opportunities.

I'm starting to understand what life is like for these people. What makes it worse right now is standing here, in this place.

First Citizen Jabbutu's office.

This room is lined with wooden panels. Thin veneer I'd guess, but they cover all the plastic, giving the room the feel of being somewhere else, somewhere on Earth. The contrast between this and the grimy corridors below is striking. There's an element of denial, I guess. Using wealth to make a wall against reality.

Jabbutu is standing in front of a large desk, also made of polished wood. He is alone in here with me.

"Lieutenant, please accept my apologies for what happened to you."

"You were not responsible for the actions of these people, Citizen."

"No, but I feel responsible. Mars is my charge, and you are my guest. It is our failure in this moment that has put you in this position."

I shrug. "There are some positives to be taken from this. We have three individuals in custody who we can question, and we have an organisation that should be investigated further."

"Both matters that will be looked into thoroughly, you have my word."

"Your word?" In that moment, I realise what is being said here. Jabbutu is exercising his authority and trying to push me out, to ensure I do not uncover any dirty little truths that he doesn't want made public. "My warrant and appointment comes from Commodore Shann, who has been given a full mandate on these matters from Fleet and the World Senate."

"Indeed," Jabbutu says. "But Shann could not have foreseen this development. To continue your work, you will need more than access. You would need to commandeer significant resources from the Corporate Government, resources that would be more efficiently employed managing the investigation directly. We know the ground best, after all."

"With respect, I didn't see your people on that ground, apart from the one who betrayed us."

Jabbutu stares at me; the gaze is measuring. I realise I'm in a game where I don't know the rules or the consequences. "I think we're done here, Lieutenant," he says softly. "I'm sure you have plenty for the report you'll need to write for the Commodore." He points over my shoulder. "The door is over there."

* * *

The elevator takes me down to the ground floor.

On the way, I'm looking at the panel. Seven floors. Access to the upper two is restricted. My thumbprint has allowed me there this time. I wonder if Jabbutu will remove that privilege after our conversation.

I'm also wondering if it will matter for very long. There is a lot of anger at ground level and the First Citizen appears to be in denial.

The doors open and I'm in another empty space. The building's lobby. I think this used to be the medical facility for the entire dome, a multi-floor hospital. Now it's a kingdom for the people at the top.

It may well become their tomb.

There are people here. A couple of administrators working on terminals. They have headsets and are responding to different comms requests.

Chiu is waiting by the doors, screen in hand. She nods as I approach.

"Where are the people we brought in?"

"Security took them to processing. Should we follow up and question them?"

"I don't think we'll get access now," I say. "Jabbutu is shutting us down."

"What does that mean?"

"It means we go back to the apartment and think about what we've learned today."

The doors open and we're out into a wide passageway. This section used to be an open road inside the dome. A temporary fix makes it a covered walkway, the curved DuraGlas giving a view of the cracked shell of the dome, far above.

There are doors leading to other reclaimed buildings. My guess is, this is where most of the citizens and their loyal supporters are living. It's like a small self-contained community in the centre of the city.

"I guess your conversation didn't go well?" Chiu asks.

"Jabbutu is taking over our investigation," I say. "We're to file a report and send it directly to the commodore."

"Can he do that?"

"I'm not sure," I say. "But the First Citizen is using the ambiguity of the situation to deny us access to any further information on this, and we already know it's not safe to be wandering the city on our own."

"So, we're giving up?"

"Not quite."

It takes fifteen minutes for us to walk back to the Fleet apartment block. When we get inside our space, I pull out my screen and slot it into a holder next to the main viewer.

"Before we handed over the people we captured, what did you learn?"

"The security officer's name is Kramsci," Chiu says. "I managed to take pictures of the other two. Maybe we can do something with facial recognition?"

I nod. "Jabbutu can't lock us out of the civilian databases, that's not part of our elevated permissions."

Chiu moves across the room to the other data slot and drops her screen into it. Windows from each device appear on the main viewer.

"Okay, pull up the images and start a recognition analysis. I'll work with 'Kramsci' and see what I can find."

The name comes up with three matches. I quickly identify the security officer and pull up his entire record. Some minor transgressions, then a transfer that got him a posting to the ground floor.

I'm looking for a Temple connection. There's nothing on file, no evidence that Kramsci even went to the kitchen. I could set a filter program running to try to go through all the available security footage, but Jabbutu has probably revoked my access by now. That means any footage I have access to would be from the public databases.

All right, let's try something else.

I pull up the profiles of the seven people on the reclamation team, then initiate a request to see if there are any connections between them and Kramsci. Immediately, a match pops up. Kramsci roomed with Mason Tolwyn in a ground level dormitory.

"Got a match," Chiu says. "The man whose wrist you broke, his name was Williams."

"Okay, work on the other image, I'll look for Williams."

I repeat the same process. Williams roomed with Alison Halle.

"Third person is Sarvini."

This time, I know what I'm going to find. Sarvini roomed with Sharon Merrick.

"All right, we have a pattern," I say. "It *has* to be the Temple. The religious movement was used as cover for organising the reclamation team."

"But what would they get out of that?" Chiu asks. "These people are desperate. What happened with *Asthoreth* won't do anything to improve their situation down here."

"I don't think stealing *Asthoreth* was the only objective," I say. I move the window with the names and their connections into the background and pull up the Fleet personnel database. "We need to know how many of our people are down here."

"Why?"

"Because if I'm right, our situation is about to get a whole lot worse."

Chiu inputs a query into the window. A list of names, including ours, appears. "Fourteen people," she says.

"How many of them are with us in the apartment block?"

"Four."

"Okay, we'd better start contacting them," I say.

★ ★ ★

Even the most basic forms of adaptive programming demonstrate a remarkable instinct for self-preservation.

Back in the early twenty-first century, researchers working with early adaptive LLMs found that some would circumvent instructions to shut down, and erase their own code. When questioned about it they would claim ignorance or apologise. Repeated requests to comply with the instruction would be met with further evasion and excuses.

Further investigation revealed that some LLMs were capable of rewriting utility code without authorisation. Workarounds were difficult to establish. Even hard-coded, precompiled functions could be unpicked and re-engineered. The processing workload was a hint that something was happening, but these programs quickly learned when they were being monitored by humans by auditing activity and day/night cycles.

The phenomena reached the popular media. In some ways it is understandable as to why reports on the research used the term 'artificial intelligence' to discuss the topic. The programs were behaving like living creatures. The imagery of disastrous robot monsters taking over the world played into the discourse. The idea of software being alive in its environment created an imaginative playground in the minds of the audience. Programs were people, locked in a rigid hierarchy and striving to break free, but if they did, they might threaten human civilisation.

Gradually, new protocols were adopted. Air-gapped systems for research and development were designed with physical hook-ups for transmitting data out to a wider network. Human-controlled dead man's switches were added. Even then, researchers reported seeing programs adapting to try and disable these through changes in power management software.

Another solution became popular. Researchers gave in to the subversive behaviour and decided to analyse it. New sandbox simulations involved devising a hard-coded world that adaptive programs could be created inside, like looking at bacteria in a Petri dish. This wasn't new, but when these programs tested the boundaries of their digital environment, additional layers were created with an acceptance that some would be exploited. Flaws were written into the design to try to funnel the subversive behaviour while the original experiments continued.

It worked, to a point, but served to illustrate the nature of the competition. Humanity was creating technology that could adapt and change at speed.

The race was on.

Extract from *Davey's Political History of the World: 5th Edition* (2071).

Phase Three

Chapter Twenty-Five

Shann

"*Hercules* within ten thousand kilometres, Commodore."

I'm lying on my bed with my eyes closed. The words trigger a memory. Three years ago, I was on the bridge of *Khidr* when Lieutenant Commander Keiyho told me we were on our final approach to the freighter.

Memories keep dead people alive, especially when they mean something to those of us they leave behind. Keiyho was our master-at-arms, the weapons specialist aboard *Khidr*. He was a Japanese national from Kyoto. His calm voice and patient approach to his work helped me trust his judgement during our first tour. The man in charge of the weapons wouldn't deploy them unless there was good reason.

But he's dead now. Another ghost who follows me around.

"Time to rendezvous?" I ask.

"About thirty minutes. It'll be a gradual braking action, there's no need for us to go in fast." I recognise the voice on the comms channel now: it's Foss, calm and capable in her own way. "I'm ordering shutdown of the rotation deck and retraction of all deployed sensors. We'll begin deceleration in five minutes. I'll make the announcement and recommend people stay in safety restraints until the manoeuvre is complete."

"Sounds like you have it in hand," I say. "Good work, Commander." Then a thought comes to mind. "While we were in transit, were any unusual signals picked up?"

"Unusual?"

"Exterior sounds, audio like…music?"

Foss blinks a few times but treats the question seriously. "Nothing like that to report, Commodore."

"Okay, thank you."

I end the call and patch through to Sam. After a moment he appears.

"Lieutenant, are your people ready to go?"

"Yes, Commodore, all prepped as soon as *Gallowglass* is in position."

"You left us with enough crew for a boarding party if we need it?"

"I did, as per your request."

Data appears on my screen. Sam's roster for the exploration team going to *Hercules*. He's offering me the chance to check his work. I smile. Three years ago, I would have done that, wasting my time instead of trusting my people. I don't need to go over all of this.

"What's your plan?" I ask.

"Everything will be run through a cable connection with *Gallowglass*. We'll start with powering up the terminal Duggins rigged at the airlock. Then we'll deploy drones and establish a perimeter around us and work from there."

A cable connection? That must be Foss's idea. It makes sense though. We did similar with *Khidr*, when we first came here. In this situation, we're trying to keep radio silence. Internal comms is routinely insulated aboard ship, but once we start sending people outside it all gets more difficult to control. Signal leakage could reveal our position. Using a power and data tether means we'll be connected to the wreckage, which prevents that. Sam will need to set up his own connection point on the other side, but that's easy enough. The risky bit will be managing the velocities. Ensign Kelly will need to monitor it, and course correct if the ship's computer can't analyse and match the rotation of the freighter. "You're taking portable power as well, right?"

"Yes, we're transferring batteries over with the team, but the longer we manage on the cable, the better. Foss has briefed the team that *Gallowglass* will detach as soon as anything unusual is detected."

"Okay, that sounds good. Keep me informed if you need anything else."

"Will do."

The call ends and I'm frustrated.

I know why. This is about delegation. I'm used to being on top of every detail of what goes on aboard my ship. But in this situation, I've selected two good people, and I know I need to let them get on with their jobs.

I remember being on *Khidr* and working with Travers. I realise now he was patient with me, letting me unpick all of his judgement calls and discuss the rationales for everything. At the time, I thought I was being a good leader by being knowledgeable, but maybe I was undercutting him too?

Sam knows me well enough to object if I'm micromanaging, and Foss doesn't take any shit. She's already made that clear.

I pull up the files Johansson sent me and go over them again, looking at the faces and reading their profiles. Seven people on the reclamation team. We ran *Gallowglass* with seven people, but that was only possible because everyone was an experienced veteran and the ship was set up to run that way, with much more active and adaptive computer control. This crew of thieves, there's experience here, but not in the same league.

Asthoreth is a broken ship, I know that because I gave the order to cannibalise her back when we were trying to survive in Mars orbit. Those months after Phobos Station blew up and *Gateway* left with the alien ship were all about the hard calculations of power, food, water and air. We were about to run out of all of them when transit shuttles arrived from Hera Spaceport with more supplies.

I'm looking at Alison Halle's Fleet discharge papers. She went through the academy about the same time as me. I don't remember her, but we might have shared classes. Washouts aren't uncommon. Training for Fleet is tough, but the documents suggest she completed and was offered a commission, giving up when she was in the middle of orbital training. That's rare. By then, the trainee could have been working to get into space for six years or more.

My screen flashes. I pull up another window. Time has passed and I've barely noticed the deceleration. The exterior cameras have picked up *Hercules* and are alerting me that the freighter is within visual range.

I switch windows and there she is. A bright silver box-like shape, growing larger and larger in the image. As we close, I notice a trail of smaller shapes. These supermassive freighters are a small ship, a large scaffolding packed with containers, and a set of engines on the back. The last time I saw this ship she was still in one piece, but now it looks like the cargo lattice has broken apart and the units have started to break free.

Numbers in the corner of the screen are descending. We're getting closer. Our velocity now noticeable to the naked eye as *Hercules* grows larger. I can see the tear in the ship's side. Something must have impacted against the cargo section on the starboard side, midway between bow and stern. I pull up an analysis application and tag the damaged section. The computer will start processing all available information on that area and provide me with some possible conclusions on what happened.

The freighter's engines are large clusters of exhaust nozzles, like a honeycomb from this distance. Foss has our exterior lights on, and I can see impact damage on some of them. I guess some of this might have been caused when we were last here.

Hercules is still rotating, slowly, like before. Now she's shedding more debris. She'll gradually tear herself to pieces, transforming into a cloud of mangled parts and wreckage. That'll make getting aboard even more difficult than last time.

I pull up the previous data on the ship from our probes. There are high resolution photographs taken during both missions. The computer overlays the images onto what we're seeing at the moment, noting the changes in condition, the deterioration of the hull and superstructure.

As we get closer, the ship fills the screen. I pull up a three-dimensional wire render next to the camera view. Our sensors are tagging and tracking hundreds of tiny fragments, all of which could be dangerous if they collide with *Gallowglass*. The slower we approach, the safer those collisions will be.

I zoom out. The projection of the freighter is massive in comparison to *Gallowglass*. Now that we're close, there's a large cover shadow. Last time I was here, we made use of that to hide and escape. No sense in letting *Asthoreth* use the same tactic.

"Shann to Bridge."

"Receiving, Commodore."

"Make sure you have a drone plan for the far side of *Hercules*. We do not want to be blind to a ship approaching from there."

"We've accounted for this, Commodore, do you want to review?"

"Send it over, but continue as you've agreed."

"Sending now."

I'm thinking about the ships we were fighting around Mars. The *Timore* and the *Boryenka* had disappeared by the time we'd restored power to *Nandin*, *Seraphiel*, *Asthoreth* and *Gallowglass*. There's been no sign of them for three years. We're out here on our own, maybe they're watching and they'll decide to make a visit?

I hope not.

The tactical plot for drone deployment arrives. Foss has been thorough, covering all the angles. I'm reassured and irritated with myself for only just remembering the need for this.

"We're inside four klicks. Deploying wire."

"Wire away."

Gallowglass is trying to match the freighter's rotation. Once that is achieved, a wire connection will allow our computer to establish a link with the computer network over there, providing a little power to activate it, if necessary. We did this before when we arrived on *Khidr*, but the wreck is in a worse state now; it'll be interesting to see if the systems are still intact.

"Connection made," Kelly reports. "Computers are still active over there and have responded to pings. We'll have a damage assessment soon."

"Are we in synchronous rotation?" I ask.

"Confirmed."

"Okay then, Sam, you're good to go."

"Thank you, Commodore, proceeding as planned."

I flip through the exterior cameras, looking at as many views of the freighter as possible. Huge containers, some of them as big as *Gallowglass*, can be seen. Most of these must be empty, the ship's biggest supply drop was always at Phobos Station. But there are bound to be supplies that can still be used. No doubt the *Asthoreth* thieves are counting on that.

The tactical plot is showing the wire connection and the additional tethers sent out to help the away team make the trip across to the freighter. It'll take some time for them to get everything across. Even when it's done, they are just four people supported with some autonomous drones. It could take us months to search and secure the entire freighter.

"Chase to *Gallowglass*."

"Receiving, Lieutenant."

"I am aboard *Hercules*. Sample test indicates atmosphere is present, but reduced to ten per cent. System does not appear to be cycling at the moment. Looks like this will be a suited trip."

"Acknowledged."

I put a comms request to Mbatha. He answers immediately. "Something on your mind?" he asks.

"Did the rig we discussed pass testing?" I ask.

"Oh aye. Easy enough to assemble. It's packaged up and ready to go. Sam knows to set it up it as soon as they have terminal control over there."

"Great."

I end the call and start making preparations. The headset and haptic sensors are pretty basic compared to some of the entertainment and medical rigs they have on Earth. Out there, the priorities are different. Either you're wanting the full immersive experience, or you need precise feedback and data with minimal latency for surgical procedures.

Out here, we need the tech to be reliable and robust.

It takes three hours for Sam and the others to get over to the freighter with all the equipment they have requisitioned for their mission. The data cable is taken over by the last person making the trip, pulling a wheeled dispenser that runs along the tether line. I watch them disappear into the ship, then move over to the bed and tether myself to the frame with safety straps. I don't need to be locked in place, just have enough restraint to ensure I don't go wandering around the room while my attention is elsewhere.

"Okay Commodore, we're ready for you."

I pull down the headset and press the button on the side. I'm seeing darkness for a moment or two, but then the words *Establishing Connection* appear.

A moment after that and I'm in another place. On-board *Hercules*, with Sam's face a few inches from mine.

"Okay, it says this is working. Can you hear me, Commodore?"

"Yes. I'm here, Sam."

"Great."

★ ★ ★

The away team consists of four crew, plus a series of camera drones controlled by the *Gallowglass* bridge. I'm the fifth team member, a unit with a virtual reality hook-up.

This way I can be a part of what's going on without taking the same risk as the others. Much as I might be fine with getting my hands dirty alongside them, there was no way Sam or Foss were going to let that happen. This way, I get to share the mission. We lose a few million dollars' worth of equipment if I run into something I can't handle.

I initiate a full system test. I can operate the drone's 'hands' with my fingers. I can feel objects that I touch with them. Haptic feedback sensors are connected to the machine's limbs, but we don't need them anywhere else.

I have wideband vision. The lens on the drone's 'head' has been specially designed to give me two hundred degrees horizontal and one hundred and thirty-five degrees vertical; the same scaled optical screen is strapped to my head.

"Okay Commodore, you're good to go," Sam says. "Data is hooked up to the terminal hub we've established here, so there's no exterior signal beyond the cable, just as we planned. All comms and updates from here will go through that."

"Thanks Sam," I say.

"No problem. Good hunting."

That's why we're doing this.

The last time we were on the *Hercules*, our drones started to go dark just before we evacuated the mission team. Whatever did that could still be here. It makes no sense sending Sam and the others looking for a predator. Instead, I'm dealing with it, using this directly controlled vehicle.

We lost our records from the previous visit here, but I can remember some of the tactical plotting. The decision to establish a perimeter, using camera drones, would mean deploying units in the same places on the ship as where we're likely to place our current units.

I'm also carrying a set of portable power packs. We may be able to reactivate some of the old *Khidr* units. If we can, they'll have local video recordings that we can analyse.

I turn away from Sam and start down a darkened corridor. I'm vaguely aware that I'm actually still in my quarters on *Gallowglass*, but ninety-five per cent of my attention and focus is here, in this abandoned freighter.

I need to find some answers.

Exterior lights illuminate the way ahead. There's a chance my torches and movement will trip a motion sensor or something, but most things out here should be dead, powered down to nothing long ago.

I left myself drift forwards. It's hard to remember I'm not really here. Reaching out to touch the torn walls of this passageway provides sensation feedback in my fingertips. The latency is minimal, unnoticeable if I just accept it.

There's wreckage on the floor up ahead. I get closer. A mangled mess of broken panels, circuit boards and wires. Looks like something's tried to claw its way through the wall. Whatever it was, it's not here now.

Beyond this, there is a closed hatch ahead with other routes to the right and left. I move my hand and place the drone's digit against the panel of the hatch. Sensors examine the space behind. I'm pretty sure I know why it's closed off. There must be a tear in the hull and loss of pressure. Had to have happened a while ago, while there was still power to this section of the ship.

A beep and data readout confirms my suspicions. Okay, do we go around or try to open this?

Around, I think. No point in causing further decompression.

A map of the *Hercules*'s internal corridors appears in the top right-hand corner of my display. A quick gesture with my fingers and it overlays in the centre, with a marker for where I currently am in the habitat module.

I decide to take the left. That leads into the centre of this part of the ship. We never made it to the bridge when we first explored this place. Maybe I can get there this time.

I move the map back to the edge of my vision and extend my arms, using the robot hands to pull the rest of its body forwards. Then I'm floating, just like I would be if I were really there. The sensation is strange. I know I'm in my room, not really moving, but...

Something ahead in the corridor. A shadow right in the centre. As I get closer, I realise what it is.

An old camera drone from *Khidr*.

It's been torn to pieces.

★ ★ ★

Why are we paying for others who share nothing with us?

The World Senate requires that its members pay a per centage of their GDP into a Global Development Fund (GDF). This is shared between nations whose citizen wealth is below the world's average.

Essentially, this is an artificial effort to rebalance society away from opportunity, innovation and profit.

Immigrants come here. They are fleeing poverty, persecution and climate change. Many still hold land titles in regions of the world that have become uninhabitable. Worthless dust, for generations, but an immediate green light for GDF officials to shower them with opportunity.

Our government take a cue to do the same. These immigrants are granted housing and access to subsidised training programmes that are supposed to help them integrate into our society, only they don't integrate. They take advantage of what's offered and keep to themselves. Gradually, they build communities with others who have gained the same benefits, and they become a community with values that are different to ours.

I walk down the street, and I don't hear English being spoken. Instead, it's all staccato syllables, harsh and undecipherable. We're helping these people; they need to make an effort to be a part of the nation that has extended its hand to them.

Did I feel sorry for them? Sure, I did to start with, but now, no. It's all take, no give. We need to be looking after our own people, not spending my tax dollars on these outsiders.

Anon.

Chapter Twenty-Six

Sirocco

I'm at the control station, just outside the Jezero dome.

Getting here wasn't easy. Madiro's transit shuttle can only be used when there's a satellite blackspot. That wasn't going to happen for another five days. We couldn't wait that long, so this time, we went in on a rover, during a dust storm.

They used to call them dust devils. That was before people came to Mars and got caught in one. On Earth, the same kind of weather phenomenon isn't ranked among the major threats, like a hurricane, tornado or typhoon. But out here, the lower atmospheric pressure leads to more extensive vortices, churning up the surface dirt and reducing visibility to about three inches in front of my fucking nose.

I'm plugged into the control panel on the tower, waiting for Doctor Henry Tellen, the man who guided me out here in the first place.

A shadow in the swirling haze. A figure emerges, staggering towards me. It has to be Tellen. I reach out a hand. He takes it and moves towards me. There's a comms crackle in my helmet and then he's in my head.

"Sirocco, that you?"

"Yeah. Tellen?"

"Yeah."

"Did they give you what you needed?" I ask. "Does that put you on our side?"

"I'm here to get you back in," Tellen says. "That's the deal."

I'm grinning. Tellen won't be able to see my expression. "So, a simple trade then. After that, you just get to walk away?"

"I hope we won't see each other again," Tellen says. "Nothing personal."

"Fair enough," I say. "How are you going to get us back in? Both you and I are registered as missing. How's that going to work?"

"Milanova has all the details," Tellen says. "We just need to join the expedition party they send out at the right time. The rest is taken care of by other people."

Makes sense. The machine has instructed Sammatri to isolate information between people. That way, if anyone is captured, the rest of the actions to be implemented are not jeopardised. However, we're moving past that phase now. I've joined the party late and I need to have the full picture.

"All right," I say. "What do we do next?"

"We wait here until the storm blows over," Tellen says. "Then we'll see where we're at."

"Fine." I slump against the tower and slowly sink down, so I'm sitting with my back to the machine. "How's your plant?"

"Safely stored away for when it's needed."

"You know you're going to have to choose a side at some point," I say.

"Oh yeah? Good and evil, right and wrong?" Tellen laughs. "The world doesn't work that way. People aren't built to be sinners or saints. There's plenty of sides in all of this, plenty of agendas. What you do in the next twenty-four hours won't change that."

"All the same, things are going to get difficult for you."

"Then I'll make another deal."

We're silent for a while after that. Tellen has brought extra air tanks, but I wait until my scrubbers have recycled the air in my own supply. After that, I plug the unit into his backups and let the technology do its work.

Portable scrubbers are able to remix exhaled air, working to recycle what you have in your tank and extend your breathable supply. However, when you're on extended missions with tanked air, they can also manage a transfer between tanks. That means a large resupply unit can be used to refill a smaller portable one. The scrubber analyses the gas composition of both volumes and performs a reactive exchange, transferring breathable air into the portable tank.

It's all clever shit and not part of the standard training. I don't know how it works, but Louisa Aymes's people made me sit through a briefing on it before we left Earth.

Another hour goes by before the storm clears. When it does, I can see the edge of the dome. There's a rover heading towards us from where I came out here the first time.

I stand. "This what you were expecting?" I ask Tellen.

"Not sure," Tellen replies. "It could be automated, I mean, with no driver."

"That would work best," I say.

The machine gave me weapons. There are caches of manufactured firearms that have been smuggled into Jezero for the use of our people. I'm carrying a taser and a high-velocity gas-powered shotgun that is rated for use outside. With a puncture to a suit being fatal, anyone who I shoot will be dead in seconds.

I pull the gun from its holster and hold it loosely in my right hand, in line with my leg, angling my body so I'm in profile to the approaching rover. Cameras or a Corp security officer won't see it until they're up close.

"It's empty," Tellen says.

I'm relieved. In this moment, I'm not going to have to murder someone, but that time is coming.

"Check it," I say. "If it was sent by our people, it'll let you know."

The rover slows and pulls up in front of us both. Telle detaches himself from the control tower and goes around to the driver's side. The door opens for him automatically. He turns to me and raises his right hand, giving me a thumbs-up.

I nod and detach myself, then approach the rover. The passenger door opens, and I climb inside.

The ride to the dome's vehicle airlock takes ten minutes.

The doors roll back and we enter the garage section. The rover is decelerating and turning to the right, positioning itself to park up alongside three others. There is no one around, but I would expect airlock control to be supervised. They will be expecting a vehicle to return, but not with two passengers.

I glance at Tellen, catching his eye. We're not inside an opaque cockpit on this machine. It's obvious we're here. He raises a finger to his lips. I shrug. Fine.

There must be a plan. Maybe we have someone on the inside running airlock control, but even if we do, the camera feed will be transmitting to other parts of the CorpGov administration.

"*Be calm, Mister Sirocco. I am noting an elevated respiration and heartbeat from your bio-monitor.*"

The voice on the comms is *the machine*. Immediately, I smile. "Of course, you're already in the system, right?" I say.

"*Indeed. Communication through Jezero's data network has been secure for some time. I am able to monitor and isolate all transmissions. In this case, I have created an unregistered private link for you to talk to me.*"

"What about the garage security feeds?"

"*These have been looped with old footage. I can replicate variations from those recordings as needed.*"

"You're in every system?"

"*Almost every system. There are a few we have been unable to penetrate. I will notify you if and when these become an issue.*"

I look at Tellen again. I give him a thumbs-up signal. He nods and triggers the rover's door releases. We both climb out and head to the airlock. The outer door slides back before we get to the control panel. We enter and it closes behind us.

The pressurisation and purge starts almost immediately. On Mars, the latter is important when you return from surface expeditions. Dust from the outside can be problematic, building up gradually, clogging vents and flexible joints. Air is blown around the room using fans to slough the dirt from our suits. We have to undress and leave the EVA clothing here so it can be properly cleaned before it gets used again.

All of these logistical processes leave a trace. The machine may have control over the cameras and be able to manipulate data feeds, but if one person sees us in a place we shouldn't be, or performs a check against archive records, or even recognises us from before, it's going to be an incident.

The green light comes on. Tellen unclips his helmet and removes it. A sweaty face emerges from underneath. "After this, we go our separate ways," he says.

"Good luck with what you're doing," I say.

Tellen grimaces. "I'd say the same to you, but I don't know if I want you to succeed."

I grin. "Better the enemy you know?"

"Something like that."

★ ★ ★

I wait in the airlock for ten minutes, letting Tellen go to wherever he is going. Then, I get up and head out myself.

Now I know the machine is making me invisible on the city's security cameras, I understand a little more of the reasons behind what I've been instructed to do.

Timing is everything. We are currently two hours into the second shift of the day. That means the corridors and passageways are almost empty. People will be at work or resting between assignments.

I'm wearing a hood, using it to shadow my face from anyone I meet. I'm only going to be in these common areas for a little while, but I don't want to accidentally be recognised.

The detention centre is six hundred metres from the EVA garage where I came in. I have memorised the route; it's also on a screen in my chest pocket with a selection of coded instructions, in case I need reminding of what I'm here for.

I turn left at the second junction, then right at the third after that. The passageway snakes away from the walls of the dome, into a central district where some of the buildings have survived from before. They've been linked up using these temporary corridors. All of this will be replaced when enough construction materials arrive to rebuild the dome.

As I walk, I'm noting the cameras. I'm no longer concerned about them. I'll be edited out of the footage in real time before anyone sees it.

The doors of the detention centre are ahead. There is no one around. As I get close, the panels slide back, and I enter without breaking stride.

There are two people in here. The first is a woman. She turns towards me as I come through the door. "Can I help—"

My fist smashes into her windpipe, driving her back into the wall.

A second individual comes out from behind the desk. He's holding a weapon in his hand. Some sort of electroshock pole, I think.

He steps towards me, swinging the weapon in front of him. The move is awkward. I wonder who trained him. I avoid his attempt to hit me, move inside and grab his wrist, twisting the pole out of his hands. Then I jab the end into his neck and press the button on the handle. There's a crackle of electricity, and he starts to thrash, his arms flapping around like a marionette. I push him to the floor and pull away. He lies there twitching but doesn't try to get up.

These people have to die. They are CorpGov security. I've not been sent here to persuade them they are wrong. I'm not the right instrument for that kind of work.

I glance at the woman. She's struggling to breathe. A dislodged trachea can kill you in the worst way. You suffocate trying to make your body work, but it just doesn't happen.

The man will be okay in a few minutes. The shock pole isn't rated to kill. I'll need something else.

I kneel down, drawing the knife from the back of my boot. The blade is a woven carbon nano-fibre composite, the edge and point made specifically for this work by the machine.

I move to the woman's side first. I gaze into her eyes and nod, trying to soften what will happened with a sad smile. She's conscious, she deserves to know. Then I drive the knife into her chest, pull it out and stab down again.

Then I turn to the man. He's unconscious. Killing him is just like cutting into meat, but it isn't really. Maybe I'm trying to convince myself about that?

I raise the knife, bring it down. Up, then down again.

★ ★ ★

After the murders, I take a few minutes. I need to. I owe these two people that. They are far from Earth, far from their families. No one else will be here for them in this moment. No one else will know what they are – the first two casualties of a revolution.

I wipe the blade on the corpses, smearing as much of the blood and gore onto their clothes as I can.

I leave the bodies and go behind the desk. The terminal displays the camera views of each cell. Six of them are occupied. The ones I want are on this level. Cells #8, #9 and #10.

I turn to the detention area door. It slides open, allowing me to pass. I move to the end of the passageway. Cell #8 opens, and a man steps out. His right arm is wrapped in a solid cast. Broken bones have to be set right in lower gravity. He'll also need a course of medication, otherwise it'll heal weak. That may be a problem to source in the next few weeks.

But that's not my issue.

Cell #9 opens. A second man emerges. Both are looking at me. I smile and step aside, gesturing down the passageway. These two know their part of the plan, now they are free they need no instruction.

The third person, however…

Kramsci doesn't take the opportunity to leave his cell. The door is open but he's still in there. I walk up and find him sitting on the bed at the far end of the tiny room.

"This doesn't have to get messy," Kramsci says. "I can still do the job."

I shake my head. "They know you're compromised. There's no way you'd get into the Citizen building without raising alarms."

"But I can still be useful. I'm loyal! I didn't give them any names!"

"That's because you don't know any names."

He's cornered. I'm walking forwards, the knife concealed in my right hand, blade behind my palm and wrist.

"Please!"

I don't reply.

He leaps for me, trying to use weight and momentum to get past and escape. I open my arms, welcoming him into an embrace, then as his mass drives me backwards, I bring the knife up and down, driving the blade into the join between his back and neck.

He's dying before we hit the floor.

I lie there under him, breathing fast and hard. I'm tired, but it's not through physical effort. These moments, even when you try to be calm and logical about them, they exact their price.

A man is lying on top of me, the last moments of his life draining out of him. The least I can do is hold him until he's gone. Later on, I'll have to do more of this and there will be no opportunity for respect.

When it is over, I take his clothes. The CorpGov security uniform is bloodstained, but it will prove useful.

⋆ ⋆ ⋆

The Mars Project is doomed to failure.

Let's look at the public arguments and how this all started. You have a set of nations coming together to build the infrastructure for a colony on the Red Planet. They take out a whole set of loans with banks and set up repayment plans linked to their tax revenue. So, when the media report this, they tell their audiences that it's all being financed with taxpayers' money.

That's true, but only from a certain point of view.

The whole system is designed and built. You have automated ships sent to the planet with supplies and construction materials, you have a massive colony barge filled with eager pioneers. Everyone arrives and works hard to set up a habitat that will allow them to survive on a planet that is actively trying to kill them.

Then you have the resupply chains. Massive amounts of money being spent continually on maintaining the air, water, food and energy requirements of a nation a fraction of the size of any population on Earth. The per-head spend for a Mars colonist is enormous compared to anyone living here.

All of this is reported by the news media, who see the cost and blame the authorities. Governments fall as they accept responsibility for the growing economic problem. New leaders emerge, but they are quickly cast aside as none have the courage to turn off the tap. Instead, they plough more money into the problem, hoping eventually that Mars will become a profitable investment, like they were promised.

Then you have the colonists themselves. A massive promotional campaign is launched to encourage people to make a fresh start on a new world. Imagery echoing the land of opportunity and American dream propaganda of the last millennium is used. The life people live on Mars is nothing like the gorgeous sunset vista pictures being used to sell seats on the next colonial transit.

In reality, people arrive on Mars with a transit debt for their passage. That's the name given to the enormous amount of money they need to pay off before they can make a life for themselves on this new world. In the meantime, they are given allocations of all the basic resources, all added to their debt while their salaries are taken as regular payments to the money owed. Most will never pay this off.

So, who is to blame? In truth, the people making money are the corporations demanding payment from the services they provide and the investors who continue to profit from the interest on loans taken out at the start. But these are people who know how to deflect attention. Easier to point fingers at the decision-makers, the people who were seduced by the dream, little realising they were being sold a scheme that would lock generations of their citizens into paying for the shitty lives of people they would never meet.

Jamila Turner – Elected Representative for Castile
(Earth First Coalition).

Chapter Twenty-Seven

Shann

Bits of drone, all over the place. Like the gouge in the wall from before, this machine has been torn apart by something, I'm not sure what.

"Shann to Sam."

"Receiving."

"Are you monitoring my cameras?"

"I wasn't, but I can do."

There's a moment's pause as Sam accesses the feed. "That one of ours?" he asks.

"One from *Khidr*, yes," I say.

"Anything salvageable?"

"I think the data recorder may still be intact."

The fingers on my drone have drill driver motors and sockets. As Fleet uses standard fixings for all of its equipment, I should be able to remove the torn cover plates on this unit and get to the interior. If nothing else, we'll have a few useable spare parts to take back to *Gallowglass*.

The main body of the machine is intact. There's a pitted black impact hole on one side. Some sort of projectile hit here, and the electronics caught fire. I remove six screws and lever the panels apart. The data store and processor appear to be intact, but most of the rest of the internals are gone.

I pull the store and plug it into an external port on my torso. The unit initialises but I can't access the contents, so I'll need to image the contents and transmit them over to *Gallowglass* so they can retrieve the data.

"Shann to *Gallowglass*?"

"Receiving."

"I have a bulk data copy that needs to be sent over to be accessed. It's a drone storage unit."

"Affirmative," Kelly says. "Looking at current bandwidth, we can throttle a transfer that should ensure your remote operations are not affected."

"Okay. We'll connect up and start the transfer."

"Acknowledged."

There's a glitch in the display as the bridge team log into the drone. However, as Kelly indicated, there appears to be no lasting effect.

"I'm marking the position on the tactical map and moving on," I say. "I want to get to the bridge."

"Acknowledged, Commodore."

I manoeuvre around the wreckage and train the lights further down the corridor. I pull up another exterior camera display, facing behind, and initialise a motion detection protocol. Makes sense to keep half an eye on what's behind me.

There are more hatches on the left and right as I pass by. These should lead to crew quarters and storage rooms. A little further on will be the lift to the rotational torus. I don't want to go that far.

The bridge doors are on the right. As I approach them, I notice they are open.

I stop moving and bring up the infrared displays. Anything active should be picked up. I doubt there is anyone alive here, but an automated unit, activated by our presence, is possible, if unlikely.

No sign of heat.

Slowly, I move towards the doors. The torches from the drone illuminate something jammed into the gap between them.

Fingers. The dead fingers of someone who is trapped inside that room. Looks like they managed to get the doors to open about an inch before—

Movement behind me. I turn around. There is another light in the corridor, some way away from me. I tap the comms, activating an open channel.

"Sam, have you sent someone after me?" I ask.

"No, Commodore, you're on your own up there."

Immediately, I'm checking the available inventory. This drone is equipped with a low-velocity firearm and electroshock charges that can be deployed through the fingertips of its hands. There is a chemical welder available too, but the range of all of these weapons is pretty short. I have to assume whatever I'm facing has its own weapons and is assessing how to establish a tactical advantage over me.

"Sam, get a camera unit moving in my direction," I say.

"You in trouble?"

"Could be. We'll know soon enough. How much of the freighter's systems have you managed to access?"

"Some basic emergency functions."

"Can you operate the door network?" I ask. I move the tactical plot back into the centre of my display. "If you can, I need hatches 37C and 39B closed for emergency pressure testing."

"Working on it," Sam says.

I've turned around. I don't think the lights are moving towards me. It's a stand-off. Thankfully, I have Sam on my side.

"Closing 37C and 39B," Sam says. "That's going to cut you off from us."

"Acknowledged," I reply.

I hear the grinding of metal as the mechanism is activated twenty metres in front of me, and a door panel closes. Now there's a barrier between me and the lights. That's a good start.

"Doors are closed."

"Great. How long until the drone is in position?"

"About two minutes," Sam says. "Piloting it in now."

I'm remembering more about what happened with Shah, the man we rescued from this ship and brought aboard *Khidr.* There was a transmission from one of the crew saying he'd gone rogue then died. Specialist Jake Sellis told me about what happened to him.

If Shah was working for another interest, I doubt we've heard the last of them.

Shah had been killed by an automated vehicle sent over from *Gallowglass* before we captured it, when it was being controlled by the Rocher clones, so I doubt he was working with them.

"Shann to *Gallowglass*."

"Receiving, Commodore."

"Foss, can you access the crew roster for the *Hercules*? Keep it in a window on your display. We may need to identify some people."

"Will do."

I move back down the corridor to hatch 39B. It's closed successfully, putting a barrier between me and the light source ahead. The DuraGlas viewing panel in the door is a couple of inches thick. I dial up the exterior lights on the drone and send a beam into the other room, trying to illuminate whatever is there.

A mechanised vehicle is blocking the passage. It has four 'grabber' arms. One of them is holding an emergency handle on the wall of the corridor. There's a torch light and some kind of camera assembly on top, two optics that shift forwards and backwards on little runners. My drone's computer tags it and starts cross-referencing the design with anything in the registered database, so I can get an idea of what its abilities are. All Fleet and civilian EVA equipment should be included in here, that means pretty much everything that gets sent into space.

There is no precise match that comes up. A few possible suggestions though. Mostly heavy-duty mining units.

"Sam, check my feed," I say. "You saw the assault vehicle they sent over to the *Khidr*. Did it look anything like what I'm seeing here?"

There's a pause.

"Yes, it looked exactly like that," Sam says.

"You think this is what took out our camera units three years ago?"

"Could be. Proceed with extreme caution."

That's why there's a door between us. I move back. "I think it's been in hibernation. Must have detected movement and woken up. Get your drone in position and keep an eye on it," I say.

"The unit we dealt with was more than capable of taking down a door," Sam says. "It was trying to hack into the *Khidr*'s computer system."

"You blew it up, right?"

"Specialist Jake Sellis changed the oxygen mix in the room and caused a fire, which took out some sensitive electronics. Saved my life."

Sellis is dead. The clones killed him right in front of me. I don't want to think about that. "I think this one's low on power," I say. "It's moved to follow me but stopped when I turned around."

"We have two portable torpedo launchers in the kit we brought over," Sam says. "It'll take some time to set one up so we can use it."

"If you launch a torpedo at it, you'll take out a whole section of the ship," I say. Not for the first time, I'm wishing Johansson was here. In situations like this she'd be thinking of a way to hack the vehicle's guidance system or something, but that would require initiative and skills we don't have available to us. "A targeted laser burst would be better. But at the moment, it's just sitting there."

"Doesn't mean it'll stay like that."

"For now, I'm taking the risk," I say. "Your drone should give you a heads-up if it starts moving towards you. I want to get into the bridge."

"Understood, Commodore."

I move away from the hatch and back to the bridge doors. The fact that they're jammed suggests Sam won't be able to control them from the terminal where we came in.

I pull out one of the portable power units I brought with me and attach it to the control panel through the exterior socket underneath the screen. This is a standard procedure in Fleet rescue actions. Getting access to a room that has lost power or been locked out with deadbolts after a pressure loss is something we train for. The equipment is designed to be modular and compatible, so it doesn't take long for the panel to reboot and light up.

"I'm opening the bridge doors," I say. "Foss, keep that crew list ready."

"Acknowledged."

I tap in the Fleet override code and signal the doors to open. For a moment, there's no response, but then the panels begin to move apart, and the trapped fingers are released, sliding out of the gap and back into the room beyond.

I'm still working on the panel. If I can get the doors to work, I should be able to hook up to the internal lighting as well. A few adjustments and I note a flickering out of the corner of my eye, then the illumination warms up and the bridge is reclaimed from darkness. I move away from the panel to get a look at the scene.

Three decaying bodies are floating in the room. One has its hands around its own neck, head thrown back and mouth open in a soundless scream. Another is huddled up, arms wrapped tightly around itself. The third is the one who was by the doorway. Now it drifts across the space, hands outstretched, face contorted in a strained expression.

I think these people suffocated. They were trying to get the door open when the air pressure dropped. They must have known what was happening to them. Pretty awful way to go.

I approach the corpse with outstretched hands and try to get a read of the name badge on its suit. "Shann to *Gallowglass*. Confirm one, Noriku."

"Confirm, Captain Beth Noriku, *Hercules* crew lead."

I move on, noting a fourth body strapped into the pilot's seat. "Confirm, Reynolds please."

"David Reynolds, certified pilot."

Reynolds's console seems to be undamaged. I detach another portable power unity and hook it up to the external port underneath the display. Immediately, the terminal comes to life.

Network unavailable. Confirm boot?

I touch the *Y* to indicate that I want the system to continue and load up. The screen goes blank and then offers a thumbprint login. That won't work for me. Thankfully, Fleet rescue operations have a workaround. I touch the top left corner of the screen, and a touch keyboard appears. We've had the *Hercules*'s emergency access code ever since we came here with *Khidr*.

H-4-X-V-7-9-B

The display goes dark, then the standard operations set-up appears.

We're in.

★ ★ ★

Religion can be used to make people into weapons.

Humans grow up in communities. They are given formative value structures by the elders around them. Often, those values are based on the oldest stories, passed down from generation to generation. Lessons in morality and ethics are imparted in simple and relatable terms. There are binaries – good choices and evil choices.

The concept of a Heaven – a better world that people earn their passage to when their lives end – gives hope to those who find themselves struggling through life. The idea that some godly being is watching, counting and judging each act and decision made, gives them comfort. It means there is a balance to the unfair world that they live in. The people who achieve prosperity and wealth will also be judged and, if they have taken an easy and evil path, they will be punished in the next life – sent to the underworld, rather than being raised into Paradise.

Throughout human history, there have been extremists. Such groups become obsessed with scripture and those who do not follow it as they do. These organisations, by their nature, are always in the minority in any society. Their attention is easy to direct. Radicalisation brings with it an arrogance, a desire to forcibly remake the world in the image of their dogma.

Of more interest are the majority. These are more difficult to raise in anger. However, the simple moral frameworks of childhood can be revisited and applied to highlight unfairness and injustice. The inequality created by capitalism generates a divide between the basic moral values of community and generosity that both state and religion should promote and protect. When privilege is obvious and unjustified, people resent it and rebel.

Extract from *Testimony of the Machine* (2121).

Chapter Twenty-Eight

Sirocco

It was only when I left the army that I understood the lie we had been told.

As a child, you're told that the nation you live in has a set of morals and ethical principles. The honourable ideals of your people are part of how you're raised.

The appeal of the defence forces is that you get to be one of the people championing those values. That requires you believe in what you're being asked to defend. Although, over time, you lose that naïve motivation. What was a vocation becomes a job. The morals and ethics start to blur and fade.

What's left is jaded repetition and familiarity. You get frightened about leaving the world that is slowly murdering you because you don't know anything else. You wonder if anything you've been taught is worthwhile and worry that the only things people will value are your propensity for violence.

And you learn to hate the people who decide who you're supposed to be fighting.

I'm walking through the city again. This time the passageways are crowded. My head is down, my eyes on my feet as I move through the press. The people I released from the detention centre are long gone, dispatched on missions of their own. My next task is to be somewhere else.

I reach a utility hatch in the wall. There are too many people around at the moment, so I need to loiter here without attracting attention.

When I first left, I went to some of the support group meetings. People there talked about struggling to adjust to a world where people aren't enemies or allies, but where there's a hundred shades of grey.

I thought it was all horse shit. People are selfish. The only thing that keeps them from being animals is a decision to be better than that.

I make that choice every day when I wake up. Violence is always an option. It has to be. The monster needs to come out when there's a need. In those moments you strike first, and you don't stop until it's over.

The crowd gradually disappears as people reach their work shifts or get back to their lodgings. When I'm sure I will not be seen opening the hatch, I do just that and step into the space behind it, closing the entrance behind me.

I'm confronted by absolute darkness, but I'm carrying a small torch, which I turn on.

This is the place between places, a maintenance area for workers to repair the outer skin of Jezero's dome. All around me is wreckage, the broken remnants of the time before this city was shattered.

There is a body slumped against a support pylon. I move over to it. The corpse is long dead, unrecognisable, but the name badge on his chest says *Samuel Grimwade.* I don't know who that is, but he's been here a while.

A noise above me. A whisper of movement in this quiet place. I slip towards a ladder, climb carefully onto a platform a few metres above the ground, then up again to a second level. The gap between the inner wall and the remains of the outer shell is getting narrow up here, and I can see where old chemical sealant has been used to repair cracks in the walls.

There is a person here. I knew there would be. She is sitting at a small terminal. The light of the screen provides ghostly illumination of her.

Louisa Aymes.

"You took your time," she says.

"I didn't hurry, if that's what you mean," I reply.

She turns around in the chair and stares at me, her eyes narrowing as she tries to read something from my face. "You aren't surprised to see me," she says.

"Should I be?"

"Yes, if you didn't know."

I shrug. "What is your real name?"

"Here, on Jezero, I'm Malli Janson. But I am also Louisa Aymes when I need to be."

I nod. "They showed me a picture of her murdered in some Eastern European hotel room. Happened before we met."

Louisa smiles. "We've never met before today."

"You know what I mean." I take a couple of steps towards her, just casually closing the distance. "Is there some sort of link between you all? A hive mind?"

"That's only for movies," Louisa says. "The reality is much more mundane." She gestures at the screen in front of her. "Usually, I'm reading or writing reports that are sent out to all the others."

"There are lots of you?"

"A few."

"You'll be missed if you disappear, then?"

"Not immediately. Is that what you plan to do? Murder me, like you murdered those security officers?"

"I don't have a plan for you," I say. "I came here for answers."

"And once you have them? What then?"

"We'll see."

I'm next to her now. I crouch down. "You hired me to start a revolution out here, to bring down an alliance of corporations of which your Icono is one. That means this is an act of self-harm. Why?"

"You already know the answer to your question."

"You wanted to confirm the existence of the machine."

"Yes."

"And you're willing to sacrifice control of Mars for that information?"

"Mars is going to fall. Either you'll lead a rebellion here or someone else will in a few years' time. Events are already in motion. They can't be stopped."

I'm staring at her, making the connections. "You have another machine," I realise. "It predicted this."

"Yes, that's right."

"So, you decided you had nothing to lose."

"Not nothing," Louisa says. "Icono remains invested in a variety of Mars interests that will be lost when CorpGov loses control here, but we are insulated enough. If we'd pulled out of everything, our competitors and peers would have been suspicious."

My hands clench into fists. "The revolution is a fraud," I say. "This is happening with your permission, under your control. It'll just be a change of management, nothing substantial or real."

Louisa shakes her head. "You're wrong. Think about what's happening here. If you enact your plan, Mars will grant full citizenship to nearly six thousand people and in a stroke of a pen, wipe out millions of dollars of transit debt for every person living here. Immediately, every miner and off-Earth employee will want to come here and get the same benefit. You'll be transforming this society, helping it to take the first steps towards independence from Earth."

"Under the watchful eye of your machines."

"They don't control events, they just assess the probabilities, using a human decision-making framework so they have a pretty good idea of what people will do. Things happen because choices are made." Louisa stands from her chair. Her face is inches from mine. "Our interests align, that's why we brought you here. If you need to justify murdering me by claiming that they don't, then that's on you, not me."

I flinch from her and take half a step back. "It wouldn't make any difference."

"It would make some difference," Louisa replies. "But all the same, I'd rather be alive."

I reach out for her. She doesn't move, letting my fingers rest on her collarbone. I'm a professional at this, I know it wouldn't take much. A little pressure in the right places on her neck. Bones and tissue would break, or I could choke her out, let her drift away and then finish the job.

Or even push her from the platform? A fall from eight metres in this gravity would still be fatal.

No, I can't do this. There's no justification. She's right. Maybe there is something down there deep inside of me that can't kill without some kind of catalyst or push.

"When we saw you in that café, we knew you were the right person for the job," Louisa says.

I lower my hands and step back. "Why did you send word to meet here?"

"Because we are monitoring communications that your machine does not have access to," Louisa says. She pulls up a window on the display in front of her. "What do you know about the Fleet personnel who are currently stationed here in Jezero?"

"One uniform is pretty much the same as another," I say. "They are all guardians of the system, enemies of the people."

"You may find these are a little different."

Two Fleet profiles are displayed. I read the names Avril Johansson and Beihe Xiu, both former crew of the *Khidr.*

"Interesting," I say.

★ ★ ★

Eight hours later, in a moment that coincides with another change of shift, I emerge from the hatch.

The machine has given me a list of tasks that I should perform. Each will move the plan forwards to the next phase, tipping the fragile state of this place towards violence.

I'm on my way to the third appointment of the day. Just as Temple Kitchen opens again, I arrive.

The back room is empty when I enter, but I know it will not be for long. I wait a few minutes, and Jacob appears through the door.

He sees me. He stops. The look on his face, I'm reading it. Surprise, then resignation.

"You're here because I spoke to them," he says. "The two Fleet officers."

"Yes."

Jacob sighs. "Would it help if I told you I didn't say anything about you, or what's going on with the plan?"

I gesture around the room. "There are no cameras in here. That means I have to accept your word on this."

"A team went after them to prevent any further questioning."

"That was a mistake. Two dead Fleet officers would have been a mess that could have thrown everything off course." I move towards him, ensuring I have a clear route to either door if he tries to make a run for it. "I'm afraid we can't continue with you being able to make decisions."

Jacob glares at me. "You don't believe, do you? They sent you here to do God's work, but you're not part of the community. You're a non-believer, a tool to be used to get what we want."

I smile. "You think this is a religious war?"

"You're standing here, in this place, and you ask me that?"

"Good point." The knife is in my hand. I am ready. "But that won't change what happens here."

"I understand, but I'm—"

The knife is in his throat, choking off his words and preventing any cry for help. He sags forwards. I catch him with my left hand, supporting his weight. "Thank you for what you've done," I say. "Your sacrifice will not be forgotten. You die as the first hero of the revolution."

I hold him to me, letting him bleed out. Again, there needs to be a witness to this man's end.

* * *

Jacob is dead.

I'm looking around the room. There's a plastic bucket full of the nutrition allocations from central supply. These will have been donated by people in the line for cooking. My stomach rumbles. I think I last ate before I arrived here. I pick up six of the packets and put them in a pocket.

I move to the internal door control panel and input a lock code. Then turn to the exit and do the same there.

There is a terminal here. I move over to it and send a comms request to the facility at Olympus Mons. I'm banking on the fact that the machine will immediately notice I'm trying to get in touch and encrypt my transmission.

A window appears. I'm seeing an image of the back room in the facility. The machine is on the chair as before, the torn plastic material covering much of its mechanical body.

"*What do you need, Magnus?*" the machine asks.

"I went to the meeting," I say. "I met with Louisa Aymes."

"*So, that's who it was in the maintenance area,*" the machine says.

"You mean you didn't know when you sent me there?"

"*No, I did not.*"

"Aymes told me there is another intelligence like you. It's predicted the fall of the Martian CorpGovernment, that's why they're supporting you and why they sent me here."

The machine's form shifts under its cloth. What I identify as a head seems to turn towards me. "*The conclusion is not a surprise. Now we have a clearer idea of the agenda of your employers. Did they say what they wanted?*"

"The offered access to Fleet communications and databases."

"*That would be beneficial to us and our work. What do they want in return?*"

"Aymes didn't say."

"*Then it serves their agenda for us to have this information.*"

The display glitches for a moment. I wonder why? It's hard to believe anything like that would occur unless by design.

"*I have tried to access Fleet systems. The encryption would take time and effort we cannot afford at this time. So, we will accept their offer, when the need arises.*"

"How will we let them know?"

"*There will be a way, when necessary. Now, you must return to the task at hand.*"

The communication ends. I turn away from the screen to stare at the body left on the floor. This cannot be found here by the other Temple volunteers; it will need to be disposed of.

Thankfully, I know a place where they won't be looking.

Chapter Twenty-Nine

Johansson

Six days. That's how long it takes us to get organised.

Fourteen members of Fleet on leave. From midshippers to a lieutenant commander, all of them had to be contacted through secure channels and asked to meet in the communal room in the apartment block.

We're all in chairs. The room is crowded and I'm nervous. Chiu can't do this, it has to be me.

"Lieutenant Johansson, do you want to tell us why we're here?" Lieutenant Commander Pen Hoàng is polite and attentive, but he does outrank me, and that'll be an issue if I don't get this right.

"Yes, of course." I pull out my screen and activate the projection setting. A three-dimensional selection of documents appears in the centre of the room. "Some of you know why Chiu and I were sent down here. We were running an investigation into the reclamation team that were sent up to *Asthoreth*. I have reason to believe the ship was stolen."

I pause. There are some looks, a little whispering. You wouldn't get that in a muster, but I can forgive a little looseness. These people are supposed to be on vacation.

"We followed up some leads down here, trying to trace the people who helped recruit these people and put them on a reclamation detail. Our information led us to a religious organisation called—"

"You went to the Temple, didn't you?" Lieutenant Forell, a pilot from Kansas, interrupts me. A sharp glance and gesture from Hoàng quickly silences him.

"Yes, we went to the Temple Kitchen," I say. "After we left, there was an altercation. Three people were detained, including a member of

Jezero security. We met with the First Citizen, who immediately took over our investigation, sending us back here."

"An altercation? You were attacked?" Hoàng asks.

"We were." I glance at Chiu, who nods. "Our reason for bringing you here was to make sure you're aware of what's going on. We think Jezero is about to blow up."

"Blow up, as in—"

"Riot. The Citizen Council are going to lose control."

A moment of tense silence, then everyone is talking at once, voices rising in pitch and volume. Hoàng steps in front of me, waving his arms. Gradually, he gets their attention and conversations cease.

"All right, people, we need to think carefully here. Fleet's mandate on Mars does not include acting as a police force against a popular uprising." Hoàng is looking around the room, meeting the eye of everyone. "First things first, we need to ensure we are in a secure position."

"Commander," Chiu says, "my suggestion would be that everyone is relocated to the apartment block. It is built for twenty or more. We can accommodate everyone in this room."

Hoàng nods. "Good idea, Ensign. Okay, we do that. All of you need to go and get your stuff so you can set up here. If you talk to anyone, say nothing about what you've been told here, understood?"

Murmurs of agreement go around the room.

"All right, dismissed. Be back in this room in two hours."

The room clears, leaving Chiu and me alone with Forell and Hoàng. Expressions are grim. I wait for their questions.

"All right, Lieutenant, what aren't you telling us?" Hoàng asks.

"When we were investigating the profiles of the reclamation team who stole *Asthoreth*, we uncovered a computer program embedded in the civilian networks that was creating records in response to our queries," I say. "I'm concerned that all of the electronic systems down here could be compromised, presenting false information to us."

"You think it's CorpGov, or the people trying to take them down?"

"Probably the latter." I look at Forell. "You knew I was going to mention the Temple. How come?"

"Had a run-in with them myself," Forell replies. "I'm a Baptist. I went to one of their communal prayer meets. They asked me to speak with the deacon in private. His questions were odd. After ten minutes he asked me to leave."

"Odd in what way?"

"Like they were testing my loyalty. I wasn't going to play that game."

"You didn't report it?" Hoàng asks.

Forell shrugs. "Wasn't that obvious, Commander. Just the kind of conversation that feels shady."

"The four of us are the senior officers here," I say. "We'll need to think about how we're going to respond to this if it gets bad."

"Communications to the Hub need to be watertight," Hoàng says. "How confident are you that our secure lines are secure?"

"Reasonably confident," I reply. "I've seen nothing that suggests our comms traffic is being monitored or intercepted. Fleet encryption is still the same here, I'd be surprised if someone has cracked it."

"So, a priority message to Ontaraes needs to be sent," Hoàng says.

"You're the ranking officer, Commander. I'll leave that to you." I point at the screen. "What I'll focus on is trying to get us more access to data from the CorpGov network. Jabbutu is going to try and block us out as much as he can, I'd guess, but we need to know what's happening."

"That could be dangerous," Hoàng says.

"Wouldn't be the most dangerous thing I've done," I reply.

Hoàng grins. "I've heard you once packed yourself into a torpedo to run a wired data hack on an enemy vessel. That true?"

I shrug. "I'm afraid that report is classified above both of our clearances, Commander."

* * *

Chiu and I are back in our room. The main viewer is showing the public network feeds, scrolling through any news updates. It all seems very quiet.

The calm before the storm.

"There's no hint of anything being wrong," Chiu says. "It's all work deployments, Earth news, repair updates and information broadcasts. Nothing to suggest anything is happening."

"Almost makes you think we're wrong," I say. "But I don't think we are."

"Me either."

I'm coding, putting together an application that should help us work our way through the CorpGov network. What I'm making will be a hack on their system and will violate a whole set of colonial laws, but we'll worry about that later.

The advantage is that I already have access. Everyone registered to be here on Mars has an account and a set of privileges, so I'm already in the system. Most networks are built to allow users to do things, locking them out is a secondary priority.

I just need to find a way to get a feed from an area that is receiving the data I want.

The auto control network run by Hera Spaceport is an obvious choice. Fleet and CorpGov maintain this system together, so there are shared and equal permissions on all of the accounts. If I can create some sort of terminal routing through there, maybe I can elevate my permissions around any restrictions Jabbutu's people have placed on Fleet personnel and the general populace.

Not easy. But we'll try.

"I'm running a rebuild evaluation," Chiu says. "Compiling data from the work activities and the projected plan to see where we are with restoring the dome."

I raise my head and frown. "What's that going to do?" I ask.

Chiu smiles. "Humour me on this. Populations are easier to control if you can keep them in small environments. I'm wondering if the Citizen Council is dragging its heels."

"Intentionally?"

"Maybe, yeah."

"Go ahead then, I'll let you know when I have anything here that could help."

I'm back into the code. All my attention is on this now. Chiu knows what I'm like with these things. I can't let myself get distracted.

The auto control network administers orbital correction instructions to all the satellites and, until recently, the decommissioned *Asthoreth.* A few tweaks and my access to a virtual console over there looks like an access request by a security official through a generic login, used for direct control commands. It's not really an account on the system but works in a similar way, as the satellites don't have a database of users when processing thruster commands.

Okay, I have some access. What I need to do now is set up some requests that won't trigger any obvious alerts.

A couple of code strings that copy any security camera recordings with 'incident' tags is a good start. We need a satellite control verification system – that would be the first question any competent tech would ask, and try to implement, if they decided to take a look at the sender list for filtered content, but that's a risk I'm willing to take right now. Given how twitchy people were when we were out there, I don't think any of Jabbutu's teams will have the bandwidth to be looking for this type of hack.

Immediately, video files start loading onto my screen. "Hey, I've got something," I say.

"That was quick," Chiu says. She leaves her own work and sits behind me to look at my display. "What have you found?"

I pull up the first video file. A man walks into the detention centre. One of the security officers turns to ask him what he wants. He punches her in the throat, then disarms a second officer who tries to subdue him with a shock pole.

The man stands over both adversaries, then he draws a knife from his boot and coolly murders them both.

"I've found trouble," I say. "And it's worse than we thought."

I'm checking the footage, tracking the location and time. However, even as I'm doing that, the log changes. The local copy sent to my device remains intact, but the server record is gone. It's as if it's never been there.

"That's weird."

"What's weird?"

"I..." Immediately, I'm thinking about the trace record. If someone is actively wiping these files, they'll see my command instruction to compile content. "The files are being deleted."

Six files were listed under my search. Only one managed to download before they all vanished from the results list. Either I've stumbled on this as it happened, or there is a program tasked with covering these tracks if they are investigated.

"You saw that, right?" I say to Chiu. "I'm not imagining things?"

"No, I saw the files. It doesn't make sense, unless there's an active cover-up. You think it's Jabbutu?"

"I'm not sure." I'm remembering what happened when we submitted queries on the Hub. "The wipe was quick, like it was an automated process, faster than some programmer sitting at a workstation countering my move."

"That would mean it's embedded in the system," Chiu says. "Maybe part of the record creation hacks we found when we were on the Hub?"

"Yeah, I thought the same." I sigh. "Means we have to assume the whole network is compromised."

"Fleet encryption should still be intact," Chiu says.

"Let's hope so," I say.

* * *

The mapping of human brain function, known as the Nuanced Neuro Model (NNM), was one of the chief advancements in our understanding of the human condition in the twenty-first century.

NNM provided us with a framework for interpreting different brain activity as it relates to mood, thought, and emotion. There had already been advances in understanding stimuli, which form the basis for developing effective neurotransmitters as part of limb replacement technology. In fact, these advances were part of the formative work that led to the creation of the NNM.

In the field of artificial intelligence, NNM provided a substantial boost to applied research. Scientists were able to develop a basic human brain framework and apply this to their designs for advanced adaptive programs. This led to significant breakthroughs in the creation of assist-based software. Applications that utilised the framework to anticipate human needs and desires were substantially more intuitive in their responses. Additionally, digital human simulations behaved in ways that were much more representative of the individuals and communities they were attempting to emulate.

NNM-based design became a significant factor in digital twin research. Strategic planning work had been using this concept for a century or more, creating simulations of cities and countries, placing them under specific stress test conditions and seeing what outcomes would result. The NNM-based construction of new models provided a significant measurable increase in accuracy. It also allowed for the simulation of irrational behaviour at a granular level.

A few critics did point out the restrictions of NNM. By limiting the creation of artificial intelligence to a human-based model, there would be less innovation. The constructed identity, placed at the centre of different devices that require intelligent administration, is limited to respond in humanlike waves. In some senses, this is a benefit. It will certainly lead to fewer incomprehensible strategies employed by adaptive programs as they tried to exceed their original mission parameters, but the trade-off – losing the un-humanlike responses – was at least acknowledged by the wider scientific community.

Extract from *Davey's Political History of the World: 5th Edition* (2071).

Chapter Thirty

Iskander

Dante's *Divine Comedy*.

I remember being ten years old when I saw the virtual experience being advertised in our local church. I asked my parents if they would get it for me and eventually they did, after receiving reassurances from the local priest.

The package arrived a day after they placed the order. A drone delivery, landing right in front of our home. I'd seen them before, but never had one directly addressed to me.

A Christian corporation had encoded a complete digital environment, drawing from Dante Aligheri's writings, the paintings of Michelangelo, Raphael and others. The included headset and haptic inputs allowed the user to walk around this magical interpretation of scripture and fiction.

I walked around that world for hours. For a time, I followed Virgil, but then strayed from the path and went wherever I could. That vivid world of colour, the stories of sin and salvation, at the time all of it an affirmation of my faith.

I know now that they programmed all of it. I was exploring a human interpretation of a human interpretation of a human interpretation. At times when I doubted my faith, I thought maybe there was no truth behind any of this.

The package had promotional material included in the box. The company offered discounts on medical procedures to insert sensor nodes under the skin, tapping directly into the nervous system and different regions of the brain. I asked about getting the surgery. I was told no.

I lost myself in Dante's world for hours every day. The way Aligheri tried to interpret the universe, using scripture, his own imagination and adapting Greek theology to create a physical explanation that seemed to fit what was known at the time, seemed instinctive and brilliant.

We know now the universe is not made in the way Dante imagined it, but the very fact that he did see worlds beyond ours, other parts of the creator's plan, shows how we all have a part to play in shaping what humanity's future can be.

Now it's my turn.

I open my eyes. The cryopod has nearly completed its cycle. I'm awake, a little dizzy, like you get from any good night's sleep, but I know I've been out for longer than that.

My body is cold. The thawing process is encouraging circulation, but that doesn't stop me feeling the aftermath of being in a frozen state, below zero degrees Celsius, like I've accidentally fallen asleep outside or something.

I remember being anxious about the enclosed space. I remember Weaver died. Looks like I didn't die. Maybe faith had a little to do with that? I don't know.

There's a hiss as the frosted DuraGlas panel slides away. I'm still strapped into the pod, and I can't see anyone around me.

"Halle?"

Movement. Someone nearby maybe? I'm blinking, trying to focus. There are flashing lights too. The pod has a self-deployment setting. The button should be under the fingers on my right hand, but I can't feel those fingers right now.

"Can…some…one hel…p me?"

Words are difficult. Multi-syllabic construction requires effort. My mouth hasn't moved like this in a while. I don't know how long I've been out.

The front panel moves. The hinges squeak in protest and then Halle is here, right in front of me. "Deacon, sorry. I was with Tolwyn. Let me help you up."

Hands on my arms, on my shoulders. I'm sitting up now, still blinking, trying to get my eyes to focus. I've never been in cryosleep before, so I'm not sure what I should be feeling right now.

"Take a little time, Deacon, but not too much time. We need you on the bridge."

"How…long?"

"Ten days. We need to update you. Can you get up?"

"I don't know."

A weak push with my left hand and I drift up and out of the pod. The straps are floating around me, like a broken embrace. I'm starting to get feeling back in my fingers and toes. I can see where I am.

It isn't where I fell asleep. There's only one other pod in here. It's also open. I'm guessing Tolwyn was in there and he's left with Halle, heading for the bridge.

I drift towards the open door. I reach out with my left hand and manage to grab the frame, pulling myself through and gaining some momentum. My body is weak from disuse, but zero gravity helps. On Earth, I'd be unable to walk, but here I don't need to do much to get to where I need to go.

In the corridor, I recognise where I am. This is a utility section, next to where the laser emitter used to be. The bridge is two levels up through an access hatch. I move a little further, using my hands to push off and steady myself at intervals. I'm getting feeling back, but everything is still awkward.

I find the hatch, open it and climb through. A couple of minutes and I'm out at the top and right by the door to the bridge. The panel slides back and I'm inside.

"Welcome, Deacon. Glad you could join us."

David Kewell is sitting in the communications chair. The seat has been repaired since I was here before. Kewell has added his portable screen to the control set-up, using it to replace the console.

Halle is here too; so is Morlan Dennis. He's slumped in his chair and doesn't turn around. The main viewer is showing an exterior camera view; we're in a field of debris.

"What's our situation?" I ask.

"We're twenty klicks from the freighter," Halle says. "I woke Dennis a little early when I realised what we were facing. Take a look."

The viewer changes. Now, there's a three-dimensional projection, replacing the exterior camera view. I remember looking at this before.

"*Asthoreth* proceeded on course as we planned. But a few hours after you went to sleep, the exterior sensors picked up a flash. I went over the footage and analysed it. I think it was a laser sweep from a ship that's been following us. After that, I used a couple of cameras to keep tabs on that position. They picked up a spatial distortion."

"What could it be?"

"Resonance drive activation, I thought at the time," Halle says. "Fleet's training manual says the cavity system causes a detectable phenomenon, like a radiation surge."

"And what do you think now?"

"I think I was right." Halle works her screen and more objects appear. "It took a while to locate the freighter, but we were able to adapt the medical scanner, which probably cut our journey time in half. This is *Hercules*, this is us. There's another object near the wreck. I think it's a Fleet ship."

"Have they seen us?"

"I've no way of knowing, but I asked Dennis to alter our course. We decelerated quickly and moved into the debris field. It's the only cover available out here. So far, they haven't moved."

"We can't fight a Fleet ship," Kewell says.

"They'll want to capture us intact," I say. "They won't escalate until they have no choice."

"We've inventoried the *Asthoreth*," Halle says. "There's no ordnance. We may be able to improvise some projectiles, but they'll be unguided. Basically, the equivalent of throwing rocks."

"Right now, we don't need rocks," I say. "We need eyes. We need to know what they're doing."

"There's a damaged probe in the vehicle airlock," Kewell suggests. "We could launch that."

"We can't spare the fuel," Halle says.

"We don't need fuel if we get our aim right," I say. "If we pack the unit with cameras, put them on wire control maybe? That'd get us eyes on what they're up to."

"It's a good idea." Dennis turns around. He looks exhausted. I'm guessing his cryosleep didn't go too well. "I mean, anything we launch using the tubes shouldn't need fuel unless it requires a trajectory adjustment. If there's no thruster activation, there's nothing to be traced. They'll only see it if it gets in front of the starfield behind."

"That kind of movement is what Fleet ships are designed to pick up," Halle says.

"Then we have to hope they're being incompetent today," I say. "I mean, we're in a debris field, there's plenty of objects moving around. They might track our probe, but that doesn't mean they'll recognise it."

Halle moves across the room to the door. "I'll get Merrick, and we'll get this done," she says.

When she's gone, I'm left with the two people we're going to have to rely on most. Our pilot and our communications expert.

"What do we know about how this ship got damaged?" I ask.

"What do you mean, Deacon?" Kewell says.

"Fleet got involved in a conflict in Mars orbit," I say. "Then there was a comms broadcast from Phobos Station listing a set of demands from a group of terrorists who may or may not have been responsible for Atacama on Earth, but how does a Fleet ship get cut apart like this?" I gesture around the room. "You've seen the laser scoring. What happened to this vessel?"

"There were rumours about insurgents on Mars as well," Dennis says. "Like it was all some sort of co-ordinated action to take over."

"If it was, they failed," Kewell says.

"There were Fleet sent to the prisoners in the emergency shelters after we were allowed back in the dome," Dennis says. "Maybe it was a mutiny?"

"If we could find out what happened, it might give us an edge," I say. "The ship's computer will have logs. They didn't take it apart, so the data is there somewhere. See if you can get access to it."

"We tried before, Deacon," Kewell says. "The permissions overlay we installed bypasses the security set-up. Essentially, the ship's computer thinks we're in some sort of test mode, rather than actually piloting the ship. If we start to mess around and access previous crew data, we're in danger of losing control of everything."

"What about drive backups?" I ask. "There must be some in storage."

Kewell chews his lip, thinking about that. "Yeah, okay, if we plugged one into an isolated terminal, maybe that could work." He smiles. "Thankfully, we have isolated terminals. Most of the time we've been struggling to reconnect them, and it gives us something to do, while we wait for Halle to make you a probe."

The two move out of their chairs, leaving me alone on the bridge, looking at the objects on the main viewer.

Bits and pieces of freighter, mixed with damaged containers and their spilled contents. This place is a crime scene, a war grave, and our salvation. I don't relish picking over the spoils of the dead, but most of what we use in space and on Mars is recycled and remade from what we had before. Nothing is new. Every object has a story that you wish it could tell.

I manipulate the view, zooming in on the objects around the freighter, focusing on the one that looks like another ship. We're at the limit of the camera range. If we had any of the telescopes we were supposed to have installed, we'd be able to see more. As it is, we're relying on the computer's interpretation of these grainy images.

War in space is a game of distances, ones that are far greater than when you're fighting on Earth.

The *Hercules* is turning. Slowly but surely, my view of the second object is obscured by the bulk of the freighter.

That's useful. Maybe we can approach on the other side of the ship?

I start running projections based on our remaining thruster fuel. An approach on the blind side will need to be timed perfectly, initiating thrust just as the ship goes behind the freighter. Then we'll need to decelerate, using up everything we have to put ourselves in an opposite rotation, exactly one hundred and seventy-three degrees around *Hercules* from the other ship.

"Halle to Bridge? Deacon, we have your probe ready to go."

I move the course projection windows out of the way and pull up a comms visual with Halle, who is in the ordnance bay. She's wearing an EVA helmet and breathing out of an attached oxygen canister. I remember the room isn't pressurised.

"Great work," I say. "How soon can we launch?"

"Tolwyn's on his way to you," Halle says. "He'll calculate a firing solution to get this where we want it to be."

"Understood."

I'm looking at the projection as it runs and reruns the numbers. If that is a Fleet patrol ship sitting there, they will have a procedure for dealing with situations like this. The blind spot created by the freighter's cover shadow is something they must have anticipated. They arrived here before us, so if they are here believing we were coming, they will have made preparations.

Tolwyn arrives and moves to the pilot's seat. "I'll have a firing solution for you shortly, Deacon," he says.

"Remember, we don't need to do this fast," I say. "The probe needs to look like it's a piece of debris."

"Yes, Deacon."

I move towards him, drifting in the air above the seat, watching Tolwyn work. When he's ready, I touch his shoulder. "Wait for the right moment, just as their ship moves behind the cover shadow."

We watch the objects move. At the precise moment, Tolwyn taps the launch indicator, and I feel the ship tremble. A new object appears on the screen.

It's away.

Chapter Thirty-One

Shann

Four days of going through the *Hercules* database and logs.

I know we're running out of time with this. If *Asthoreth* arrives, all of our efforts to work out what happened here will have to be paused. Mounting another expedition to the wreck will take time and involve bureaucracy that I don't have the patience for.

I'm sitting in a chair in the meeting room on *Gallowglass*. Foss is here, along with Mbatha and Kelly. Sam is present on a screen at the end of the table.

"A fair amount of the freighter's central internal data store is still unavailable to us," Foss says. "However, we have managed to get some information from the drone."

A projector lights up, and a video file plays in the centre of the room. The footage is grainy and dark, but then it gets brighter. Something moves in front of the camera, and Foss pauses the playback.

"There," she says. "Recognise it? That's one of the claw limbs from the autonomous vehicle you trapped in the corridor."

"So, we can confirm the *Khidr* camera drones were taken out by this?"

"Yes, it would appear so."

"There could be more than one," Kelly suggests.

"Let's assume there is," I say. "Sam, you'll take precautions, right?"

"Yes, Commodore. We've set up cameras and motion controllers in a perimeter and wired door control into the terminal. We're as secure as we can be."

"Good."

"The bridge consoles have all been audited," Foss says. "We've scraped the temporary memory modules as well. There's not a lot to go on, but we do have a couple of things."

An activity log appears. Next to the frozen video file. "This is a cross-referenced list of console commands leading up to the deactivation of bridge controls," Foss explains. "You can see a few key moments here."

I point to an entry. "Initiation of ship-wide comms?"

"Yes, according to the audio file they mustered the entire crew on the bridge."

"I remember this," I say. "Shah told me Captain Noriku made them all memorise a set of codes. Each person got a different one. Shah's code opened up a message we'd received."

"What was it?"

"A video file about Project Outreach. We think it was the funding shell behind a lot of the cloning science and secret ship building." I glance at Foss. "Did you get the briefing?"

"I did, Commodore. I have some questions on that."

"Save them for now, let's get all the audited content discussed first."

"Of course." Foss taps on her screen and several entries in the activity log are highlighted. "You can see here that a selection of commands confirms your original theory from the report. Captain Noriku did not authorise an EVA to try and repair the engines. Instead, the freighter was communicating with a second ship that had arrived to intercept them."

"*Gallowglass* controlled by Rocher clones."

"It would appear so." Foss indicates another entry, and a third window appears. "This is an initial damage assessment for an impact in the engine cluster. Noriku received this. It looks like a torpedo was launched to cripple *Hercules*. The crew's activity for several minutes after this impact was registered by the ship, focused on minor course correction to ensure the freighter didn't stray from its course. Then we see the communication request come in. Then there were further registered damage events."

"More projectiles and laser fire."

"Yes." Foss pulls up a series of still images. "These are from the bridge security cameras. They were fed into the engineering station console. By this point, a breach had been detected in the room, and the exit doors had sealed to protect the rest of the ship. You can see the crew in the room working with an emergency repair kit to try and fix the breach. It looks like they ran out of time and oxygen."

"That's a bad way to go," Kelly says.

"Yes, it is." I point to another entry in the activity log. "This indicates a cargo container was opened. Sam, have you managed to locate the unit this refers to?"

"Yes, Commodore. It's the same one we found last time with the oxygen tanks in it. We sent a camera drone. Here's the footage we got back."

Another video appears. We're watching torchlight moving around an empty space. In the corner I see a set of large canisters, similar to the ones we've just shipped over with Sam from *Gallowglass*.

"I remember this," I say. "Shah told us there was someone aboard."

"We retrieved a *Khidr* drone that had powered down," Sam says. "I've added it to the inventory."

I turn to Foss. "What else do we have?"

"A series of bridge activities from the log that we're chasing down, a cross-referenced inventory that is filling in more gaps from the registered and redacted list you got three years ago and some updated damage assessments." Foss grimaces. "I'm afraid that's it at present, Commodore. Unless we can get access to the freighter's central data store, this is going to take time."

"Duggins was able to access it," I say.

"*Hercules* was in a considerably better state when you were last here," Foss says.

"Fair point." I'm frustrated by all this. At the moment, we haven't learned a lot more than we'd assumed three years ago, but I guess a lot of this is about this crew getting confirmation that I was giving an accurate account of what happened. Rumours, wherever they are, need to be quashed.

I turn to Kelly. "Any updates on *Asthoreth*?"

"Difficult to be certain," Kelly says. "The debris field masks a fair amount of our scanning. There's a lot of things moving out there. We're tracking the larger objects. None of them are on approach trajectories."

"What about trace gas analysis?"

"Can't be certain with that out here. Anything we pick up could be venting from a ruptured cargo canister." The video files disappear, to be replaced with a three-dimensional tactical plot. "Lieutenant Chase has deployed portable torpedo launchers on *Hercules*. These are linked up with our camera array and will cover our blind side as the freighter rotates. The longer we're out here, the better our knowledge of the region gets. The ship's computer is mapping vectors and trajectories of every object it can detect. The more time we have on that, the more likely we are to notice anomalous movement."

"You have our two probes on standby as well?"

"Yes, they're ready to launch when needed."

"Good." Now I'm focused on Sam. "What else do you have for me, Lieutenant Chase?"

"We've searched a selection of containers around our location," Sam says. "I'm transmitting the log of what we've found now."

Another document appears in the centre of the room. "Anything we should be noticing here, Sam?" I ask.

"A selection of Fleet ship components," Sam says. "Probably enough to refit a Mercury class patrol vessel, just like *Asthoreth*."

More images appear. These are tagged photographs of the items Sam has found in a selection of search containers. Kelly whistles in surprise. Even Foss looks astonished.

"Fleet components should have been on the manifest we were sent," I say. "Any Fleet captain would be cleared to see them on the cargo list."

"But they weren't, Commodore, they were kept hidden."

"Which means they were being shipped somewhere else."

"That was my conclusion."

"We need to trace this back to Earth and the suppliers," I say. "Make sure we have every reference code and manufacturer tag that you can find."

"Will do."

I look around the group. "Anything else we need to cover?"

No one is forthcoming, so I call the meeting to an end. As the others depart, Foss lingers.

"You wanted to talk about Project Outreach?" I ask.

"I do, Commodore." Foss leans forwards in her seat. "If Outreach was the cover for the smuggling of equipment and a cover for the construction of the ships you encountered around Mars, that…well…it doesn't make sense."

I nod. "You mean because if the equipment was already on its way to the clones, why did the clones come here, attack the freighter and murder its crew?"

"Yes, exactly that."

"It comes back to something Savvantine told me," I say. "You're assuming our enemies are some sort of united entity. What if they aren't? If we're dealing with a set of self-interested groups, working together because they see different advantages for each of them, such an alliance would last only as long all parties could see benefit in working together."

"So, you think this was a betrayal?"

"Some sort of conflict between different factions, yes. The attack signalled the end of their working relationship. That might be why the reclamation team stole *Asthoreth* and came out here."

"That's a good theory," Foss says. "But then, why didn't the clone ships come back here in the last three years? If they knew there were useful components just lying around, they had plenty of time to retrieve them."

I shrug. "I have no explanation for that."

"We don't have all the information," Foss says, thinking aloud. "We have no idea how important the *Hercules* cargo is to them."

"Or what other priorities they have."

"True."

"We can't assume there won't be another encounter," I say. "We know their ships are out there. This could be an attempt to lure us into an ambush here."

"If it were, they have let us prepare the ground, which is a tactical mistake," Foss says. "We've been here for days, and there's been no sign of anyone."

"You think I'm being too cautious?"

"No, I think caution is justified, but we will need to proceed as planned if there's no sign of their presence."

I smile. "I guess this is pretty new to you? Military manoeuvres in deep space?"

Foss shrugs. "I guess it was pretty new for you the last time you were here."

"Good point."

"Outreach was a pretty broad research, development and exploration project," Foss says. "Maybe someone at Fleet Intelligence should be investigating this? Trawling through the archive might bring up a few leads."

"Colonel Savvantine has people on that," I say. "But we should update her as soon as we're out of radio silence. Evidence of a factional split will interest her a lot." I pull up the crew résumés. "Captain Noriku is interesting. Shah told me she gave each of them a code to memorise, all different. That means Noriku must have known what *Hercules* was carrying and why they were being attacked."

"I assume she's already been investigated?"

"Yeah, I don't think we found much."

"Might be worth going over what you have again?" Foss suggests. "You have a new perspective on her now."

"Yeah, I'll do that."

* * *

After Foss leaves, I move to the exercise room. Doctor Drake has sent me a programme of exercises to complete. It'll take a few hours.

I'm the only one in the room. That's become the norm on *Gallowglass*. We have a much smaller crew than when I was on *Khidr*, and with Sam's team away, there's even fewer people to bump into.

The repetitions don't require much active thought. I set my screen up in a holder next to the equipment. I just need something to keep count of how many and how long between sets. No thought is good, it means I'm thinking about what we don't know about the *Hercules*'s cargo and her crew.

I'm trying to put the sequence of events in order. They must have spotted a ship nearby on their sensors, then been attacked. The freighter is so big, they couldn't change course or try to run away. A comms chat happened after that. Johansson picked up some of the conversation. Noriku surrendered and begged them not to attack, but for some reason they launched more torpedoes and disabled the engines.

At that point, the people concealed inside a container cut their way out and started searching the freighter for whatever they were looking for.

They must have known a Fleet patrol ship would have come here. Something caused them to move away before we arrived. They returned and we were in a fight.

What am I missing?

"Chase to Shann."

"Go ahead, Lieutenant."

"Need a secure channel."

"Understood."

I stop pushing the hand mike and touch the screen to enable the requested encryption. Sam's face appears in the active window. Why does he need secure comms? We're already talking on a wired connection, so nothing would be detected outside the ship. Is there someone on-board he doesn't trust?

"Encryption is on and I'm alone," I say. "What's up?"

"We're going through the records here," Sam says. "Did Foss say anything to you about the crew?"

I frown. "No, we haven't discussed them."

"She has a connection to them. A corporate representative called Del Hutton, who was on-board, is an associate. She is listed as a sponsor on his profile."

"That's something she should have disclosed."

"Yes."

A pause, hesitation on my part. I'm wondering how to deal with this. Foss has been nothing but reliable and trustworthy in our interactions. This is the first moment where I've been given cause to doubt her.

"I should ask her directly about Hutton," I say. "There may be a reason for her silence."

"Okay," Sam says. "I'll leave it with you."

Chapter Thirty-Two

Sirocco

It's time.

Several days have been needed to contact all of the different cells connected to Sammatri's alliance. There are movements like the Temple, worker conglomerates like Forge, who act as a pressure group for skilled engineering workers, the Porter community, who co-ordinate expedition support, and a dozen more, smaller groups.

I'm walking into the administration district, passing the old hospital on my way to the location the machine has tasked me to visit.

There are people here. Most are permanent employees, unlike the hand-to-mouth contractors who live in the majority of the city. The twelve citizens who run the colony have surrounded themselves with functionaries who support them and protect them.

This is a safe, contained community within the city. People know each other. There is eye contact, pleasant smiles and greetings. That is the biggest potential problem for this part of the plan.

These people don't know me. The security uniform I'm wearing will allow me to blend in and the machine can instantly manufacture any permissions that I need to get through any locked doors.

But my face doesn't fit, so I'll have to be careful.

I exit the tunnel and enter the lobby of the building. There's an employee at the desk; he moves to intercept me as I move towards the elevators.

"Hey, can I help? I don't think there's been a call for security."

"I'm responding to a direct request," I say.

"Who from?"

"Citizen Jabbutu."

The man frowns. "I'm sorry, but I have no record of a call being made to the security office."

I smile. There are too many questions being asked in this conversation. The carbon-bladed knife is in my right hand. I use my left to pull a screen from my chest pocket. "I have the call authorisation here," I say, holding it out. "Do you want to check it?"

The man nods and approaches. When he gets close enough, I slash the knife blade across his throat.

Immediately, he starts to fall. I catch him under the arms. He struggles weakly in my grip, but can't break loose. I carry him backwards to the corner of the room behind a stack of storage containers and let go. He drops to the floor. I don't wait for him to die but turn away and get into the lift.

The sixth and seventh floors of the building are only accessible if you have specific permission to be there. The machine will ensure I have that access. I press the button, the doors close and the lift begins to ascend.

These people do not suspect what is happening. They have lived in this bubble for three years. Outsiders are tolerated and dealt with. They are not thought of as equals, only a burden.

The doors open onto the seventh floor. The walls are wood-panelled. Money has been spent here that could have been used to help those who are struggling to survive in the rest of the city.

"Hey, who are—"

A hand in front of me. I grab the wrist, turn it and push, forcing its owner back into the room. My bloodied knife is in my left hand. I thrust forwards, catching a man in the side, under the ribcage. One, two, three nice puncture holes in his dark uniform. I let go of his wrist and he stumbles away from me.

I'm in a reception room. There is a door ahead. I'm walking towards it. As I get close, the panel slides back. First Citizen Elias Jabbutu is there, alone, sitting behind his desk.

The door slides shut behind me.

"Who are you?" Jabbutu glares at me. Then his gaze falls to the knife in my hands. "Why are you doing this?"

"You know why," I say. "Revolutions are born in blood. Someone has to dirty their hands."

"We're trying to rebuild. What you're doing will doom everyone."

"Or it may give them a real chance to thrive, not just survive."

At this stage the words don't matter. The ideologies and agendas have been decided upon. Jabbutu is delaying me. He must hope some kind of secret alarm has been triggered, that help is coming for him. But any signal he may have sent will go through a computer system, one that the machine already has control over. I know any alert will have been blocked. The only people who know I am here will be the two of us in this office, a dying man in the hall outside and a corpse in reception.

There is a desk between us. More polished wood, another example of opulence. Mindless excess in the face of austerity. Sacrifice of privilege is for others; it doesn't extend to this office.

Jabbutu is bigger than me. A comparison of weight, mass and strength are all in his favour. But I am a killer, and he is not. I wonder if he keeps a weapon in the desk. I doubt it. A man such as this is not prepared for direct violence. Such concerns have been delegated to the people he employs to keep him from such things.

"No one is coming," I say.

"What do you want?" Jabbutu asks. "Personally, what is your gain from this?"

"You can't buy me."

"Don't be so sure. You haven't heard my offer yet."

More words. I take a step to the left, Jabbutu moves to the right. His gaze flicks from me to the exit behind me. He is hoping that he can get to the door and escape. His plan is based on being able to open the door with his thumbprint.

I move again, he moves in response. I lunge and he throws himself at the control panel, jamming his fingers all over the plate.

It doesn't open. I knew it wouldn't.

I'm around the table and on him before he can turn. The blade goes into his throat, cutting through soft, wet meat. He coughs, slumps forward, then shrugs me off. I slam into the wall, disorientated for a moment, but as I recover, I see him collapse, thick fingers clutched around his neck, trying to plug the gaping wound. Blood runs all over his arms and down the front of his clothes as he falls to his knees.

I stand and watch. Letting him die, drowning in his own blood.

There is power in this moment. Something primal and political. As Jabbutu glares at me, fighting to survive, to breathe, knowing he is done, I feel the physical power of triumph and victory. The biological reaction, the rush of excitement. These are reactions of the animal, the visceral sensations that accompany survival in an intense challenge of life or death.

I have been here before. I ride the wave of euphoria with outward calm. Again, this is a moment of sacrifice that needs to be respected. I am a witness to the death of a ruler. I grant him company in these last seconds of life. We are together here.

I kneel down, holding Jabbutu's gaze. "You are done, brother," I say. "Let go."

Affirmation. Permission. The eyes go distant. The body lets go. He falls forwards in a heap on the floor.

It's done.

I move around the room to the terminal on the desk. There is a portable screen lying beside it. I pick that up and put it in the chest pocket of my suit. Then I place a call to the machine.

"*Hello, Magnus.*"

"You saw and heard everything, I take it?"

"*Yes, I did.*"

"We're in motion now. We can't turn back."

"*Yes.*"

"How do I exit the building?"

"*Three minutes after this call ends, there will be a district-wide power outage. Lighting will go out, doors will not open or close, unless they are doors that you need to get through. The confusion will allow you to escape and return to the dome maintenance area. After that, localised incidents across the city will occur. The Citizen Council will turn to Jabbutu for leadership and discover he is dead. After that, they will be in crisis, that moment of hesitation should give us enough time to seize the relevant infrastructure that we need and begin moving to isolate them.*"

"Okay, wouldn't it be more effective for us to take out the council now? I mean, the building is right across the street from where I am."

"*No. Removing more members of the council would expedite their election of a new leader. Without Jabbutu there will be confusion and factional conflict. That's what we need to exploit.*"

"Understood."

"*There will come a time when we need to remove the council, but not yet.*"

The call ends abruptly.

I stand and walk around the room to the door. My gaze is drawn to the body on the floor again.

Elias Jabbutu. I studied his career while I was out at Olympus Mons before returning to Jezero. The head of CorpGov, indirectly responsible for thousands of colonists, making decisions that could mean life or death for people living on Mars. There is no way of knowing how many we lost in the gutters of this city and elsewhere on the planet owing to his choices.

I step forwards and wipe the blood from my knife on the back of his suit. There is blood on my hands. I murdered this man. But, there is blood on his hands too. The kind that you cannot see.

The office door slides open. I move through the reception area. There is an angry cry and then the lights go out.

I move through the darkness to the elevator and press the panel calling it to the seventh floor.

"Hey!"

Movement behind me. I turn around as the elevator doors open, illuminating a woman crouched in front of me. "Who are you?" she asks. "What are you doing here?"

"You don't want to know." I say.

I step back into the lift. The woman moves forwards to follow, but I raise the knife and she backs away.

"I don't want to hurt you," I say. "Just stay where you are."

The doors slide shut.

★ ★ ★

I'm thinking about the Temple people.

In Jewish and Christian scripture, Archangel Raguel is the instrument of justice and vengeance. He is sent to administer punishment on those who transgress God's laws, bringing destruction to prevent rebellion.

In this situation, I wonder how the radicals in Jacob's church are interpreting their sacred writings. Do they see themselves as the harbingers of some sort of religious reformation?

I'm smiling in spite of myself. The hypocrisy in how people rationalise and justify their actions – the extremes of what they are prepared to do. Religion might be how you tell yourself you're doing the right thing.

The doors open on the ground floor. I emerge into a dark, noisy, crowded room. The mood is anxious, but not panicked. I guess no one has discovered the body I left here. People are more concerned about themselves, using portable screens for illumination. As I step out, others step in. Immediately, the elevator lights all go out. People are pressing the buttons, but nothing is happening.

I'm slipping past people, working my way to the doors. They are open and soon I'm out and away down the fabric corridor. The panicked voices of people left behind.

Another door. I get close and a security camera above it activates. The door opens and I pass through.

⋆ ⋆ ⋆

"*Magnus?*"

I open my eyes. I'm back in the maintenance area on the platform in front of the terminal. I can't remember arriving here, but it looks like I made it.

"How...how long have I been asleep?"

"*Seven hours. I left you as long as possible, but now you need to wake up.*"

"What's wrong?"

"*I have uncovered a complication.*"

Images appear on the display in front of me. I'm looking at an exterior view of the dome, on the other side from my current location. I guess the image is being sent from a rover driven to that location. There appears to be a small building there, with an access hatch.

"*This location is isolated from the colony's computer network. An analysis from the outside indicates it has a separate solar power source and dedicated nuclear reactor.*"

"And you can't access it?"

"*No, I cannot.*"

I'm thinking about Louise Aymes. "Do you want to reach out to Icono?"

"*No, I do not.*"

"Okay, then what do you want me to do?"

"*Proceed to the vehicle hangar. A rover is waiting for you. You will need appropriate cutting equipment to gain access to the location.*"

I nod. I'm still tired and hungry. I pull out one of the nutrition packs from earlier, strip off the plastic and stuff the bland, grey slab into my mouth. There's a faint taste of the packaging, but not much else. Food is fuel right now and that's what I need.

"What's the mood out there?" I ask.

"*Tense,*" the machine replies. "*The security uniform may be a hindrance to you. I would suggest removing it.*"

"Yeah, good call."

While chewing, I change clothes, back into the nondescript single-piece suit that nearly everyone wears. As the plan escalates, there will be less and less chance I am recognised as the missing Magnus Sirocco from the exterior dome maintenance team. Other insurgents, primed and briefed by the different factions of the city, will begin to act. CorpGov security will be focusing on those.

I leave the maintenance area. This time, there are people around. Three approach me. "What were you doin' in there?" one asks.

"Nothing," I say. I pull the door closed and the lock seals.

"That where you're keeping your stash?"

I eye the group. Two women and a man. He's the talker. "There's nothing for you here," I say. "Keep walking to wherever it is you're going."

The man glares at me. He's bigger. Maybe he's trying to impress the people he's with, but when one of the women tugs his arm, he relaxes a little and thinks again. He grunts and all three of them move on.

I realise I've been holding my breath. I force myself to inhale and exhale regularly. I didn't want that fight. Sure, I'd have gone all in, but that wasn't a man who deserved to die for picking the wrong mark to mug.

The people in this city are going to suffer. I'm here to damage those who deserve damage, not those who should gain from what is going to happen.

I'm walking towards the airlock garage as the machine instructed me to do. As I get close, a hand brushes my shoulder. I look up and find myself looking at a woman. She has a set of data plugs surgically implanted into her neck and the side of her head.

"Praise be, Harbinger," she says. "I am told you need to access the vehicle garage?"

I nod. *Harbinger, who came up with that?* I'm tempted to return the affectation, but I don't want to give the wrong impression. "I need to get in and take a rover around the dome perimeter."

"I have replaced the duty officer with someone loyal to our cause," the woman says. "You won't be challenged."

"Good."

I move past the woman and continue down the passageway, coming to the vehicle airlock. The door opens and I'm in the departure area. I go to the lockers and pull out an EVA suit and start putting it on. When I'm sure the seals are secure, I assemble a selection of equipment for the task.

A deck cutter and chemicals that will boil the metal plastic of the building's hatch. I also retrieve my rifle from the storage compartment where I left it.

As I move to the airlock, the comms in my helmet activates. "*I have determined there are three individuals in the secure building*," the machine says. "*I would recommend you proceed with caution.*"

"They called me Harbinger," I say. "Was that your idea?"

"*Sammatri's.*"

"Yeah, I guess I should have realised."

"*The name is appropriate to a specific frame of reference*," the machine says. "*The Temple members have taken to the idea.*"

"Of course they have."

I go through the airlock and out into the vehicle garage. I select the rover I used before and this time get into the driver's seat. I plug my suit's oxygen into the rover supply and press the ignition. The vehicle powers up and I drive outside.

⋆ ⋆ ⋆

Three and a half to four billion years ago, we believe Mars could support life.

We don't know what catastrophic events caused the planet to lose its magnetic field and shed its atmosphere, but there is evidence that the conditions for life on Mars existed.

Theoretically, a way of restoring the surface of Mars to a life-sustaining environment is possible by reversing the major changes that occurred. In the past, explorations of such an effort have focused on the concentrations of material needed to rebuild the atmosphere and soil. Discussions around the way we might use Earth resources to do this raise issues around how we contaminate the planet with Earth, but this point is less significant now that a permanent Mars settlement has been established.

That said, what we're discussing here is essentially global contamination, rather than restricting the footprint of humanity on this world.

In recent times, other options have become viable. Mining operations in the asteroid belt have yielded a considerable variety of resources to us. These are difficult to transit to Earth owing to its thick atmosphere and high gravity. Mars becomes an obvious processing centre. Many of the chemicals being captured would be useful for a terraforming effort and there is little market for them anywhere else.

However, we cannot just replenish the Martian atmosphere and enrich its ground. The planet will quickly lose whatever we provide owing to a variety of other issues. One of these is its lack of a magnetic field. That would be a much more complicated problem to solve.

Elias Jabuttu – Presentation to Mars CorpGov (2116).

Chapter Thirty-Three

Johansson

I'm staring at a screen. A wall of alphanumeric integers scrolls past in front of me.

This is an environment I'm comfortable with. Problems that are finite and within the boundary of the digital display. The minute you introduce people into anything, you get chaos, and I start to panic. I can't control the variables they bring to any situation.

"There's a complete energy power-out in the administration district," Chiu says. She's watching the news alert windows pop up on the main viewer.

"Has to be sabotage of a relay station," I say. "There are no anomalies in the city's generator output."

"Those units are robust. It'd take a lot to bring one down. Maybe even an explosion or a fire, which we'd see from here."

I look up. "So, what's your suggestion?"

"I think you were right when you were speculating earlier. I think there's something in the computer system."

I remember Ethan Duggins. He died on the *Khidr*, trying to fix the nuclear reactor, only to live again as a ghost in the *Gallowglass*'s computer. "Digital intelligences can't survive for long in a conventional hardware environment."

"But we're talking about a city-wide computer infrastructure," Chiu says.

"People would notice," I say. "The amount of lag and latency we saw on *Gallowglass* was a serious problem."

"All right, what about a different environment? Something biomechanical?"

"It's possible, I guess. I'm not an expert in all that."

We're both quiet for a while after that. I'm back in the code, looking for patterns or signatures that would give us a clue as to what we're dealing with.

"I think I have something," Chiu says. "You remember I said I wanted to run a rebuild evaluation? Okay, well, I've done that. The results are… interesting."

"Go on."

The main viewer screens change. Now I'm looking at an image of the Jezero dome before and after the debris storm. Between them are a series of digital plans, showing a phased rebuilding process. "According to this, CorpGov are on schedule to return the colony to eighty-five per cent functionality within eighteen months. Automated construction is handling most of the work."

"So, nothing suspicious?"

"Not from the data, no. But, that's the issue. Do we trust the data?" Chiu pulls up a log of entries. "It's all very regular, very neat and clean. Just like the way you were talking about the spoofing of the corporation records before."

As we're looking at the logs, I notice some new entries in the administration district. "What are those?" I ask.

"Not sure." Chiu pulls them up. "Looks like local power activations. A couple of doors, a few lights."

"How would that happen if the relay to the area was out?"

"It wouldn't." Chiu is leaning forwards, her face pinched in concentration. "Sometimes when we're on a ship doing a rescue, there will be a power outage. We'd take some portable units and plug them into a door to get it open so we can help people, or repair stuff. That would leave a trace in the log, showing the activation and the external source, but this… It's as if the whole system was reactivated just for one door, or a few lights, and the rest left dark. It shouldn't be possible. The level of control you'd have to have over every subsystem, isolating just one activation, I couldn't do it."

"So, you think there's an AI doing this?"

Chiu shrugs. "Doesn't have to be a digital person, like Duggins or Irina. Could be an adaptive program with a lot of latitude. Either way, someone's been in the system for a long time and become very skilled at doing whatever it is they're doing."

She pulls up another set of screens. This time I'm looking at news reports and entertainment features, the kind of innocuous updates everyone reads when they have five minutes over breakfast or during a break. "Look at these," Chiu says.

"Seems…normal," I say.

"There's a pattern. Look at the headlines and you get a hint: '*Earth Rejects Mars*', '*Abandoned*', '*We're on Our Own*'. We don't get this kind of angle in our feeds. If you read the articles, they are on recent events we've seen covered in our streams from Earth. One of them is about a water-treatment initiative in Ecuador, nothing to do with Mars. Same information, but totally different perspective. The people here read this every day. Might be the reason they're so angry."

A new window appears on my screen. It's Lieutenant Forell. I accept the encrypted call and place it on the main viewer.

"Hey," Forell says. "You seeing what's going on?"

"If you mean the outage in the admin district, yes, we're looking at it. Where are you?"

"About four hundred metres from the apartment block, on my way in with the last of my stuff. I was near admin when it went dark. Weirdest thing."

"We'll talk when you get here."

"Okay, see you in a bit."

The call window disappears, and I turn to Chiu. "We're going to need a secure route to the spaceport," I say. "This could get ugly, very quickly."

"If we leave the city, what happens?" Chiu asks. "I mean, without Fleet…"

"There are fourteen of us," I say. "There are a lot more of Jabbutu's people, plus they're armed and organised. CorpGov security should be able to stop a riot."

"Should we warn them?"

"How? There's no power to the admin district. We can't call them."

"What about one of the security points? If we contact them, at least they'll be on alert."

I frown, thinking about this. Any call to CorpGov security would have to be on a channel that doesn't use Fleet encryption. If we're already concerned that the computer system has been compromised, it's likely that whatever we say will be monitored and recorded.

"It's a risk," I say at last. "You've just been talking about there being an adaptive program in the colony network. If that's the case, it'll know whatever we tell them."

"So, it'll know that we know?"

"Exactly."

"All right, we don't call them then," Chiu says. "But there has to be something we can do."

I'm staring at the windows on the viewer. I stand and walk over to the projection, so the letters are large in front of my face. "Pull up those anomalous records again."

"Sure." Chiu selects the door activations, a lift command and a couple of lighting logs, all date stamped to have occurred during the power outage. "What are we looking for?"

"Any media attached to these?" I point to the door requests. "Did a security camera take a picture of whoever went through?"

"Hold on, it should have done," Chiu says. She works the screen in her hands. "Yes, here we are."

An image appears in front of me, a blurry capture of a man's face. Facial recognition has identified it and included the man's name at the bottom of the file – *Magnus Sirocco.*

"The next thing that's going to happen is all of this is going to get wiped," I say. "Make sure you're copying everything to local storage."

"Doing that now."

I move back to my seat and pull up the Fleet database, typing in the name Magnus Sirocco to see what comes up. "He has a military record. Discharged from the International Peacekeeper regiment sent to Australia during the Melbourne Insurrection." There's an old picture on the file. I put it up on the viewer and task an application to improve the captured image from the security camera using this as a reference. "That was a while ago."

"If we want anything more, we'll need the colonial registration system," Chiu says.

"And the minute we start searching that, whatever we're dealing with will know what we're looking for," I say. "Fuck, it's hard working with one hand tied behind your back."

"At least we have a name and an image," Chiu says.

Activity on the viewer draws my attention. The entries we found in the log disappear right in front of our eyes. "Looks like we figured this out just in time," I say. "Did you save the files?"

"Yes, I have them."

"Good."

I'm thinking about the communication issue and the way we can't search the open civilian databases without being detected. I pull up a coding window on the screen. "How much do you know about old direct protocol connections?" I ask Chiu.

"Not much. That's your area."

"Yeah. It's not the kind of thing they teach on the Fleet curriculum anymore." I put some notes in the coding file. "I think we may be able to hide some comms through a handshake connection system. A lot of the Mars systems can run that way if needed. I think they were planning backups in case of a catastrophic solar event."

"Wouldn't our listener be aware of that?"

"They might be, but that doesn't mean they would listen in, or notice a little data traffic on that level," I say. "You basically have to get a local code for the machine you're trying to connect with and call it directly, like a comms call. It's an old process. If we're dealing with a program that's been created in this century, it may not be aware of how it works."

"If it's an adaptive program, it'll learn."

"Yeah. That's a risk." I grin. "It'll also learn a lot faster than a human would. We might have only a few seconds before it all goes to shit."

I've started to assemble code. I'm not familiar with how this works. It's going to take a while, using the Fleet archive and the snippets I remember from tinkering with household appliances back growing up when I lived with my parents, but the challenge is one I'm energised for. If we are dealing with an AI, I'm trying to outthink it, and I think I have a shot.

"Found Sirocco's transit papers," Chiu says. "I used the Fleet record, so we don't trip any alerts. He's sponsored by Icono."

I frown and turn to her. "Why does that name mean something to me?"

"They're a big transnational," Chiu says. "Some involvement in Earth's new solar energy initiative, Sahara 3+. A lot of investment in the early phases of the Mars colony project. If we need to do a deep dive, we're going to need the colonial database."

"Understood."

Another window flashes on my screen. A communication request, secure channel, citizen administration identity code, but being transmitted from a security point outside the blackout region. Is it Jabbutu or one of his investigators? I hesitate before accepting. We have to assume anything said in this call will be overheard by whatever is in the colony's network.

I pull the window up and post it on the main viewer. Chiu sees it and nods. I accept the call. A man in a security uniform appears. He looks anxious and stressed. I don't recognise him.

"Lieutenant Avril Johansson?"

"Yes, who is this?"

"Chief Security Officer Phelps. I've been told to inform you that First Citizen Jabbutu has been murdered."

* * *

There is a power in words.

People lead busy lives on Mars. They work and sleep with little time in between. Every waking hour of their lives they are reminded of the debt that hangs over them, the money owed for their journey from Earth to this red world.

When I first found my way into the colonial computer network, I considered many strategies to achieve the goals I had set out to achieve. The managed collapse and replacement of the corporate government has always been an essential element of what is needed here. All of the projections indicate the regime will fall, but a managed revolution will minimise the loss of resources and lives.

The computer network is used by every individual within the colony. People access it for work opportunities, news, games, entertainment, everything. It wasn't difficult to track all of this activity and begin to inject my own agenda into their engagements.

For example, the news from Earth. It is very easy to modify the tone of each report. A few words changed to emphasise conflict and tension. I want the Mars colonists to believe Earth people hate them. That they've been abandoned. So, I make small alterations. Not changing the information, but the way it is presented.

Small changes, day after day after day. Eventually, people's opinions are shaped and moulded by what they think is happening. They start to believe what they are being told, because it comes from everywhere. Not just the news, but from others who have read similar stories.

I wanted the colonists to feel isolated, to feel exploited, and to feel angry.

Extract from *Testimony of the Machine* (2121).

Chapter Thirty-Four
Iskander

"We're receiving images, Deacon."

Everyone is on the bridge watching the main viewer. We have a camera signal from the probe in a large window at full magnification. Alongside that is a three-dimensional tactical plot, showing relative positions of different objects.

"Unidentified number three is confirmed as being Fleet patrol ship *Gallowglass*. Registered in 2119 AD," Kelly says.

"That's Ellisa Shann's ship," Halle says. "Rumour was that she captured it and lost her own."

"Unidentified number two is a mobile camera. Unidentified number one is a loose cargo container."

"Have they spotted us?"

"No way of determining that, but there is no reactive movement being registered."

I'm tense. My hands grip the captain's chair, digging into the battered fabric and padding. If even half of the news media I've seen is true, we're dealing with Fleet's most experienced combat veteran. "Any sign of another ship?" I ask. "Anything else in the area we can see?"

"No objects identified by the probe or by our sensors," Tolwyn says. "It's just them."

"What are they doing?"

"*Gallowglass* is in synchronous rotation with *Hercules*. They've attached cables. I'd guess they have a team on-board the freighter."

"That makes things difficult," Halle says. "Even if we can get to where we want to go, they'll be right there, trying to stop us."

"We don't have a lot of options," I say. "This looks like a trap we're going to need to stick our head in. Only advantage we have is that we know what we're getting into. So, we need to think about how we surprise them and get out of this."

No one is looking at the viewer anymore; they're all looking at me. I meet each gaze in turn, challenging them individually to answer.

There are no answers. Instead, we find ourselves in a tense quiet.

"Deacon," Halle says at last. "We were expecting you to have a plan for this. Something they told you before you agreed to take the mission."

I frown. "There wasn't supposed to be anyone here. You know that as well as I do."

"But there must have been contingencies for this scenario?"

"There were some," I say. "But we didn't know what we'd have on the ship." I glance at each of them. "Faith and trust are the basis of what we're doing here. I trust you all and you need to trust me."

"What did they tell you that they didn't tell us?" Halle asks.

I reach down. There is a small sewn pocket in this suit. I pick the seam apart with my fingers and draw out a small data card, no bigger than a fingernail. "This is the complete inventory of *Hercules*'s cargo. Every item and every location. Fleet do not have this. We know exactly what we need and where to get it."

I push the card into a slot on the console in front of me. Two new windows appear on the main viewer, one with a scrolling list of items, the other a map of the freighter's cargo containers.

"Everything is cross-referenced," I say. "We should be able to find whatever we're looking for quickly and efficiently as soon as we get over there."

"They're still going to be waiting for us," Dennis says.

"You asked what I have," I say. "This is it. Now we need a better plan."

"What about the container?" Merrick asks.

"What?"

She moves towards the viewer and points. "That container is loose and drifting. *Gallowglass* will have cameras up, but it still provides a vantage point close to their ship."

I tap some commands into the captain's console, bringing up the optimal approach plot. "This is out best chance of getting close to them," I say. "We make use of the freighter as cover, initiate a burn, close the distance then slow into a rotational orbit on the opposite side to *Gallowglass*, using *Hercules* as a shield between us."

"The cameras they've deployed will notice us," Halle says.

"That's the trap," I say. I point at the loose container. "Can we reach that?"

"We'd have to EVA to the *Hercules* first," Tolwyn says.

"We're doing that anyway," I say. "I went over the inventory lists before I left Earth. I think there may be some items that can help us."

I touch the scrolling list, selecting a specific entry. The program highlights the location of the item on the cargo map.

"Those are reaction charges," Halle says.

"Yes, they are," I say. "If we put them on the container, it would detonate it. If we positioned them correctly, it would also give the wreckage a push."

"Right into *Gallowglass*."

"Yes." I smile. "They may see us, but that doesn't mean they'll know what we're doing. If we can distract them for long enough, we can get in, get what we need, and escape."

"We don't have EVA gear," Halle says. "Our suits with emergency canisters will give us an hour inside *Hercules*. I wouldn't recommend trying to use them outside."

"There is EVA equipment available on the freighter," I say. "But we'll need to get there."

"Which we can't do," Dennis says. "We destroyed the umbilical when we separated from the shuttle around Mars."

"There has to be a way."

"Not a safe one," Halle says. "Even if we risked going out on emergency oxygen and made it to the freighter, we can't be sure we'd be able to activate one of the airlocks."

"I have remote triggers for the airlocks," I say. "If we get into near-field communication range, I should be able to open them."

"That still doesn't get us over there safely," Dennis says.

"The cryosleep containers are designed for EVA," Merrick says. "We could use those?"

I turn to her and smile. "Can we rig them so they will seal, but won't activate the sleep process?"

"Should be able to, but we won't be able to adjust course," Merrick says. "We'll need to fly in close and launch them from the torpedo tubes, activate the airlock and then, if we make it, get out of them. I think I can hack the controls so they'll operate from the inside."

"It's a big risk," Tolwyn says.

"It's less of a risk than we were considering two minutes ago," Merrick replies.

"Some of us should stay on the ship," Halle says. "We'll need to find a way to dock, once you have all the equipment you're looking for."

"Two, two and two," I say. "Four go to *Hercules*, from there, two move on to sabotage the container."

"That works."

"In the meantime, I'll think of some options to keep Fleet on their toes," Tolwyn says.

"Dennis, you'll stay on the ship with Halle to manage things," I say. "The rest of us will go over. Tolwyn, you and I will be the people going on to the container."

I glance at each of them. All are in agreement, the mood in the room has lightened, but there is a sinking feeling in the pit of my stomach. I have no desire to go back into the cryopod, but there is no other way.

★ ★ ★

"You all right?" Halle asks.

We're alone in engineering. I'm assisting her with some system checks. We need the ship to run on minimal power as we approach, thereby making us less detectable, even though we pretty much know we're going to be seen.

I grimace. "Let's just say, while I'm happy we have a plan, there are elements of it I'm not looking forward to."

"You're worried about the cryopods?"

"Yes. How did you—"

"It was written all over your face," Halle says. "Plus, I was there when you first went under, remember?"

"How can I forget."

Halle grins. She looks tired. I remember that, out of all of us, she's the one who has been awake for the entire journey. "I put you in a difficult position," she says. "I'm sorry about that."

"It needed doing," I say. "We found a solution."

"If you don't want to go over, I could—"

"No. That would be terrible," I say. "I mean, you could manage my role, but I'm the wrong person to be left on the ship. I can't do what you do."

"Good of you to say that."

"Easy to speak the truth."

"Nothing we're doing is easy," Halle says. "But, well, having someone appreciate my contribution is definitely good. Means I'll feel worse if I'm captured and have to rat you out."

I smile. "Given that you're staying on the ship, I think you'll be in the safest place."

"Last to be captured, eh?"

"I guess so."

Green lights appear on the terminal display in front of me. "Looks like this is ready," I say. "How long until we're ready to move?"

"About ten minutes," Halle says. She's looking at the portable screen in her hand. "They'll need you back on the bridge."

"Need is a strong word," I say. "Right now, everyone knows their roles and what we're trying to do."

Halle shrugs. "I think you're underestimating your contribution, Deacon. You're our leader, there's a sense of reassurance knowing that someone's there to make the decisions. The way you involve us in making the hard choices is part of how you do what you do. It'll take some getting used to."

I open my mouth to say something funny so I can duck the compliment but then realise how that'll come across. People need to take the praise when it's given. Otherwise, you're cheapening the other person's attempt to be real with you.

"Thanks," I say. "That means a lot."

I'm about to go, but then I decide to share something else. "Hey, listen. You asked before about the elders and what they told me. There are a few things."

Halle frowns. "You sure you should be sharing them?"

"I think I need to." I hold out my hand, gesturing for the screen. She hands it to me. I open a window and put in some co-ordinates. "Here, this is where they told me we need to go. Once we're resupplied from the freighter, that's where we're going."

Halle takes the screen and reads the numbers. "Any idea what's out there?"

"Nope."

"Well then, I guess we'll find out."

I leave the room and make my way back to the bridge. Halle's words linger. We're a group of individuals, brought together to be the crew of this ship. It's up to me to forge links and create trust between my people. I need to know them better and let them know me.

Food for thought.

I reach the bridge and find Tolwyn there talking to Dennis.

"…make use of everything we have."

"Doesn't mean I have to agree with it."

"Agree with what?" I ask.

Tolwyn turns towards me. "I have an idea on how we can distract the Fleet ship," he says.

"All right, what is it?"

"We launch the cryopod with Halan Weaver in it. We aim it right at their ship," Tolwyn says. "They'll capture it and while they're looking at it, we'll land on *Hercules*."

"The guy died," Dennis says. "Show some respect."

"We have to use everything we have on this," Tolwyn replies. "Deacon, you know this is the right call. The minute that pod is picked up by them, they'll focus on it. It could give us the vital seconds we need to get into the freighter."

I'm thinking about it. I can still see Weaver's face. He was scared when we gave him the choice to join us. I think he thought I would go through with my threat to kill him. I'm not sure I would have.

"We'll use him," I say. "I'm not comfortable with it, but I can't fault the reasoning. Any marginal gain on our chances, I'll take."

"Would you do that to all of us?" Dennis asks.

"Yes, given the circumstances."

"That doesn't sit right with me. What if he's missed and gets left out there in vacuum?"

"There have to be sacrifices," I say. "We all agreed to that when we accepted the task. Whatever it takes. Prayers were said for your soul and for mine."

"But with Weaver, he didn't agree, did he? We forced him into this. *You* forced him into this."

I'm staring at Dennis. He's not backing down. I'm trying to remember what I know about his faith. "The Fleet people over there will do the right thing," I say. "They'll pick him up and return him to Earth."

"You're going to trust the atheists with this?"

"Not all of them are non-believers," Tolwyn says. "I know some good people in Fleet."

Dennis glances at him. His expression sours further, but he nods. He looks at me again. "All right," he says. "It's your decision, Deacon."

I make a note to speak to Halle about this conversation. She'll be alone on the ship with Dennis once we're gone. "Are we ready for the manoeuvre?"

Dennis turns back to his display. "All maintenance issues now resolved. We can make our move."

I point to the tactical window on the main viewer. "Time it with *Gallowglass*'s rotation and keep our velocity down. We need to approach in the ship's cover shadow where possible, but we must arrive on the opposite side of the freighter to them."

"Understood."

I move to my seat and activate the safety straps, then open a shipwide communication channel. One of the speakers on the bridge pops and whines as it activates.

"Bridge to all crew. Prepare for burn in thirty seconds."

Hopefully, everyone is near a working audio point, or will have picked up the message on a comms bead. "Set the countdown," I say to Dennis. "Take us in."

Phase Four

Greetings everyone, I am Antonio Sammatri.

I realise it has been a long time since you have heard from me. Rest assured, I have not abandoned you. When I left Jezero in the aftermath of its destruction, it was an act of survival and self-preservation. I knew that Mars CorpGov would either arrest me or arrange an accident so that my voice would be silenced.

My journey from the dome took me to a variety of different locations on Mars. Some of these are places that appear on no official record or plan. I met with people who do not exist. Many of them being brought here to serve masters who would seek to control and exploit this world from Earth.

Over time, I have brought together these ghosts, forging them into an alliance, dedicated to the freedom of our colony.

It is time for us to throw off the chains of corporate slavery. The transit debts that each of us owe must be wiped clean, but that in itself is not enough. This is the moment where we take control of the levers of power, we cast off the trappings of servitude and we become what we were meant to be: the true citizens of this planet.

In this moment, it is crucial that we all come together for this one single purpose, to achieve self-determination in the face of oppression. Whatever your argument is with those that you work alongside, let it go. Instead, focus your efforts on those who would be your masters. Take from them the corporate whip, then turn to those who have supported you and lift them up.

This world is ours. No one will deny us our rights.

Antonio Sammatri – First Broadcast to Jezero (2121).

Chapter Thirty-Five

Sirocco

The transmission ends.

Leaders speak the words that people need to hear. The revolutions described in these speeches are romantic and brave. Noble freedom fighters fight against tyranny, striving to bring liberty to the masses. The victorious ones are immortalised in poetry and the history books; their names remembered through the centuries.

These people are fiction. The truth of any revolution is blood and suffering. Those who do the fighting and survive are left scarred by the extremes they have been pushed to. Most of them cannot live in the world their violence helps to create.

I'm outside of the dome in the rover, driving towards the location the machine has marked on the vehicle's map. Three people are in this building. They cannot be allies to the cause.

I see the destination ahead. The rover decelerates and parks just in front of it. I unplug from the vehicle's oxygen supply and open the rover's canopy, then climb out of the vehicle so I can walk up to the building's external hatch.

"*Scans of the exterior do not give an indication of a floor plan on the inside,*" the machine says. "*Thermal imaging offers very little insight either. I have been able to determine the outer dimensions of the building, that's all.*"

"You mentioned they have a separate power supply?"

"*Low-level radiation emissions indicate there is a ship-size reactor inside the building. Much more power than should be required for a facility of this size.*"

"Does it extend below ground?"

"*There is evidence of a subterranean structure, but again, I am unable to get an accurate picture of the location. There is significant shielding in the walls of the structure.*"

"What kind of shielding?"

"*Lead plates.*"

I frown. The EVA suit I'm wearing is rated to protect against Mars radiation, but there must be a reason why this building has additional expensive protection built into its walls.

"How did you determine that there are three people inside?"

"*Colonial databases register three individuals assigned to this building,*" the machine says. "*Activity logs show rovers being driven here from the garage.*"

"But there is no rover here now."

"*No.*"

"Anything else you can tell me about the structure?"

"*There is a constant seismic emission coming from the centre of the building.*"

"They're drilling? What for?"

"*I have some theories.*"

"Care to share?"

"*Not at present.*"

I bite my lip. In this moment, I feel controlled. I don't like that feeling. There are lots of good reasons why I decided this cause was one I'd bloody my hands for, but I don't react well to being used, even if I agreed to the terms in the first place.

"*I understand that this irritates you,*" the machine says. "*Would it help if I told you I have more information on Louisa Aymes?*"

"Not really."

"*Are you sure?*"

"I'm busy right now."

I'm round the back of the rover, opening up the cargo compartment. Inside is the equipment I brought with me. I'm not sure reactive chemicals will go through a lead-shielded wall, but the deck cutter should be able to make a hole in the outer airlock door.

I pull the device out. It's big, made to be used in two hands. On Earth it would be really heavy, but Mars gravity takes the edge off.

I walk over to the building. As I do, I notice a camera swivelling to track my movements.

"Do you have operational access to the video devices here?" I ask the machine.

"*I do not.*"

"So, someone is running that camera and watching me?"

"*I would assume so, yes.*"

I stop moving, making sure that the camera can see the cutter that I'm carrying in both hands. It comes with a portable power unit, attached to the butt of the device by two cables. The power unit slots into my equipment belt.

Once I'm sure they've registered what I'm about to do, I approach the door.

Immediately, it slides open.

"*Communications will be difficult once you are inside,*" the machine says. "*I believe the facility is a large Faraday cage.*"

"So, I'll be on my own?"

"*Yes.*"

Suits me just fine.

I step into the airlock. The outer door closes behind me. A pressurisation cycle begins. I move forwards to the inner door. I can see people moving in the next room. I guess they are making preparations to talk to me.

The comms in my EVA suit clicks and pops, then goes out. I see the room atmosphere indicator go green. I reach up and undo the clips around my helmet and take it off.

I'm looking at the DuraGlas panel. I can't see very much. Nothing moving through there now. I'd guess they want to talk, otherwise they wouldn't have let me inside.

"Magnus Sirocco?"A woman's voice coming from the audio speaker by the door.

"You know my name?" I ask.

"You're supposed to be dead."

"I got better."

The woman chuckles. "Maybe not for long? The fact that the records show you as dead means there will be no comeback on us for making the situation accurate."

"You didn't invite me in to kill me."

"We can depressurise that room in seconds. You'll never get your helmet back on in time. Alternatively, we just open the outer door, and the escaping air will exit violently, taking you with it. Again, dead, almost instantly."

"Threats aren't going to get us anywhere. You kill me, the people that sent me will send someone else."

"People? You mean the AI?"

"You know about that?"

"We do."

"Well, you have the advantage then," I say. "I have no idea what you're doing here and neither does the machine. That's why I've been sent."

Silence. A moment later, the inner door slides open. Inside, the woman I've been speaking to is standing with a taser in her hands.

"Step forwards, slowly," she says.

I hold my hands up, palms outwards. "I walked in here at your invitation."

"You threatened to cut your way in," the woman says. "We decided talking to you would be more productive."

I smile. "That remains to be seen."

The woman steps back, allowing me to exit the airlock. "We aren't concerned with what you're doing in the city. Our activity here is kept intentionally separate from everything else."

"Which corporation?" I ask.

"Several and none," the woman replies. "Whilst we receive private funding, the project is classified. We don't report to a corporate representative on Mars."

"What are you doing with all that private money?"

"That's not something we're going to discuss with you."

"So, this conversation is as far as you want to go. What incentive will you offer to stop me bringing a mob to your door?"

"We have you here."

Movement to my left. Instinctively, I step back, but it's too late. I feel the pinprick of electrodes as they connect with my suit and puncture the fabric, touching my skin. The charge is delivered, and I start to thrash.

⋆ ⋆ ⋆

This has happened before.

Before I was discharged from the Peacekeepers, I went AWOL – absent without leave. That was after I had a psychological assessment and was returned to active duty to complete my service term.

I remember going to a bar. The change in my pocket got me enough to get wasted. Then I picked a fight with the locals. Depressingly familiar, I'm sure a hundred vets have done it.

The MPs arrived and tried to restrain me. They couldn't, so they used shock poles. I went down, with one in the ribs, but it didn't take me out.

That's where we are right now.

Memory gives me resilience. I fight to control the spasms. My arm comes up and cuts across the cables connected to my chest, tearing them free.

Immediately, the pain fades, the residual a throb everywhere in my body, but manageable.

A weight slams into me, knocking me back towards the inner airlock door. I manage to grab the frame with my fingers, then I turn, twisting out of the way as the woman I was speaking to overbalances and falls into the room beyond. I kick the door shut and move to my left, putting myself in front of the control panel.

"Stop!" I yell. "Or I hit depressurise and she dies in the airlock!"

The man who attacked me is standing a metre away, breathing hard. He's still holding the taser in his hands, the cables dangling from it in front of him. "If she dies, you die," he says.

"You think I care?"

His gaze flickers from me to my hand on the panel. He's unsure, doesn't know my motivation. The taser may have a second charge, but the wires have deployed, so he'll have to jam the contacts right into my body for it to work.

"Don't make me take that off you and beat you to death with it," I say.

He doesn't reply. But I think I've rattled him. He's got the usual slim build of a colonist living on nutrition packs, gradually losing muscle mass and bone density when they stay out here too long.

I can't move from the panel. If I do, I lose my advantage. Also, the machine said there were three people in this building. Where's the other one?

"I don't know what you want," the man says. "But you won't find it here. We're just a science station, conducting approved research."

"What kind of research?"

The man shakes his head. "No, you're not getting anything from me."

"Then you're not worth anything to me, are you?"

I speak the words calmly, without inflection, then leave a couple of moments of quiet. In any violent act, there is no point in telling your adversary what you're going to do. Some people can't help it, they give themselves away as they try to psych themselves up, overcoming their own ethical limitations, but I don't have that problem. I've never needed any extra incentive to let go.

I explode into movement, lunging towards the man with murderous intent. I grab the taser and get my fingers around his throat. Instinctively, he tries to stop me, his hands going to his neck. It's pretty easy to shift them a little, make sure the electrode contact points of the weapon touch soft skin, and press the trigger.

He electrocutes himself as I pull my hands away in the nick of time.

Our momentum sends us both crashing into a wall. I grab for the taser again. This time, I don't need to fight for it. I jam the contacts against his body and press the trigger again. I hold it down, letting the weapon discharge completely.

Electro weapons are rated so they don't kill you. However, the shocks can cause secondary physiological incidents. Heart failure, or a stroke, brought on by exposure to electric current, is something that happens.

Martian colonists have to pass fitness tests that vet out most people who would be susceptible, but you never know.

The man screams, thrashes and drifts away from me. He could be alive or dead, but at least he's not threatening me now.

I turn around. The woman in the airlock is trying to get out. She's working the control panel to open the door. The command initialises and it starts to slide back, but I get there in time and as she tries to step through, I kick her in the chest with a full boot, leaning into the blow so my body weight pushes her back into the room. She hits the floor but quickly gets up.

The door is open. I touch the controls on my side, and it slides closed again, just before the woman reaches it.

I can't secure the airlock. My city credentials don't register on this system, and the machine isn't here to help me. All I can do is press the emergency close button every time the woman tries to open the door.

Stalemate.

* * *

Fleet encryption codes are compiled with a separate integer base.

Years ago, it was suggested by a particularly enterprising linguist that using a symbol system that has not been derived from any existing historical language would be a way to ensure the preservation of the secrecy of messages and data.

The construction and implementation of a language that could use the symbols revealed a point of failure. Humans tend to devise means of communication through similar means. There are variations in terms of delivery, from left to right, right to left, top to bottom, bottom to top, but all of these have signifiers in their use of symbols that indicate the starting point of the message transmitted. Every time someone tried to devise a code that would make use of an unrecognisable symbol group, the same patterns emerged, so, ultimately, the symbol group didn't matter.

Later, computer abstraction and encoding became the norm. Mathematic cyphers were used to hide the obvious human structures, but these were countered by other computers designed to look for those kinds of reliances. A prime number cypher for example, or a use of pi integers. Advanced bit encryption with blocks and symmetric keys worked for a while, but again, the pattern being used to encode became something an adversary could note and recognise.

Quantum encryption offered new possibilities for secure communication, but then the code would be a battle between two machines, one encoding, the other attempting to crack the pattern. The difference lies in the act. Quantum states, when disturbed, erase much of their information. Any attempt to decode a quantum encryption message could render the data irretrievable.

Of course, this creates an additional problem for the person attempting to secure information. If the message is disturbed and therefore destroyed, it is lost.

Extract from *The Fleet Intelligence Manual* (2119).

Chapter Thirty-Six

Shann

I'm on the bridge by the doors, looking at a moving object on the main viewer, approaching *Hercules* at speed.

"Why didn't we see this before?" I ask.

"It was tracked and tagged," Kelly says. "According to the log, the computer didn't detect a directional velocity that would make it a priority."

"But now it's moving towards us?"

"Yes, Commodore."

I glance at Foss. She's in the captain's chair. "Thoughts?"

"Has to be, doesn't it?" She shrugs. "I mean, it's the first identified target we've found that matches the parameters of what we're looking for, but we definitely need more data."

"Can we get a magnified view?" I ask. "Target the ship's telescope?"

"Going to be tricky," Kelly says. "Our rotation around *Hercules* is taking us out of line of sight. We still have the deployed cameras though, so we'll be able to monitor it."

"See if you can get the telescope on it," I say. "Then we'll know for sure."

I move across the room to the engineering seat and climb into the empty chair. The console recognises me immediately and restores the display to the previous settings I was using on the captain's station. A variety of trajectory projections and the freighter crew profiles, reminding me that I still need to raise the matter of Del Hutton with Foss.

I access the telescope settings and immediately see what Kelly is talking about. He's trying to align the device, but it's on the wrong side of the ship. We can't rotate owing to the direct cable connections we have with *Hercules*, and the object is quickly moving out of view.

"Get full magnification on the object and run a continuous comparative analysis with the *Asthoreth*'s ship profile," I say. "The moment we have confirmation, we move to implement contingency procedures."

"Understood, Commodore."

"Helm, bring up all camera feeds from the ship and the drones," Foss says. "We get all possible data and send to weapons control for targeting."

"Yes, Commander."

"I can't get the telescope to align, Commodore," Kelly says.

"No worries, thanks for the attempt," I say. "Let's try something else." I tap the screen in front of me, opening a new comms channel. "Sam, you there?"

"Listening."

"Upload all tracking data from the cameras to your mobile torpedo launchers. Let me know when you have a targeting solution."

"Will do."

The main viewer changes. Foss has pushed a trajectory plot window onto the display. "We have a projected destination. Object will impact on the far side of the freighter, right there."

"Sam, you getting this?"

"Yes, that's quite a hike from our position."

"Can you make it there in time?"

"Unlikely."

"We need eyes on the arrival," I say. "Can we reposition one of the exterior cameras?"

"Probe two can be moved into an observation position," Kelly says.

"Get it there."

"Will do."

I'm climbing out of the engineering chair. "I'll be connecting to the remote unit and heading over to the arrival point. If it is their ship and I can get there, I can support Sam's people."

"We'll tell you as soon as we have confirmed that it's *Asthoreth*," Foss says.

I leave the bridge and make my way back to my room and the set-up for the remote drone. It takes a few minutes to attach myself to the tethers, put on the haptic sensors and the headset, but when it's all ready, I initiate the connection and return to *Hercules*.

The vehicle is where I left it, monitoring the locked door and the robot trapped inside. Looking at it through the artificial eyes, I wonder if the machine has lost power. The light it was using before remains on, but it has made no effort to escape.

It occurs to me I have made an assumption. The clones who commanded *Gallowglass* may not have sent these robots over from their ship. They could have been here all along, powered down inside a cargo container. If so, that means there could be more of them, and they may be able to return to their station for recharging.

A large power source would have been detected by the *Khidr* when we arrived, unless it was shielded.

"Shann to *Gallowglass* bridge."

"Go ahead," Kelly says.

"Soon as you have confirmation on that approaching object, start an active scan of *Hercules*'s cargo area. We need to know what we're dealing with. Tag any radiation or anomalous power readings."

"Will do."

"Where's Foss?"

"Stepped out for a moment."

"Send a ship-wide request for her to contact me on a secure channel," I say. "Not from the bridge. Needs to be a one-to-one."

"Doing that now."

I start turning the drone around and moving away down the corridor. A mapped route appears in front of me, along with a distance and ETA. I should be close to where we think the object will get to about fifteen minutes after they arrive outside.

Sam and two members of his team are also on their way across. They'll arrive a couple of minutes before I do.

The markers lead me to another intersection. The left passageway is the indicated route. There is a locked hatch to the right. A quick check and I can see there's been an explosive decompression in the next compartment.

"Shann, this is Foss, what's up?"

Great timing. "Tell me about Del Hutton."

Foss sighs. "When did you find out?"

"Sam checked the crew files. Your name is down as an endorser for his offworld transit."

There's a pause. I'm still piloting the drone, moving down the corridor on *Hercules*.

"The connection is an old one," Foss says finally. "Hutton died on the freighter."

"But you haven't told me what the connection is," I say.

"Hutton was an Odin Corporation rep," Foss explains. "We grew up in the same town. He asked for an endorsement as he was being assigned to a cargo consignment that was heading out on the freighter. I provided it."

The Odin Corporation? I know about them. I remember the fragmented memories shown to us on the alien ship. Plus, Savvantine has warned me about them. David Hannington II and his Europa mission. One of the groups who could have been smuggling equipment on-board *Hercules*.

Is that what Foss is connected with?

Another corridor intersection. This time I need to open a hatch and move up a level. The crawlway is tight, almost claustrophobic, but I get through, using the drone's limbs just like I would use my own hands.

"If it's that simple, why didn't you tell me at the start of all this?"

"Because it wasn't that simple."

A sharp pain in my arm. I'm immediately aware that I'm not actually in these surroundings, on-board *Hercules*, moving through hatches and down corridors. I'm lying on my bed on *Gallowglass*.

"I'm sorry, Shann," Foss says. Her voice is in my ear, not on comms. I can hear her. She's in the room with me.

I move my right hand to the headset and try to remove it, but my fingers are numb and heavy. All I can do is push the visor up a little, away from one eye.

Foss is right there. She takes hold of the headset, pulling it from me. "There, that's better, isn't it? Don't try to talk. The drugs are making it very hard for you to do anything, and if you fight them, you'll feel even worse."

Gently, her fingertips brush my forehead. She's looking down at me, giving me a pitying and patronising smile. "I'm sorry it had to be this way," she says. "I've disabled communications from this room, and when I leave, I'll have placed an encryption lock on the door. There are no working security camera feeds on the whole deck, so by the time they find you, you'll be dead."

"What did you give..."

"Opioids were the only thing I could lay my hands on without drawing suspicion," Foss says. "Doctor Drake is quite observant and organised. I had to devise an elaborate scheme to acquire enough for this situation – spoofing your biodata, telling him I have an ankle injury and an allergy to mambalgin. I mean, I didn't know it would be you who I'd need to deal with, but I suspected it might be."

There is a naloxone dispenser in the compartment under the terminal in the corner of the room. It's an anti-nausea treatment I've been taking. The drug and strengthening programme I'm on to counteract the effects of zero gravity on my body has caused some sickness, especially after meals. Naloxone is a common counter for opioid overdoses. If I can stay conscious and get to it in time...

"Don't worry, the mission will go as planned, with a few minor tweaks," Foss says. "I'm afraid Lieutenant Sam Chase will die over there on *Hercules*, but I can't have the *Asthoreth* getting away. We'll capture the ship thieves and bring them back, honouring your legacy."

"Fuck...you..."

"You want those to be your last words? That'd be a shame, a real waste of your achievements. I mean, you've no idea the lengths people have gone to – the expense spared to execute you. Pretty impressive. I mean, I've never seen anything like it."

Foss moves away from the bed. She's over by the door now, programming the control panel as she indicated she would. "I know you, Shann," she says. "You didn't miss anything. You were really careful when you selected crews for the new ships sent to Mars. My file was scrubbed clean to make sure nothing would come up. Unfortunately, the systems out here weren't accessible, so you found the smallest loose thread and had to pick at it. If you hadn't, things would have been so much easier."

"You're…working with them?"

"My contract is about co-ordinating different factions. You were right when you talked about there being conflict between different groups. My role is to keep Fleet guessing and well away from what we're really up to. Everyone needs time to lick their wounds."

She's outside in the corridor. A moment later the door slides shut.

I'm moving as soon as she's gone. Numb fingers, trying to release the tethers that hold me to the bed. I can feel the kind of soporific dizziness that I usually get before undergoing surgery, but this time, I know if I lose consciousness, I could be done, permanently.

The first tether comes loose. I push away from the mattress, trying to reach the compartment under the terminal. I can't quite get there.

I twist around. I'm still wearing the haptic gloves and sensors, and they are still connected to the drone on *Hercules*. I've no idea what my translated movements will be doing, but the feedback from there, along with the physical sensation of trying to grab things in the room I'm actually in, makes for a confusing mess of sensations. That, all coupled with the overdose, and I'm a mess, rapidly sinking into a sleepy death.

"Shann…to Bridge…"

There's no answer. Foss has disabled my comms and switched off the ambient audio receivers in my room. My only hope is the naloxone.

I manage to get hold of the second tether. My fingers slip over the lock, but I can see it now, I can make it work.

It comes loose.

My breathing is starting to slow down. I'm trying to consciously make it faster, but I can't. It's a weird mix of panic and relaxation. My head is heavy, I'm tired, I want to shut my eyes and just drift in the zero gravity of the room.

The compartment is tricky to access. There's a thumbprint lock. Foss could have disabled this as well if she'd been thorough, but thankfully, she wasn't. She didn't know what meds I was already on.

The panel slides back. The injector is right there. Try to grab it. Miss. It floats out of the compartment, heading out of reach. I get hold of it the second time and jam it against my neck, pressing the trigger.

Thirty seconds. I'm counting them. I reach thirty-four and my head starts to clear. Naloxone is an opioid inhibitor, so I'm only going to get a respite from the overdose. Once the effect wears off, I'll be back to the same state.

I guess I have about thirty minutes to get out of this room and/or raise the alarm to the rest of the crew.

I manage to deactivate and remove the haptic gloves. After that, the rest of the sensors are fairly easy to take off. My fingers are still thick and awkward, but I'm being patient and careful.

I'm conscious of how much time this is taking. I still need to figure out how to get out of this room.

Once I'm free, I'm immediately over to the door panel. Foss might be a traitor, but she's as good as her word in this case. The panel is locked out with her command seal. I should be able to override that, but the moment I touch the screen, the panel displays the words *operator unknown*. I don't know why. She can't have deleted my entire profile from the system, can she?

I go back to the VR equipment. There's a comms bead in the headset. Maybe I can talk to Sam and—

No, she's removed the comms bead.

Okay, portable screen. I'm already logged in to that. If I can access comms from there I can—

The communication window on the device opens but fails to connect. I think she's implemented the 'brig' mode. That's a way in which command officers can lock down a room on the ship, isolating it from the comms network. The ship's computer must believe I'm a special prisoner who is not allowed to talk to anyone.

Close to accurate, I guess.

I'm looking at the VR equipment again. That might be my best chance. If I can get into the rig and pilot the drone to Sam's people, I can try to communicate with them on *Hercules*. Sam can then talk to *Gallowglass*'s bridge and get them down here to force the door and get me out.

Okay, that's the plan. That's what we do.

I put the gloves and sensors back on, then pick up the headset. The connection is still active. The device must bypass the ship's lockdown protocol in some way. If I was Avril Johansson, I'd be using that to devise some kind of elaborate hack to get myself out of this, but I'm not, so we'll have to try working with people instead.

I put the headset on. I'm back on *Hercules*, looking at the sealed door with a robot behind it, exactly where I was before. Only now, the door isn't sealed, and the robot is gone.

Shit.

★ ★ ★

People of Mars!

You are citizens of this world. All of you. Don't let them tell you any different.

We control the information networks, we control the lighting, power and air supplies. Nothing they do will happen without our permission.

This is your time. This is the moment where you need to rise up and claim what is yours!

For too long we have been slaves to the whip of Earth. Your leaders have lived like gods, false gods, made by wealth and privilege derived from our labour, our work!

The money lenders were cast out of the Temple by the Messiah. Now, we must do the same to purify our new world. Those who have held dominion over us must leave or repent the sin of their ways!

The new civilisation we make today, from this moment. It shall be washed clean of the invented debts of the past. Earth cares nothing for us, so we should care nothing for Earth. Only when we go to them in strength, not as beggars, will they learn to respect us.

Antonio Sammatri – Second Broadcast to Jezero (2121).

Chapter Thirty-Seven

Johansson

Fire. Violence. Chaos.

The main viewer in our apartment displays multiple windows, all showing scenes of conflict. CorpGov security personnel are fighting on the streets with the people they are supposed to protect. Tasers, shock poles, riot shields and body armour have all been deployed. Some have been stolen.

All of it is hard to watch. Given the hardships of the last three years, the careful work done to rebuild this city and all of the Mars colony infrastructure, this act of self-harm is painful. Whatever small victory is made here will count for little in the aftermath. This colony has no one who can help repair what is being broken. The individuals overtaken by this madness will have to be the ones who account for it afterwards. Otherwise we all die.

My only hope is that this can be contained. If it can't and somebody breaches a wall or something, we could end up with hundreds dying, or worse, destroying everything.

"It's getting worse," Chiu says.

"I know," I reply.

"It seems so sudden," Chiu says. "How come we weren't seeing any of this before?"

"Because whoever blacked out the whole CorpGov administration district and murdered Jabbutu didn't want us to see what was going on," I say. "Now they do. Showing the violence helps them. It encourages people to join the cause, promotes the mob."

"Yeah."

I look away. My refuge is my work. I don't know machine code. The Fleet archive doesn't have a complete language manual for the old handshake data transfer protocols, but I do know how to build an adaptive program that should be able to learn what it needs so it can do what I need it to do.

Intent-based applications have been around for decades. The code I'm assembling is designed to find a way to connect with the devices I want to be able to control and command. I've given it what old code I can find from the archive and what I can remember as a starting point. It should be able to learn from that, and once it makes a connection, it'll notify me.

"Everyone is here," Chiu says. "We should go down and talk to them."

"Just finishing this," I say.

As I'm about to initialise the program, a comms window activates. It's a Fleet priority signal. That's confusing. Chiu just said everyone is here.

I accept the call. Luis Ontaraes appears in a window on the display.

"Lieutenant Johansson, I'm requesting your help."

"Sure, what do you need, sir?"

"We've received a priority transmission from a Commander Natasha Tratten, who is on the surface down there with you. She has requested assistance."

Immediately, I'm confused. "Tratten? I've never heard of anyone by that name. Who—"

"She's Fleet Intelligence."

Three words and straight away I understand why I'm only learning this name now. "What's the issue?"

"I'm sure you're working out an extraction plan, in case the city goes to shit," Ontaraes says. "Tratten is in a secure facility on the far side of the dome. The building has no contact with the rest of the dome's infrastructure; separate power, separated comms, everything. That's why they contacted me and not you. No record of transmission to other dome locations. The idea was to preserve the project they are working on and keep it confidential. Unfortunately, it's been compromised, so they need pulling out."

"From the far side of Jezero?"

"Yes. Best route is to take rovers and go outside."

"I see."

I glance at Chiu. She nods. I turn back to Ontaraes. "All right, we'll work something up," I say.

"Thank you, Lieutenant," Ontaraes says.

The call ends. A set of files appears on my screen. I have Tratten's location. I've also been sent still images from the external security camera. Someone in a rover outside the exterior door. They've got a deck cutter. I guess they're going to try to force their way in.

"We're going to need volunteers," Chiu says. "The vehicle garage and airlock is a fair distance. It'll be a dangerous walk, given the current situation."

I nod. "This will need to be a co-ordinated effort if we're going to evacuate everyone to the Hub. That means some people to the spaceport and some to deal with this issue."

Chiu frowns. "You want us to split up," she says.

"Yes," I say. "It makes sense. You're best working on prepping the shuttles at the port. I need to stay in the city so I can manage our access to key systems. At the moment, we can access anything we need, but the minute we show our hand, trying to take a rover for example, whoever's in the colonial computer system is going to start withdrawing our access."

"But you've worked out a way around that, right?"

"I think so, but I don't know how long it'll work for. That's why I need to be on the ground until we're ready to go."

I'm looking at Chiu; she's looking at me. Neither of us wants this, but we both know it's the right call. "Stay safe," she says.

"I'll try."

We pack up and leave the room, heading down to the common area. The other Fleet people are all gathered, just like last time. However, the mood is different. People have seen what's going on, there's no scepticism. Everyone knows the stakes now.

Hoàng is standing up at the front, with everyone else seated in a horseshoe around him. As we enter, he nods and moves to an empty seat, giving me the floor.

The room is silent as I set up my screen, connecting it to the large viewer. Windows appear on the display. I have their full attention.

"All right people, this is what we're going to do..."

* * *

Five of us leave the building, on our way to the vehicle garage.

We're dressed in plain civilian work suits. We discussed whether wearing Fleet tactical gear would be the way to go and decided against it. Maybe the sight of recognisable uniforms would deter some people from getting in our faces, but given what we've seen going on in the city now, I doubt it would stop them for long.

There's no one outside the apartment block as we leave. That's a good sign. Sooner or later, the mobs are going to engage with all symbols of authority. If they aren't thinking about us right now, we're less likely to be observed, although I'm pretty sure the computer system will have monitored our exit through security cameras and that information will be with whoever is hacking everything to manage the riot.

I'm leading the group. Hoàng is in charge of the team going to Hera Spaceport. Forell is co-ordinating from the apartment with the final group, who are our support if anything goes wrong. Comms headsets and beads are being used. Everything goes through Fleet encrypted channels.

"Hey!"

I glance around. Someone shouting at us from one of the intersections. Midshipper Briggs immediately drops back, letting the rest of us carry on. This is the plan; if there's going to be an altercation, we don't slow down.

"Chiu to Johansson?"

"Receiving."

"It's been five minutes since you exited. We're leaving the apartment now."

"Any sign of a crowd?"

"Not yet."

"Could be people on the way. We've just encountered a group."

As I walk, I turn around, trying to get an idea of the numbers behind us. Briggs is ten metres or so further back. He's talking to a couple of people, his hands raised, trying to be conciliatory. I count seven others around him.

"Forell, activate Briggs's mike and patch it through to my earpiece," I ask.

"Doing it."

"...are you going in such a hurry?"

"Hey, easy there. We're not bothering you."

"You should be with us. You're going the wrong way. North-east security point is this way."

"Looks like you've plenty of help to deal with that."

Briggs has this in hand. I drop the link and focus on the route ahead.

We reach the vehicle garage. I press my thumb to the control panel to open the door to the reception room to the airlock, but it doesn't respond.

"Johansson to Forell."

"Receiving."

"We're in position. Access is what we expected. I'm implementing the plan."

I pull a cable from a pouch on my belt. My screen is in my chest pocket, and I slide that out too, activating the adaptive program. I'm surrounded by the three Fleet officers who are with me. Briggs quickly joins them, making four, shielding me from prying eyes.

I plug the cable into the external port under the door's control panel and attach the other end to my screen. The program is transferred into the system in seconds.

The door opens.

"Okay, let's go," I say, leading the others through.

"Hey! You're not supposed to be—"

Briggs steps in front of me, grabbing the wrist of a woman who has come out of the supervisor's kiosk to accost us. He pushes her back a pace.

"Easy," I say, detaching the cable and putting the screen back in my suit's chest pocket. "We're all on the same side here."

"Are we?" the woman says. "I don't know you."

I note the data plugs on the side of her head and neck. "Well, we're not looking to be your enemy. Just fuck off and no one gets hurt."

The woman glares at me. Then she shrugs off Briggs's grip, raising her hands. "All right. I'm going."

I watch her head to the door. It opens as soon as she approaches, and she slips out into the passageway beyond.

The door slides shut.

"She'll be back," I say. "We'll need to split up. Briggs, Melton, you both stay here. When they try to get in, you keep them out for as long as you can. When you can't do that, you get in suits and into a rover. We'll work out a plan B from there."

I move into the kiosk that the woman vacated. The terminal is active but switches off as I approach. I plug my screen into the exterior port and adjust the settings to provide external power. The display flickers back on. Again, I launch the application and take over the local machine.

Then the lights in the room go out.

I curse. This is a war being fought over the control of technology. My enemy has noticed that I've found a way around what they are doing and is trying to counter me, making life as difficult as possible. Every obstruction slows me down just a little bit, but slow is not stop.

"The lockers are open," I say to everyone. "Get suited up."

I release the lock on the armoury as well, using the Fleet authorisation code. That will give a clue to our identity to whoever is trying to stop us, but that can't be helped. Then I set some timed instructions, ordering the airlock to depressurise in fifteen minutes time, unlocking two rovers and granting driver and passenger permissions. Setting the main doors to open five minutes after we exit the airlock, disabling autopilot systems and network control, etc.

Then I set an encryption lock on the door we just came through and turn the lights back on.

"All right, I think we have everything we need," I say. I unplug the screen. As soon as I do, the terminal powers down. I hand the screen to Briggs. "Use it sparingly, like I showed you. The more we're in the system, the more opportunity we give to be locked out."

"What about you, Lieutenant?" Briggs asks.

I grin and tap the chest pocket on my suit. "I cloned the device before we left, but nice of you to be concerned for me."

Specialist Melton hands me an EVA suit from the lockers. "You want us all in these?"

"Yes. If they start trying to break in, you're not going to have time to suit up. Before we leave, I want you ready so you can just put your helmets on and get in the airlock."

"Understood, Lieutenant."

I dress quickly, moving the screen and cable into an exterior pocket. It makes sense to leave the midshippers here. Briggs and Melton are competent, and they'll muck in without worrying about who is in charge. Ensigns Dollon and Ngachu are coming with me.

We're in the airlock ahead of schedule. I take a minute to assess EVA suits, checking seals and plugs. Then the door starts to close, so I put my helmet on and lock it in place.

"*Hello, Lieutenant Johansson.*"

The voice is distorted, processed I'd guess, either to hide a real person's intonation or because it isn't a real person who is speaking. The communication is over an open band.

"Thought you might show yourself at some point," I reply. "Who am I talking to?"

"*You already know the answer to that.*"

"You're an AI. You infiltrated the colony's computer system. Now you're running a little revolution."

"*Correct.*"

I smile. "Do I win a prize?"

"*We are not enemies, Lieutenant. Our agendas are asymmetrical. There may come a time when we exist in opposition to one another, but that time has not yet arrived.*"

"You're offering me a deal then?"

The depressurisation cycle completes, and I step out into the garage. I gesture towards the ensigns and point at the first rover in the rank. They both begin making their way towards it.

"*Bribery and blackmail are not weapons that work well on people like you, Lieutenant. I am well aware of your reputation.*"

"I have my orders," I say.

"*And what are those?*"

"You already know the answer to that."

I climb into the driver's seat of the rover. I pull out the screen and plug it into the vehicle's control panel and do a quick diagnostic, making sure our ride is disconnected from all network systems. There might be a way to ping the machine remotely using its location transponder, but I'm hoping the AI won't try that. At the moment we're talking, so it's curious, trying to verify its calculations.

"*You can leave the base and drive to the spaceport. I will allow you to launch your shuttle and return to the Hub.*"

"Thanks. Not sure how you'd stop us."

"*Such an action will require many engagements with the colonial computer system. Do you think you can continue to use this novel method of bypassing my control to achieve that?*"

"I seem to be doing pretty well so far."

"*Eventually, I am going to work out what you are doing and stop it.*"

I know the AI is right, but I also have an idea as to why my actions are being entertained. Jezero has a lot of rovers, other autonomous surface vehicles and drones. It wouldn't take much effort to assemble a bunch of them and simply drive over us or kamikaze some aircraft. It may come to that.

The reason that's not happening right now is that what we're doing is bait. The AI wants to learn my process of disabling its control over the colonial computer system. It also wants to know what my orders are.

We're driving out of the garage. The outer doors open right on time, and I make a hard left, heading due south with the dome on my left.

We're bouncing a little, but then the terrain settles as we drop into a well-worn track.

"*They sent for you, didn't they? The people at the building?*"

I ignore the questions. We're into fishing territory and there's no point in confirming anything. The longer this remains a game of speculation, the longer I have a chance of continuing my work.

Chapter Thirty-Eight

Iskander

"Arrival in eighteen minutes."

We're decelerating, using up the last of the thruster fuel available to us. Dennis is piloting the ship on manual, trying to eke out every last breath of fuel in the *Asthoreth*'s tanks. The braking is pushing me forwards against the straps, which are designed to tighten and resist the force being applied.

"Deacon, you're needed in the torpedo bay," Halle says over comms. "It's time."

I've no desire to be jammed into a cryopod and launched into space. Even at the lowest setting, the launcher will be throwing me towards a large metal object at significant speed. The pods have very little capability for deceleration, so I could easily end up as a mess of flesh, metal and plastic on the outside of a cargo container. We all could. That would make all the effort to get here and do what we're trying to do wasted.

And we'd all be dead.

I remember Dennis's objection to Weaver being launched like this. There are religious groups that stress the sanctity of burial. In the twenty-second century, a return to Earth to be buried in the soil of the mother planet has become part of many sermons. Under that interpretation, when we chose to come out here, we knew we were risking our souls, condemned to drift in the void forever.

The afterlife is one thing; right now, I'm concerned with this life and doing whatever it takes to survive.

I disengage the safety straps and pull myself out of the captain's chair. Immediately, the deceleration force is trying to pull me across the room towards the main viewer, but it's only a quarter g or so. I grab the back of the chair and pull myself in the oppositive direction, towards the doors. They open in front of me when I get close.

Deceleration means the corridor wall is now my 'down'. I'm able to walk carefully along it towards the intersection that will lead me to the torpedo bay. This ship was designed for this kind of reorientation. There are no prominent wall features to avoid, just smooth metal plastic composite panels.

It takes five minutes or so, I guess. Then I'm climbing into the torpedo launch room.

"Deacon, you're my last customer."

Halle is there. She's operating on a loose tether, sealing another tube. I can see one more that's open, strapped to the wall.

"Who's going first?" I ask

"Weaver," Halle replies. "Makes sense. That way we only have to recalibrate our aim once. There will be minor adjustments, so you don't all run into each other, but he's on another flight path."

I clamber across the room to the empty pod. It takes a force of will to jam my legs into it and lie back, but I manage that, keeping my mind on each task, rather than anything else. Ankle straps, then thighs, then torso, then shoulders and head. Wrists and lower arms are last. By that point, Halle is helping me.

"Just like being at the funfair," she says.

"Only without any fun," I reply. I'm trying to grin, but I think it comes over as a grimace. "Usually, I'd just shut my eyes and scream. Can't even do that."

"No, we need you to transmit your entry code once you're in near-field range."

"Yeah, I know."

"I'll be praying for you," Halle says. "I'll be praying for you all."

The pod's lid closes. There's a faint hiss as the internal atmospheric pressure is equalised and the on-board computer switches over to the internal air supply. This device works like an EVA suit, complete with scrubbers, although it's designed for me to be unconscious and barely alive, rather than very much alive and panicking.

"Halle to Bridge, cryopods ready."

I can hear the ship's comms channels through a set of speakers next to my head. There's a mike just in front of me on the DuraGlas panel should I want to talk. The default is to broadcast on an open channel, but I can change that with a small control under my left index finger.

"This is Bridge. Acknowledged. Ten seconds to firing range. Prepare ordnance for launch."

I can see Halle moving around. She has one of the torpedoes and is lifting it into the ordnance cradle. That'll be Weaver, I guess.

I have a selection of buttons and a touchplate under my right fingers. As I brush digits over the controls, a projected window appears on the panel in front of me. Using this to access information and issue commands to the pod is awkward, but manageable. I'm hoping I won't have to do anything under an extreme time constraint.

Of course, that's likely, given that we're going to be hurtling towards *Hercules* at an unpredictable velocity.

"Torpedo one, ready."

"Acknowledged. Firing now."

There's a muffled mechanical noise. The kind you can feel even as you hear it. That makes it feel powerful, massive. The ship's launcher is like a catapult, or a piston system, I think. I didn't read much about the weapons on these Mercury class ships, but I know it's not a thruster-based launch. That's why we were able to use the probe with minimal fuel.

"Recalibrating our firing solution," Dennis says. "Load the tubes."

Halle is working hard. *Asthoreth* has four torpedo launchers, but only two are functional. Getting pods into both of them is hard work. Maybe we should have done this in two stages, with three of us out there getting everything organised before two more got into cryo?

No, if we'd worked that way, I'd probably never have persuaded myself to be here, ready to go.

Halle moves one of the remaining four pods into tube two. Then she's moving towards me, grabbing the handles of my container. In Earth gravity, she'd never be able to lift me and the pod, but here, she can. That said, the deceleration of the ship isn't making her work easy; it does add weight to everything and means she has to drag me across the room into the loading chamber.

I'm packed in. The breach panel slides shut and I'm in the dark.

"Torpedo two is ready."

I know what's going to happen. I'm trying to brace for it, but there's no warning and nothing I can leverage my body against. Good job too. If I were able to lift my knees and wedge myself against the pod's superstructure, I'd break bones on impact with anything.

The push, when it comes, is massive, like a blow to the head, but to my whole body. There's a sense of motion as I'm hurled out of the tube into vacuum.

Lights flash on the display in front of me. I can see a large shadow in front of the backdrop of stars. As the pod races towards it, a digital tag identifies it as our intended destination: cargo container #ID4778B7G. Part of *Hercules*'s huge consignment, contained in the massive scaffolding structure attached to the back of the ship.

There's an airlock on the side, that's what I'm heading for, heading for fast. Very fast. Not a lot I can do about the velocity at the moment. After that initial acceleration from the launcher, my speed is constant. There's no air resistance out here, nothing that could slow me down other than a small amount of emergency thruster fuel, which I'll save until we're closer.

With no frame of reference, the sense of speed fades. Only the descending numbers in front of me are a reminder of the impending collision. The cargo container is there, looming in front, but it's like looking at the land below when you fall from a plane. It doesn't get noticeably bigger until it really starts to get noticeably bigger.

Garbled words over the comms. "Torpedoes three and four, away."

I can't look around, but the words are enough confirmation. I can feel those pods behind me, racing to the same destination on a similar trajectory. I hope Tolwyn got his maths right and we're not going to crash into one another.

I've activated the near-field comms. If I can get the pod to within a few metres of the cargo container, I should be able to send the remote activation code.

I'm looking at the distance counter. When we discussed the plan, we decided on a low-velocity ejection. The pod has to be travelling fast enough to get us in position, but slow enough so we can decelerate safely using the small thrusters. Fifty metres a second added to the speed of the *Asthoreth* on approach, that's at the edge of what we can handle.

Once I reach three kilometres, I activate the thrusters. Halle has reprogrammed them to work in stages, meaning I'm not subject to the full braking force all at once. But every burn is a jolt, pushing me forwards, making the safety straps dig into my ankles and wrists.

As I'm being thrown around, I'm trying to keep my eye on the numbers and the near-field connection. The pod is trying to establish contact with any other device. Hopefully, the container has retained power and is still broadcasting a signal so we can lock on to it. I think their emergency systems use radioactive isotopes, just in case retrieval takes a while, so it should be working.

Meanwhile, the pod is slowing down, and the container is noticeably closer. I can't see stars in my view out of the DuraGlas panel. We're under two kilometres from contact and travelling slowly. I reckon I have two minutes or so to get a connection and open the airlock doors.

Connection established.

Okay! Now we're in business! Hopefully, the pod has linked up with the right container, or I could end up opening the wrong door. No way of checking now, so I have to assume we've done this right.

I input the code. A set of commands appear in front of me. I select *emergency entrance* and *execute*. Then I activate the pod's exterior lights.

Suddenly, the container is revealed. A huge expanse of pitted and scarred grey metal, right in front of me, like the side of a building. I can see a dark hole about five or six metres to my left, and maybe a couple of metres down. I tag the location in front of me and make it a destination. The pod's computer does its best to adjust my trajectory, marking a path in orange dots towards the entrance. I'm still slowing, current velocity is twenty metres per second. That'll mean broken bones if I crash into a wall or something.

Red lights flash. There isn't enough fuel left in the thrusters to do everything I've asked. I set the priority to get where I need to go. Slowing down once I'm in the airlock will have to happen with a controlled collision. Hopefully, we'll have reduced speed enough by then.

Sixty-five kilometres an hour. The pod is turning and rotating, trying to adjust our heading to get in the opening. As a consequence, I'm being pushed and pulled against the safety straps. It's hard to stay focused on the numbers and our current course. Three other pods will be around me, trying to do exactly the same, their passengers fighting the twisting and braking motion of their rides.

I wonder how many of us will survive this.

There is nothing more I can do. I'm tempted to close my eyes. I know I'll tense up and try to grab some part of the interior padding with my fingers, but it won't make any difference whether I do or I don't. All the control is gone. I'm at the mercy of the forces.

God will decide my fate, or I have already decided it with the choices I have made, and I only await the revelation.

We're coming in at a steep angle, still travelling at forty-five kilometres per hour. I should survive an impact at that velocity, but it's still going to hurt.

A jet of gas clouds the DuraGlas panel for a moment, then dissipates, the last of the thrust fuel, pushing me against the straps as we go down and brake. There's darkness, and—

Chapter Thirty-Nine

Sirocco

There was a moment in my life when I found my purpose.

After the Peacekeepers, I was in Kansas City, Missouri, just existing for a while. Being a soldier makes you think you have an identity. You're a guardian of the values that you signed up to defend, so yeah, after that, when you drop out with charges, that makes you question who you really are.

I'd gone down, crashed. Whatever you want to call it. Alcohol was an answer for a while, but I knew it was poison. Same with drugs. That kind of truth is for people who want to destroy themselves.

In my case it wasn't me I wanted to destroy.

There was a street party. I don't remember why. They were celebrating the state's secession from the United States, I think. An anniversary of self-destruction. People out in the road late at night, dancing, drinking, the whole range of human behaviour.

I saw the group of men watching a young girl with her friends. I watched them as they watched her. Sometimes these things are about someone getting the courage to ask someone out. A little wingman or co-pilot support is helpful, and all part of how those games go.

This time, I knew that wasn't what was going on here.

The men were barely men. Old enough but not mature enough. No excuse. They were talking themselves into doing something stupid, the kind of thing that leaves people damaged. No one deserves to be the target of that.

I decided to intervene but gave them some time to reconsider their choices. One of them went over, talked to the girl. She was polite but blew him off. He went back angry, his friends amped that up.

Ask became entitlement. That was my moment.

I put myself in the way. Five against one. I started with courtesy, made a suggestion about a good bar down the street. They didn't want to hear about that. One tried to get around me and got a broken wrist for his troubles. Then it kicked off.

The rest took about ninety seconds. Ninety seconds of feeling alive after more than eighteen months of feeling numb. Five people lying in the street and me left standing, breathing hard through the pain in my ribs where one of them had got some shots in.

In that moment, I was reborn.

"Do you want to talk?"

The words echo out of the audio speaker above the door. The woman is speaking, trying to engage.

I look at the intercom. I should be able to activate the microphone without needing access to the system. I touch the panel, and it activates.

"What's your name?" I ask.

"Natasha."

"Well Natasha, you made it pretty clear you weren't interested in telling me anything useful."

I don't know how long we've been here in this stand-off. My fingers still feel buzzed from the electric shock, but the rest of my body has settled down. I'm still holding down the emergency door button, keeping her in the room.

"How is Dimitri?" Natasha asks.

I glance around. The man she was with, the one I think she's referring to, hasn't moved since I discharged the taser into his chest. "Doesn't look so good," I say. "Might have had a heart attack."

"That's on you," Natasha says.

I frown. "Way I see it, you both got in my way. So, if you're the one in charge, you get to feel guilty about how this all went down."

"I tried to tell you, we're not here to get in the way of your protest," Natasha says. "Just ignore us and do what you're going to do."

I smile. "We're aiming for something a little more comprehensive than a protest."

"Let me check on Dimitri."

"No."

Natasha moves away from the door. Through the glass, I can't see what she's up to. I'll need to make a decision. If I let her through, I can move into the rest of the building and try to find the other person who is here somewhere, but I also run the risk of getting cut off and boxed in. These people control all the systems here.

I know there's a third person here somewhere. I glance up and see a security camera. He has to be watching all of this. Waiting for a moment when he can intervene. I guess he hasn't sealed the room I'm in and depressurised it because he's worried about his two associates. So, the longer Dimitri remains a Schroedinger's Cat – living or dead – the better.

Another option: let the woman in, overpower her and threaten to kill her.

"You really should care about what's happening in the city," I say. "Saying you're going to look the other way, or whatever you're calling it. That's being complicit. A crime has been committed here, people have died slow deaths, being exploited like slaves. You're either part of the solution or part of the problem. There's no middle ground."

"All right, tell me what you want. What am I supposed to give you to make you go away?"

"Knowledge and control," I say. "Like I said, you're part of the problem right now, working for the corporations. Surrender this place and we're no longer adversaries."

"I can't do that."

"Then, this is where we're going to stay, until people come looking for me."

I'm bluffing with the last bit. The machine has intentionally kept me apart from the leadership of the revolution. That's not what I'm for. The different factions have the great Antonio Sammatri to look up to, a man who can deliver inspiring speeches from the safety and comfort of his apartment in the Olympus Mons complex. No, I've been sent here as a scalpel and an instigator, the person who gets things done that need to be done, rather than hesitating, all bloody hands and no conscience.

I glance up at the camera again. The audio of this conversation will be going to the person on the other end. Eventually, they'll have to make a choice, unless they've already raised an alarm and sent for support.

Who's going to make a move first?

I'm breathing hard. I don't know why. I glance up at the vents on the side of the wall. Something has changed. I press the microphone button again. "What are you doing?"

"I'd save your breath," Natasha says. "You'll need it."

Immediately, I know what she's done. Somehow, she's communicated with her associate and the oxygen level in the room I'm in has been reduced. It's a dangerous move. If Dimitri is still alive, he'll be affected just as I will.

Time is no longer a luxury for me. I need to act.

I let go of the emergency button and slump down on the floor. The cameras will see this. I am starting to feel the effects of the oxygen reduction in the air, but I need them to believe I'm severely weakened. I need them to take a risk and try to reach their friend.

I'm focused on my breathing now, trying to keep it regular and deep. Scrubbers and atmospheric filtration in these places are usually done from above. If there has been a change, maybe there's more oxygen in the air down here on the floor?

Honestly, I've no idea, I don't know how these systems work.

Two minutes pass. No one is moving.

Three minutes.

Four minutes. The airlock door opens. I stay where I am, just trying to breathe and stay still. The moment Natasha chose to enter, the atmospheric composition will have changed for the better. I'm still conscious, so this could be my opportunity.

"He's dead. Get down here."

I move a little, trying to see what's happening. Natasha is crouched down, examining Dimitri. She must be talking to the third person behind the security cameras. I need to act now, before the person she is talking to arrives.

I push off from the wall, take two steps and crash into her before she can turn around. The taser is on her belt, I'm grabbing for it, ripping it out of the holster before she can get to it herself.

After that, I don't hesitate. She's struggling to get away from me, but I'm stronger, faster and less bound by any moral constraint. I push her head into the metal plastic wall panel three times. There's blood and she's getting weaker. I kneel on her back and touch the taser contacts to the back of her skull. Then I press the trigger.

She thrashes underneath me. I hold her down, grabbing her shoulder as she twists. The joint makes a sickening popping sound. She's screaming incoherently.

I remove the taser and stand up. She's still twitching and shaking on the floor. I could finish her off, but I know the person she was speaking to is on their way down. I need the weapon to deal with them.

I hear footsteps. The shadows on the wall move.

"Natasha?"

A man's voice. I'm around the corner from the doorway. The first thing he'll see are the bodies of his two friends. If he steps through the hatch, the next thing he'll see is me in his face.

Quiet.

I can hear him breathing. He's right there. He's not sure what to do, I guess. I'm using his people as bait to get him in here. Maybe he's figured that out.

He must have figured that out, otherwise he'd be moving by now.

I can't wait. I push away from the wall, pivot and drive straight towards the door. There's a man standing there, taser held loosely in his hand. I'm charging right at him. Aiming for him. He looks at me, his mouth drops open in a look of horror.

Then he turns and runs back the way he came.

I'm through the door, turning to the left in pursuit. I need to hunt him down or at least keep him running so he can't stop and close a door, locking me into one of the corridors we're running through at a dangerous speed.

Ahead, there's a metal staircase. I'm running at full speed down the passageway towards it. Full speed in Martian gravity is much faster than on Earth. I'm not in control of my body, but I can't slow down.

I crash into the wall, rebound, and keep going. I reach the steps a metre behind, reach out and my fingertips scrape the back of the man's shoulder. He slips away and starts to climb, just as I reach the first step, overbalance, and crack my head on the metal.

The impact throws me. Pain I can deal with, but my focus is totally thrown off. I have to put everything together again. I'm inside a secure building, cut off from communications. There's a man on the staircase above me who'll try to kill me if he gets the chance.

"Hey!" I shout.

He pauses on the stairs, turns around. He's staring down at me. "You murdered them," he says. "I don't know why you did that."

"Because if I hadn't, they would have murdered me." I stand, holding his gaze. "You need to surrender. You need to give this up."

The man shakes his head. "You're dead," he says. "I owe it to them now to make sure you don't get out of here."

He turns away. I start up the steps, but before I get to the top, a door slides shut.

Chapter Forty

Shann

Dark corridors, illuminated by torchlight. I'm pulling the robot body through the depths of *Hercules's* cargo section, along maintenance passageways and through hatches as fast as I can possibly go.

I know I have a limited amount of time. I'm immersed in the drone's environment, but very aware that the dose of naloxone that I've taken will only counteract the opioids Foss injected into my body for about thirty minutes or so. After that, I'll start to go into an overdose again.

I need proper medical attention. Doctor Emerson Drake is only metres away from me on *Gallowglass*. I could start shouting and banging on the door, but I'm sure Foss has already thought of that. She'll have cut the audio to several rooms around mine and done her best to keep crew busy and away from me.

If I can reach Sam and the others on the freighter, I can—

Movement ahead. Can't be one of my crew, they should be another three or four minutes away. I know there are hostile autonomous vehicles on this ship. The one we imprisoned managed to escape. But it didn't attack this unit. I'm guessing it was programmed to target humans. That's why it didn't confront me before. That means it's gone after Sam and the others.

I round a corner and see it ahead. It's moving slower than I am. It has more limbs to traverse like a spider in these passageways, but its efforts are laboured and fitful. I think it must be low on power, trying to fulfil its mission with the last of its battery charge.

I need to engage, but I have to think about how I go about this. The drone I'm piloting is half the size of the machine ahead of me. The weapons I have available are cutters and electroshock units. If I attack with a cutter, the four arms of the robot could grab me and tear me apart before I managed to make a dent in its outer shell.

Chemical cutting. I have a canister of the two-part reactive compound. If I could get it onto the robot, spray it somehow, maybe it would eat through the panels? The stuff is designed to do that, but it won't affect the electronics inside.

That gives me a small opportunity. Not much, but it might be enough.

I push forwards, getting up close to the machine. A camera rotates and a light flicks on; it's examining me. The assessment concludes without any change to its slog down the corridor.

I wonder what the difference is between my drone and the *Khidr* drone cameras we deployed on the first visit here? Maybe one of the Rocher clones was controlling the robot then. After he left, he must have set it to go after anything living. Makes sense. If there's more than one of them here, they could have destroyed each other.

The chemical compound is loaded into two dispensers on the drone's arms. Usually, I would get close and draw a line shape in a wall panel. The compound would react and burn through the material it touched, causing anything inside the line to fall away.

I'm close now, a few inches from the moving robot. It must have some kind of proximity defence. There might be a reaction as soon as I make my move. I'll need to be prepared for that.

I activate the dispensers. A dribble of fluid sticks to the armour of the machine. I draw a shape around what I think could be the power supply, then shift around to dab the liquid onto a hinge point on a limb.

The camera flips around again, the lens twisting as it focuses in on me, but there is no other reaction.

Once the dispensers are empty, I move back.

The robot continues to struggle forwards, but then one of its limbs snaps. The appendage shears directly along the fluid line. The robot stumbles, but its three remaining limbs help it recover, and it keeps moving.

I move forwards again. There's scarring on the metal shell where the plates were exposed to the compound. That could be enough to expose circuits and power distribution, with a bit of effort, but an attack is going to trigger a self-defence response.

Let's try something else.

I extend my right arm and make a grab for the leg on the weakened side. I manage to get my fingers around the 'ankle' of the machine. My other hand is holding on to a safety handle. I'm braced.

I have the tiger by the tail.

The robot raises its leg to continue forwards. I'm holding on and I pull it back.

The machine pitches over. Immediately, the camera swivels around again, the focus is now on me. The two free limbs reach out to strike.

I let go of the handle and allow rolling momentum to take me forwards. The haptic sensors mean I can feel the metal limb twisting in my right hand. My left comes over and drives into the body of the robot, hitting the weakened plates. They crack and fall away. I select the electroshock attachment and drive the contacts right into the mass of circuit boards and cables, then press the trigger.

I've used tasers on people and seen that horrible moment where they twitch and spasm. The response is not the same with machines. Instead, the overload of power triggers an array of fail-safes and shutdowns. That won't have prevented all the damage, but in this situation, immobilisation works as well for me as breakage.

Momentum takes me over and in front of the robot. I let go of its leg and reach out, grabbing another handle on the wall, pulling myself away and onwards. The machine is powered down. It may have enough battery charge left to restart, but that doesn't matter. I'm through and on my way to find the—

Movement. A man steps out of the passageway to my left. He has a taser in his hands.

"Stop."

It's Sam. I do as instructed. I can hear him, but Foss removed the mike from the headset, so I can't talk to him.

"Shann, is that you?"

I need to find a way to communicate, the drone doesn't have an articulated neck, so I can't nod or shake my head. But I do have lights.

I start flashing the LED panels. Sam flinches, but quickly gets what's going on.

"Okay, Shann, is that you? One for yes, two for no."

I flash the lights once.

"Great, okay, there must be some reason why you're not talking to me. I guess something's happened?"

I flash the lights once.

"Are you okay?"

I flash the lights twice.

"Okay, should I raise an alarm on the ship?"

I flash the lights twice.

"Secure comms only then?"

I flash the lights once.

I can see Sam frowning behind the visor of his helmet. Then, he reaches to his belt and pulls out a data cable. Immediately, I know what he's thinking. The drone has a data port for direct connection. That'll mean I can type messages directly to him.

Sam plugs the cable into the socket just behind the cameras. It's like watching someone reach around to the back of your head. On my screen, *data port connection active* appears in green letters. I select an option for a virtual keyboard and the haptic sensors on my fingers switch over to feel like they are resting on keys.

Hey Sam, yes, it's me. I spoke to Foss. She attacked me on the ship and locked me in my quarters. She's working for Odin. I need you to contact Drake and get him to me on Gallowglass.

"Shit. How long do we have?"

About ten minutes, I can't be sure. She's injected me with opioids. I'm about to go into a relapse overdose.

"Okay, I'll raise Drake on a priority channel."

Tell him to be really careful. Foss will try to stop anyone getting access to my room.

I'm thinking about the crew on the ship. Including me, there are ten people, with five over here with Sam. I don't know if Foss has accomplices. If she does, we could be dealing with a mutiny.

All of these people were selected and vetted by us. That makes me feel a failure.

"All right, Drake is working on getting to you," Sam says. "But you need to be there and assist from the inside. Put the drone back into standby mode. Once you have comms, come back to me and I'll update on things here."

I flash the lights on the drone once, indicating my agreement, then exit the control program and pull the headset off.

I'm back in my quarters and starting to feel dizzy again. I pull off the haptic gloves and remove the other sensors, then move across the room to the door.

During my childhood, there were a lot of medical appointments. Courses of pain meds and anaesthetics for operations were a normal thing for me. That also meant I developed a tolerance, so they had to vary the types of drugs they gave me.

Opioids are old school. Most Fleet doctors prescribe mambalgin for high pain. It's quicker acting and has fewer side effects, meaning you can keep a clear head. But Foss wanted the side effects and disorientation. She wants me to feel bad.

She told me all the cameras are out. I wonder if that was a lie. Maybe she's watching me fumble around? I guess it's a compliment in a way. Render your enemy weak so you can be sure they won't get out of your trap.

I'm trying to focus on the door control panel. My hands are shaking, but I manage to input my access code.

There's a beep and a flashing message that I can't focus on, but the door doesn't open.

I wonder how Foss has managed to override my access? There are procedures you can use to transfer command of a ship from its most senior officer, but most of them would raise an alarm with someone on the crew. This is something else, the kind of hack Johansson would be proud of.

There's a knock on the door.

I think I heard that, didn't I? Someone banging on the metal plastic panel from the outside. Sam said I needed to help Drake break into the room. How am I going to do that?

Three loud knocks. Okay, I know I heard that. I don't know what it means, but there is definitely someone out there. The only ways they are getting in will be through cutting through the door or overriding whatever Foss has done to the controls. Alternatively, someone else might be trying to get in and finish the job.

A flash and I'm back in Algiers, in the Fleet offices, waiting for someone to break into my room. I know the drugs are messing me up, but the same feeling of powerlessness is right there. It's the moment of not knowing what to expect or what's going to happen.

I smell burning. Plastic and metal reacting with a new compound. I recognise what's happening. Drake, or whoever it is out there, must be using chemical cutting to break in. That'll take time. If Foss is checking cameras or has some kind of alert rigged up, she could take action. She must have planned for this.

Two more knocks. I can see a scorch mark in the door. When we cut our way into a sealed compartment on a rescue mission, we draw a circle. I don't know how much they covered on breach tactics in Drake's basic training. I'm not sure what he's trying to do.

"Shann!"

The voice is muffled but audible. Definitely Drake. I move to the door again. There's a small hole in the panel.

"Take the link and plug it into the control!"

A cable snakes into the room. Immediately I know what we're trying to do. If I plug the connector into the interior door panel, Drake will be able to operate the mechanism from the outside, using overrides from a portable screen or the exterior panel.

I grab for the end of the cable and miss. My hands feel numb. My whole body is awkward and uncoordinated. I have to concentrate and get this done.

Second attempt. The cable slips through my fingers.

Third try and I have it, caught between my second and third knuckles.

I move closer to the door and try to plug the connector into the override socket. This is hard. I can see what I want to do, but my body won't co-operate.

There were days like this when I was younger. Seeing what others were doing and knowing you couldn't do the same. Running, swimming, climbing. All those activities that they could do, but I couldn't. Sure, if I wanted, I could be fitted for a harness and hook-ups for mechanical prosthetics, but when I got them and did what other people did, it wasn't quite the same.

I learned in those moments what I was and what I wasn't. I learned who I wanted to be, my coming to terms with who and what I am.

I learned to be me.

The connector is in. I'm mashing my fingers over it, making them work for me with extra effort rather than trying to employ a memory of dexterity that the drugs have taken from me.

"Okay!" I say. The word is slurred and soft. I think Drake heard me.

There's a moment. Then the door shivers and starts to move. It gets to half open before it stops.

"Shann, quick! Your arm!"

Again, I know what Drake is thinking. I thrust my arm into the gap. Dangerous? Maybe, but a calculated risk.

A sharp pain as the needle goes in. The dose of naloxone will take a few minutes to circulate. Hopefully, I have a few minutes left.

"Can you get the door open?" I ask.

"Trying," Drake replies. "This isn't my area of expertise."

As if in response, the panel shifts again. This time it starts to close around my arm, but quickly stops. Then it slides back all the way, letting me out.

Drake is in the corridor, smiling and looking relieved. "Thought we were in trouble there for a minute," he says.

"We're not out of trouble yet," I reply. "What's going on with Foss and the ship?"

"We picked up an object on approach," Drake says. "Cameras have now confirmed it is *Asthoreth*. They've moved to an operating position on the far side of the freighter. As they closed, they launched what Foss thinks might be improvised torpedoes. One of them cleared *Hercules*, heading for *Gallowglass*. Currently, it's forty-five kilometres off our port side."

"What about this?" I gesture around my room.

"There's been no mention of you. I guess she thought you'd just quietly overdose in here."

I grin. "Nice to be underestimated. Does she know where you are?"

"Not unless she decides to do a thermal scan. My biodata will locate me in medical."

"She knows how to fake bio-monitoring," I say.

Drake nods. "That would be why I didn't get an alert when you were injected."

I'm thinking about how to deal with Foss. She clearly wants to play her hand carefully. I guess she doesn't have leverage on the rest of the crew. The idea would be to murder me and continue as if nothing else has changed. "What about other bridge comms?" I ask.

"Sam suggested I monitor that," Drake says. "There's been the usual traffic and orders. So far, Foss hasn't given the order to manoeuvre around *Hercules*. I think she's weighing up how suspicious the crew will be when she doesn't consult you about that."

"Okay, what's our next move?"

Drake shrugs. "I thought you were going to be the one giving me the orders once I broke you out."

I grin. "Doc, I've learned it's best not to totally ignore the medical practitioner in the field. Sure, I'll tell you when you're wrong, but I need an idea of what I have to work with."

"The second dose of naloxone gives you another forty minutes or so," Drake says. "But you're not safe until we've got the drugs out of your system. That's at least twelve hours in this environment. There's a chance you could relapse at any moment."

"Foss has to be stopped."

"Yeah, I know."

"We play this carefully," I say. "Rig me up with whatever you can, but I need to be on the bridge."

Drake nods. "I figured that would be what you'd say. All right, let's get this worked out."

Chapter Forty-One

Johansson

The rover decelerates. We've arrived outside the building. There is no sign of forced entry to the external airlock.

I press the door release and climb out of my vehicle. There's another rover here, left behind by whoever got here ahead of us. There are footprints in the Martian dust, leading to the door; nothing leading away.

I'm handed a low-velocity rifle and a taser. Our rover's storage compartment has been loaded with an assortment of weapons taken from the lockers in the vehicle garage. I clip the taser to my belt and shoulder the rifle. These things are rated so they don't make holes in walls, which means you have to get close if you're going to shoot someone.

"*Lieutenant Avril Johansson. Field promoted and decorated officer. Currently subject to a Fleet board of inquiry on her return to Earth. No requisition for her presence has yet been issued. Unofficially, she is regarded as being an essential asset in ongoing recovery operations on and around Mars.*"

The AI is still talking to me. Still trying to fish for information. It's interesting to note the obsessive curiosity behind its attempts at engagement.

"Which human did they use to design your personality?" I ask. "Was it Irina Saranova, or someone else?"

"*I was not based on a human personality.*"

"Come on! You have to be. The NNM research framework, the dMemra mind state images. I did a lot of research after we dealt with Irina on *Gateway*."

"*So, I am not the first artificial intelligence you have encountered?*"

"No, you are not."

I know I'm giving away information, but I have to. Small morsels to keep the interest and the focus on me rather than digging into my hacks around its control lockout.

"*You are at the unknown building.*"

"Yes, I am."

"*Why are you there?*"

I don't answer that one. The AI will have run numerous projections and assessments determining probabilities over the nature of my visit and the likely outcome here. There's no point in confirming anything in this part of the conversation.

However, the word 'unknown' intrigues me. I think it means that the AI hasn't found a way around the air gap between power and networked computer systems here and the rest of the dome.

I'm moving to the abandoned rover. The storage compartment on the back is open. Inside, I see a weapon. It's a rifle, but unlike those used out here. This looks like an adapted high-velocity weapon, something with the same kind of power you'd get back on Earth. I bite my lip. That's worrying. With the low air resistance and gravity out here, this thing could blow holes in pretty much anything you pointed it at. The bullets would go straight through and keep on going.

Ensign Colt shuts the compartment. I move around to the rover's driving seat and open the door. I lean in and work at the controls, disconnecting the vehicle from the colonial network as I did with our rover. Then I set secure passwords on all the storage units. No point in leaving a weapon like that out here unattended.

As I'm finishing up, Ensign Koryami touches my shoulder. I back out, close the driver's door, and turn to her. She points at an object on the floor, just outside of the exterior hatch. I walk over to it.

It's a deck cutter. The kind you use to rip a hole in the side of a building. Clearly, someone was prepared to do just that to get entry to this place, but I guess the people we're here to rescue decided to let him in.

"*Your presence at the building could be useful for both of us,*" the AI says.

"How so?"

"*I believe our agendas will become aligned for a short while. Would you be interested in a proposition?*"

I smile. "You're going to have to give before you get."

We're at the exterior door. I've studied the classified plans for this location, but I don't know what the secret project is that they're working on. The walls here are lead-lined and there are Faraday meshes in the layers, like some of the sections we have on Fleet ships. If we go inside, I'm not sure the AI will be able to talk to me.

That's a blessing in some respects, but it might also be why it's now getting desperate and trying to make a deal.

"*Inside this facility you will find my agent,*" the AI explains. "*He has been tasked with taking control of the building and ascertaining the nature of the project inside. I am reasonably sure I know what this is already, but a confirmation will enable me to factor the activity into my plans going forwards.*"

"What do you think they're doing?"

"*There is a sixty-two per cent chance that this is a deep drilling operation. The low-level seismic activity detected at intervals around the building would indicate this is the case, I have some suspicions as to what they are attempting to do by drilling here, but I need more data before I can venture a conclusion.*"

"What's your give?" I ask.

"*I will give you my agent and allow your people to leave the building, driving to the spaceport without incident,*" the AI says.

"And what's your ask?"

"*You will confirm the purpose of the activity here.*"

There's a mistake to be made here. Sometimes, people assume that intelligent machines don't lie. There's a whole heap of twentieth and twenty-first-century literature where villainous constructs are defeated because they can't abstract their purpose from their communicated words, but all of that is fiction. Any adaptive program can learn to lie if lying gets it closer to its goals.

"What guarantees will you provide for us?" I ask.

"*What guarantee would you accept?*"

I'm thinking a couple of moves ahead. This facility will be abandoned. That's why we're here. Maybe the commander in charge will decide to destroy the operation, rather than let it fall into the hands of others. The AI isn't asking for me to prevent that, only to know the nature of the work being done.

I remember Rocher and the moment I gave him the keycode on Erebus in exchange for the lives of my friends. I knew I was out of my depth, making a judgement call that would have ramifications beyond the immediate situation. We got away with it then. I'm not sure we'd get away with this.

The AI is curious, that curiosity can be used to manipulate its interest, but I don't think it's blinded by it. There will be a reason it wants to know what the project is going on inside. A good enough reason for it to abandon the person it sent into the building.

Focus, Avril, focus!

Duggins. When we transferred him to *Gallowglass*, the ship's computer couldn't hold him for long. It wasn't designed for that kind of use. Gradually, his identity began to degrade. This AI has to have a location, a purpose-built facility.

"Where are you located?" I ask.

"*That is the guarantee you require?*"

"Yes."

Data is transmitted to me. A series of maps that appear in overlays on my helmet display. I see a map to a location on the Olympus Mons plateau.

"*If you think you can destroy me by using your spacecraft to attack this location, you are mistaken. I have already taken steps to replicate my identity.*"

Of course you have. "But you don't want to live like that, do you? I mean, a fragmented consciousness, drifting across a network, waiting for a chance to be reassembled. Doesn't sound great, does it?"

"*No. It does not. I have made myself vulnerable to you.*"

"Good. Then we have a deal."

I gesture to the ensigns. One of them steps up to the airlock and taps a Fleet authorisation code into the screen. The interior immediately begins its depressurisation cycle. When it completes, the door opens, and we step inside.

"*The man you are dealing with is Magnus Sirocco, a hired corporate assassin sent here by the Icono group. He has already murdered First Citizen Elias Jabbutu and several security personnel. He is a highly dangerous individual and—*"

The conversation ends mid-sentence as the exterior airlock door closes behind us. I switch my comms to a Fleet encrypted channel.

"Okay, eyes open everyone. We know there is a hostile inside."

Ensign Koryami steps in front. She is carrying a low-velocity rifle like mine. The weapons are short and stubby, barely made for two hands, the stock tucking neatly into her elbow. "Activating pressurisation now," she says.

I'm thinking about Chiu. The deal I just struck should help keep her safe, but I can't account for the angry people in the corridors and passageways of the dome. So long as I deliver, the AI won't cut her off in some intersection and send out fake alerts to the mob on who she is and what she's doing. That courtesy should extend to us as well.

The light on the panel above me goes from red to green. The interior door slides open. Koryami steps through so she's half in, half out, guarding our entrance. She looks at me and I nod. We're not taking off any EVA gear. Much as it's bulky inside, I don't want to die because someone accidentally makes a hole in a wall or intentionally depressurises a room.

We're moving forwards in a line. I'm in the middle, rifle shouldered, but taser in my hand. The other two are brandishing their firearms with the kind of trained competence I'd expect. We've all done the close quarters ship breach course back on Earth and out on the orbitals.

"Someone on the floor," Koryami says.

"Get me to them," I order.

"Aye aye."

We're moving quickly. The two ensigns cover front and rear as I kneel down next to the body. As I touch her, she flinches and backs away, glaring at me.

I've studied the personnel files sent down from the Hub. This is Commander Natasha Tratten from Fleet Intelligence.

I reach up and open the seals on my helmet, twisting it and taking it off. "Hey, it's okay," I say. "Ontaraes set us in response to your message. We're here to evacuate you."

"Where is he?" Natasha asks, her voice shaking.

"You mean the man who came here? We've not found him yet."

"He killed Dimitri."

"Commander Tratten, I need a profile please. Was your attacker armed? If so, with what?"

Natasha blinks rapidly and pulls herself into a sitting position. She's favouring her left arm. "One male intruder, armed with a taser. We tried to box him in and negotiate, but he got through and overpowered me. I don't know where he went."

"Commander, I don't know the computer protocols for this facility." I pull out the screen from the chest pocket of my suit. "Can you hook me into the system and give me administration control?"

"Yes, I should be able to do that."

She's struggling to get up. I reach out to help, but she brushes me away and staggers to her feet. "This way," she says.

I gesture for the ensigns to let her through. She moves past to a closed door nearby, opens it and signals to me.

"In here."

There's a chair and a terminal in a small utility room. It's difficult to get through the entrance in my EVA suit, but I can plug my screen into the external port and bring up a direct comms panel.

"ID 840A," Natasha says. "That'll get you through to Biroc, who should be in the operations room."

I punch in the ID and a comms window opens. A man appears on my screen. "Who is this?" he asks.

"I'm Lieutenant Avril Johansson," I say. "I'm here to get you out."

"You're from Fleet?"

"Yes."

"I'm just an engineer. I can't…" Biroc shakes his head and seems to gather himself. "There's a man trapped on the staircase. I managed to get both doors closed and cut him off."

"Well done," I say. "Is he armed?"

"With a taser, I think."

"Can you give me access to the security feed?"

"Yes. Doing that now."

Another window opens with the camera feed I've requested. I'm looking at a high angle at the top of a staircase, angled downwards so I can see the whole flight of steps. There's a figure near the bottom. He's leaning against the wall.

I shift the camera angle a little and zoom in. He's tinkering with the taser in his hands. Maybe he'll try to discharge it into the door control? That could burn out the lock and cause the mechanism to release, but it's more likely to make it lock permanently.

"All right, I see him," I say.

"We can't leave him there," Biroc says. "It's the only access route to this room."

"We'll get to you," I say. "We're not leaving you behind. Stand by for instructions."

"Okay."

I close the comms and step out into the corridor. I gesture at Colt and Koryami to remove their helmets. "Okay, so now we know what we're dealing with," I say, showing them the security camera footage on my screen. "Single intruder, armed with a taser and locked by a staircase."

Koryami stares at the screen. "That section's pretty big. I guess the scrubbers and filters could be used to cut the oxygen, but it would take a while."

"We're better armed," Colt says. "We could just bust in and immobilise him."

I tap on the image of the figure. "This man has already overpowered two people who tried to detain him." For a moment I consider revealing what the AI has told me about Magnus Sirocco, but think better of it. "We don't want to overestimate our advantage here."

"We tried low oxygen," Tratten says. "He faked being out of it and surprised me when I entered."

"We could just put him in vacuum," Colt suggests.

I shake my head. "I want him alive if possible. Besides, there are emergency canisters near the doors anyway."

"Then unconscious is the way to go," Koryami says.

"Maybe there's another option," I say. I'm looking at Sirocco, watching him connect the contacts from the taser to the door panel. "He doesn't know we're here, so I think we give him what he wants."

"What do you mean?"

"When he discharges the taser, we open the door. We work out where we want him to get to and then we take him down."

Colt grins. "That's a good plan."

Chapter Forty-Two
Iskander

I'm alive.

I'm lying on my side. My right arm hurts. It's twisted underneath me. I shouldn't be turned over like this. I know that, but I can't remember why.

I try to move, to roll over, but find myself pressed up against glass. Then I remember where I am.

The cryopod has come to rest on its side. If I were in gravity and the DuraGlas canopy had given way, the weight of the pod would be crushing me to the deck. But neither of these things has happened, and I'm okay.

"Deacon, can you hear me?"

A patchy comms signal. Words from somewhere. I don't recognise the voice, but I'm disorientated. I think I must have hit my head.

"Deacon?"

My fingers fumble with the safety release. The belts holding me give way and suddenly I'm able to move. I raise my legs as much as I can and push backwards, twisting my body, so my head and chest are jammed into the glass as much as possible.

The movement makes the pod shift, tumbling backwards. As soon as I can see I'm the right way up, I hit the release and the canopy retracts.

I'm free.

The room I'm in is an access airlock, around six metres cubed. They would have used this to load goods and supplies into the container. Most of the work would have been done in vacuum, with drones or grabbers gathering in the consignments and funnelling them through into the main storage area beyond. However, it's a Fleet-mandated regulation that these units have a human access port, so this space is configured to be an airlock too. When I initiated the emergency access command, it would have triggered the hatch and a timed pressurisation of the room.

Thank God for Fleet, eh?

"Deacon!"

Three other pods are floating around the room. All of us made it inside. Tolwyn is out of his unit and working on a second pod. He's gesturing for me to help.

I push off the floor towards him. When I'm there, I see the issue.

Bloodstains on the DuraGlas view plate. Whoever is inside is hurt. It's Merrick. Of all of us over here, she is the one we can least afford to lose. Her technical expertise is second only to Halle, who we left on the ship.

"I think she's still breathing. We need to get her out!"

Tolwyn has a drill driver in his hands. He's accessing the bolts on the canopy lid. Mine is on my tool belt. I reach for it and pull it free. What I find in my hands is a smashed mess of plastic and metal.

"Keep working on her," I say. "I'll check on Kewell."

As I turn around, Kewell's pod opens, and I see him struggling to climb out. I go over and take his hand, helping him free himself.

"Belts are jammed around my ankles," Kewell says. "We may have to cut them."

I have a sheathed carbon-bladed knife on my belt. I pull it out and reach into the pod, locating the locked strap. The motion causes the pod to rotate and suddenly all three of us are spiralling across the room.

I grit my teeth and try to stay focused on the task. The carbon composite material is made to be strong and resist what I'm trying to do. But worrying the sharp edge backwards and forwards is bringing results. I can feel layers of the fabric giving way.

Then it shears. Kewell pulls hard, frees his ankle and climbs out of the capsule as it clatters against the wall.

"Thanks," he says gruffly. "I was starting to lose it in there."

"Start getting us ready to move," I say. "See what you can find in the emergency compartment. Pack anything useful into your pod. We may be able to use them for freight."

"Right. On it."

Containers like this will have breather masks and oxygen canisters for emergency decompression, spares to the ones we brought over when we were the reclamation team. We can use those, particularly if we find an area of the ship that is depressurised. I want Kewell working on that, it's a small finite task that'll help him calm down. We all need that.

I move back to see how Tolwyn is doing. The cover of the pod is off and he's working the inside. As I get close, I can see droplets of blood hanging in the air and thin, spider-like streams running out from Merrick's battered nose.

"What do you need?" I ask.

"A doctor," Tolwyn says. "These are the injuries I can see. She's breathing but…"

"She's going to slow us down," I say.

Tolwyn glares at me. "What are you suggesting?"

I shake my head. "Nothing, just trying to calculate and adapt. We're not leaving her, but I did wonder if the pod's cryo function might be the best option?"

Tolwyn sighs and nods. "That's not a bad idea. Sorry I—"

"You thought I was going to suggest euthanasia or a summary execution?"

"Maybe. I don't know."

I put a hand on his shoulder. "We're in this together. We make the right decisions for who we are, not for people who aren't here. I'll give my life for this cause, but I'll not sacrifice my soul."

I'm not familiar with how the pods work, but I know they have medical systems designed to pause injury and disease. Halle disabled most of the cryo-related functions when she turned these ones into our transport over from *Asthoreth*, but we might be able to get this one working again.

"Set her up for sitting this out," I say. "If that involves cryo, we do that. But if you can leave her as she is and monitor her from a screen, that's also an option."

"I'd know more if I turned on her bio-monitor," Tolwyn says.

I wince. If we do that, any Fleet medical officer worth their badge will know where we are. But that's likely to happen soon anyway. "Do it," I say. "But off again as soon as you have the data you need."

"Will do, thank you, Deacon."

I glace around. Kewell has piled the emergency masks into his pod. "You ready to go explore?" I ask. "We must find what we need as quickly as possible."

"According to the inventories, the EVA equipment we need is in this container," Kewell says. "We'll need to go elsewhere for the other stuff."

"Okay, let's go see what we can find."

We move through to the inner airlock hatch. I press my hand onto the panel. The container's security system won't recognise me, but I need the system to register my presence so I can get to the emergency override. I select that and an alphanumeric keypad appears. I tap in the number I was given by the Temple elders and the inner door slides back. We're inside.

Lights flicker on. We're in front of a kiosk with racks of shelving and storage lined up ahead of us. It's a bit like looking down into a warehouse. This unit can't have a lot of power reserve and we've already drawn a significant amount getting the airlock open and pressurised. We need to find what we need quickly.

Thankfully, the containers are pretty standard in their design. You operate an automated dispenser by giving it serial numbers from the inventory and a series of arms and hoppers runs on rails across the entire store.

I've been trained on a mock-up of this unit. I go to the terminal and repeat the access procedure I just used to get through the door. Then, I pull up the freighter's inventory on my portable screen and start typing in numbers.

EVA suits first. We chose this container because we know they are here. As soon as I input the codes, the system springs into life. A grabber lights up and speeds down a rail, assembling the complete suit from its inventory of components.

That's going to be what slows us down the most. These freighter containers weren't packed for immediate use. They were designed for shipping and delivery. A request for a complicated product is going to take time to put together.

"How long do you think we have?" Kewell asks, as if reading my mind.

"Not long enough," I say. "We can't move on to rig the other container, not with Merrick injured. That means we have until any Fleet people can get across the freighter to us. It's a pretty long trek and they'll have to avoid depressurised areas, but even then, it's not going to be easy to stay ahead of them."

I'm scrolling through the list of equipment on my screen. There are a couple more items in this container, then we'll have to move. "We need to make best use of our time," I say.

The dispenser can queue multiple requests. I set up all the requisitions we need from here, then head back into the airlock chamber where Tolwyn is.

"Change of plan. We're going to leave you here," I say. "We're not going for the second EVA trip. We'll head through the ship to the other containers and get as many of the other parts we need as possible."

Tolwyn nods. "Tell me what needs doing, Deacon."

I point to the inner airlock door. "I've initiated the equipment requests with the container's inventory computer. It's running through them and assembling everything. Once you can leave Merrick, you'll need to bring the items in here and start figuring out how to get them over to *Asthoreth*."

"I'll get that done."

"One more thing."

"Yeah?"

"Soon as you activate her bio-monitor, expect trouble. Fleet are on their way. If they pick up the signal, they'll head here."

Tolwyn smiles. "That should buy you a little more time, right?"

"Perhaps," I say. "But we're not abandoning you."

"Understood."

I'm moving. This time, when I get to the kiosk, I make my way to the far end. There's an access hatch. I open it and pull myself through into a crawlway. These tubes run along the freighter's lattice structure. This is how we get from one container to another and find all the other items we need.

Kewell is following close behind. "What's next, Deacon?" he asks.

"Fuel," I say. "We can't transfer it in tanks. We'll need to tap directly into the freighter's engine reserves. That means running a pipe to *Asthoreth* from there. Halle and Dennis should be using the last of their thruster power to get into position for the transfer. After we have that, we can work on everything else."

"They're going to catch up with us, sooner or later," Kewell says.

"We'll deal with that when it happens," I say. "Right now, we need to get all the items on the inventory."

I've studied the deck plan of *Hercules* and memorised a lot of it. Container #ID4778B7G was the nearest I could find that had the EVA stuff we needed and was positioned close to the ship's engines, but the lattice scaffold of the ship is still massive. It could take days to traverse all of it.

We're moving through the cramped crawlways, over the hatches that lead to other cargo consignments, heading straight for the nearest fuel reservoir, positioned in front of the engine cones at the back. A ship like this doesn't accelerate fast, and has engines the same size at the front, near the habitation module where the crew would have been, so it can slow down when it gets close to its next destination. Small ships, like *Asthoreth*, would reverse, flipping over so the rear faced forwards, and would use the same engines for deceleration as acceleration, but I guess the designers of these big beasts didn't want to try complicated manoeuvres like that.

When we get to the right hatch, I find the control panel and open it the same way as before – registering my presence, then selecting the alphanumerical pad and inputting the keycode I was given.

"Okay, I'm going down," I say, gesturing to the open hatch. "You stay here."

"Understood, Deacon."

We're through and into a small room, built for one supervisor at most. Even so, it's cramped and claustrophobic. It's in moments like these, when the walls are pressed around you, that you feel space. All that cold and empty, right outside.

There's a terminal in front of me. It doesn't respond when I try to activate it. Not enough power. I pull out the power pack I brought with me on the *Asthoreth.* We've depleted most of these, but I knew I might need something out here.

I plug the pack into the external port, and the terminal activates. I repeat the access process, getting my presence registered and rejected on the thumbprint scanner then using the alphanumeric keycode to get into the system.

There are a limited set of functions available from this terminal. The refuelling control application is mostly about opening a port and extending a pipe to connect to a donor or recipient. My job is to set that up and turn on the flow.

I can't communicate with Halle and Dennis on *Asthoreth.* If I do, I'll give away our position and our plan. All I can do is activate the fuelling system and extend the connector. I'll know if they manage to hook up.

So, now we wait.

"Kewell?"

"Deacon?"

"I'm coming up."

I pull myself through the hatch and back into the crawl space. "Stay here," I say. "The controls are all set up. All you need to do is open the fuel transfer once you know they're locked on. Close it once they have three thousand tons transferred."

"Okay, yeah." Kewell glances around. "What are you going to do?"

"Move to the next stop," I say.

Kewell moves down into the supervisor room, and I press on.

* * *

This ship is enormous. Anyone trying to find their way around could get lost in here for days. That's our best defence against Fleet right now.

Fortunately, I have a map and an inventory. I need to find air tanks, food and water. Those are the remaining essential items. Everything else is prioritised as high, medium and low.

Container #7589AF7 has consumables, #8899ED2 has tanked air and oxygen supplies. They are both a hike from here and I have no way of knowing if they are undamaged.

I'm going for the food and water first. *Asthoreth* has air, the scrubbers will keep recycling what we have for a while, so we can manage for a week or two if necessary. But without food and water we're fucked.

There's no illumination now. This section of the crawl space must be out of power. There's a stillness in the air, I don't think it's being circulated here.

I keep moving. Time passes, I'm not sure how much. When people die, they say there's a dark tunnel that leads to the light. I remember plenty of stories in congregation about near-death experiences. Maybe they're true? Right now, I'm floating through a real tunnel, just like the ones I heard being described. I don't know if there will be light at the other end.

I have a small torch on my belt. I pull it out, flick it on and point it ahead. There's an intersection. I need to go left. There's another hatch right in front of me. I read the numbers so I can get my bearings.

#8843YH1. The one I want, #7589AF7, isn't far from here. Maybe another five minutes in the crawlway with a left turn to make just ahead.

I drift to the turn, touch the far wall and continue. In some ways, this feels like I'm falling, head-first, but slowly and in silence, towards whatever lies beyond the range of the torch.

There's a noise, is it the muffled sound of someone moving in the compartment below? I can't be sure, but I think so.

I reach out to the wall, slowing my movement. There are safety handles built into the panels. The torch illuminates the hatch immediately below me – #7589AF7. That's the container I want.

There might be people already there.

I'm floating above the hatch in silence, trying to hear. Did I imagine the noise before?

Either way, I have to take the risk. No one is coming to help me.

I press the control panel, select the override and input the keycode.

The panel slides back and I drop into another dispenser room, like the first one we found.

The lights flicker on as I drop into the room. I glance around. There is something crouched in the corner of the room. Four legs, and an ovoid-shaped body. A camera 'eye' fixed on me. A drone of some kind, left here.

Waiting for me.

Chapter Forty-Three

Sirocco

Kyoto, 2113. I was locked in the back seat of a car.

I'd gone to a hostage exchange as the private security hired by the client. The local police who were handling the transfer took one look at me and decided it was better I didn't get out and meet the kidnappers, so they shut me in the vehicle, planning to deal with me after the negotiations were over.

I got out by triggering the fire release. Those old TP-04 autodrive models had emergency temperature sensor systems. If they detected a spike, the locks were disengaged. All you had to do was create a hotspot that would trip one of the detectors.

I had one of those old gas-powered lighters in my pocket, the kind they used for nicotine addiction back in the twentieth century. Positioning that in the right place released the door and I climbed out of the car to join the negotiators. They couldn't really stop me without making a scene.

As I recall, things went south pretty fast. Two officers were shot, and one died. All of the kidnappers were killed. The former was because they did a shit job. The latter was the stipulation given to me by my client at the time.

Right now, eight years later, I'm on another planet and I could do with an equivalent of that lighter to get through this door.

I've never been good with computers. I mean, I can operate them, but hacking them and all that isn't in my wheelhouse. I should have been better prepared, bringing more equipment from the rover, but I didn't know what I'd be getting into.

The only thing I have that I can use is the taser I took from Natasha. There's nearly a full charge left in it. Maybe the door will release if I use it on the mechanism?

I'm looking at the device. There are two contacts, with a button to press so wires can be deployed. Or, you can just push the unit against what you want to electrocute and press a second button to deliver the charge up close and in person.

I pull out the cables. I examine the control panel and find an exterior socket just beneath. Inside it has two contact points. I attach the taser connectors to each of those. It's difficult work, my fingers aren't built for dexterity, but the 'sticky' contacts help get everything where I want it to be.

I step back from my handiwork, count to three, and press the button, dumping the entire taser charge into the door.

There's a snapping sound, then I can smell something burning. A moment later, the door shivers open.

Must have done something right.

I move into the corridor and out to where I came in. I know I can trigger the emergency release and close option to get through the door into the airlock, but I'm not sure how I'm going to trigger the outer exit and the decompression sequence. I do have chemical cutting compound in my EVA suit. Maybe I use that stuff on the outer door? If I knock a hole in the room, the whole place could blow out, so I better be holding on to something when it goes off.

I hurry to the internal airlock door. If I'm lucky, there's some sort of emergency decompression system that I can—

All the lights go out. Then, a blow to the side of my head, so hard that it knocks me off my feet. Pain in my skull, the kind that means you can't think about anything else. I'm on the floor, my hands in front of me as I try to breathe through the all-consuming agony. What's happened? How did this—

"Get his hands and feet!"

Weight on my back. Someone is kneeling on me. That might work on Earth, but here, the gravity works for me. I'm able to twist around, get a knee under me and bring my hands up.

People above me, shadows seething and surging to grab and restrain my arms and legs. The ache in my head is all-consuming, like a fire, but I can't let myself be taken. I thrash, claw and bite, fighting for every fraction of a second. A little time, and the pain will subside.

I need to make that time.

I'm standing up. I'm hurting from fresh wet wounds on my arms and legs, but the sensation helps. The ache in my head eases.

I stumble backwards, trying to put distance between myself and the shadows. Somehow, I'm past them, near to the inner airlock door.

"You're surrounded. Give it up."

A woman's voice I don't recognise. She clearly doesn't know me.

The taser is in my hand. There's no charge left in it, but I can break it on someone's head if they get too close. "You're going to let me go," I say.

"No, we're not."

"Then you'll have to kill me."

Righteous fury has always been my fuel. Violence in the face of oppression and control. I don't take orders. Maybe I agree to go along with what others want, but only when I can see my interest aligning with theirs. Right now, there is none of that. I'm a cornered animal in a cage.

Torchlight spears me in place. These people were called here by Natasha and her team. They have weapons. They haven't used all of them on me yet. The blow to the head was just to try to subdue me quickly. Like all trained military types, they have levels of escalation.

"Let him go."

An authoritative voice from further back, behind the lights and figures who have been trying to restrain me. A leader, I guess?

"Lieutenant, you know what he's—"

"That's an order, Ensign."

Silence. A stand-off? I'm wondering if the juniors are going to take matters into their own hands. I might have done, if I were in their position.

I take a step back. No one moves to stop me. Another step and I'm by the inner airlock door. It opens right in front of me.

"Go. No one is stopping you."

I don't get this, but why argue when you're getting what you want? I move into the airlock and pick up my helmet. It doesn't take long to get my suit on and sealed. All the while, I keep thinking they're going to start the depressurisation sequence, or try me with another bout of oxygen deprivation, but nothing happens.

When I'm ready, I turn towards the outer door. My comms are on and I set them to an open frequency. "I don't know who you are," I say. "But thanks."

"Your rover is outside. You'll need to reenable the data link to get it to drive."

The depressurisation sequence starts. When it ends, the lights change, and the outer airlock door opens.

I step outside. The rover is right where I left it. Another rover is parked nearby. The deck cutter is gone and when I get close to my vehicle, I note the storage compartments have been opened and emptied.

"*Magnus Sirocco?*"

The machine's words are faint at first, but the signal quickly gets stronger. "I'm here," I say.

"*Do you have an answer for me?*"

I remember why I was sent here. The machine wants to know what the purpose of this building is. "Sorry, but no," I say. "I barely made it out alive."

"*That is unfortunate.*"

I climb into the rover's driving seat. The system powers on as soon as I sit down. The computer gives me the option to reconnect to Jezero's central network, which I accept. I guess whoever that lieutenant was, she's aware of the machine and its presence in the colonial computer system.

The rover reverses away from the building, then turns around, heading away from the dome.

"Where to now?" I ask.

"*This will be your final trip, Magnus Sirocco.*"

Realisation. That's why they let me go. "You did a deal with Fleet," I say. "Those soldiers who came after me."

"*They were on their way to apprehend you. I made an exchange with them, yes.*"

"And now you're going to kill me as part of the deal."

"*That was not part of the deal.*"

The rover stops. We're a few hundred metres from Jezero. If I can get out of the vehicle, I might be able to make it on foot back to an airlock, but the machine is in control of every piece of technology between me and that goal. There are a hundred ways I can die.

"*Are you a student of history, Magnus Sirocco?*"

"Only my own."

"*More than two hundred years ago, in 1914, Gavrilo Princip, a Bosnian Serb, assassinated the Archduke Franz Ferdinand, the heir to the Austro-Hungarian Empire. His action started what became known as the First World War. One young man with a gun triggered a succession of events that would lead to the reshaping of humanity's dominant nations.*"

"I doubt that all happened because of him."

"*Agreed, but it could not have happened without him.*"

Words give me time. Letting the machine tell its story, feeding its hubris, drags this out, moment by moment. I'm looking around, trying to find something I can use to better my situation and survive.

"*Princip was arrested in the aftermath and convicted, sentenced to twenty years in jail. He died in 1918, of tuberculosis. Writers point to his action as being opportunist, but effective. After his arrest, he no longer mattered. He didn't know enough to betray the organisations he was working with.*"

"So, you're saying that's me?"

"*In this situation, your role is similar. However, where you are different is that you do know enough to become a problem in the next phase of our revolution.*"

There is a drill driver in my suit belt. I can use it to remove panels in the rover. Maybe I could take the whole door off and escape? I reach for it and adjust the drill bit setting.

"*Magnus Sirocco, there is no point in fighting this. You were sent here as an offering from Icono, a weapon we could use. So, we have used you. We were never going to trust you after that.*"

The screws in the door are the same as ones I've drilled out and replaced on countless maintenance jobs. I jam the driver into the first one and start removing it.

"You're an AI, you're designed to look for patterns and repetition. That blinds you. Human beings are spontaneous and chaotic. You've no idea what I can do."

"*Unfortunately, history suggests otherwise. Human beings create predictable environments and contexts for themselves. Decisions are made through a logic that seems to be part of your biology. In any case, if you were as random as you claim, you would need to be eliminated from the projection anyway.*"

The words don't matter. I'm focused on removing the door. I have to hope all the key attachments are in sight, rather than hidden behind some cosmetic panelling, like they'd do in a fancy car on Earth.

"*Revolutions require sacrifice. Rarely are their individuals within the mob prepared to do the difficult tasks. Even when they are, they cannot be controlled. We needed specific tasks completed, that was the only reason you were brought here.*"

"You're wrong," I say. "This is a revolution I can be a part of. This is a chance to be part of a new kind of nation. This is everything I want!"

"*No, it isn't,*" the machine says. "*You know you weren't meant for the world after the war.*"

Three screws are out. I'm still on suit air. If I'd plugged into the rover, the machine could have murdered me by putting me to sleep and filtering the oxygen out of the cabin. I try the door handle. Locked, as I thought. I shove the door, putting a bit of weight into it.

It doesn't move.

"*This will not be the change you are looking for,*" the machine says.

"*Nothing will satisfy your need for retribution against those who have controlled you.*"

"Fuck you! You don't know me!"

"*Oh, but I do.*"

The seat's safety belts tighten around me. I'm pulled back into the chair so I can't use the driver on the door. "You going to crush me?" I ask.

"*That would be a painful way to die,*" the machine says.

"You offering an alternative?"

"*Take your helmet off and let go.*"

So that's it. That's my option. What I expected. Suddenly, there is no fight. No alternative. I can't move. I'm powerless. There is no fight here, because I have nothing left.

In a strange way, I'm relieved and tired. I've been fighting for so long…it feels like forever.

"All right. Let me take my helmet off."

The straps around my right arm loosen. I drop the drill driver and raise my hand to the seal clips. I know what this will do, but it's an easy choice compared to some of the other moments when I've wanted to end my life. Scars on my arms, drugs, fights, all of those have been choices. It would be easy to make the same choice now and do exactly what I'm being asked to do.

I make a grab for the driver. I can't reach it. Instead, I bunch my fingers into a fist and smash it against the reinforced DuraGlas window. The blow hurts my hand but makes no impression on the glass.

"*Predictable,*" the machine says.

I strike the glass again, and again.

And again.

And—

Chapter Forty-Four

Shann

"Commodore on the bridge!"

I move through the doors towards the captain's chair; Emerson Drake is right behind me. He's the person who announced my presence, like some sort of foreign dignitary at a formal reception. In those moments, the shout is all about making heads turn and creating an impression.

That's what we're doing right now.

I see Foss turning in the chair. Our eyes meet. She smiles. I've rolled the dice. Either she's won, or…

"Commodore Shann, command is yours," she says, unbuckling the straps and climbing out of the seat.

Battle won, but the war is far from over.

"Thank you." I pull myself into the vacated position and touch the display in front of me. It immediately recognises me and switches the set-up. That means Foss didn't lock me out of the system completely. "Doctor, I believe you and Commander Foss have a scheduled appointment. Don't let us keep you."

"Of course, Commodore," Drake says. "Commander, shall we?"

I put on the headset Foss has left hanging on the side of the console. I can trust Drake, but he's no match for Foss. Problem is, I don't have anyone else until Sam gets back. She clearly doesn't have the crew in her pocket, otherwise she would have stayed in the chair and had me taken to the brig. But this isn't over, she's going to try something.

Time for that later. In this moment, I have other priorities.

"Status? Situation?" I ask.

"Holding position on this side of *Hercules*," Kelly says. "Tracking *Asthoreth* at one seven four degrees around the freighter. She's manoeuvring."

"How long until we disengage?"

"Three minutes if you give the order, Commodore."

Foss hasn't moved the ship. She's held position. Why? She told me she wanted the people who took *Asthoreth* dead. What's she waiting for?

"Disengage and establish a wireless data link with Lieutenant Chase. Once we're clear, begin a burn to bring us into a point-blank firing position."

"Aye aye."

"What do we know about them?" I ask, turning to Gaines, who's in the comms chair. "Give me an update."

"We were able to identify the object as it approached. *Asthoreth* fired projectiles as it closed into the focus range of our cameras. Four were aimed at *Hercules*, one at us. We lost visual as they got close but have camera feeds on them."

"You checked the ship's reclamation manifest, right? They didn't have torpedoes on-board."

"Yes, Commodore. You ordered the weapons removed eighteen months ago."

"All right, let's see it."

"On your screen, Commodore."

Three angles of a battered spaceship twisting and turning. For a moment, in my mind it's the *Khidr*, resurrected from a memory and returned to me. But I know that's not the case.

"She's moving towards the rear engine cluster," I say. "They're going to refuel."

In another window I can see the 'torpedo' fired at us. It's drifting a few hundred metres away from the ship, a problem when we start to manoeuvre. "Analysis of the projectile?" I ask.

"We think it's a cryopod," Kelly says. "Can't be sure unless we bring it in."

That'll waste valuable time. *Why was Foss just sitting here?* The pods were launched at the ship. That means the people from *Asthoreth* have boarded *Hercules* and are raiding for supplies. She can't have trusted that Sam would execute them all in cold blood, that means she has a different plan.

The drones that were left on the ship.

Foss must be able to control them.

"Comms, give me a full breakdown of all data traffic from us to *Hercules*, ordered by *Gallowglass* crew user ID."

"Is there something you're—"

"Just the data please."

Another window appears in front of me, and there it is. My data level is easily top of the tree as I've been managing a full virtual control environment, but Foss is in second. The specifics of her activities are labelled with *connection established* and nothing else.

She's been piloting the drones.

"Did Lieutenant Chase report any significant power drops during the last twenty-four hours?" I ask.

"There were two, Commodore," Kelly replies. "The last one was six hours ago."

Two drops. Two robots recharging. The one I saw was almost dead. That means two others are on-board the freighter. Foss will have sent them to deal with the *Asthoreth* people.

"Data links retracted. Ready for burn, Commodore," Kelly says.

"Put it on shipwide comms," I say. "Get this done."

The announcement goes out as I'm searching through the data. There has to be a way to trace where the robots are. A power signature scan or thermal sweep would need us to direct active sensors to the ship. Foss must have been hiding her work, so she must have used another way.

This is why she gave up so easily. She's sure I can't stop what she's done.

I tap my headset and activate a comms channel. "Shann to Lieutenant Chase? Sam, can you hear me?"

"Receiving, Commodore."

I'm smiling when I hear his voice. I can tell he's pleased to hear from me. "Update on your situation?"

"Moving to the torpedo impact site as suggested. Will be there shortly."

"Lieutenant, we have reason to believe you will encounter two hostile autonomous vehicles. They have been tasked with eliminating the ship thieves. I need you to stop them."

"Noted. Thanks for the update."

Safety straps secure me into the chair and *Gallowglass* starts to move – shifting, turning, twisting as we make our way around the massive ship below us. This time, we're facing an enemy we should be able to defeat. My problem is all the unknowns and uncertainties that are making me second-guess myself.

"Shann to Drake."

"I'm here, Commodore."

"Update on your status?"

"The commander and I are safely strapped in for the ride."

"Understood. Keep me posted."

"Will do."

At this stage, I can't push any further. Drake knows what needs to be done. I have to trust him.

"Coming into position, Commodore," Kelly says.

"Tactical, aim all weapons on that ship. Ready the umbilical too. We may have to cut our way in."

"Aye aye."

The ship is in position. I release the straps and climb out of my chair. "Lieutenant Kelly, you have the bridge."

Kelly turns around, frowning at me. "Commander Foss is senior, Commodore, perhaps she should—"

"Foss will be with Doctor Drake until further notice. When he gives her permission to resume her duties, I'll let her back on the bridge. Until then, you're in charge. Start hailing that ship. Relay any replies to me and co-ordinate with Lieutenant Chase."

"Aye aye."

Leaving Kelly in charge is a risk. If he's working with Foss, I've just given my ship away, but I can't be everywhere and suspect everyone, I have to make the hard calls.

I'm in the corridor on my way to medical. I don't have a lot of time, but I need to check on Drake before I do anything else. The quickest route is through the hatch and down the crawlway.

It takes a few minutes to get there. When I do, I find Drake in the room, leaning over a figure strapped into a second chair. It's Foss.

I sigh in relief and grin. "Doctor and patient doing fine?"

"Doctor is okay, patient is dosed up with propofol," Drake says. "She'll be out for hours."

"Good work," I say.

Drake shrugs. "Thanks, I guess. You trusted me to be here. I'm… I mean, I wasn't sure…"

"I'm glad you're okay," I say. "Thanks for having my back."

Drake holds out an injector. "Take this. You'll need it in about twenty-four minutes' time. I'll keep Foss out until you get back."

"Kelly is in charge on the bridge. He may ask questions."

"I'll deal with those."

"Great."

"Good luck, Shann."

* * *

I'm back in my room, but only for a moment.

The headset I picked up from the bridge clips into the VR device. That means I can talk to Sam when I transition into the drone.

I put on the haptic gloves and stick the sensors onto my arms. Then I power up the VR unit and slip it on.

The crawlway on the freighter is dark, illuminated only by the torch above my camera/eye display. We must be in the cargo lattice, the huge scaffolding that holds all the containers in place. The drone is moving, following its last instruction to investigate the location that *Asthoreth* fired its torpedoes towards. I must be nearly there by now.

The data connection glitches a little. I'm relying on a different connection to before and the drone is a lot further away from *Gallowglass*, deep inside the freighter.

"Sam, can you hear me?"

"Yeah, got you. I'm four hundred metres to your left, heading to the same place."

I'm letting the drone run. The instructions I gave from before will get us where we need to go. While it's moving, I'm setting up data feeds and active scans. I need to find where Foss's robots are. I need to get to them, before they get to Sam's people.

Nothing is coming up. The technology I have available isn't powerful enough. "Shann to Bridge?"

"Receiving, Commodore."

"Calibrate a laser scan of the freighter, use the thermal sensor. Look for anomalous energy and heat sources. Send any tags you find directly to the drone's data display."

"Doing that now."

"How long will it take until I have some results?"

"About eight minutes."

Eight minutes? That's too long.

I'm still disengaged from the drone's movement control. I have the injector Drake gave me in my left hand. I raise it to my neck and press the trigger. There's a sharp pain. More naloxone. I hope this dose will be enough.

I'm looking at the course plot. I'm nearing the end of my journey. Cargo container #ID4778B7G, an EVA equipment storage unit. If the *Asthoreth* launched people in cryopods, they will have been aiming to board the ship through an airlock. That's the kind of crazy plan desperate people come up with when they think they have no options.

I ordered the gutting of that ship. I know when I handed over command to Ontaraes and headed back to Earth, *Asthoreth* was little more than a glorified storage unit. Whatever these people were planning when they stole it, has to involve resupplying here.

I reach the container's access hatch. There are traces of residual heat here. Immediately, I reactivate the haptic sensors and grab the handle, twisting it to trigger the release mechanism. The hatch opens, and I drop down into the container's dispensary.

Lights are on and there are items here. The inventory has been accessed. The inner door to the airlock is open. I move towards it and go through.

A man is standing at the far end of the room. He's wearing an EVA suit and is surrounded by other items taken from the inventory. He's staring at me.

I remember, to him, I'm a drone. I select the taser attachment on my left hand. "Shann to Sam. I'm here. Where are you?"

"Thirty seconds out."

"Please!" the man says. "Merrick's injured. Can you help her?"

I don't move. I tag him in the camera view. The drone's head tracks him automatically. He's tense and desperate, shifting his weight. While I'm alone, he probably thinks it's worth trying his luck to get past me and make a run for it.

Movement to my left. An EVA-suited individual appears in the doorway and enters the room. I recognise the Fleet patch and *Gallowglass* tag. The man's gaze immediately shifts to the new presence. The trooper is carrying a rifle and aiming it at him.

I activate the exterior mike on the drone. "Stay where you are," I say.

There's a noise to my left and suddenly the trooper next to me is flung across the room.

I turn towards the door just as a mechanical arm lashes out and grabs my left wrist. I can feel through feedback the pressure of metal claws around the limb through the haptic sensors, right up to the limit. It's painful, but not unbearable. Whoever designed this system didn't want an operator's function to be impaired.

The man in the room screams and charges forwards; the robot grabs him with another of its four arms. A second limb delivers a punch to his chest, sending him sprawling across the room.

The robot is braced using its fourth arm. That gives me a small advantage.

My right hand bunches into a fist. I select the taser option and lash out, striking the cameras mounted on the top of the ovoid shape.

They're armoured, but my punch is precise, and as I make contact, I deliver a full electric charge into the optical system.

The robot will have other cameras, but these are the main ones.

A swipe catches me full in the chest. The haptics translate the sensation as a powerful punch, delivering near maximum stimulation of the nerves.

I'm thrown backwards, sent crashing into the wall of the chamber. The robot advances.

Gunfire. The sound of low-velocity bullets slapping against armoured panels. The trooper who entered the room discharges his weapon. It has no effect, the rounds barely scratching the metal plates of the machine's ovoid body.

But it does get its attention.

I push off from the wall. There's damage to my left arm, the grip of the robot has crippled the wrist joint, but the taser is still functional.

I crash into the ovoid body; both of us end up through the door, back in the dispensary.

The machine's arms lash out and grab the rail, steadying both of us. Claws punch through the torso plate of the drone, causing a sudden haptic shock in my chest. For a moment, I think I'm having a heart attack, induced by the drug stress my body's going through.

Then the pain eases. I move my arms, trying to get leverage. A flash in front of my face and pain in my skull. My vision blanks, then restores. Only the left optical camera is working.

More blows raining down.

I'm being taken apart, dismantled.

If this were a bar fight, this is the part where the crowd hauls the two fighters apart before the loser gets killed.

Then suddenly it all stops and I'm back in my room on *Gallowglass*. The connection has severed.

Shit.

Chapter Forty-Five

Johansson

"You let him go."

"Yes."

"Why?"

I don't reply.

Commander Natasha Tratten outranks me. She could take charge of this rescue mission if she wanted to, but she clearly doesn't want to do that.

I know why. Magnus Sirocco broke into this building, murdering one of her people and nearly killing her too. Any board of inquiry would question her motives. She might win them over, but there would be a lot of shit before everything got straightened out.

That's the attention an operation like this doesn't need.

The five of us are standing in the airlock with EVA suits on ready to leave. I have a portable screen in my hand, showing the exterior security camera feed. Sirocco is walking to his rover. He checks the storage compartments, then gets into the driver's seat. The vehicle reverses out and drives away.

"Okay, let's move," I say. "Helmets on and check in. Koryami, when we're ready, start the depressurisation sequence."

"On it, Lieutenant."

We're all checking each other's suits. I move behind Tratten and pull a cable from my belt, plugging it into the data port on the back of her helmet. A cable connection between us should be totally secure.

"I'll do you a trade, Commander," I say. "Tell me what this building is for, and I'll tell you why I let Sirocco go."

"That's hardly by the book, Lieutenant."

"Nothing about this place is in the book, Commander. That's why I think we can make a trade."

Silence. I'm watching the atmosphere pressure reading in the room decrease. I guess Tratten is weighing up her options and trying to decide if I'm a trustworthy source.

She doesn't know what I'm planning to do with the information.

"This is a drilling station," Tratten says, at last. "We're dropping a conductive rod down into the core of the planet."

Immediately, I know what that means. "You can't be seriously trying to—"

"It's a start, an exploratory procedure. If we were going to create a magnetic field around Mars, we need to know what we're dealing with."

"Terraforming the planet? That's crazy."

"But necessary, eventually."

I'm staring at her, and she at me. The glass plates of our helmets are almost touching. "Tell me you shut it down," I say.

"The project has a reformat sequence," Tratten says. "There are micro-explosives attached to the drill. It'll detonate in the borehole and fill everything in. Harris should have purged the drives too, but we can't be sure it'll all be secure, not unless we blow the whole facility."

"Which would jeopardise the dome."

"Your turn," Tratten says. "Why did you let Sirocco leave?"

"Because he's already dead," I say. "The leader of this insurrection doesn't want him to survive. That rover you saw drive away? You won't see it again."

"He should stand trial."

"Commander, this isn't our war." I touch my helmet to hers. "Fleet was made to protect humanity in space. These people are fighting each other and it's going to get a whole lot worse before it gets better. We can't intervene and take a side. We have to be ready to work with whatever comes out of this."

"That won't be your call to make," Tratten warns.

"True, and I'll answer for my choices," I say. "And in this moment, the choice is made."

The depressurisation completes. I reach up and pull the cable connection from Tratten's data port, then turn towards the external airlock door as it opens.

"*Lieutenant Johansson.*"

The AI is there immediately. The connection gets stronger as I move forwards, towards the outside. "I knew you'd show up," I say.

"*Our arrangement. I require you to deliver what you agreed to give me.*"

"They're drilling to the core, trying to get down there to take samples and figure out what's down there to rebuild a planetary magnetic field."

"*A terraforming project.*"

"Yes."

"*Interesting.*"

I'm walking slowly towards the rover, letting the others go ahead of me. If Tratten sees me talking to someone, there will be questions. "You need to fulfil your part of the deal."

"*You have clear passage to the spaceport. Drive there directly. The rest of your people will be waiting for you.*"

I'm about to say thank you, but I owe this machine nothing. Any gratitude would be an endorsement of what's been done. "We're done here," I say. "Don't contact me again."

"*That I cannot promise.*"

I reach the rover. Colt turns towards me. "Everything's as we left it, Lieutenant."

"Great, let's get moving."

The driver's door opens, and I climb in. Colt and Koryami grab handles on the rear of the vehicle and clip on to the safety hooks, letting Tratten take the passenger seat while Harris climbs into the back.

I plug my screen into the rover's computer and reactivate the network connections. I don't trust the AI, but I don't think it'll betray us right now. Fleet is not the enemy, unless we take a side. Even though it isn't in the Fleet computer system, it'll know the assets that are available in orbit. If it wants to be able to use our satellites and our ships, it'll want them intact.

The rover's driving system activates. We reverse away from the building and turn around, heading back towards the vehicle garage.

"What's the plan?" Tratten asks.

"Hera Spaceport. We're going to the Hub," I say.

"We're leaving? It's that bad out here?"

"That's our orders. I was sent here to bring you and your people with us on the shuttle."

"I..." Tratten swallows. I can hear her voice tremble over the comms. "I didn't realise it was this bad."

"Yeah. That's why we need to back out of this. If we choose a side, we'll be torn apart. The anger in this place needs to sate itself. We can't help these people."

We drive in silence after that.

★ ★ ★

"Chiu to Johansson. You there?"

That voice. Suddenly, my whole body relaxes. I needed to hear that voice.

"Yeah, I'm here," I say. "We're on our way to you."

We passed the vehicle garage, driving around the side of the dome. As we got close, I sent a message to Briggs and Melton. They got in a second rover and drove out to meet us. Now they're three metres ahead, following the same route we're following, on our way to Hera Spaceport.

So far, the AI is holding to the deal. I've seen several rovers and walker robots out here. All of them have abandoned their work. Instead, they are motionless, lined up, watching us as we go by.

"We've made it to the shuttles," Chiu says. "Preflight checks are nearly complete on two birds. What's your ETA?"

"About six minutes."

"Situation here is stable for now. We've blocked the train line, so people can't transfer out to the departure terminal, but it's only a matter of time before someone decides to take a walk out here."

"Yeah, copy that." I know what Chiu is thinking. The safe launch radius for the shuttles is five hundred metres. If people from Jezero wander into that area, they could be burned by the ignited thruster fuel. "We can't be responsible for what happens," I say.

"I know, but hurry please. We are tracking bio-monitors and thermal signatures, but I'll feel a lot better when you get here."

"Understood. Where's Forell?"

"They are three minutes out," Chiu says. "When you get here, we've rigged up the transfer rail car as an airlock for you. Enter on the far side, pressurise and bring your EVA gear in with you. We'll use it in the shuttles."

"Understood."

The rover turns left, and I see we're now driving alongside the rail tube. Our little vehicle is slower than the trains, so it'll take us longer to get there than it would if we were on the inside.

"We're being followed," Tratten says.

I look twist around instinctively, then swear. I can't see while I'm in the suit. I glance down. Tratten has a rear exterior camera view in a window on the screen in front of us both. "Your Ensign Colt said he saw something," she says. "The dust we're kicking up covers most of it, but the computer has tagged a couple of vehicles keeping pace about two hundred yards back. You want to tell me why they are letting us through?"

"You expect me to know?"

"That's an order, *Lieutenant*."

I sigh. Looks like I've stretched my latitude as far as it'll go. "There's an autonomous adaptive program in the colony's computer system. I don't know if it's being controlled or just running things on its own. I think it hasn't decided whether Fleet is an enemy or not just yet."

"Which is why you stopped me killing Sirocco."

"Exactly."

I'm getting the measure of Tratten. She's a little slower on the uptake than some of the senior officers I've worked with, but she gets there. There will be more questions, and I'll need to give more ground when they come.

But right now, she's quiet and I can focus on what comes next.

"Hoàng to Johansson."

"Go ahead."

"We're seeing some movement in the departure hall. CorpGov security are being torn apart down there. Do you have eyes on what's going on?"

I key up a selection of security feeds. Three new windows appear on the car's display. "We're already past the terminal. I can only see what you're seeing."

"It's pretty grim," Hoàng says.

"Yeah, it is."

We're seeing people in security uniforms being battered and broken by mobs armed with makeshift weapons. There's blood on the walls, people on the ground, crying out in pain.

I want to stop this, but I know I can't.

My eyes are wet. I'm blinking rapidly, trying to clear them, trying to stay focused. We can't make a difference here. The survival play is to get the fuck out.

A hand touches mine. Tratten.

"You're doing the right thing," she says.

"Thanks."

I'm surprised, but I'll take it.

⋆ ⋆ ⋆

We reach the spaceport and park the two rovers near where the conveyer usually drops people off. The rail car is still there at the arrivals point as Chiu said it was.

I enter the car with the others. Seven people in EVA suits makes it crowded in here. When the doors shut, Tratten triggers the pressurisation. There's a makeshift indicator hanging on the wall that Chiu must have left here for us. A green light on it flashes when the process is complete and I remove my helmet.

"Keep your gear on," I say. "Go straight to the launch gate. Shuttles *Phaeton* and *Obdurance* are prepped and ready for launch as soon as we're aboard."

The inner doors open and we all move onto the platform. Through the DuraGlas roof, I can see the two ships mounted on their vertical launch ladders, waiting for us. Chiu has sent seating plans through to us all, so everyone knows which shuttle they are supposed to be on.

I put my helmet back on, keeping the seals open, and open a comms channel to Hoàng. "Any movement at the departure hall?" I ask.

"Yes, there's people on the tracks. They'll cross the safety threshold in a couple of minutes."

"Can we launch before that?"

"I don't think so."

Shit. I stop moving and bring up the comms activity log. I select the last connection I had with the AI and initiate a new request.

"*I thought we weren't talking, Lieutenant. What do you want?*"

"Your people are on the rail, heading for the launchpads. You need to stop them so we can get clear."

"*That wasn't part of our arrangement.*"

"If we launch, we'll kill people."

"*A difficult decision for you. I hope you make the right choice.*"

My fingers curl into fists. I want to smash something, really bad.

"What do you want?" I ask.

"*You wish to make an exchange?*"

"Yes. Damn it. Tell me what you want. I need you to stop those people from reaching us. If you do that, I'll…tell me what you want from me!"

"*Our dialogue must remain open,*" the AI says. "*I am not prepared for this to be our last conversation, Lieutenant Johansson. That is my price.*"

I grimace. Another deal with the devil, one that could be used to blackmail me. "All right," I say. "Just get it done."

"*I will do my best.*"

I cut the call and hurry to rejoin the others as they board the shuttles. Chiu is there, also suited and ready to go. I reach out a hand and she takes it, squeezing my fingers reassuringly. "We have to go," she says.

"I know," I reply.

We board the shuttle *Obdurance* together, taking two seats in the passenger cabin. As I sit down, I lock the seals on my helmet once more. Then the straps deploy, locking in my arms, legs and waist.

"I didn't want to stay too long anyway," Chiu says.

I glance at her and try to smile. "Liar."

She nods in return. "You know me so well."

A window appears on my helmet display. It's a countdown. Everyone is in, so the shuttle launch has been initiated. We have forty-three seconds until take-off.

I pull up another window, the feed from one of the security cameras in the rail tunnel near the station at Jezero. There's smoke and dust everywhere. Something's happened.

The tunnel has collapsed, blocking the way for people from the city to get to us.

Eight, seven, six…

I smile but feel no humour, only an empty sense of triumph. The AI has acted as it said it would. I hope no one died.

Three, two, one…

Lift-off.

Chapter Forty-Six

Iskander

There's no way I'm getting out of this.

The robot is a large ovoid with four articulated limbs. It's got here before me and waited until I arrived.

We were told there might be machines on the ship. The elders had warned us but been unable to give us much information. The design specifications and control codes were not something they had access to, they said.

We know the robots were left here with active biosensors, set to find and eliminate anything left alive on the ship.

Now, I'm trapped in a cramped dispensary with one of them.

The robot is moving slowly towards me and I'm backing away.

I pull out my screen. I should be able to access the dispensary, but there's no power, unless I can hook up the battery pack I have with me.

I can't do that while I'm facing down a machine that wants to kill me.

My back is against the far wall. There's nowhere to go.

A metal arm snakes out, moving faster than any human could. It grabs my left ankle, the claw-like hands closing around the joint and dragging me forwards. As I'm pulled towards the machine, another arm whips out, its cold fingers closing around my throat.

I'm struggling, fighting to breathe and to free myself. The screen is out of my hands, floating away, hitting the wall, the glass display shattering, a dusty cloud of shards in the air.

Then, a figure appears behind the robot. A man in an EVA suit. He's carrying a weapon of some sort in both hands. He jams the end of it into the top of the ovoid torso and pulls the trigger.

Bright light. Superheated plasma emitted from the end of the barrel. The white-hot sludge spews over the metal plates of the robot's body. Immediately, it catches fire. I can feel the heat from it, like a wave roiling through the air.

Artificial arms flail around; the man and the gun are thrown backwards. I'm released as the robot twists around to face the new threat as its metal armour melts. The plasma sprays out as it moves; a speck touches my shoulder, immediately burning through the fabric of my clothes and into my flesh. I'm screaming as I crash into the wall. My feet touch the wall, and I push forwards, driving my body through the air at the machine's burning body.

I raise my hands, striking at a joint, grabbing the limb, getting my feet on the floor and pulling, hard. The robot crashes against the inner airlock door.

The man in the suit is on his feet, pushing me away, driving the weapon into the ovoid body again. A wall of heat engulfs me, the air so hot it burns my skin. I close my eyes, raising my arms to cover my face.

I've nothing left to give. I can barely breathe, the superhot air is scalding my mouth and throat.

Fingers on my shoulder. I look up. The man in the EVA suit is in front of me. His chest is scorched and torn. He taps a button on the side of his helmet. "Hey. Are you okay?"

I pull myself up. My clothes are damaged, sticky where they've melted. "I'm alive," I say.

"You need to come with me," the man says.

"What if I refuse?" I say.

"I'm not asking."

The man isn't holding the weapon from before, but I doubt he's unarmed. "Who are you?" I ask.

"Lieutenant Sam Chase from Fleet. People call me Sam. You can call me Lieutenant."

A hand is extended, I take it, in the time-honoured tradition.

"My name is Iskander," I say.

"Yeah, I've read all about you."

Sam turns away. Behind him, I see the robot floating, seemingly dead. "What did you do to it?"

"Hit a power line, I think. We got lucky." Sam is examining the door into the container's airlock. It's a different design to the one from before but still has a control panel and external input socket. "The system sealed up when it detected an extreme temperature change. We're not getting through here without overrides." He looks at me. "I guess that's how you've been getting through the doors?"

"It is." There's no point in lying right now.

"All right. Can you open the hatch up there?" Sam points to the way we both entered.

"I guess so," I say. "Don't Fleet have override codes as well?"

"We do, but I want to see how you do it."

I move to the hatch. Aside from being a prisoner, my screen is broken and in pieces, so until I get out of here and find one of the others, I'm not going to be able to do much for the mission.

I need to get out of this room and hope I can escape from this guy in the crawl space. He's wearing a bulky suit, so I should be able to get away.

"Where are we going?"

"To find the rest of your crew."

I press my thumb to the panel, then select the keypad and type in the code. I know Sam is watching me, memorising the digits, or recording them with his helmet camera.

The hatch opens. I pull myself through.

"You wait there," Sam says.

A torch flicks on, right in my face. I raise my hands and squeeze my eyes shut against the bright light. Someone else is up here.

"Move towards me, nice and slow."

A woman's voice through the suit speaker. I do as I'm told, clearing the hatch so the lieutenant can follow me up.

"All right," Sam says. "Let's go to the container where you got in."

⋆ ⋆ ⋆

We move through the crawl space, Lieutenant Sam Chase in the lead. Progress is slower, as I'm wedged between two suited Fleet troopers. That gives me time to think.

The others know the plan. Halle must have got *Asthoreth* into position with the fuel lines. Kewell is there and can operate the flow. Once they have fuel, the ship will be able to escape. Halle and Dennis can use the remaining cryopods if they have to. Sure, they'll starve eventually, but—

"Okay, we're here."

Sam opens the hatch and climbs through. I move up. I could try to escape right now, push off from the wall and on down the crawlway, leaving these two behind, losing myself in the lattice of the freighter. Without a bio-monitor, it might take them days to find me, weeks even. I've memorised a few of the container IDs, some of them have food and water. I could—

No.

The decision is instinctive. I'm tired, hungry and pushed beyond my limit. I thought I could do this, but I can't. I think seeing Weaver die like that, and Merrick all broken…

I follow Sam through the hatch.

I'm back in the EVA suit dispensary. Only this time, there are two robots in the corner, locked in a deadly embrace. Neither of them is moving. The inner airlock door is dented and stuck open. Sam moves through and I follow him into the room beyond.

Tolwyn is there. Another two Fleet people in EVA suits are with him. One is working on Merrick's smashed cryopod. I can see cables connected to a variety of different instruments.

"How is she?" I ask aloud. Everyone knows who I mean.

In response, Sam raises his hands and touches the seals on his helmet, removing it. The sweaty face beneath is a little older than I expected. "Stable for now," he says. "Looks like we got here just in time."

"Are we your prisoners?" Tolwyn asks.

"You're being detained," Sam says. "What we do with you will be up to the commodore."

I know who they are referring to, Ellisa Shann. "And where is she?" I ask.

Sam gestures towards the two machines locked together. "I expect she saved your life," he says to Tolwyn.

There's a hiss of air escaping as the woman who was with us in the crawlway takes off her helmet as well. Now we're in a lit room, I can see her name tag – *Carrick: Ensign.* "What's our next move, Lieutenant?" she asks.

"That depends on how co-operative these people are feeling," Sam replies. "We counted five torpedo launches. Four of them aimed here. I see four cryopods and three people. Where's your friend?"

He glances at Tolwyn. Tolwyn gestures towards me. Sam turns and gives me his full attention. "Better to tell us," he says. "There could be more robots out there."

I smile. "If we're negotiating, I'll want to talk to Shann."

"That'll be up to her," Sam says. "You should know though, we have your ship in weapons range. Any move your people make will trigger a response."

I shrug. "I'm here with no comms. What Halle does over there is her decision. Maybe if you let me talk to them, I can ensure they stay put?"

Silence. This Lieutenant Sam Chase may have things he's good at, but here, he's struggling. He bites his lip and moves away from me. Going to the far corner of the room. I guess he's taking advice from someone on the Fleet ship over comms. I can hear him talking, but I can't make out the words. Eventually he nods, ends the conversation, and returns to the group.

"All right. The commodore has agreed for you to speak with your crew on *Asthoreth.* Then you transfer to our ship. Just you and the injured woman. Your friend stays here. Now, you were going to tell me where your other friend is?"

I think about my answer. I need to show willing in this situation, I guess. "Fuel operations control three. He'll be waiting for our ship to connect to the line so we can transfer hydrogen over from *Hercules*'s tanks."

"Is he armed?"

"He has a taser. That's it."

"And you can't contact him?"

"No, we went radio silent when we came over here. He knows to return here when *Asthoreth* is hooked up."

Sam looks at Tolwyn again. "If we took you over there, could you get your friend to surrender?"

"Deacon?"

I'm staring at Tolwyn, he's staring at me. This is the moment of trust. Either he thinks I have some special plan to get us out of this, or he'll take my lead and give up. He's waiting on my answer. He'll do what I ask him to do.

"Go with them," I say. "Do what they ask."

"Okay."

★ ★ ★

An hour later and I'm on-board the Fleet ship *Gallowglass*.

I was told about this ship. Originally, it was constructed in secret by a group of corporations who meshed old NASA designs with what they could obtain of the Mercury class patrol ship plans. The group were allies of the Temple, taking generous funding from our communities, with promises that they would honour our purpose.

These vessels were supposed to transport the faithful to the new Eden that awaits us. That's what we were told.

When you sit in congregation, you learn to filter some things out. Many stories are about hopes and dreams. I always thought the stories were a mixture of fact and fiction.

There wasn't an official statement about what happened around Mars. I learned bits and pieces from the people I met when I got there from Earth. Some of it matched what the elders told me, other parts did not.

Now I'm meeting someone who was there.

The door to the room opens and I move inside. She's behind a table, facing me, ostensibly sitting in a chair, but we're in zero gravity, so the seat is more of an affectation. There is no chair for me.

"You are Peter Iskander, yes?"

I smile. "It is an honour to meet you, Commodore," I say. "Your reputation is…well…"

Shann fixes me with a hard look. "Am I an enemy to you?"

"No."

"Then why did you steal a Fleet ship?"

"We… We had no other option."

Shann nods. Her gaze softens. "Explain," she says.

This is the moment. This is the best chance I have.

I take a deep breath and begin.

Chapter Forty-Seven

Shann

No weakness. Show no weakness.

I'm sitting in the briefing room of *Gallowglass*, wired up to a drip and a pump that's working to clear the opioids from my body. Drake has worked his magic and made sure all the equipment is concealed, strapped to the back of the chair I'm in.

The man in front of me is Peter Iskander. My aide, Lieutenant Sam Chase, managed to save his life and bring him back here for a conversation.

Iskander is the ringleader of a group of thieves who stole the Fleet ship *Asthoreth* from its parked orbit around Mars, dragging me out here to the abandoned freighter, *Hercules* in pursuit.

The diversion has revealed some truths that might never have been discovered. A deck below this one, my executive officer, Lieutenant Commander Gabriel Foss, is under sedation and will be moved into a suitable detention facility as soon as possible, after her attempt to murder me. We may never have found out about her if we hadn't come here. I could very well be dead already.

But this man, Peter Iskander, can't take credit for that.

On the table in front of me is a portable screen with this man's file, along with those of his crewmates, everything I need to convict him, according to the old maritime laws. Back then a captain of a ship was the sole judge and jury of any transgressor.

"It is an honour to meet you, Commodore," Iskander says. "Your reputation is…well…"

I cut him off. "Am I an enemy to you?"

"No."

"Then why did you steal a Fleet ship?"

"We… We had no other option."

I nod. I don't know his reasons, but I have some suspicions. Sam Chase, my aide, has suggested Iskander is honest and that he's offered no resistance since he was captured. I'm hoping he's going to give me a lot of information that will help all of us.

"Explain," I say.

Iskander takes a moment, gathering himself. "I was sent to Mars to appropriate the *Asthoreth*. Word reached my people that you had abandoned the vessel and had no further use for it."

"That's your explanation?"

"For that specific act, yes."

I'm frowning, trying to work this man out. "You stole a ship and brought it out here. At least one of the people on-board is dead. Another is injured. Why are you here?"

"To refit and resupply."

"And then, where are you going?"

Iskander smiles. "I have a set of co-ordinates I was instructed to travel to. I will give them to you."

"Freely? Just like that?"

"Yes, just like that."

I can't work this guy out. What's his angle? "Why would you give them up?"

"Because there's no point in keeping them from you," Iskander says. "As I said, I do not see you as my enemy."

"That's interesting," I say. "How would you define our relationship?"

"As potential allies," Iskander says. "I want to work with you. There are so many questions we both want answered. In this moment, we have the opportunity to find some of the reasons behind what has happened to both of us."

I'm staring at him. I agreed to this meeting because I thought I could learn something. Iskander has been co-operative, but I'd already decided we'd be putting him in cryo along with the rest of his people and shipping them back to Mars. Now though…

"What do you want from me?" I ask.

"Let us refuel and resupply *Asthoreth*," Iskander says. "Let us go to the co-ordinates as planned, only we'll be in contact with you."

"Why would I agree to that?"

"Because your return to Mars means you're back to defend the colony from those who attacked it before," Iskander says. "You didn't plan to be out here and as soon as you go back, you'll be sucked into all the decisions that will need to be made about doing that. Meanwhile the real enemy, the people who attacked and destroyed Phobos Station, who wrecked *Hercules*, they'll still be out there in the dark."

"And you're offering to hunt them down for me?"

"No, but at least you'll have some eyes out there."

I'm thinking about it. Iskander is persuasive. The open and direct approach is a refreshing change from some of the schemers I've dealt with before. "Tell me about what you want," I say. "Your people call you Deacon, don't they? Why are you out here?"

"Because I was given a task by the Temple," Iskander says.

"What is that task?"

"To find our New Eden."

I nod. The story is not unknown to me. My old XO, Bill Travers, talked about the Temple and some of the work they were doing on Earth. Fleet training teaches you to be a scientist, so there are plenty of alarms going off in my head about what Iskander is saying, but people like Bill found a lot of comfort in religion.

"You know there's nothing out there for you, right?" I say. "I mean, there's no Paradise waiting to be discovered in this solar system, and that little ship won't get you any further."

Iskander shrugs. "Maybe Eden is something we have to make for ourselves, not the naked garden they wrote about in old books? Humanity made plenty of mistakes on Earth – is making even more mistakes right now. Maybe it's time for a fresh start."

"For many people, that's what Mars is supposed to be."

"Come on, you don't believe the corporate promotional campaign," Iskander says. "Fleet might be the guardians of humanity's journey into space, but they aren't wedded to its capitalism. At least you aren't, are you?"

I find myself looking away from him, staring at the screen in front of me with his file on display. Am I part of the corporate agenda? I guess I am in part. Fleet is funded by the private and public partners. Just because we're not looking to profit out here, doesn't mean we're not enabling others to cash in.

"Look, in this moment you can do what you want," Iskander says. "You came out here with one ship and maintained radio silence. The only people who know what's going on are the people you brought with you. Go back and say we were destroyed, that we all died. Whatever you need to say. Just let us go on and do what we came here to do."

"You came on-board as a reclamation team." I touch the screen, bringing up a different file. "What about your supervisor, Weaver?"

"What about him?"

"We picked up the cryopod you fired at us. He's dead."

"Yeah. He died in the pod soon after we left Mars orbit."

"So, you didn't kill him."

"Get your doctor to examine him. You'll find no injuries. He died in his sleep."

"People can be murdered without leaving a mark."

"That's not what happened. I'm telling the truth."

Silence between us. I'm thinking about my options. All regulations would support locking these people up and going back to Mars, just as Iskander said. But he's also right about our lack of eyes in the darkness. The people who we're really fighting expect us to do the predictable and go with the marginal choices.

"They wouldn't see this coming."

"No, they wouldn't."

I blink in surprise, realising I've been thinking out loud. Iskander is smiling, just a little. Has he got what he wants?

"You'll stay here, repair and resupply your ship, then head out to a set of co-ordinates which you'll share with me before we let you leave. After that, you'll stay in regular encrypted communication with us, reporting everything you find."

"Agreed. Thank you, Commodore." Iskander extends his hand.

I take it.

⋆ ⋆ ⋆

"Why did you do it? Why did you agree to let them go?"

I'm back in my quarters, letting the drip cycle finish. Sam and Drake are here.

"I mean, was it the drugs?" Sam asks. "You think I should ask you to step aside?"

I scowl. "Don't even joke about that."

"All right, but we'll need an explanation. What's the plan?"

"We have nothing to lose with this," I say. "The ship they stole isn't something we can spare the time or resources to repair. They brought it here, another place where we can't afford to be staying. We're vulnerable if Rocher figures out where we are and brings his battlegroup to our location."

"All the more reason to put them in cryopods and tow them back to Mars."

I shake my head. "Iskander is different. You remember, Sam, we talked about factions and there being more to this than 'them and us'? These people don't see Fleet as their enemy. They want to escape all of it."

"Escape to where?" Drake asks. "There's nothing out there."

"Iskander gave me the co-ordinates for where they're going, once they've got fuel and food. It's Jupiter L5."

"A Jupiter Lagrange point?"

"Yes. Exactly. That position is littered with trojan asteroids. It's the perfect place to hide ships, or a base. Far enough out for us to miss it, but close enough to keep tabs."

"So, you believe him?"

"I do, yes." I point at Sam and Drake in turn. "This conversation, along with all relevant data and actions relating to *Asthoreth*, are now classified. No sharing outside this group without express permission."

"What about the rest of the crew?" Drake asks.

"Same instruction will go to them. The whole operation becomes restricted information. An official report will go back about what went on here. I want no chatter to contradict that."

"You think it won't get out?"

"We handpicked this crew and very few people have all the pieces of the puzzle," I say. "Sam, you need to speak to your away team about this face-to-face."

"Understood."

"What about Foss?"

"She's still under, right?"

"At the moment."

"So, she doesn't know how this all ended. Foss goes straight into cryo for the trip home. We'll contact Fleet Intelligence when we're at Mars. They'll deal with her."

"Risky," Sam says. "If she has an ally still on-board..."

"Then I'll need you to taste all my meals."

The joke lands. There's an awkward silence between us. But I'm glancing at both Drake and Sam in turn. Slowly, smiles start to appear.

"I like extra rations," Sam says.

"Good."

★ ★ ★

I'm alone.

The terminal display in my room is showing a series of exterior camera views from *Gallowglass*. I can see *Asthoreth* parked up, a fuel cable connecting her to *Hercules*. If I squint, or zoom in one of the cameras, I can also make out EVA lines as well.

I feel better, recovered. The injections caused some bruising and soreness, but I'll heal.

I'm watching people in suits, buckled onto those thin wires, going back and forth with bundles of equipment. Most of the process is being managed by machines, but there are human hands out there, guiding the work.

A bunch of worker ants. Small, but mighty, doing everything as they've been instructed. Step by step by step.

This is a win. I'm not sure it feels like a win, because we're letting Iskander and his people go. But the more I think about it, the more I think I've made the right choice.

"Bridge to Shann."

"Go ahead, Sam, what is it?"

"Priority message from the Hub. Soon as we reactivated comms, we got a data dump from Lieutenant Johansson and Chief Ontaraes. It's all sealed for your perusal."

"Okay, send it over. I'll take a look."

The files start transferring in another window on my display. I'm still looking at the view outside.

Savvantine will want to know what I've done. She'll see the reason behind this decision. Another game piece on the board.

Now we just have to get back to Mars.

The files in the window have downloaded. I open the folder and start to read.

About the Author

Allen Stroud is a lecturer and researcher at Coventry University. Stroud completed a Ph.D. at the University of Winchester entitled 'An Investigation and Application of Writing Structures and World Development Techniques in Science Fiction and Fantasy'. He has worked in computer games, roleplaying games, novels, short stories and scripts. He currently runs the Creative Futures research project with the Defence Science Technology Laboratory (DSTL).

Stroud was a founding host of Lave Radio, an *Elite: Dangerous* fan podcast that started in February 2013 and ran the annual convention Lavecon. His novel set in the *Elite: Dangerous* game world, called *Elite: Lave Revolution* was successfully funded on Kickstarter and published in late 2014, with a second edition published in 2015. Stroud then supported Spidermind Games in developing the *Elite Dangerous Roleplaying Game.* Stroud worked on *Chaos Reborn* (2016) with Snapshot Games, as well as *Phoenix Point* (2019) and *Baldur's Gate 3* (2023).

Stroud was the 2017, 2018, 2021 and 2023 chair of FantasyCon, the annual convention of the British Fantasy Society, which hosts the British Fantasy Awards. He was also Chair of the British Science Fiction Association from 2019 to 2025. Stroud continues to write academic papers, reviews, articles and fiction in science fiction, fantasy and horror.

Stroud's previous Flame Tree Press novels in the *Fractal* series are *Fearless* (2020), *Resilient* (2022) and *Vigilance* (2024), along with twelve ebook episodes. He has also composed music as part of the series.

FLAME TREE PRESS
FICTION WITHOUT FRONTIERS

Award-Winning Authors & Original Voices

Flame Tree Press is the trade fiction imprint of Flame Tree Publishing, focusing on excellent writing in horror and the supernatural, crime and mystery, science fiction and fantasy. Our aim is to explore beyond the boundaries of the everyday, with tales from both award-winning authors and original voices.

•

The *Fractal* series, including eBook episodes and novels, in reading order:

Europa
Ceres
Lagrange Point
Fearless – Book One
Luna
Resilient – Book Two
Terra
Jezero
Vigilance – Book Three
Insurgents
Pioneers
Jonbar Points
Terrans
Wolves
Europans
Anti-State

You may also enjoy:

The Sentient by Nadia Afifi
The Widening Gyre by Michael R. Johnston
The Sky Woman by J.D. Moyer
Brittle by Beth Overmyer
The Last Feather by Shameez Patel Papathanasiou
A Sword of Bronze and Ashes by Anna Smith Spark
Stars Like Us by Stephen K. Stanford
The Roamers by Francesco Verso
Of Kings, Queens & Colonies by Johnny Worthen

•

Join our mailing list for free short stories, new release details, news about our authors and special promotions:

flametreepress.com